BLOOD ON THE MOON

BY JENNIFER KNIGHT

Books published by Running Press are available at special discounts for bulk purchases in the
United States by corporations, institutions, and other organizations. For more information,
please contact the Special Markets Department at the Perseus Books Group, 2300 Chestnut
Street, Suite 200, Philadelphia, PA 19103, or call (800) 810-4145, ext. 5000, or e-mail spe-
cial.markets@perseusbooks.com.

ISBN 978-0-7624-4117-4
Library of Congress Control Number: 2011923645

E-book ISBN 978-0-7624-4386-4

9   8   7   6   5   4   3   2   1
Digit on the right indicates the number of this printing

Cover image by Steve Belkowitz
Cover design by Ryan Hayes
Interior design by Ryan Hayes
Typography: Verlag, Knockout, and Mercury

Published by Running Press Teens
an imprint of Running Press Book Publishers
A Member of the Perseus Books Group
2300 Chestnut Street
Philadelphia, PA 19103–4371

Visit us on the web!
www.runningpress.com

BLOOD ON THE MOON

BY JENNIFER KNIGHT

RP | TEENS
PHILADELPHIA • LONDON

7

To Brittany, for the hearts in the margin.

PREFACE

I am surrounded.

A dozen pairs of manic eyes glitter at me underneath the cold light of the full moon; the odor of death hangs over the bloody snow at my feet and tears trail slowly down my face.

I am begging.

Not for my own life, but for the life of a boy I've both loved and mistrusted for ten years. I hear the gurgling, retching sounds of his breath, and I look up into the mad eyes of the beast looming above me, begging for his help.

But the eyes are indifferent, not just to my pleas, but to everything. Everything but blood. Blood coats his world in a crimson film, blurring reality into madness. He can't think, can't rationalize. All he knows is blood. Blood and that orb hanging over our heads—waxing and waning—as unstoppable as time, and just as cruel.

I cover my face in my hands, knowing that nothing I do will help. The beast has already resisted the one pathetic chance I had. I know in my heart that I will die tonight. Alone. The only way I can be.

FIRST LOOK

I had always imagined that college would be different than high shool. I thought that I would enter the Colorado State campus and feel this wonderful sort of enlightenment, like just being there would make me an adult. Or at least that I had some purpose in life besides using up the air that was meant for those greater than me.

But no, college seemed just as confusing and frustrating as high school. In fact, it was harder because I didn't have my mom around to take care of me. No home-cooked meals, no laundry folded on the corner of my bed. If I wanted to go someplace, I couldn't just borrow her car, I had to wait twenty minutes for the bus to come wheezing up. If I ran out of food, I had to trek out to the store. If I wanted my roommate, Ashley, to turn her music down, well, I had to suck it up because she wouldn't, no matter how nicely I asked.

I'd only been on campus for a week, but I was already beginning to feel scared and alone, and somewhat nauseous. If Derek hadn't been with me, I don't know what I would have done.

Derek had been my best friend since the third grade when he beat up Roger Miller for knocking me off the swings. We'd tried dating a couple of times, but something always screwed it up. Usually it was Derek's wandering eye or maybe it was my inability to admit having any feelings for him stronger than friendship. Eventually we decided to keep our tongues out of each other's mouths because we cherished our friendship too much to let stupid crap like that ruin it.

Derek followed me to Colorado State. Sure, he said he chose CSU because he got a football scholarship to play first string for the Rams, but Derek also got a scholarship to play running back for the Florida Gators and the University of Alabama. I knew the real reason he came with me was because the thought of going someplace new, totally on your own, was scary as hell. I guess he thought having one other person to be alone with was better than having nobody. I was definitely with him on that. Until Derek told me he was going to CSU, I had been in a constant state of hyper-anxiety.

Not that I felt any steadier after having "acclimated myself" for the past week. Even after moving into my dorm room, meeting my roommate, touring the campus and the surrounding town, and attending several freshman mixers with Derek, I still felt out of place. Mostly I craved the start of the term when my coping mechanism would begin: track team.

I was a runner. It was how I dealt with stress, with disappointment, with anything really. Running was rhythmic, steady, dependable—things I usually lacked in my life. It felt good to have something I could count on, even if it was as menial as running.

I'd been jogging around campus a few times since arriving—trying to stave off the nerves—but there was something about running full-out. Sprinting. Heart pounding, sides splitting. Pushing myself as hard as I could to beat the person next to me.

I missed that.

I couldn't wait until cross-country team try-outs the following week, but now I had to get through my first day of classes. I wasn't sure how hard the work would be, if the people would be nice, if my professors would be cool. I was a bundle of nervous energy, but one thing calmed me—the only thing that ever soothed my tattered nerves besides running—Derek. I knew talking to him would calm me down.

I walked in my new suede boots and red jacket toward the Union where Derek had told me to meet him at nine thirty on the dot. Derek's a punctual guy, while I'm one of those people who is perpetually late—just one of the many reasons we would never work out.

The sky was gray. Nasty, cloudy, elephant skin-gray and I could tell it was going to rain, so I hurried down the walkway and dashed up the cement steps. I shrugged off the twenty-seven people who tried to thrust flyers at me and entered the Union. It was warm inside, making me instantly happier.

Shaking my hair out from under my hood, I did a quick scan for Derek.

The Union housed a coffee stand packed with groggy college kids and professors craving caffeine, a Panda Express, more people passing out flyers, an information desk with two bored employees, and a little café that sold bagels.

I found Derek sitting at Bagel Place, the ever-so-cleverly named bagel café, where the waitress was hovering over his table. She looked ready to pull her skirt up right there. Derek usually had that effect on girls. He had the perfect combo of tan skin, blond hair, and ultra-blue eyes. He was seriously good-looking and knew it—hence his obvious flirting with the waitress. Rolling my eyes, I rushed up to him.

"Hey," I said, giving Derek a smile.

Derek turned and stood when he saw me. He was wearing the green and gold jersey of the Rams and my heart started beating a little harder. I had a thing about football jerseys. I don't know why, but guys just look good in them, especially Derek. He wasn't huge and hulking like most football players, but lean with a thin waist and broad shoulders—the perfect body for a running back. His wide grin when he spotted me did nothing to slow my pulse.

"Faith, hey!" He hugged me briefly and pecked me on the cheek, our customary greeting. Derek was drenched with cold, clammy sweat.

"Ugh!" I groaned playfully. "You're soaking."

"Oh, sorry," he said, looking down at himself. "Just came from morning practice."

The waitress scowled, clearly sensing that Derek was no longer interested in flirting with her, mumbled something about getting me a drink, and left. I sat down across from Derek.

"So, what's up?" I asked. I reached over and stole a piece of his whole wheat bagel with cream cheese.

"Nothing," he said. "I just, you know, wanted to see you before you had your first class."

I gave him a skeptical look and snagged a sip of his OJ.

"Well, actually," he said. He picked at the remainder of his bagel and swallowed hard. "I did want to ask you something."

"Sure. But hey, make it fast because I have class in like ten minutes."

"Right," he said, nodding. He took a swig of his juice and looked me in the eye with his baby blues. I instantly warmed to whatever he had to ask. His innocent charm almost always got to me, no matter how hard I tried to resist. "I heard about this river not too far from here, the La Poudre, I think it's called? Anyway, it's great for kayaking and camping or whatever. A lot of people go there to chill, so I thought maybe you and me could, I don't know . . . go." He gave me that shy, vulnerable smile that showed just a hint of his sparkly white teeth.

But I didn't turn to mush like usual. I was floored. Derek couldn't mean he wanted a date, could he? We had decided against that a long time ago, and I thought we were both happy about it. Maybe I had just misunderstood. I decided to play it cool.

"Sure," I said. "We could invite your roommates and my roommates and make it a get-to-know-you type of thing. It'll be fun." I smiled brightly.

Derek furrowed his brows and looked at his plate. "Ah . . . I guess we could do that. But I think Mark has lacrosse and Pete has some band thing. Might be easier if we just go together. Better even?" He looked up at me, hope in his eyes.

My heart dropped to my shoes. "I don't know, Derek. You know how I feel about . . ." I looked at his sad, sweet face and was swayed. "Okay fine, we can go, but don't—"

"Really?" Derek's eyes lit up. "You want to go, really?"

"Yeah, I want to go. It's just—"

"Awesome!" He stood and pecked me on the cheek. "We can go this weekend, it'll be great! I brought some camping stuff up so we can spend the night and everything. It's gonna be a full moon on Saturday, totally beautiful. This is gonna rock, Faith."

My mouth fell open as I groped for something that would bring him down from his high, but wouldn't crush him completely at the same time. Where was this coming from? What had I done that prompted him to try and change our relationship after a year?

Did coming here together give him some signal that I wanted to be with him? Moreover, why after a week of hanging out had this suddenly come up?

He grabbed his helmet and tucked it under his arm. "I gotta go change before class. Meet me for dinner at Spoons? Six o'clock?"

"Ah . . . sure?"

"Sweet. See ya later." He kissed me on the cheek one more time and sauntered off.

I sat there at the café, stabbing Derek's uneaten bagel with a fork. This was not what I needed right now. I was stressed enough without having to worry about Derek's feelings as well. He had already been hurt by me more times than I cared to count. Granted, he'd hurt me, too. But I didn't want to be responsible for causing him any more pain because while Derek loved me, I could never love him back. And he knew that.

The redheaded waitress came back and cleared the table.

"Excuse me," she said. "If you're not going to order anything, we need the table for actual customers."

I grabbed my bag and left without a word.

As I made my way outside, I huddled into my jacket, trying to ignore the fifty-three people who threw flyers at me, and made it to my first class—Intro to Psychology—just as the first icy drops of rain hit the cement. I rushed down the abandoned hall and snuck through the door three minutes late.

The class hadn't started yet, which was a relief. The room was a huge auditorium with a massive screen up front; it was dark and packed with students. I made my way into the center of the room and took a seat at the edge of the row.

I had barely settled into my chair when I heard, "Faith! Faithy, down here!"

I looked in the direction of the voice and there was my suitemate Courtney. She waved me down so I got up and made my way over, cursing life. I didn't like Courtney. She had a trashy, nasty vibe about her. I'd only known her for a week and already she'd had three different boys in our dorm. Luckily, I didn't share a room with her, but we did share a wall, and I heard everything.

Everything.

So more nights than not, I would call Derek at two a.m. and we would go for a walk around campus, freezing our butts off and thinking up clever ways to murder Courtney.

"Hi, Faithy," Courtney said when I sat next to her. Another reason I didn't like her: she called me Faithy. Her deep blue eyes crinkled into an excited smile. "I didn't know you were taking this class, too."

"Yep." Her bright pink lip gloss was burning my retinas so I busied myself with getting out my notebook and a pen.

"Oh, this is so great!" she cooed. "Now we can walk to class together every Monday, Wednesday, and Friday."

"Awesome," I said, unenthused.

"So what's up with this guy, huh?" She gestured to the front of the class, so I assumed she meant the absent professor. "I bet he'd be all over us if *we* were ten minutes late."

"Uh-huh."

Suddenly Courtney gasped loudly and a few people around us turned. She leaned in and said, "Oh my gosh, Faith! What if this guy's the killer?"

"What are you talking about?" I asked, frowning.

Courtney lowered her baby voice to a whisper. "Didn't you hear? Oh my gosh, there was a murder in Denver last night. I bet you anything that's why he's late."

I wasn't so sure. Courtney came from a small town in southern Colorado, so maybe she didn't see many murders, but in my hometown of San Diego it happened all the time.

"Courtney, the odds that Professor Lamb is a murderer are so minute, it's not even funny. I'm sure he's just caught in the rain."

Courtney mulled this over for a second and then said, "Oh, yeah. You're probably right. But wouldn't that be cool? We could go home and say our professor murdered someone!" Her eyes lit up like sapphire fireworks and I smiled despite myself.

"So what's your major anyway?" Courtney asked. "Mine is psychology, so this is a prerequisite course."

"Ah . . . cool," I said, deciding to avoid her question. I had no clue what I wanted to major in and I didn't exactly feel like discussing it with her. "So you want to be a shrink?"

"Oh, totally. I've wanted to do it ever since my dog died when I was five. . . ." That was all it took to get her going. She was like a line of especially chatty dominos; you flick over one and an endless chain of talking ensues. Luckily, the professor arrived two minutes later and Courtney dissolved into silence along with the rest of the room.

Class wasn't as difficult as I had anticipated. Professor Lamb seemed enthusiastic, which was a definite plus—I had been picturing the whole *Ferris Bueller* scenario complete with him droning in monotone for two hours and me drooling on the desk. He went through a PowerPoint presentation introducing the course and then launched into a way too in-depth explanation of the syllabus. It would have been tolerable if Courtney hadn't been bugging me throughout the whole thing. Asking me about this book, that author, did I understand this or that? I wanted to stab her with my pen.

But I refrained.

After class, I walked with Courtney to the manicured front lawn where a huge evergreen tree stood with a bench underneath. It was freezing without the warmth of the sun, and the sky was still slate gray. I was just thankful that the rain had stopped.

CSU was more like a minicity than a college—there were a ton of people around. Students rode by on bikes and buzzed past me on skateboards. Some loafed near the front door smoking, which I hurried to get away from with Courtney hot on my heels. She was blabbing about the reading list for class when all of a sudden she started waving frantically.

"Oh! Oh, hi!" she squeaked. Then she turned to me. "Faithy, that's my boyfriend over there, you see him?" I didn't look. "Oh, he's waving me over. Will you wait for me for a second?"

"Actually, I have class—"

"I'll just be a sec. Thanks, you're a doll!"

Courtney skipped off in the direction of a tall boy standing near the parking lot. I didn't bother to take a good look at him, knowing that whoever it was wouldn't last more than two days. Instead, I shuffled over to the towering evergreen to wait on the bench. I pulled my phone out of my bag, cursing under my breath as the stupid thing shocked me. Ever since coming to CSU, I'd been a magnet for static electricity. People's skin, door handles, and anything metallic would shock me. Every. Single. Time. Grumbling to myself, I texted Derek:

Hey. How's ur class?

Fine. Boring as hell. U?

Same. Guess who was there.

Megan Fox?

I laughed to myself.

No, idiot. Courtney.

Lame!! That chick is hot tho.

You'll get a disease if you go out with her.

**I'm not going out w/her.
I'm going out w/u remember?**

Oh, jeez. I had to set this straight before Derek got the wrong idea—not that he hadn't already. But I couldn't do it over the phone, so I told a little white lie:

Gotta go. Class starting in a sec.

He didn't text back so I looked up, my eyes scoping the lawn for Courtney. I found her in the parking lot wrapped around a boy.

A frightening boy.

He was well over six feet tall with serious muscles, standing near a blood-red foreign car that could have fit in his pocket. He looked so out of place beside it that I almost laughed.

But then my eyes hit his and all thoughts of hilarity flooded out through my open mouth. His eyes were dark, black even, and they burned into mine with an intensity I didn't know was possible. There was something about him that spooked me, although I couldn't begin to guess what. I was too caught up in his stare.

His skin was tanned and his black hair was styled in this oh-I-didn't-know-I-was-sexy sort of way. He was handsome, but too brooding to be cute. And he was staring at me while he kissed my suitemate. His lips were encircling Courtney's glossy pink mouth and his hands were plastered to her backside, but he was staring at *me*.

What a psycho.

Disgusted, I tore my eyes away, but I could only resist the temptation to look back up for so long. *Was he still staring at me?* I risked a look at Courtney and saw that her kiss-fest was over. I watched as the gigantic boy lifted a book from the roof of his car and strode away down the walkway. Afraid that he'd lock eyes with me again, I tried not to gawk at him as he disappeared behind the cover of the bright yellow elm trees sprawling across campus. But he never looked back at me, leaving me thinking that the whole encounter had been in my head. Who stares at other people while they're making out? It was absurd.

Courtney danced up to me, beaming.

"New guy?" I asked. I was mad at myself for caring, but I had to know who he was after that unnerving incident.

"Yeah," she said, sitting down next to me. "Isn't he just the hottest thing you ever saw?" She leaned in like she was telling me a secret and said, "You know, I hear he's like, loaded. Richer than the Queen of England or something. He's got this castle off in Scotland or Ireland or someplace, filled to the ceiling with jewels. How cool is that?"

"Cool," I said, though I didn't believe her. I was pretty sure either Courtney or her freakjob boyfriend was lying about that. "What's his name?"

"Lucas something or other." She waved her hand flippantly. "Who cares, you should see his abs!"

I laughed a little and said, "No, thanks. I'll leave that to you."

She grinned devilishly, eyes alight. "Wish I could, but he won't even spend the night! *So* weird."

"Weird," I agreed. Staring at other girls while he was kissing his girlfriend and not wanting to have sex? There was definitely something strange going on with that guy.

As I watched Courtney cake on some blush, I suddenly had a wonderful, terrible idea. Maybe if Courtney came with Derek and me on Saturday, I could keep him at bay without totally crushing his soul. Before I could talk myself out of it, I asked, "Hey, do you have anything planned this weekend?"

"Nope. I was just going to go out to a club or something. Why?"

"Well, on Saturday me and my friend Derek are going to the river. La . . . La . . . I forget the name, but it's supposed to be fun. Maybe you and our roommates can come and we'll make it a thing."

"Oh, that sounds like a dream! I'll ask Lukie if he wants to go."

I almost snorted with laughter. That guy was so not a Lukie.

I only held it together because I so loathed the idea of Lucas coming along. After what I just witnessed, I was convinced that he was some sort of psychopath and I didn't exactly relish being out in the woods with him. But I couldn't think of a reason to deny Courtney. "Yeah," I said reluctantly. "Ask Lukie and I'll ask Ashley."

"Super. He's on his way to class now, so I'll catch him after." Her phone rang and she slapped it to her ear. She began to laugh loudly, which made people turn to glare at us like we were the rudest people on campus.

"I have to go," I said urgently. "Humanities is next and it's halfway across campus."

Courtney nodded and waved, still laughing like a nut job.

I was late again, and this time the professor had already started class. I tried to sneak in through the back, which at first I thought might work since this class was in another darkened auditorium, but then I got the death stare from the professor. I dropped into the first seat I could find and pulled out my things, readying myself for another dull hour.

But the next hour was far from dull, because sitting right next to me was none other than Courtney's new boyfriend, Lucas.

2

GOSSIP

I was stunned. And in a grand show of coordination and feminine grace, I promptly knocked my books onto the floor with a loud smack. I picked them up quickly and tried to act like it had never happened, but I felt my face redden as several people glanced back at me, snickering. Lucas wasn't looking at me, which was the only thing that saved me from total humiliation.

We were at the back of the classroom, high above the professor. The lights were out to make the screen more visible, so all I could see of Lucas was his profile. I tried not to look at him, but it was hard. There was this peculiar vibe coming off of him.

I'd always been good at reading people. Kind people. Bad people. Boring, angry, loving people . . . there are a thousand types out there and they all give off a distinct *vibe*. Maybe it was nothing more than just acute observation skills, but I could usually tell what a person was like as soon as I met them.

Lucas had a vibe rolling off of him like nothing I'd felt before. It was like every inch of his skin was trembling with pure unveiled anger. But he just sat back in his chair looking bored.

I stole a glance at him, and I was surprised to see that his eyes were closed. I tried to be discreet as I leaned forward in my desk to get a better look at him. His face was like polished stone—smooth and utterly emotionless—except for his slanted black brows, which were knitted together just slightly. It was such a stark contrast to what I was sensing that I was instantly fascinated. *How could someone so agitated look so calm?*

I continued to stare at him until his eyes snapped open. The lights flicked on at the exact same time and I jumped back as though I'd been burned. He looked dead at me.

His eyes were wild—like an animal's. Intense and angular, they were so light they were almost silver. It freaked me out for a second, but then he blinked and they returned to the black I had seen while he was kissing Courtney.

Then I was really freaked. No way had that just happened! His eyes could not have just changed color. . . . It must have been the lighting. I tried to be calm and rationalize. *Don't pupils dilate in the dark? Yes . . . that must be it.*

Lucas's eyes left mine and fell to the front of the room. I, too, returned my gaze to the professor and struggled to pay attention.

"So," said Professor Polk, "Next thing on the agenda is the group project, which is explained in detail on page three of your syllabus. You'll all need to pick a partner. Go ahead and take a minute to choose someone."

I was still reeling from Lucas's eyes so I looked around half-heartedly. Unfortunately, I was sitting at the end of the last row and the girl in front of me had already chosen her partner. *Oh great . . .* I knew what that meant: Lucas. I stared at my papers, avoiding looking up at him. Maybe he'd gotten someone else and I'd be able to find a partner next class.

"Hey," I heard a voice say. I turned and realized Lucas was speaking to me. Or, at least I thought he was. He was as motionless as a statue. Part of me wondered if I had imagined him speaking. But he was looking at me, his eyes, not black as I'd first thought, but dark brown, like molasses. "You want to partner?" He had a deep grating voice that was oddly pleasant. It suited him.

I searched for an excuse. My bird died and I'm dropping out of school? I'm planning on taking a trip around the world? I'm going to go back to my room to turn into one of those crazy old ladies with twenty-five cats?

Lucas's eyes collapsed into a frown. "Hello?" He sounded irritated beyond belief.

I glanced around one last time searching for some way out of this, but seeing none I said, "Sure, I guess so."

"Good." He turned away from me and reclosed his eyes.

"So . . ." I tried to make my brain work normally. "What's the project on?"

"It's on the syllabus," he said. His eyes remained closed.

"I—I didn't get one." I looked around for a stack of them, which should have been somewhere at the front of the room, but wasn't.

"That's because you were late." He opened his eyes and picked up his syllabus. He handed it to me. "Keep it."

"Thanks." I frowned and looked away.

I spent the remainder of the class alternating among shooting nervous glances at Lucas, wondering why he was so mad, telling myself to stop obsessing over Courtney's boyfriend, and trying not to do anything stupid like drop my pen on his white sneaker and get blue ink all over it. Which, I did. Twice.

Finally, mercifully, the professor released us and I gathered up my things. Lucas stood in one swift movement and looked down at me. I gaped up at him.

Lord, he's tall.

"When do you want to do this thing?" he asked.

"Huh?"

Lucas rolled his eyes.

"The project?" he said, enunciating every syllable like he was reading to a three-year-old.

"Oh! I'll meet you in the library so we can work out who's doing what."

"Fine," he said. "I can't do it this week. I got plans."

"That's okay," I said. "How's next Monday at three?"

"Busy."

"Tuesday then?"

"Make it the week after next."

"Okay," I said. "Can I have your number?"

His eyes flashed down at me.

"In case I need to reschedule," I said quickly.

He just glared at me, looking right past my eyes and focusing somewhere around my ear.

"Maybe just an e-mail?" I tried.

He bent, snatched up my pen, and scrawled something on my notebook. He shoved it at me and then straightened.

"Thanks," I said, feeling my face flush from his nearness.

He nodded curtly and walked away.

I wrinkled my nose after him. What a grouch.

I looked down at what he'd written on my notebook and saw a blob of scrunched up numbers, none of which resembled a phone number or e-mail address in any way.

Awesome.

I headed off to my next and final class for the day. It was another long hour of the professor explaining the syllabus, so I passed the time by texting Derek to tell him about my weird encounter with Lucas. He was just as upset by it as I was, which made me feel slightly better about the whole thing. At least I knew it wasn't in my head.

When six o'clock rolled around, I practically flew down the walkway toward the Union, where Spoons was located, eager to see Derek. I hurried to the restaurant and found that I was there before him. Odd. Derek was always on time.

But within five minutes, he arrived and I discovered the reason for his tardiness. He was being followed by his two roommates, Mark and Pete. Mark was a short, stocky guy with heaps of thick muscles from his years of playing lacrosse. Pete, on the other hand, was tall and gangly with bright orange hair and no eyebrows. When I'd first met them, I remembered feeling their vibes envelope me and knowing that they were opposite in more than just looks. While Pete had a quirky, kind vibe, Mark's was laced with a sour smugness that made me dislike him before I'd even heard him speak.

As they came closer, I noticed that there was also a girl with blond hair and freckles attached to Pete, whom I assumed was his girlfriend.

"Hey, guys," I said when they strolled up.

Derek stepped up and hug/kissed me. "Sorry we're late," he said, glaring at his roomies.

"Yo, Faith," Pete said. "Meet Heather." He gestured to the girl standing next to him.

"Hey, what's up?" I waved at her.

The girl smiled and said "hi" so softly I could hardly hear her over the noise in the hall. Her sweet, gentleness washed over me like a desert breeze, and I could immediately imagine myself being friends with her.

"Let's grab a table," Derek said as he put his hand on my back and led me inside. I felt his fingers zap my skin, which made me jump. *Stupid static electricity.*

I leaned over to him. "I didn't know you were bringing Mark and Pete."

"They wouldn't take the hint. Sorry, I know I said it'd just be us." His eyes softened into mine.

Uh-oh.

"No," I said waving him away. "It's cool. This'll be better; I can get to know them some more."

Derek looked put out, but he didn't say anything.

The hostess seated us in a corner booth at the back of the restaurant, and I slid in between Derek and Heather. We ordered drinks and everyone stared at the menus for a moment. Then Mark piped up.

"Anybody hear about that murder in Denver?"

"Yeah," I said. "My suitemate said something about it in class today."

Derek's eyes shot to mine. "What murder?"

Suddenly I was uncomfortable. Four pairs of eyes were staring at me expectantly.

"Ah . . . I don't know," I hedged. "She just said it happened last night."

"It's the fifth one since June," Mark said. "Totally random. All girls in their twenties."

"That's sick," Pete said.

"Nah," Mark continued. "That's not even the sick part, man." He seemed all too excited about this, but I was repulsed. "When they found the corpses," Mark said. "They were exsanguinated. Like dried up old prunes."

I let out a noise of disgust and Derek put his hand on mine. I was so grossed out that I didn't even try to remove it.

"What's . . . exsanguinated?" Pete asked.

Mark rolled his light brown eyes. "Means they didn't have any blood in their bodies, idiot."

"Well, 'scuse me, Mr. Vocabulary."

Mark guffawed and said, "Hell, yeah! I got a 2100 on my SATs."

"Oh, yeah?" Pete challenged. "I got a 2250, and 99th percentile on the math portion."

I glanced at Derek; he was concentrating very hard on his drink. Derek had done pretty badly on his SATs last year. He had to take it four times to get a decent score. If it hadn't been for his athletic scholarship, he probably wouldn't have gone to college at all. It was a sensitive subject for him. But before I could say anything, Heather cut in.

"Who says that test is any measure of intelligence anyway?" she said softly. "Pete got a high score and he thought Nebraska was a city in Arkansas."

Everybody laughed and I smiled up at Derek, liking Heather more and more each minute.

The waiter came by and took our orders and then Pete said, "So did they say who killed those girls?"

Ugh, back to this. It was such a nasty topic for dinner.

"Jeez, Pete," I said. "Morbid much?"

"Nah, just curious. We never had much of this in Missouri. It's kinda exciting, you know?"

"It's exciting that five innocent girls are dead?" I asked skeptically.

Pete looked down at his plate. "I didn't mean it like that."

"You know what I think?" Mark said grimly. "I think it's got something to do with that Whelan clan. Those guys are freaks."

"Never heard of them," Derek said, looking like he couldn't care less.

"They're this huge family that lives out in the Rockies," Mark said. "Smack in the middle of nowhere. The town's got some creepy name . . . ghoul or something."

"Gould," Heather supplied.

"Whatever," Mark said, waving her off. "They've been there forever, but up until recently, hardly anybody knew about them. Got this whole . . . *community* thing going. I think it's a cult, personally, but what do I know?" He started tearing up little bits of his bread as he spoke. "Once a month they have these gigantic parties, real loud and raucous. I dunno . . . there's just something weird about them."

I resented that. Just because people were different, it didn't make them killers. I knew lots of people who were labeled weirdos because of the way they looked, but were actually really nice people. Usually nicer than the *normal* people, who most of the time, were mean and heartless. "So," I said. "Just because they happen to have parties once a month, they're automatically suspects for murder? Maybe they're just family-oriented."

Mark sniffed and his thick nostrils flared. Something superior played in his eyes, which only incited me further. "Maybe you have to be *from* here to understand," he said. "People from big cities usually don't get stuff like this. They're jaded."

I gave him a cold stare. "Maybe there's nothing wrong with the Whelans and it's just people from small towns inventing cruel gossip to make their boring lives more interesting."

Mark pursed his lips and glared at me.

"Chill, Faith," Derek said in my ear.

"Why?" I said, refusing to back down. "Just because someone is different, doesn't make them weird or strange. It just means they're different. It's those kinds of small-town ideas that perpetuate the evil in this world, and it makes me sick."

"Yeah, well," Mark said. "If you knew what the Whelans were up to in the mountains, you'd think differently."

"Oh, really?" I said, dripping sarcasm. "Do *you* know what's going on up there or are you just spreading gossip?"

Mark leaned back in his seat, a smug smile on his lips. "Yeah, I know what goes on up there. I used to date one of the Whelan chicks senior year of high school . . . Beth or whatever." He shrugged. "She took me up there once to meet her folks, and let me tell you, it was weird." He glanced at me and said quickly, "Not weird like, different. Weird like . . . scary. Everyone there looks alike, same shaped eyes, same noses, same hair. . . . I think it's inbreeding, personally. They have like, fifty kids living up there but hardly any of them go to school . . . all homeschooled, I guess." He looked at Heather, who nodded like she agreed. "And when I met her parents," Mark continued, "they started yelling at her saying she wasn't supposed to bring me there—that it wasn't safe." He shuddered a little. "I don't know. I didn't stay much longer after that."

Everyone fell silent and I couldn't find any more ammunition to argue back. I had to admit, that did sound freaky. But maybe Mark was reading too much into it. "Maybe you just had some preconceived notions when you went up there, so everything just seemed strange when it really wasn't."

Mark sniffed haughtily. "Yeah, well how's this for strange? Two of the Whelan boys came to our high school in my junior year—first time anyone had ever even heard of the Whelans, let alone seem one of 'em. Just showed up out of the blue, like they'd been going to school with us all their lives. One day, somewhere in January, one of them fell off the roof of the gym."

"Oh yeah!" Heather piped up. "I remember that! I felt so bad. There was blood everywhere and some girl got sick over it."

"I saw it happen right in front of my eyes." Mark said. "I swear to God, that kid's back cracked in *half.*"

He paused for us to react. Which we did, horrified.

Mark continued, looking satisfied. "Took him to the hospital; stayed only two nights in a dead coma. He was back in school on Monday. Not a scratch on him. They said the Dumpster broke his fall . . . load of crap, in my opinion. And nobody ever explained what he was doing on the roof to begin with."

I raised my eyebrows, and a tingling feeling tickled my spine. "That *is* odd," I murmured.

"Yup," Mark said. He took a sip of his soda and leaned back in his chair, happy that he had finally convinced me that the Whelans were freaks.

"What was his name again? The boy who fell?" Heather asked, frowning. "I get them all confused."

"Lucas," Mark said. "Lucas Whelan."

My heart stopped.

"What?" I spat, choking on my drink.

"His name was Lucas," Mark repeated.

I felt my breath coming in ragged heaves. Lucas? Could this be the same Lucas that Courtney was dating? How many Lucases were there in Fort Collins? A hundred? A thousand? What were the odds that this Lucas Whelan with the superspeedy healing skills and the spooky family was the same grumpy, menacing guy from my humanities class? I knew deep down that it was definitely the same guy. But I had to be sure.

"What's he look like?" I asked, trying to sound casual.

I didn't fool Derek, though. Never could.

"Why?" he asked, turning to me.

"Oh, ah . . . nothing. It's just that Courtney's new boyfriend is named Lucas, so I was just wondering if it was the same guy." I kept my voice nonchalant to try and play it off like it didn't matter who Lucas was. But it did. I'd just invited him to go out into the woods with us this weekend. I had to do a project with Lucas for the rest of the semester. I had to be alone with him. Many times. And if this dude really was a psycho, I needed to know about it.

Mark's tan eyes swept the room and a smile crept into the lines around his mouth. He inclined his head toward something in the distance and said, "Don't gotta tell you. He just walked in."

I whirled around and saw that Lucas was standing in the doorway of the restaurant. He was leaning casually against the doorframe wearing dark blue jeans and a white shirt topped off with a black leather jacket. He reminded me of Colin Farrell—brooding and dead sexy.

I turned away.

"That him?" Mark asked.

"Yeah," I said. "That's the guy."

"Wait," Derek said. He shifted in his seat and turned to face me full on. His eyes were crinkled up into angry little slits. "That's the guy who was staring at you while he was kissing Courtney?"

I could actually *feel* the eyebrows rise around the table. I was definitely regretting texting Derek during my stat class to tell him about the incident. *Way to blab, man.*

"Yeah, that's him," I said at last.

Derek's jaw clenched and he made to launch himself out of the booth.

I grabbed his arm. "Wait. What are you doing?"

"I'm gonna go kick his ass, what do you think?"

"Sit down and *calm* down." I pulled him back into his seat. "Since when have you been violent?" Unless he was on the foot-ball field, Derek was usually a pretty easygoing dude.

"Since some random jerk-off practically sexually molested you."

"Aw, come on," I said, attempting to sound soothing and con-fident, two things which I definitely wasn't. "He was probably just . . . I don't know, staring off into the distance and I happened to be sitting there."

I knew that was a lie. Derek seemed to know it too because his lips drew up into a snarl.

"Whatever," he said. He shook my hand off of his arm and glowered at his plate.

"Told you that guy was a wackjob," Mark said with a meaningful look.

As I sneered at him and then looked away, my eyes fell on the hulking form of Lucas Whelan. He was walking toward a table with a girl I didn't know. I watched his face, set into an oddly attractive scowl, his eyes as dark as ever. They flickered to mine for just a moment, and in that moment, they were silver.

BREAKING POINT

I was in an awkward position. I was sitting in the middle of the Cache La Poudre River—on a kayak no less—squished between Derek, Heather, and a guide with too much aftershave. It was late afternoon so it should have been warm, but it wasn't. It was freezing.

At least, *I* was freezing. Heather and Mark seemed to think this weather was perfect. They kept commenting on how warm it was and how there was no need to wear a jacket. Derek and I were popsicles. I found myself staring up at the sky, the color of ice, and praying for just a sliver of blue to shine through the clouds. Or even better, of yellow—the sun.

"So, Heather, you and Pete are in band together?" I asked, trying to make conversation.

"Mm-hmm," she hummed. Her hair was tied up in a long ponytail that kept smacking me in the face whenever she turned her head. But I didn't say anything; I didn't want to embarrass her.

"Did you two meet in band?" I asked.

"Yes. We've been together since July. We came early for band camp."

"Cool."

"How long have you two known each other?" Heather asked.

Derek jumped in before I could answer and said, "Me and Faith have been together since elementary school."

I wrinkled my nose. He made it sound like we had been *together* since elementary school. Which we definitely hadn't.

Heather turned and gave me a little smile. I returned it and tried to keep my eyes from watering when her hair smacked them again.

"You two are so cute," Heather said.

I turned and glared at Derek, who grinned smugly. I wanted to punch him in the gut. But I didn't. He might've thrown me overboard and that water looked glacial.

"We're just friends," I said to Heather.

"Oh," Heather muttered. "Sorry, I just assumed . . ."

"It's fine," I said quickly. "We've known each other forever, so I can see how you'd get it confused. But we're friends."

I thought I heard Derek say something under his breath, but I didn't catch it. He was probably pissed, but whatever. I needed to set everything straight. He had to deal.

"What's your major, Derek?" Heather asked.

"Oh—umm . . ." Derek sounded surprised at having been asked a question.

I hid a snicker as he worked up a response. Derek was majoring in computer engineering, which was basically code for nerd—something Derek wasn't. He was only doing it because he liked to play video games, not because he actually knew anything about computers. Derek might have been a genius on the football field, but he was far from that when it came to academics.

"Computer engineering," Derek finally answered.

With that I let out a snort, just to tease him.

"What?" Heather asked.

I snuck a glance at Derek in time to see him give me a sarcastic smile. "Faith thinks it's nerdy," he said.

"Well, come on, it is!" I defended myself. "You're only doing it because you like to play video games, but I'm telling you, it's not going to be like that."

"How would you know?"

"Because I, unlike you, actually read the brochure when we went to Freshman Orientation."

Derek grumbled something unintelligible.

"And you're going to end up all gangly and pale with two-inch-thick glasses," I went on, mainly just bugging him now. "And then who will marry you?"

Derek had finally found his voice again.

"Yeah, well, at least I *chose* a major," he shot. "Unlike some losers I know."

I made a face at him and he stuck his tongue out. He knew he'd hit my sore spot. After attending Freshman Orientation a week ago, I was feeling a ton of pressure to pick a major. The university made a big deal about staying on-track and setting goals so we could graduate in four years with our class. They even required us to choose a major in order to sign up for classes. I'd randomly picked liberal studies, but I was sure it wasn't for me. I didn't even know what liberal studies meant.

"What do you mean?" Heather piped up. "You don't have a major, Faith?"

"Not really," I admitted. "I'm just kind of waiting to see what fits."

"I'm a music ed. major," she said.

"I'll bet you make a great teacher." I hoped I sounded kind rather than resentful. At orientation everybody had jumped to pick majors, leaving me feeling like the only one who didn't know what they wanted to do.

"What do you *think* you want to major in?" Heather asked after a short silence.

I rubbed my fingers into my eyes and winced from the cold

that spread from them. "I really have no clue."

"Didn't you have a favorite subject in high school or some-thing?" I could hear the concern in her voice. The confusion. Like she was trying desperately to figure me out.

"I liked photography," I said, trying to make my voice light. "But that was mainly because there was no homework."

She laughed. "In any clubs?"

"Nope."

Heather's shoulders slumped a little.

I was being difficult on purpose, mostly because I was frus-trated with myself for not having chosen a major. But that wasn't Heather's fault. I decided to throw her a bone.

"I was on the track team," I said. "Cross-country."

Heather straightened and I could hear renewed enthusiasm in her voice when she said, "Well, there you go! Maybe something with that?"

Derek sniggered behind me. "Major in running?"

"Exercise science is a major," I said. "But it's not something I'm all that passionate about. I just run because it makes me feel good."

"There are other things you can do with exercise science besides running, though, right?" Heather asked.

"Well, yeah. But I don't really like the idea of training juiced-up body builders for the rest of my life or teaching war vets to walk. So depressing."

"Yeah, I guess that would be sad," Heather admitted. "Well, maybe something will just come into your life when you're not expecting it." She gave me a warm smile. I heard her nice words, but I couldn't buy into it. Without a major, I felt lost.

She whipped back around and I shielded my face with my hands. I heard Derek laughing at me under his breath.

"What's San Diego like?" Heather asked. "I've always wanted to go to California. Do you guys surf and stuff?"

I'd been getting that question a lot since coming to CSU. It was like everyone from California had to be a surfer who says *radical* and *gnarly* and smokes pot in the back of some love van.

"Nope," Derek and I said at the same time.

"You do, too!" I said. "Derek surfs. He just sucks at it and he hates to suck at anything, so he pretends he doesn't."

Derek splashed some water at me and I shrieked.

"No yelling," the guide said sternly.

"Sorry," I mumbled and glared at Derek. He smiled his sweetest smile, and I couldn't help but smile back at him.

"San Diego is cool," I said to Heather. "It's a lot different than here, that's for sure."

"I'll bet it's nice and hot there," she said wistfully.

"Too hot sometimes. But Colorado is like an ice bucket. I don't know how you guys stand it."

"It's not so bad. Wait until you see the first snow . . ." She continued to ramble about taking us skiing later in the year, but I couldn't concentrate.

I wanted to ask Heather what she thought about the murders in Denver. I heard people murmuring rumors before and after class, and Courtney never shut up about it. At first, I had written it off because Denver was miles away and the odds that the serial killer would trek all the way over to sleepy Fort Collins were remote. But all the hubbub over it was starting to leak into my brain. I was beginning to get worried. And scared. So much so that I brought it up to Derek a few times. He had just looked at me like I was losing it—which I probably was—so I let it drop.

But late a few nights ago, when the trees were scratching on my window like fingernails tapping the glass, I Googled the news reports on the murders. Unfortunately, I didn't find out much. Just that all five were young college girls.

Like me.

To make matters worse there was no lead on the killer. He left no fingerprints, no shirt fibers, no footprints, nothing. And I knew they could find out a lot about a crime scene from just a tire print or an eyelash or something. I watched *Forensic Files*. I was informed. But I guess the killer watched that show too, because he was supercareful about not leaving anything behind.

Not only was I scared for myself, but I also felt bad for those innocent girls. There had to be a reason the killer chose them, and I wanted to know what it was.

Maybe Heather, having come from Fort Collins, knew something. But as I opened my mouth to ask her about it, Mark, Pete, and Ashley's kayak came up next to ours.

"Hey, y'all!" Pete called. "We're going back to shore, you wanna come?"

I closed my mouth shut and glanced at Derek. He looked ticked. Probably at me for telling Heather we were just friends. *Well, tough, dude. We* are *just friends.*

"You done?" I asked him.

His gaze stayed locked on mine. "Not even close."

I rolled my eyes and turned back around.

"Yeah, let's go in!" I called to Pete.

We started to paddle toward the dock, where a mass of ancient pine trees stood, shading a rental shack and some decrepit picnic tables. We'd driven out here at the crack of dawn and spent the morning hiking through the nature trails that snaked through the woods. Then we'd staked out a campsite and set up our tents so we wouldn't have to do it later. I was glad for that now, since my arms were killing me from paddling.

The guide grabbed the dock and jumped on. He began roping the boat to the little metal stake as I threw my paddle down on the dock and started to unstick myself from the boat.

"You know," Heather said, wrestling herself out of the boat as well, "we should all go out sometime."

"Yeah, sure." I launched myself onto the dock and jumped up and down a few times, trying to get the feeling back in my legs.

"No, really." She clambered onto the dock after me and rubbed her hands over her thighs. "Me and Pete wanted to check out Zydeco's. It's this club that's supposed to be fun."

"That sounds fine." I smiled and watched Derek leap out of the kayak in one nimble movement. *Darn him and his athletic grace.*

"Perfect, actually," Derek said. He came up to me and wrapped his arm around my waist. I didn't make him stop because the warmth felt so amazing. "We can all go. All four of us. Like a double date."

I glared up at him for a second. Then I turned back around to see that Heather looked uncomfortable. I smiled at her again, but this time I could feel the tremendous effort it took to do so.

"Sounds perfect," I ground out.

. . .

Late that night, everybody sat around a campfire the boys had built. It took them literally an hour to get it going, but I was so grateful when they finally accomplished it that I hugged all three of them and even kissed Derek on the cheek. He'd blushed, which I thought was adorable.

I sat next to him, huddled into his side and curled into a big quilt I'd brought from my dorm. It was an old one my mom had made with my grandmother. It was my favorite because it always smelled like my mom, even after I washed it.

Heather and Pete were sitting across from us, intertwined like an intricate Boy Scout knot. Mark and Ashley seemed to be hitting it off. They sat next to each other and I thought I saw their hands clasp a couple times. I'd have to tell Ashley what a jerk Mark was, even if I only thought so because of his oily vibe. And because he'd said all those mean things about the Whelans.

But even though I didn't like what Mark had said, I actually believed him. At least partly. I'd had to sit next to Lucas Whelan for three days last week and I could feel him raging beneath the surface of his calm exterior, prompting me to constantly ogle him like a total spaz. If he noticed, he never said. Actually, he never spoke to me at all.

Not that I wanted him to.

He was so grumpy the last time we talked, I wasn't too eager to start up again. But after all that talk about his family, I wanted some kind of signal that he wasn't as creepy and sinister as Mark had said he was. Unfortunately, I was more convinced than ever that there was something seriously wrong about him.

I was relieved when Courtney had told me she and Lucas weren't coming with us to the La Poudre. Courtney said Lucas had some family thing, which made sense since apparently Lucas was some bizarre, silvery-eyed, mysterious party-having freak. His excuse didn't really matter to me, just so long as I didn't have to be around him and his manic vibe any longer than I had to.

After my stressful first week, I wanted to enjoy myself, and for the most part, I was. Mark and Pete had brought a bottle of Jack Daniel's with them, and it was already half gone between the two of them and Derek. I hated the way Jack Daniel's tasted, so I'd refused it along with Heather. Ashley, on the other hand, dove right in, so by midnight, everyone but Heather and me were drunk.

"Oh my gosh," Ashley said, colliding with Mark. "Anybody know any ghost stories?"

"Seriously?" I asked. "That's so lame, you guys."

"No, no!" Ashley said. "You don't understand, you don't understand, Faith. These ghost stories are true. Like, so true they actually *happened*."

I hiccupped from the effort of holding in my laughter and looked up at Derek. He smiled down at me and shrugged.

"You know some, right, Mark?" Heather asked. "I remember you telling one on the senior trip to Disney World last year."

"I know one," Mark said. "But it's dumb, and it's not true or anything."

"Oh, but it'll be fun!" Ashley gushed. "Come on, Mark." She batted her eyes at him and I could tell these stories were going to be told whether or not I wanted to hear them.

"Okay, okay," Mark said. He looked around at us and said, "Once upon a time on the night of the full moon, there was this group of chicks who went skiing up at the summit." He pointed to the giant mountain looming over us and I looked up at it. "They were all friends," Mark continued. "There was a good girl, a bad girl, a mean girl, and a dumb girl." I smothered my laughter. This sounded like a bad joke, not a ghost story. Mark shot a dirty look at me but went on. "They all spent the day skiing when suddenly the dumb girl goes missing. The other three friends get scared and start looking for her in the woods and calling out her name. But they can't find her. They decide to split up and meet back at the ski lift at nightfall. So they search and search . . . but they can't find her. Then night falls and they meet up at the ski lift. But the bad girl is missing now, too.

"The other two are really freaked. They call 911, but the dispatcher thinks it's a prank for the full moon, so nobody comes to help. Now it's really dark, even though the moon is shining bright. They know the woods are dangerous, but they can't leave their friends out there alone. So they take off into the trees, hoping against hope that they'll find them.

"Hours pass and the girls are freezing. They decide to go back to the ski lift and try again with the 911 call, when they hear this growling in the trees. They stop and look around. They hear snow-crunching foot falls coming their way." Mark's voice had become low and dramatic. I leaned in like Pete and Heather and peeled my ears to hear him.

"They look down at the snow and see it's stained red with blood. There's nasty, gnarled-up guts dragged all over the place and the girls start screaming. They know it's their friends mangled up in the snow. They start to run, and they can hear those foot falls crunching after them. The mean girl looks back over her shoulder and trips on a root. She falls and the good girl tries to help her up. They freeze and see this huge beast standing in front of them.

"It looks like a wolf, but bigger. Meaner. It's got pale eyes like the moon and it rises up onto its haunches like a human. The girls are so scared they can't even scream. The thing runs at them and the mean girl pushes the good one in front of her to save herself. But the beast bats the good girl aside and rips into the mean one, tearing her body to bits. Blood sprays the trees, the snow, everything. Then the beast turns on the good girl." Everything was silent save Mark's deep voice, softer than the trees rustling around us. "The beast looks into her eyes, walks toward her, fangs dripping with blood and then . . . IT BITES HER HEAD OFF!!"

Ashley screamed and I yipped because she did. Heather gasped too, and Derek started laughing his ass off. Pete and Mark guffawed like jerks as I beat my fists against Derek.

"Shut up!" I yelled. "You're all ass bags, seriously!"

"Oh, man," Mark said. "That was great. I so had you going. You were all laughing and then you screamed like an idiot."

"I only screamed because Ashley screamed," I argued back.

"Uh-huh," Mark said. "Suuure."

"That's a true story too, Faith," Ashley said, still giggling wildly.

"No, it's not," I said dismissively.

"Well, it sort of is," said Mark. This guy seemed determined to make me wrong about everything. "The whole part about the four girls going missing on the full moon is true. The scary beast in the woods got made up after this crazy dude swore he saw Bigfoot out here once."

"Bigfoot?" I said skeptically.

Mark chuckled and took a swig of Jack Daniel's. "I think it was a wolf that got 'em," he said.

I gulped and glanced around into the dusky shadows of the surrounding woods. "Are there . . . wolves out here?"

"Yup," Mark said. "That's why you gotta bring a gun when you come camping out here." He jerked his head toward his tent, and my eyebrows jumped up.

"You have a gun?" I asked incredulously.

"Uh-huh," Mark grunted. Then he must have seen my expression because he said, "I got a permit, don't have a heart attack."

I exhaled a little, but I was still nervous about having a firearm out here. I rubbed my hand over the scar on my thigh, remembering with a shiver the feel of the bullet ripping through my flesh. Five years and the scar was still sore. Derek gave my shoulders a little squeeze.

"Jeez, I'm beat," Pete said, yawning. "And we gotta get up early tomorrow and get back to campus. Band practice."

I heard Heather groan and watched them shuffle into their tent together.

"Night," I said.

"Night," they both replied.

"Yeah, I think I'm gonna hit it, too," said Ashley. She stood and gave Mark a come hither look. "Goodnight," she said breathily. I rolled my eyes.

Mark watched her go into the tent Ashley and I were sharing. I prayed he wouldn't be making any midnight visits. *Yuck.*

The three of us sat there for a while, and I listened to Derek and Mark talk sports. An hour later, having reached the bottom of the Jack Daniel's bottle, Mark tottered into his tent, leaving me and Derek alone in the moonlight.

I was exhausted. Spending the day hiking, kayaking, and worrying about serial killers will do that to a person. I leaned over Derek's lap and didn't make him stop when he began to run his fingers through my hair. He liked to do it and I liked to let him. It wasn't a big deal.

"Hey, Faith?" he whispered.

"Hmm?"

"I'm a little . . . hurt that you invited all these people. You know I wanted it to be just the two of us."

I squeezed my eyes together and tried to think of something to say that wouldn't sound totally mean. I listened to the fire crackling and popping. Minutes went by.

"Faith?" he asked. "You awake, baby?"

I felt my heart skitter.

"Yeah. I'm awake."

"You gonna talk to me?" His voice was gentle.

"I don't know," I said honestly. "I just . . . you know how I feel about us. I don't want things to change."

"They don't have to," Derek said. "We can stay friends, just like we are. We'll just be . . . more. Wouldn't that be better?"

I didn't answer for a moment. I was tempted to say yes. I was always tempted, but giving in was wrong. It wouldn't be fair to

Derek to tie him up in all my messed up crap. Besides, we had tried being together once before and he proved to me that he couldn't handle it. In middle school, I'd turned to him when my life had felt like it was unraveling and he'd been there for me. He'd been the only reliable thing in my life for three years while I pulled myself together. My mom was always leaving on business, my stepdad was in prison, girlfriends were flighty at best, and Derek was always, *always* there. Day or night, thick or thin, he always understood, always calmed the storm. I could have gone on like that forever. Best friends until we were old and gray. But when we were sixteen Derek had wanted to take things further. And I'd agreed because for me, there was no one else but him. And if he wanted more, it was the least I could do to repay him. He'd been my best friend and my first kiss.

And then he cheated on me. The one guy I never thought would break my heart did just that. The ordeal had almost destroyed our friendship forever. But being without Derek had never been an option. Because without him I had no one.

So although I was still hurt inside, I kept it pent up to preserve our friendship. But that still didn't mean I could trust him in a relationship. Derek knew our dating days were over—I'd told him that more times than I could count.

"No," I said finally. "It wouldn't be better, Derek. And don't ask me why not because you know the answer to that."

I felt Derek's hand clench around my hair. I snatched it away and sat up, looking into his bright blue eyes.

"We have to be friends," I said. I reached out and touched his cheek. He grabbed my hand and held it there. He brought it closer to his lips and closed his eyes. I heard him inhale over my wrist, the sensation bringing butterflies to my stomach. I swallowed hard and tried to gather myself.

His lips touched my skin and my heart sputtered. I forced myself to pry my hand away.

"No, Derek," I said as firmly as possible. "You know why. I don't want to hurt you."

Derek's brows drew together. "Why don't you let me decide whether or not I want to hurt myself, for once? You're not my mother or my babysitter or whatever. If I want to be hurt, I'll be hurt."

"That's dumb," I said, because I didn't know what else to say. "It's dumb to hurt yourself for no reason."

"I have a reason," he said angrily. "You're my reason. I love you, Faith."

My pulse sped up at those words. I'd heard him say them before, but they didn't mean any less now. They meant everything. How I wished I could say them back. But I couldn't love Derek. I couldn't love anyone.

"Stop it," I said, looking away. "It took me a long time to get over what you did when we were dating and now we're friends. I don't want to ruin that." I saw the pain in his eyes and my heart ached. That look was exactly what I was trying to avoid.

"I came here with you," he said, "because I thought maybe you could learn to love me back—that you'd finally gotten over everything that happened with your stepdad."

"That has nothing to do with why I can't be with you, Derek. I can't fall in love with you because I can't trust you."

"That's not true. Even back then, before I screwed up, you wouldn't love me, you'd never even say the words."

I started to protest, but Derek cut me off.

"I get why. I get that what he did to you guys ruined your faith in love, but I just thought that you'd get over it eventually and that one day you'd forgive me; finally be able to trust me again. But now I can see that that'll never happen." He stood up and looked down at me, his face a mask of torture in the hazy light of the fire.

I reached my hand out and grabbed hold of his.

"Don't do this," I begged. "You know I . . . love you, I just . . ."

"You don't love me the way I love you, Faith. You don't *want* me." He pulled me up by my hand and did something I never expected. He took my face in his big hands and pressed his lips against mine. I felt my knees buckle and I held onto his arms to keep from falling.

He deepened the kiss, spreading my lips apart with his tongue. I couldn't resist. I let him kiss me, let myself fall away. He'd kissed me this way before, but somehow it felt different now. It felt like the last time. There was desperation in the way his hands raked over my body, the way his lips pressed against mine hungrily, as if he was trying to fit a lifetime of kisses that would never come into this one stolen moment. The thought broke my heart and I was filled with the need to kiss him back— to give in . . . just one more time.

He drew back and looked down at me, the flames glinting in his eyes. He wiped my face, and I was surprised to find that I was crying.

"Let yourself love me, Faith," he whispered, almost begging me.

But I knew this would end the same way it always did. There would be tears and yelling and months of not speaking. It would end with pain. I couldn't take the chance of falling for him again and him changing his mind

"I—I can't," I choked.

Derek's face distorted in anguish. I wanted to reach out and smooth it away, to take it all for myself. He held me for a long time and finally whispered, "I don't want to lose you, but I can't keep doing this to myself." His eyes hardened and he let go of me. "There's only so much a guy can take, Faith, and I just reached my breaking point."

He turned slowly and stalked into his tent. I watched, clutching the quilt to my body as he zipped up the flap behind him, closing his heart as well as mine.

SUSPICION

I lay awake for hours after that. Derek's face haunted me behind my closed eyelids. I kept hearing his voice, feeling his lips over mine.

I couldn't take it anymore. I unzipped myself from my sleeping bag, shoved my sneakers on, pulled on a jacket, and stole outside.

The air was frigid. I almost went right back inside my tent, but the prospect of being alone with my thoughts was too horrible. Instead, I charged forward, hoping to warm my rigid muscles with movement. I walked along the edge of the river and stared out at the thick band of pine trees rustling on the opposite side. The moonlight played games with their branches, contorting the shadows into creepy shapes. I got the feeling that evil things were lurking within the darkness of those trees. Big, scary, hairy things that bit girls' heads off at the full moon.

I looked up and froze.

It *was* the full moon.

For a moment I couldn't breathe as my mind flooded with images of white snow stained with blood. I took in a long breath and calmed myself. It was just a dumb story. It was about Bigfoot, for God's sake. I turned around to walk back toward camp anyway, keeping my eyes on the trees. No matter what I told myself, I was still afraid of them. It was like they were watching me. I could almost see glinting eyes peeking out from between every limb. I walked faster and glanced around to make sure nothing was following me. The wind blew from behind, sending my hair billowing in front of my face. I watched the brownish-black of it snake before my eyes and stretch into the night.

I tucked it into my jacket and walked even faster, almost jogging.

My breath turned to mist in front of my face and my feet stamped hard on the pine needles choking the ground. As I ran, I watched those pines. Those staring pines.

It was then that I saw it: a shadowy form painted against the tree line. It was almost the same shade as the trees, deep green, close to black. I stopped.

There was something big on the edge of the trees. Something alive. It moved, and I took a step back, heart throbbing. I ducked down behind a boulder and hid. Edging around the side of the rock, I squinted my eyes to see through the gray night. The figure was still there. It looked like it might be a person. Then it split in half and I realized it was actually two people.

One I recognized as Mark and the other . . . maybe Ashley? Were they having a make-out session on the opposite side of the river? But how would they even get over there?

I crept slowly around the boulder, staying low to the ground. I wanted to know what Mark was doing out here so late, who he was talking to, and how he'd gotten over there. I didn't see a boat, and God knows he couldn't jump twenty feet across the icy river.

The other person shifted at the tree line and came closer to the moonlight. It seemed to be a man, tall and slim. I could hear them talking about something. Arguing, it sounded like. I caught stray words like *hungry, witnesses,* and *imbecile.* . . .

I inched closer, heart racing loudly, making it difficult to hear.

The mystery man shoved his fingers into Mark's shoulder, jabbing as he spoke harshly. Then he pointed in the direction of our camp and snapped his fingers.

I frowned and strained my ears.

Mark hung his head and swept his jacket aside to stick his hands in his pockets. As he did so, I could see the silver glint of his gun in the moonlight. My eyes widened. If Mark felt threatened enough by this man to bring a gun with him when they met, then this was definitely a conversation I wanted no part of. I continued to watch them for a moment longer until the mystery man vanished into the woods.

Mark stood there for a minute and then he, too, seemed to just blend away into the shadows.

I let my breath out.

I got up and began walking to camp, trying to think of a logical reason for Mark meeting someone in the woods in the middle of nowhere.

I couldn't think of any.

As I was getting close to camp, I stopped to give the trees one last glance. They still seemed to watch me, knowing secrets I could only imagine. I turned around to go back to my tent, but there was suddenly something blocking me.

Mark.

I gasped when I saw him, tripped over my feet and fell backward. My butt hit the frozen ground with a thump and I looked up at Mark, eyes wide.

"What are you doing?" he asked. His voice sounded different. Menacing.

"Nothing," I stammered. "Taking a walk." I stood and gathered myself. "People are allowed to walk aren't they?"

"Just odd to be out walking at three in the morning."

"Yeah, well it's even odder to have mysterious conversations with random people on the other side of a freezing river."

Mark's gaze sharpened on me. I was suddenly all too aware that he had a gun in his pocket. Maybe revealing that I'd been spying on him hadn't been too smart.

"But I'm sure you had your reasons," I said, forcing out a smile. "Just like I have mine."

He continued to stare me down, eyes like knives.

"Okay, then," I said, scooting around him toward camp. "I'll just . . . go . . ."

He grabbed my arm and pushed me into a tree. The back of my head hit hard against the harsh bark, and his beefy hands pinned my arms with an almost inhuman strength.

"Say a word to anyone," he warned, "and I swear I'll kill you. Slowly."

I tried not to be afraid, but it was hard. I knew he had a gun. My mind flashed with memories of gunshots, of my mom screaming. Mark's fingers pressed into my arms, bringing tears to my eyes.

"I didn't see anything but you talking to an old buddy," I managed. My voice warbled despite my try for composure.

He shook me.

"No. You saw *nothing*. You never took a walk. You stayed in the tent where you were supposed to be and you never saw a damn thing. Got it?"

My head jerked a nod.

"Good."

He removed his hands, and I winced as I rubbed my arms. I would definitely have bruises. Mark began to turn and then stopped. He faced me again and before I knew it, he'd punched me in the gut. The breath rushed out of my lungs and I folded over to the ground.

"That's for defending those mongrels," Mark said from above.

I looked up in time to see him drift into the forest like a ghost.

I stood, using the tree for support, and waited for the pain to ebb. Slowly I felt every muscle in my body relax as though I'd been dunked in a hot bath. Tears sank down my face and I wiped them away. I'd never been punched before. I felt like I was going to puke.

I couldn't understand what Mark had meant about mongrels. What mongrels? Surely he couldn't still be pissed about the Whelan thing. And why would he call them that of all things?

Not wasting another moment trying to decipher Mark's insane ramblings, I ran back to camp, climbed into my tent, and zipped it behind me. I crawled into my sleeping bag and curled up.

For a while, I thought about going into Derek's tent and telling him what had happened. Maybe he would go beat up Mark or better yet, tell me everything would be all right and hug me until the tears stopped. But the memories of our fight earlier halted me. Nobody would believe me anyway. And Mark would deny it, of course. I'd just have to keep an eye on him myself if I wanted to be safe. Nobody around here was going to protect me—that was for certain.

I lay awake for a long while, listening to the tree branches creak and groan around me. I don't know if it was minutes or hours that passed, but somewhere between listening to the trees and falling asleep, I heard the low, distant sound of a wolf's cry to the night.

It sounded lonely, just like me.

• • •

Cross-country tryouts came and went the Monday after our trip to the La Poudre. Derek was supposed to come to watch me run, but he never showed. After our fight, I hadn't really expected him to, but I still found myself looking up into the stands every few minutes to check. Even without him, I kicked ass on the track field. It was like every time I started running, the pounding of my heart erased the thoughts of Derek. And the harder I ran, the better I felt. I was so pumped full of adrenaline that I won all my heats and made the team.

It didn't completely eliminate the sting of Derek's absence, but it was something.

Over the next two weeks he called me less and less. He only met me for lunch when I forced him and we hardly ever spent any time together after class. I knew I was losing the only true friend I had at CSU and I felt cheated. As though Derek was throwing away ten years of friendship just because I didn't want to be his girlfriend. Had those years meant so little to him that he could cast me away so easily? It was backward and probably wrong, but even though I'd been the one to reject Derek, I felt jilted. I had said I didn't want to be his girlfriend, but I never said we couldn't be friends. I'd forgiven Derek after he cheated on me in high school. Our friendship had meant more to me—did mean more to me—than one stupid fight. I just wished he felt the same.

The Tuesday on which I was supposed to meet Lucas Whelan in the library arrived much too quickly for my taste. It wasn't an event I was looking forward to, especially after hearing all those sinister rumors about his family.

I walked up the stone steps, halfway hoping that Lucas wouldn't show. He hadn't been in class yesterday, which was a good sign. But I didn't want to be the irresponsible group member, so I had to at least go and check.

I went inside the library and was instantly hit with the aroma of coffee, copy paper, and overdue books. We were supposed to meet next to the research computers so I did a quick scan of the room and realized that Lucas wasn't there. I delved further into the library, peering around in corners and looking over my shoulder. *Maybe he forgot? I wished I could read the illegible phone number he'd given me so I could call him and guilt him into coming.* I'd tried several times in class to get up the guts to ask him for it again, but the intense heat of his vibe always quelled me.

But I did have Courtney's number. Maybe he'd blown me off to be with her. That seemed like something he'd do. I texted Courtney:

Hey, are you with Lucas? He was supposed to meet me for a project but he's not here.

A moment passed before Courtney responded.

OMG, no! I broke up with that weirdo a week ago. LOL!

I blinked, staring at my phone. I was tempted to pry and ask her why she'd dumped him, but I decided it wasn't my business. I was ready to forget the whole thing, when I saw a set of stairs to my left and thought that he might be on the second floor. So I jogged up the stairs and did a scan.

No Lucas.

I went up the third and fourth floors, but he wasn't on any of them. Annoyed beyond belief, I checked the topmost floor, peering behind each and every desk until, finally, I found Lucas lounging in the last one.

"Lucas!" I gasped when I saw him.

He jumped and looked around. His big brown eyes fell on me and they crumpled into a scowl.

"What the hell did you do that for?" he asked. He sat up and cracked his neck.

I shifted my weight and said, "I've been looking for you for the past twenty minutes. I went to all five floors."

He didn't seem to care. He wasn't even looking at me.

"Why are you way up here?" I demanded, still fuming.

"You said meet in the library." His eyes remained on the window beside the desk. I wondered what he was looking at.

"I said next to the computers on the first floor."

He appeared completely unconcerned.

I took a big breath to steady my temper and sat down at the table shoved haphazardly into the bay window. I busied myself getting organized but I could feel Lucas's eyes on me and that boiling energy rolling off of him. I wondered why I seemed so attuned to his vibe—usually I only felt it when I first neared someone. I looked up at him, but he was still staring calmly out the window, totally at odds with his vibe. *Am I imagining things?*

I cleared my throat and he turned his head toward mine, but still didn't look directly at me.

"Are you ready?" I asked.

"For what?"

I faltered. "For . . . you know, to work on the project."

"I'm ready whenever you're ready."

I watched him twirl his pen between his long fingers, fascinated by the seamless motion of his hands and the way his angular eyes followed the pen—focused, unblinking. I broke my trance and said, "Well, Professor Polk has this whole thing broken up into sections, so if we each take two, then we can be done faster." I paused, waiting to see if he'd object. He didn't, so I continued. "I'll take the first two and you take the last two. Okay?"

"Yep."

I nodded and began to reread what my part of the project would be: just some research, a PowerPoint presentation, and a bibliography. Lucas had to compose the actual paper. I hoped he didn't think I gave him the harder part on purpose. I began to obsess over whether or not I should offer to swap sections with him, when Lucas suddenly asked, "What's your name?"

It took me a moment to gather myself. It seemed so odd that he didn't know my name. I knew his name much too well.

"It's Faith," I said. "Faith Reynolds."

"Pretty."

More shock. "Thanks," I muttered.

"Belief," he said intently, his eyes cast carefully away from me. I stared.

"That's what your name means, didn't you know?"

I nodded my head.

"Belief in the unbelievable," he murmured. His eyes jumped to mine for an infinitesimal moment and then refocused on the desk.

I'd heard this about a million times, but somehow it felt different coming from Lucas. While others joked about my name or quoted biblical verses at me, Lucas's tone was melancholy and almost . . . hopeful at the same time. As though he wanted me to agree that I could believe in the unbelievable. His vibe had even calmed, becoming somber for once.

It was a stark contrast to his usual grumpiness, and I was surprised to see a different side to him. I hadn't expected it. I tried to smile at him, but he still glared at the desk. The muscles in his cheek twitched, and when he spoke his voice was rough.

"My name is Lucas," he said at last. "But I think you already know that."

I was relieved to switch topics and get back to something normal. "I did." Then I felt compelled to explain myself—it sounded like I was a creepy stalker girl. "My suitemate is your ex."

"How do you know she's my ex?" His voice wasn't angry, or sullen. Just curious—like he didn't expect me to be so knowledgeable about his life, or something.

"When I couldn't find you, I texted her and she told me you guys split." I paused, wondering if this was a sore topic for him. "Sorry." I didn't know what else to say.

"Why are you sorry?"

"I—I'm," I stammered like an idiot. "I'm just sorry that you broke up. It sucks to break up."

"Nah," Lucas said, shrugging. "It only sucks when you actually liked the girl. It wasn't anything serious."

I narrowed my eyes at him, but he wasn't looking at me. Still.

I held in my words for a while, but after a few minutes, I

couldn't help but spit them out. "Listen, don't think I'm rude or whatever, but how can you date someone you don't even like?" As far as I knew—and I knew a lot thanks to thin walls—he and Courtney had never had sex, so why would he bother being with her at all?

Lucas flipped through the glossy pages of his textbook and said, "I date a lot of girls I don't like."

I wrinkled my nose. "Why?"

"Why not?"

"Because that's dumb. It defeats the whole purpose of dating."

"And what do you think the purpose of dating is, oh wise one?" Sarcasm dripped off his words.

I said in my calmest voice, "The point of dating is to go out with people you actually like so that you can see if they fit."

"Fit," Lucas said slowly. His slanted brows knitted together in an irritatingly handsome way. "Fit what, exactly?"

"Your life."

"And what if there isn't one girl on this planet that's gonna fit my life? Then am I free to date girls I don't like?"

"Well . . . yeah, I guess. But there has to be at least *one* girl that fits your life." I laughed a little, trying to lighten the mood. "I mean, there are a lot of girls out there. You shouldn't give up. You're only, what? Nineteen?"

To my surprise, Lucas's mouth curved up in a rueful smile. His eyes remained on his book. "Believe me, Faith. If I thought there was even a remote chance that there was one girl on this earth that would . . . *fit* in my life . . ." His eyes flickered to mine for an instant and he sighed deeply, looking down at his books once more. "Let's just say it's not going to happen for me."

I wished I could see his eyes, read what was really behind that statement. What could have happened to this guy that would make him so cynical? So like me? And why did I even care if he dated girls he didn't like? It was no bother to me. Besides, trying to convince him of something I didn't believe myself felt like a lie.

"Well," I said, eager to put an end to this topic. "I'm sure you'll find somebody." The words sounded hollow, even to me.

I heard the low, growling sound of him laughing, but it was bitter and hard.

"No," he said. "I won't." There was a note of defiance in his tone that I didn't quite understand, almost like he was forcing himself to believe the words. I itched to know more, but I couldn't make myself speak. Instead we remained entrenched in silence, only speaking when we needed to ask questions on the project and never—not once—looking at each other.

VIBES

It was nighttime when we emerged from the library. Yellow lamps cast an eerie glow over us as we meandered down the campus walkway. I racked my brain, trying to think of a way to shake Lucas without being rude.

Nothing came to mind.

"Where do you live?" Lucas asked gruffly.

"Ah—right over there," I said, pointing off to the left vaguely. "Edwards Hall."

"It's kind of late . . . do you want me to walk you?" I saw him sneak a glance at me.

In truth, it would have been nice to have someone big and strong walk me to my room with all this talk of murders, but I shook my head.

"It's not far," I said.

"I don't mind."

I looked up and found him looking off into the night with shifty eyes, almost like he was nervous. I wondered if he was thinking about the murders, too.

"All right, then," I agreed. I couldn't think of any reason for him *not* to walk me.

The old pines and dying elms lining the campus walkways seemed to glare down at us as we walked quietly past. I stared into the shadows, shivering, and not just because it was freezing. The darkness had made me nervous ever since the incident with Mark on the La Poudre. I never ran at night anymore.

"What are you thinking?" Lucas asked softly.

I was momentarily thrown by the languid tone of his voice. It took me a moment to come up with a feasible lie.

"I was thinking that I have to wake up early tomorrow for track," I said. Though I hadn't been thinking it, it was still true.

"You any good?" Lucas asked.

"It's about the only thing I *am* good at."

His expression was skeptical. "When's your next meet?"

I looked up at him with a half-smile. "Why? Are you going to come watch?"

Instead of answering, he asked another question. "What would happen if I did?"

I'd probably pass out from nerves, but I couldn't tell him that. "You'd see me win," I said instead, letting my confidence show through in my voice.

He cracked a small smile. "Then maybe I'll show up."

We were outside my building now. Lucas leaned casually against the brick wall, looking down at his shoes. He was so sexy I forgot to be stunned that he might go to one of my track meets. All I could do was admire the way his black hair fell across his forehead and remind myself firmly that reaching out and sifting my fingers through it was out of the question.

"Well, I guess I'll see you at class?" I said. I didn't mean it to sound like a question, but he was so seldom in class that it almost made sense to ask.

"I suppose you will," he said. "Night, Faith."

For inexplicable reasons my heart actually skipped a beat when he said my name.

"Night," I managed, brushing past him to unlock the door. I felt his eyes on me the entire time that I fumbled with the lock and staggered over the threshold. I waved one last time as I shut the door behind me, hoping that he would at last meet my eyes.

He didn't.

After our meeting in the library, I did start seeing Lucas in class more often, though he never showed up at any of my track meets—thank God. But his mood was just as pissy as always. Part of me had been hoping that would change—that I'd cracked a layer of his armor that afternoon at the library—but he didn't speak to or look at me unless he had to. Any hope I'd had of fostering some kind of friendship was quickly eliminated. We dissolved into what we always had been. Nothing.

September passed in a blur of homework, classes, and track meets. It seemed that Derek was not going to get over what happened at the La Poudre. The few calls I did get from him petered away to nothing. I never even saw him anymore, never bumped into him on campus.

Derek's absence had created a hole in my heart. He'd been my best friend since elementary school, been with me while I'd dealt with the unthinkable, and now he had left me like I was nothing. Just because I didn't want to be Derek's girlfriend didn't mean we still couldn't be friends. He'd broken my heart and I'd gotten over it for the sake of our friendship. Why couldn't he do the same for me?

The Saturday before Halloween, I was forced to go into humanities class for an extra study session where—hopefully—we would be getting the answers to the test next week. But the study session was a complete a bomb. Not because Professor Polk didn't give an excellent review. He did. But I could barely breathe, let alone copy notes, with Lucas sitting beside me. Staring at me, more precisely. It was the first time since the disaster in the library that he'd so much as acknowledged my existence. Now he was staring at me with beautiful unblinking eyes. Making my spine tingle, my breathing turn to shallow, ragged heaves and my fingers go absolutely numb.

I got zero notes accomplished.

In an act of supreme kindness, Professor Polk let us out early as our "Halloween treat." I looked over at Lucas out of habit and did a double take when I saw that he was still sitting down. Normally he vaulted out of his seat and left as soon as possible. And not only was he still sitting, but he was also looking in my direction. Not at me—he never looked directly at me—but toward me.

"So, I'll see you on Monday?" I asked tentatively.

"Sure." He bit his top lip, creasing his eyebrows together, and then stood up. "I'm hungry." He shoved his hands in his pockets and looked around. "You wanna come with me to get some food?" he asked in a rush. I thought I saw his eyes flicker toward mine for a second, but it was too fast to be sure.

I was taken aback.

"I thought you didn't like me," I said before I could stop myself.

This time his eyes *did* look down at me. He sat back down in his chair and leaned in a little.

"I never said I didn't like you."

"You don't talk to me," I said. "You don't even look at me."

"I'm looking at you now, aren't I?"

"Well, yeah. But you look like you're in pain."

And he did. His face was rigid and the veins in his neck were pulsating. He looked away quickly.

"Do you want to come or not?" he asked stiffly.

I looked at his profile for a beat—took in the hard set of his jaw, covered in dark stubble, the tension surrounding his mouth and his perfectly straight nose. . . . I was worried that if I said no, I'd upset him. Make him explode.

And despite the fact that he was rude, brusque, and generally miserable, there was a part of me that wanted to go with him. I remembered the way he'd mentioned the meaning of my name the way so many people had before, but with that gentle, almost hopeful tone. And the moment outside my dorm when he'd asked me about track. Could there possibly be more to this guy then he was letting on?

For inexplicable reasons, I wanted to find out.

"Okay," I said.

To my delight, he actually smiled.

Lucas and I walked over to the Union together. The sky was deep blue above our heads and, for once, I didn't need my jacket. As we passed through the crowded, noisy yard in front of the Union, a lady walking a Chihuahua crossed us. I curled my lip at it—I couldn't stand dogs.

I heard Lucas mumble a curse underneath his breath and he slowed his pace considerably, eyeing the tiny dog with unease. I slowed down with him, halfway hiding behind his giant body. As the lady came closer, her dog began to growl at Lucas. It barked loudly, which drew a lot of attention our way. I gasped and danced away from its tiny snapping jaws. Lucas narrowed his eyes at the dog and sped up. I scurried behind him, casting a last glance at the animal to make sure it didn't follow us. *They're like miniscule gremlins,* I thought with a shudder.

"What was that about?" I asked, holding in a smile. "Are you afraid of dogs or something?"

Lucas let out a short laugh that actually sounded somewhat like a bark.

I stared; it was the first time I'd ever heard him laugh.

"I'm not scared of them," he said. "But they're scared of me."

"That dog didn't look scared. It looked like it wanted to bite your head off."

"Please," Lucas scoffed. "I could field goal that thing."

"You looked scared," I teased.

"No, *you* looked scared. You got a thing against Chihuahuas?"

"Oh, it's not just Chihuahuas. I hate all dogs."

Lucas snorted with laughter.

"You've gotta be kidding me," he said, lips spread into a little grin.

"No. Why?"

"Nothing, it's just . . ."

"What?" I asked. I searched the side of his face as we walked. "Oh," I said, suddenly clueing in. "You're a dog person, right?" *I must have offended him with my anti-dog agenda.*

Lucas smiled broadly, revealing a set of straight white teeth that stood out nicely against his tanned skin. "Yeah," he said. "I guess you could say that."

He held the door of Panda Express open for me, but I was still staring at how cute he looked when he smiled. He should really do it more often. Much more often.

"You going in?" he asked, his smile fading.

I went through the door, tripping on the sticky linoleum as I did so. We ordered our food and sat down at a table by the window. At first, neither of us said anything. I stirred the fried rice around on my plate and then decided I couldn't stand the silence any longer.

"Can I ask you something?" I said.

Lucas grunted and took a humongous bite of his egg roll. He had about ten of them piled on his plate.

"Why are you angry all the time?"

Lucas's angular brows drooped into a frown. "Who said I was angry all the time?"

"Nobody . . . it's just. You seem angry whenever I see you, so I—"

"Well, you don't see me all the time, so how would you know whether or not I'm always angry?"

I looked down at my plate. "I wouldn't. It's just that . . . I can tell you're angry whenever you're around me."

"How can you tell that?"

"Well, you're rude to me, for one thing." I gave him a pointed look. "But also . . . you have this angry vibe about you. Like you're bursting out of your skin or something."

"I have an angry *vibe*?" he asked incredulously.

I blushed. "Yeah, that's what I call it. I've always been able to tell a lot about a person just from being near them. I get these vibes, like waves of emotion that shoot off from people. Nice people have gentle, sweet vibes. Mean people have pointy, jagged vibes. And people like you—angry people—have raging, crushing vibes that make me feel small and smothered."

"So you read peoples' vibes? Their emotions? Is that what you're telling me?"

I blushed harder, worried that he'd start laughing at me. "No," I said. "Well, yes, sort of. But it's not like some psychic ability or anything. I don't believe in that stuff. I just get these feelings about people sometimes." I studied my plate. "I've never told anyone about it before."

"Why not?"

"Because I was scared they'd think I was crazy."

Lucas cocked his head to the side. "So why'd you tell me?"

"I don't know, maybe I don't care whether you think I'm crazy or not." I crooked a wry smile at him.

He nodded and leaned back in his chair, twirling his chopsticks between his fingers.

"So what did you feel when you met me?" he asked. "Just anger? Nothing . . . else?"

I wondered at his melancholy tone. Did he want me to have felt something else? But that would mean . . . "Don't tell me you actually believe any of this," I said aloud. "I don't even believe it."

"Of course I believe it," Lucas said. "You wouldn't lie to me." He didn't say it like a question or a warning. He said it as a fact.

"No, I wouldn't," I agreed. "You'd be able to tell if I did, anyway. I'm a horrible liar."

"So what'd you feel?" Lucas asked, ignoring my nervous chatter. "Or was that it? Just violence . . ."

I stirred my fried rice some more. There it was again. That sadness. I wanted to know more, so I told him the truth in the hopes that it would get him to open up to me in return. "Well, like I said, you were angry. But there was something else. Something I'd never felt before. Like . . . this bright, effervescent energy. It was odd."

"Energy," he repeated slowly. He seemed a little upset by this, but nodded to himself as though he'd expected it all along. "That makes sense."

"It does?" It made no sense to me.

Lucas looked up at me as though just noticing that I was in the room. He averted his eyes and said, "Never mind."

"Aw, come on. I told you something, now you have to tell me something back."

His expression was noncommittal as he looked down at his hands.

"Why are you so angry when you're around me?" I asked stubbornly. "Did I *do* something?"

Lucas looked up again, but his eyes didn't meet mine. "No. You didn't do anything. I just find it . . ."

"What?" I urged. I felt like he was on the verge of spilling something and I didn't want him to stop himself before I heard what it was. If he wasn't angry like this around everyone then I wanted to know why he was like this around me. "Tell me," I said gently.

Lucas stabbed an egg roll with his chopsticks. "I don't know," he grumbled. "It's just hard to look at you."

I felt my mouth drop, partly from rage and partly because I couldn't believe what I was hearing.

"What? You think I'm ugly or something?" I asked, hardly able to get the words out through my outrage.

Lucas's lips twitched, almost like he was hiding a grin. "Nah, that's not it. It's just . . . I don't know. I don't wanna talk about it, all right? Can we just eat?"

I pursed my lips and said, "Fine."

I glared down at my plate, but my appetite was gone. I couldn't get his words out of my head. *It's just hard to look at you?* What did that even mean? Just because he looked like a freaking European underwear model didn't mean he could make the rest of us normal people feel bad for not being as devastatingly perfect as he was.

The silence stretched between us, but I'd be damned if I'd be the one to break it.

"So how's track going?" Lucas asked awkwardly.

"It's fine," I forced out.

"Have you won any heats?"

Though, I still felt like punching him in the face, I could tell he was making an effort to be nice, so I tried to get over my anger. "Yes. I won one at the last meet. But the other girls were scrubs. Anyone could have beat them."

"Or maybe you're a better runner than you give yourself credit for."

I frowned at him as he carefully avoided my gaze. "Why are you being nice to me?"

"I'm not allowed to be nice?"

"Not if it's because you feel bad for saying it's *hard to look at me.*"

"Well that's not why."

"Then what is it?"

"Nothing," he snapped.

"Tell me," I demanded, furious with him now. First he insulted me, then he was nice to me, and now he was back to being irrationally grumpy. I couldn't keep up with his mood swings.

"I don't want to talk about it!" Lucas yelled with what looked like a shiver. I looked around furtively, embarrassed by his outburst. The cashier glanced at us worriedly, but busied himself with the register when he saw me looking.

I heard Lucas take in a deep breath.

"Sorry," he said. "Bad temper."

I reigned in my own temper and said, "Me, too."

"That's a bad combo," Lucas said.

"What is?"

"Two people with bad tempers."

I looked down at my plate and realized I'd made a heart shape out of my rice. I took my fork and broke it up quickly. "Well, it's a good thing we don't have to be together for very long."

"Yeah," Lucas muttered. "Good thing."

I took a bite of my now cold, fried rice and decided we needed to change the subject.

"So," I said. "I heard you went to high school in Fort Collins? This guy I know, Mark Gates, went to school with you?"

"Yup."

"Have you always lived here?" I knew his family had supposedly lived here forever, but was trying to make polite conversation.

"Just over a year." Lucas took a bite of his eggroll, and I watched the muscles in his jaw move as I took in his answer.

Someone was lying. Mark said Lucas's family had lived in some creepy town in the woods for years. But Lucas was saying he had just moved here little more than a year ago.

"Where'd you live before you came here?" I asked in what I

hoped was a casual tone.

"Russia."

I made a face. "Russia? As in the country, Russia?"

"Is there another Russia I'm not aware of?"

"Shut up," I said, smiling at my idiocy. What kind of person moves from Russia to Fort Collins? And why didn't he have an accent? There was definitely a story here. I only wished I had the guts to pry further. Instead I just said, "That's pretty cool. Did you like it there?"

"Yup. Tons of good hunting . . . nice and cold and remote. Not like here."

"I came from San Diego. It was nice and hot and full of people."

"Yeah, you've got the tan of a Californian." His eyes fell to my arms, sweeping down them like he could see my tan through my shirt.

I felt my heart rate climb. He'd actually paid enough attention to me to notice my tan?

"Yeah, well, it won't last long, here," I said. "Not with all these layers I have to wear to keep my toes from turning blue."

Lucas chuckled deeply and took a gulp of his drink.

"I heard you had an accident," I said delicately. I didn't know if it was okay to ask him about that. If he was still shaken up about it.

"You've heard a lot about me," he said, sounding slightly amused.

He avoided my question. I tucked that info away.

"Mark likes to gossip," I said, curling my lip.

"You don't?"

"Not really. Not if it's mean."

Lucas leaned back in his chair, fiddling with his chopsticks again. "What'd he say that was mean?"

"Nothing. Just that you got hurt, but that you healed really fast. Like . . . too fast or something."

"You believe that?"

"I don't know," I said honestly. "It sounds like dumb gossip to me. Except everyone seemed pretty certain that you were on the roof of the gym."

He remained silent, spinning his chopsticks.

"*Were* you on the roof?" I pressed.

He just nodded slowly.

"Why?" His evasiveness was making me apprehensive of the answer. I almost wanted to drop the whole thing. Almost.

"I was drawing," he said at last.

I felt my eyebrows rise, betraying my shock.

"Drawing," I repeated with more than a hint of skepticism.

"It's . . . peaceful," he said quietly. "Above everyone. No noise. No chaos. It's almost like you're in a different world. A different time."

I frowned, put off again by his sudden openness. "But you fell," I said. "Why?"

He exhaled, then, seemingly annoyed at my interrupting his thoughts. "I tripped," he grunted.

I narrowed my eyes at him, disbelieving.

"Wasn't as bad as everyone makes it out to be," Lucas went on. "I just got knocked out is all."

"Mark said you were in a coma."

He sat forward and the chair hit the tiled floor with a loud smack. "That's a lie," he said sharply.

"Okay," I said in a small voice. My eyes strayed to his hands lying on the table clenched up like rocks. My gaze roamed upward, along his bare forearms. They were so smooth and muscled. Not too muscled, like I'd first thought, but long, lean, graceful muscles. I gazed at the shadows and contours of his skin and then saw something unexpected. He had a thin, white scar in the crook of his elbow. There were two of them, jagged and short like puncture wounds.

"Is that scar from the accident?" I asked, pointing to the marks on his otherwise perfect arm.

He shoved his sleeve down.

"Nah," he said. He gave me a playful smile that showed just a little bit of teeth. "Dog bite."

I smiled back, feeling the tension between us release. "Do you have any soy sauce left?"

"Yeah, sure," he said and handed me his extra packet. As I reached forward to take it, my fingers brushed his. I gasped as his skin zapped me.

Without warning, a flash of fear surged through me, consuming all thought, all reason. Only one thing penetrated my mind: *Get away. Now.*

But as quickly as it happened, it was gone and I was staring blankly up at Lucas as he sprang out of his seat. I could see that his eyes were silvery even though he wasn't looking at me. "I gotta go," he said. He threw his hand to his forehead to shade his eyes.

"What?" I asked, alarmed. "Why?"

"Migraine. Bad one." He grabbed his pack. "Sorry."

He flew through the door and I watched him race out of the Union, almost stomping on the Chihuahua. I heard its high-pitched barking even from inside the restaurant.

I was confused by the flash of fear I'd felt when his skin brushed mine. It had left me with a sensation similar to a head rush—I was dazed and disoriented. I couldn't understand where the irrational fear had come from. I wasn't afraid of Lucas. . . .

At least, I thought I wasn't.

STONE

Not long after Lucas left, I set out for my dorm room. It was already close to dusk and the temperature was dropping fast, so I hustled through the frigid courtyard in front of my building. I was just about to stick the key into the lock when I heard my name. I turned around and saw Heather jogging toward me. She was clothed in mesh shorts and a tank top. Her arms were full with a water bottle and a black instrument case.

"Hey," I said as she approached me.

"Hi," she said breathlessly. "I'm glad I caught you. I just came from marching practice and I don't have my cell phone with me."

"What's up?" How could she be wearing shorts in this weather? I was so cold my nose was freezing off.

"Pete and I are going to Zydeco's tonight and I wanted to invite you and Derek like we talked about before."

I felt my face fall at the mention of Derek, but I picked it back up quickly. "Ahh . . . I don't know." I bounced on my heels, eager to get away, to get inside, to get warm. To spend the rest of the night trying to figure out why contact with Lucas's skin had made me want to run away screaming.

"Oh, did you have plans already?" Heather's face fell too, but she didn't pick it up like I had. She let it hang down to the floor, sad and crestfallen.

Immediately, I felt guilty.

"No," I said. "I don't have plans." Other than possibly taking a run at the gym to shake off my jitters. . . .

"So you'll go?"

I looked around at the evergreen trees, benches, and deadened flower beds, hoping that somehow one of them would give me an excuse.

"Yeah, I'll go," I said at last. "But Derek can't come. He's got . . . some football thing."

"Yeah," Heather said. "Pete told me you two are having . . . problems."

I cast my eyes away. I didn't want to talk about it.

"Hey, listen," she said, "I'll get my roommate's brother to come with us so you won't feel like the third wheel or whatever."

"No," I said loudly. "No, please don't do that. I won't feel like the third wheel."

Heather rolled her eyes at me and juggled her water bottle and the case around. "Don't be dumb," she said. "You'll love him."

"I'd rather you didn't."

Heather's face spread into a sly smile. "Live a little, why don't you?"

I watched her turn and walk toward the building next to mine.

"What time?" I called out.

"An hour! Meet us out here."

"Okay," I grumbled. I thought briefly of calling Derek, so I wouldn't have to endure a blind date, but I knew that would be wrong. I didn't want to lead him on.

I went upstairs and found Ashley sitting on her bed, talking loudly on her cell phone—to Mark, probably. Giving her a wave, I threw my bags under my bed, which I had raised to its highest setting so that I could fit all my junk underneath.

After showering, I stood in front of my tiny closet, doing the I-don't-have-anything-to-wear-that-looks-good thing. I did that for ten minutes before deciding on my low-riding jeans with the accidentally-on-purpose hole in the thigh and a dark red shirt that had little veins of sparkly thread in it. I straightened my hair so that it lay in a glossy sheet down my back and took care lining my eyes with makeup. I grabbed my black leather boots and a small purse to keep my keys and phone in and shrugged on my jacket.

I entered the courtyard outside my dorm and spotted Heather and Pete hugging near a bench. As I reached them, their vibes mulled over me, both excited and warm.

"Ready to go?" Heather asked.

"Yep," I said briskly.

"Cameron's meeting us at the club," Heather explained.

Oh, goody.

We took Pete's car into Old Town and parked on the side of the road in front of a small park, a few blocks from the club. I jumped out of the back seat and wrapped my arms around my body, freezing. Heather and Pete walked hand in hand down the brick sidewalk; neither of them were wearing jackets.

I could feel my teeth chattering.

Heather must have heard it too because she laughed and said, "It's only fifty-five degrees outside, Faith. It's not that cold. Wait until winter hits. Now *that's* cold."

"I'm not cold," I said.

"You're a bad liar." She looked backward at me and I gave her a strained smile that took an enormous effort to carve out of my frozen face.

As we approached Zydeco's, I saw a large crowd out front where people were squashed together, trying to get in. Heather,

Pete, and I pushed our way into the throng. It wasn't more than five minutes before a male voice in my ear made me jump.

"Sup, girl?"

I turned and felt a wave of revulsion roll over me.

Mark.

I turned away without saying a word.

"What's your problem?" Mark asked.

I was so outraged that he was acting like he never threatened me that I actually gave him a response.

"You know exactly what my problem is," I said, edging my way closer to the entrance. Mark was pressed up against my side, jostled by the crowd. I elbowed him away.

"No idea what you're talking about," he said pleasantly.

Then I whirled around on him and whispered fiercely in his face.

"You threatened me and punched me in the stomach. Don't think I forgot just because I never reported you to the police for assault."

Mark was unfazed.

"Well, it's a good thing you didn't report me," he said. "Because you have no proof. And as far as I'm concerned the whole thing never happened. Maybe you had a nightmare."

"You can't be serious," I said. "If I'm not going to get you arrested, don't you think you at least owe me an apology?"

Mark turned his ugly face toward mine. He had this aggravating look of innocence as he said, "Apologize for what?"

I just about smacked him right then and there, but Heather grabbed my wrist and pulled me to the entrance of the club. I heard Mark guffawing as the bouncer stamped our hands to signify that we couldn't drink. I was seething as we walked inside.

The room was decked out in Mardi Gras colors, green and purple lights streaked across the crowds and unnecessarily loud techno music blared. But the blob of rhythmically throbbing bodies dancing did look inviting. I hoped this Cameron guy would dance with me—at least that way we wouldn't have to have that awkward first-date conversation.

"I wonder where Cameron is!" Heather shouted over the music.

Heather took my hand and led me to a table at the back of the club. There were only five or so tables, so we were lucky to find one available. All three of us sat down and scanned the room for Cameron.

"Oh, there he is!" Heather yelled after a few minutes. "See him, Faith? With the curly hair?"

I turned and looked in the direction of Heather's waving. There was a mildly attractive boy walking toward us with dark curly hair that fell to his chin and a thick goatee. He had a nice smile, very white and sparkly, like a toothpaste ad.

He walked up and smiled at me.

"You must be Faith," he said. He had a deep voice, even and steady.

"Yeah," I said. "You're Cameron, right?"

"Uh-huh," he said, nodding. He looked over at Heather and Pete and waved.

"You mind if Pete and I go dance?" Heather asked eagerly.

I shot a furtive glance at Cameron. "Yeah, go ahead."

I watched Heather and Pete abandon me and then meld into each other on the dance floor.

I kept my eyes on them to avoid looking at Cameron as he sat down next to me. I felt his vibe and I could tell he was sweet, a nice guy. Like Derek.

"So," he said. "Where're you from?"

"San Diego."

"Aw, cool!" he said. "You surf?"

I tried really hard to keep from rolling my eyes.

"Nope," I said shortly. "Where're you from?"

"Denver."

Suddenly I perked up and turned toward him. If he was from Denver, maybe he'd heard something about the murders.

"Denver, really?" I said, sounding as friendly and interested as possible. "You go there to visit a lot?"

Cameron shrugged his skinny shoulders and said, "Yeah, I just went to visit my . . . my *ex*-girlfriend last weekend. We broke up."

"That sucks, I'm sorry."

Cameron looked away and fiddled with the chain hanging around his neck.

"No biggie," he said. "I'm all moved on." He smiled stiffly. "That's why I'm here, right?"

I forced a laugh out. "So did you hear anything about those murders while you were there?"

"Oh, yeah," Cameron said, nodding solemnly. I watched his hair flop into his eyes as his head moved. "Five so far, right? My dad's a cop, so he's got all this inside info. But that's all classified." He laughed a little. "Man, I feel like such a nerd saying 'it's classified, ma'am.'"

I laughed too. This time it wasn't fake.

"I won't tell anyone," I said. "You can tell me the classified stuff."

He bit his top lip for a moment and then said, "Aw, what the hell, eh?"

I leaned in, eager to hear this classified info.

"They have a special investigator on the case. He's seen all the crime scenes and says that it's impossible to drain a person of their blood without leaving traces of it around someplace." I must have made some kind of confused expression because Cameron said, "There wasn't even a single drop of blood from the victims at the crime scenes. Not a single drop. My dad said the special investigator's never seen anything like it. The whole thing's got him stumped."

"Wow." I shivered.

Cameron looked away. "I feel bad for those girls. I get worried about Alex sometimes, my ex. She still lives in Denver."

I put my hand over his bony arm and gave it a comforting squeeze. The skin to skin contact zapped me and I stifled a surge of annoyance.

"I'm sure she'll be fine," I said, even though I wasn't sure. I was worried for Alex now, too.

He looked up at me, blind hope in his eyes. "Yeah?" he said hoarsely.

I smiled and nodded.

"Listen," I said. "I can tell you still like your ex—"

"No, I—" Cameron sat up straight and started to interrupt me, but I held my hand up and he stopped.

"It's okay. I can tell you still like her, so we don't have to make this a thing. If you want to go, that's fine, too. I'm not looking for anything here." I gestured between our bodies, to show I meant us.

Cameron made a face like he was impressed.

"Wow," he said. "No girl's ever been so cool about stuff like this. They usually get all crazy and go off on me."

I let out a puff of laughter. "Well, I guess I'm just easygoing." I'm stubborn as hell, but whatever.

Cameron smiled this little half-smile and he stood up.

"Thanks," he said. He held out his hand and I shook it, feeling completely dumb and awkward. I watched him zigzag his way to the front doors and disappear.

At least that whole thing was done with. I hadn't been looking forward to putting up a happy façade all night long. This was better. Alone was better.

But it looked like I wasn't going to be alone for long because Heather and Pete came barreling back to the table only minutes later.

"What happened to Cameron?" Heather asked, wiping the sweat from her forehead.

"He had to take off."

"Oh, I'm so sorry, Faith! I thought he'd be great for you."

"He was fine."

"Do you want to dance with Pete?" she asked.

I laughed at Pete's horrified expression. "No," I said. "Don't worry, Pete, I won't put you through the torture of dancing with me."

Pete laughed nervously.

"Well—I feel so bad!" Heather said, grabbing my arm. "Do you want to leave?"

"No. You guys go dance. I'm good here."

Heather gave me one last "I'm sorry" look and took off with Pete. I returned to staring at the table for a while, brooding over things I couldn't change when I felt a presence standing behind me. I turned and saw a wall of blood red fabric. I looked up . . . and up and up . . . and saw a face grinning down at me.

A sexy face.

"Hello," he said. "I noticed that you were sitting alone, and I thought I might keep you company?" He had a soft, gentle voice. Like harp strings plucking. But I noticed he had an unusually cold vibe.

I nodded and stared as he lowered himself into the seat previously occupied by Cameron. He was holding two martini glasses, and he placed one in front of me. He didn't look like he was twenty-one.

"I am Vincent Stone," he said. "What, may I ask, is your name?"

I swallowed and tore my eyes from him. I looked at the table instead. The table was much safer.

"Faith," I said.

"Lovely to meet you."

I glanced up into his eyes, which were deep, dark brown, like bitter chocolate. The tips of his chestnut-colored hair fell into them, and I smiled and blushed, looking away again. *Why is this guy talking to me? He should be sitting on a throne somewhere with throngs of supermodels throwing themselves at him.*

"Why so sad, Faith?" Vincent asked, leaning in a bit so that his eyes were level with mine.

I looked away yet again, this time to try and hide the truth in my eyes. He didn't know my past, the reasons I had to be alone. Derek was the only one who knew about that and now I'd pushed him away. For good, this time.

"You'd be surprised," I said. I picked up the martini glass, stared at it for a second and then took a sip. I wrinkled my nose at the taste, but took another sip anyway.

I felt Vincent's eyes on me and I stole a look at him. He seemed to be waiting for something. Waiting for me to . . . what? *Tell him why I was sad? Well, I wasn't about to get into all that with a stranger.*

"My date took off," I said.

Vincent's eyebrows twitched upward. "What an imbecile."

I laughed nervously. "It was a blind date. No biggie."

"I see," Vincent said. "So, you are . . . unattached?"

I took another sip of the martini. "Yeah. I am *so* unattached."

"Wonderful," Vincent said. He smiled widely and my stomach churned as I felt his cold vibe roll over me again. But that wasn't all that made me feel sick. Vincent's smile revealed something . . . gross. He had abnormally pointy teeth, like shark teeth but less exaggerated. Strangely enough, they fit his handsome face, and I found myself thinking he'd look wrong without them.

"So, unattached Faith," Vincent said. "Are you a student?"

"Yeah, I go to . . . to . . ." I couldn't remember the name of my school. His cuteness must have been sucking my brain out.

"CSU?" Vincent supplied helpfully.

"That's the one."

"Freshman?"

I winced. "Am I that obvious?"

"No," he said, smiling. "Just young."

I nodded and stared into the blue liquid of the martini, thinking that Vincent wasn't much older than me.

I heard Vincent's chair slide against the tile, and I looked up at him. He held his hand out and said, "Would you care to take a turn on the dance floor with me?"

I smiled at his funny wording, figuring he was trying to make a joke. I debated for a second, and then thought, *What the hell?* I threw back the rest of the martini and jumped down from the chair. I tottered for a moment as the alcohol hit me and felt Vincent's hand on my upper arm. I looked down and saw that he was wearing black leather gloves. I could understand that. It was cold in Colorado. But wearing them inside . . .

Vincent took my hand and towed me to the dance floor. There were bodies everywhere. Drunk, sweaty, stinky bodies. But I didn't care. I loved to dance.

After a while, Vincent placed another drink in my hand and I downed it. Now I was tipsy. Tipsy and trying to make myself forget about my issues with Derek, about my strange obsession with Lucas Whelan. Tipsy and throwing myself at Vincent. Sexy Vincent that talked funny and wore leather gloves inside.

He moved like a snake, smooth and flowing, but seductive at the same time. It was fun to move with him, to dance with someone I didn't know. I felt myself relaxing, succumbing to the dulling effect of the alcohol and Vincent's too-cute-for-me smile.

"Faith?" I heard someone yell from behind me.

I turned around and my heart froze in my chest.

Derek and Courtney were standing there hand in hand, so obviously on a date that I didn't even register Derek's expression at first. He looked like he'd never seen me before in his life. Like he couldn't believe it was really me he was seeing dancing with Vincent. But as shocked as he was, it couldn't have begun to compare with what I felt.

"Derek?" I yelled over the music. "What are you doing here?"

He blinked, glancing from me to Courtney and back again. "What are *you* doing here? And who is that?"

I ignored his question. "Are you on a date? With *her*?" I was all but screaming at him. I knew I sounded borderline psycho, but I couldn't make myself calm down. Something inside of me was protesting, raging at the thought of my disgusting suitemate dating my best friend . . . or what used to be my best friend.

Derek just stared at me, apparently unable to answer my questions, so Courtney took over. "Our first date ever!" she gushed. "Isn't it fab? I wanted to tell you, but you'd already gone out."

Derek took a step closer to me. "Who *is* that, Faith?" His eyes shifted to Vincent. I heard the twang of envy in Derek's voice— the same envy I suddenly felt—and all I wanted to do was make it worse. Make him hurt worse than I did.

I slapped a smile on my face and drew in closer to Vincent, stumbling slightly in my high heels.

"This is Vincent Stone!" I said with a sickening sweetness that rivaled Courtney's.

Derek scowled at me.

"Are you drunk?" he asked.

"Not yet," Vincent said, leering at Derek.

Derek shot him a dirty look and said, "Faith, can I talk to you for a sec?"

"Oh, now you want to talk?" I said. "I've hardly heard from you in a month! Well, sorry but I'm busy."

"Quit it, Faith. Come here and talk to me."

"Why don't you go talk to Courtney," I said acidly. "She seems to be the only one you care about now."

As if on cue, Courtney bounced forward and thrust a clear plastic cup in Derek's hand. "Come on, sweetie, let's dance!"

She pulled Derek away and I glared at him for as long as I could see him.

Vincent put another drink in my hand.

"Who was that?" he asked in my ear.

"Nobody," I said. I tossed the martini back. I was now drunk, which did nothing to tame my unstable emotions. And I had to go to the bathroom. I yanked Vincent's shirt and pulled his face close.

"I'll be right back!" I hollered over the music. "Don't go dancing with anymore strangers while I'm gone."

"Wouldn't dream of it." He flashed a pointy smile and I tried to hide my grimace. *Those teeth*—I wondered if he'd had them sharpened on purpose. Some people did freaky stuff like that.

I weaved my way through the crowd toward a hallway in the back of the room. I stumbled a little and grabbed onto the side of the brick wall. I'd just about made it to the bathroom when I felt a hand on my shoulder. It turned me around and I was facing another wall of fabric. But this fabric was black and shiny. Like leather. I looked up.

"Lucas?" I shouted incredulously.

Lucas stood over me, looking just like his normal sulky, good-looking self. He seemed totally out of place in this corny Mardi Gras club. I would have laughed, but I had to pee and I might have embarrassed myself.

"What are you doing here?" I asked. I reached up to remove

his hand from my shoulder, but before I could touch it, he slipped it away. "What happened at lunch today? Why'd you run off so fast? I know you didn't have a migraine because—"

"What are you doing with Vincent Stone?" he asked roughly.

I blinked and took a step back. "How is that any of your business?"

"Because that guy's a jerk. A major jerk, okay?"

"Doesn't seem like a jerk to me," I said. "He's a hell of a lot nicer to me than you are, that's for sure!"

Lucas took a step toward me and leaned down so that his face was very near mine. Even with all the smoke and sweat in the club, I could smell Lucas's skin. He smelled like the woods and fresh pine needles and something vaguely sweet.

"Faith," he said. "You gotta stay away from Vincent, okay? Trust me on this."

"Trust you? I don't even know you."

I saw Lucas's face break into something resembling a snarl. "You think I want it that way?" His voice was low and guttural— like a growl.

"Want it what way? What are you talking about?"

Lucas seemed to awaken from some kind of stupor I didn't know he was in. He blinked and straightened. "Nothing," he said. "Just stay the hell away from Vincent and—and stay away from me." He turned and strode away.

I stared after him for a second and then fury overtook me. "Well, fine!" I screamed to his hulking form, fading into the shadows of the club. "Who asked you anyway!"

A girl with bleach blond hair looked at me like she thought I was crazy, so I stopped yelling and spun around too fast. I tilted and grabbed the wall. I made it into the bathroom, did my business and then washed my hands at the sink, still fuming over what Lucas had said. Just as I was imagining all the fantastic comebacks I should have said to him, the bathroom door squeaked open and, of course, Courtney came toppling in.

"Faith!" she squealed and went flying at me. She surveyed herself in the mirror and played with her hair. "How's it going with that cutie I saw you dancing with?" She winked at me in the mirror.

"Fine," I said.

"What's his name?"

"Why? You want to date him, too? Derek isn't enough for you, so you have to screw every guy in the universe?"

She paused with her fingers stuck in her hair.

"I was just trying to be nice," she said, acting hurt.

"No, you were trying to steal Vincent just like you stole Derek."

"You weren't even dating Derek," she said coldly. "Don't be pissed at me because you didn't take him while you could get him."

I watched Courtney drag her lipstick across her pouty mouth and pop her lips.

"Gotta go," she said. "Derek's waiting." She spun on her skinny black heel and sashayed out of the bathroom. A group of girls came in behind her and huddled around the sinks, discussing boys.

I stared at my reflection. My face was ashen with shock. I knew what Courtney had said was true. I was mad at Derek for finally moving on, but that wasn't fair. Derek was doing a good thing. He was distancing himself from me. He was healing. I should've been happy for him. I tried to tell myself that I was only ticked because he was moving on with Courtney. But that only lasted a few seconds. I knew that wasn't true. I'd have been hurt no matter who he had decided to date. Yes, I was crushed over our screwed-up past, but I still cared deeply about Derek and the thought of Courtney's lips on his. The thought of what they'd be doing on the other side of my wall tonight.

I suddenly felt sick.

I flew into the stall behind me and threw up.

When I'd emptied my stomach of the alcohol and my heart of foul thoughts, I exited the bathroom. I stopped by a water fountain and sucked in some water to get the vomit taste out of my mouth. I still felt drunk. And now I felt even worse because I had vomit on me.

"Hello there," said a voice from my right.

I turned slowly and looked up. It was Vincent. He was leaning on the wall, arms crossed over his chest. A grin twisted his gorgeous lips and a mischievous light played in his eyes. He was just too hot to be allowed. I grunted at him.

"You look ill," he said. "Are you feeling well?"

I shook my head.

"Would you like me to take you back to your dorm room?"

I thought for a moment about what Lucas said, about staying away from Vincent. But then I decided that Lucas was way more of a jerk than Vincent so I should listen to the nonjerk one, right?

Right?

I was too drunk and too sick to care. All I wanted was to be in my bed, warm and safe and alone.

Alone. The only thing I was good at.

I looked up at Vincent's pretty, smiling eyes and said, "Yeah. Please take me home."

T he inside of Vincent's car was nicer than anything I'd ever been in. The seats were soft, black leather and the dashboard was sprinkled with neon blue lights that cast us both in this eerie ghostlike glow. Vincent was so pale that he looked almost transparent beneath it. Staring out the window, I watched Fort Collins roll by. I watched the couples strolling along the brick sidewalk, watched the lights of the store windows flicker off for the night, watched the trees zip by, and by.

"You know," I said to the silence. "My mom would kill me for this."

Vincent glanced at me as he drove. "For getting drunk?"

"Well, that too. But I meant, for getting into a car with a stranger."

"I am not a stranger," Vincent said. "You have known me for . . ." He checked his watch hidden beneath his black jacket. "Four hours now." He smiled at the windshield.

"Four hours is nothing," I said. "You could be the psycho serial killer for all I know."

Vincent chuckled deeply. "Would it help to know something about me?"

"I guess."

"Ask me anything."

I thought for a second. "Why do you wear those gloves?"

I saw a muscle in Vincent's cheek twitch. "Burns," he said.

"Burns?"

"I have burns on my hands from an accident."

"Oh . . . I'm sorry."

"Don't be. You did not burn me."

"Who did?"

Silence for a beat. "No one of consequence." There was an edge to his buttery-smooth voice, and he shot me a small smile that didn't reach his eyes.

I returned to staring out the window, worried that I might say something else too forward and ruin the night further.

But Vincent didn't seem to mind my drunken questions. "What else would you like to know?" he asked as we pulled up to the half-moon driveway next to my dorm room.

I turned to look at him as he yanked the shifter into park and clasped his hands together. He looked back at me, a pleasant smile on his devilishly sexy face. If I hadn't been so messed up and angry at Derek and Courtney and Lucas, I probably wouldn't have said what popped out of my mouth next:

"Do you want to eat lunch with me tomorrow?"

Vincent's pointy smile widened. "I'd love to," he said. "But better yet, how would you like to do something special for All Hallows Eve?"

I hadn't been planning on doing anything for Halloween, but the prospect of having such a cute date to go out with—not to mention a distraction—was impossible to pass up.

"Sure," I agreed.

"Eight o'clock. I'll pick you up here."

I started searching around in the dark for the door handle, accidentally rolling the window down and locking the doors twice in the process. Vincent reached over and pulled the door handle for me. I felt his chestnut hair tickle my cheek as he brushed by me and I smelled the perfume of his pale skin. I inhaled sharply as his wintry hand brushed my arm, zapping me. A rush of his emotions hit me along with the electricity—it was all desire. I figured it made sense since we were so close, but the intensity of the vibe was star-tling. I'd only had this happen with one other person—someone I definitely didn't want to think about just then.

I clambered out of the car and leaned down so I could see Vincent's face.

"Thanks again," I said. "For the ride."

"Anytime." He bowed his head slightly. "Until tomorrow, Faith."

"Bye," I said and shut the door of his shiny little car.

He rolled the window down and a wide grin split his face, illu-minated by the dash. "Don't forget your costume," he said wickedly.

And he was off. I watched him rumble away and stood outside in the cold for a while, shivering and grinning despite myself.

FOREWARNING

I will never drink alcohol again, for as long as I live.

Those were the words that ran through my head as I blinked my eyes open in the late morning sun. Everything seemed too bright. Too real. Too painful.

My head hurt. My stomach hurt. Even my arms and legs ached, though I couldn't begin to think why. I rolled over and tried to continue sleeping, but Ashley was snoring next to me and I'd always been a light sleeper—even with a hangover, it seemed.

I crawled out of bed, feeling very much like the creature from the deep, and locked myself in the bathroom. I showered with the hope that the steam and hot water would ease my headache. Unfortunately, it didn't so I flicked the lights out. I began brushing my snarled hair and sat on the toilet with the lid down. I didn't want to go back into my room. My room was bright and snore-filled and mean. There was homework out there, and laundry and garbage and other things I didn't feel like doing. It was better in the bathroom. It was warm and dark. And I was alone.

But my small measure of comfort didn't last long. I heard my cell phone ringing in my room and I sprung to the door, catching it just in time.

"Hey, Heather," I said into the receiver.

"Faith! Thank God you're okay!"

I winced at the loudness of her usually soft voice. "Why wouldn't I be okay?" I asked, confused.

"We couldn't find you last night to take you home. I tried calling a million times, but reception was horrible in the club and I couldn't get through."

I felt guilt wrap around me. "I'm sorry. I wasn't thinking. I felt sick, so Vincent drove me home. I should have told you . . . I'm really sorry."

"It's okay. I'm just glad you're not hurt." She paused. "That Vincent guy was hot! Do you think you'll see him again?"

"Ah . . . actually, I have a date with him tonight." I just remembered. I couldn't believe I asked him out.

"Awesome!" Heather said.

I smiled. Sudden inspiration dawned on me—a way to hopefully make it up to Heather for bailing on her. "Do you want to go someplace with me today? I have to get a costume for tonight and I could use someone else around to tell me if I look too idiotic."

Heather giggled. "Sure. I'll take Pete's car and pick you up in . . . ?"

"Give me five minutes."

"Okay. Glad you're not dead."

"Yeah . . . thanks. Sorry."

Heather clicked the phone off and I put my hands over my face. *I am such a jerk.* I cast a look at Ashley and found her still snoring away. At least one of us was a deep sleeper. I rushed around as silently as possible getting dressed and blow-drying my hair—something that is impossible to do quietly.

I was ten minutes late as I fluttered down the stairs to meet Heather at the driveway. She was even later than me, so I had to wait a bit before Pete's car wheezed up. Heather and I chatted about school and our Halloween plans as we drove to the only store that carried decent Halloween costumes within a ten mile radius: an ancient theater shop painted neon green.

We spent over an hour trying on costumes in various degrees

of ridiculousness. Heather had fun picking out the most hideous for me—robot, bar wench, clown, hobbit—while I focused on trying to find something that wouldn't make me look too absurd. Preferably something with a little sex appeal, so I wouldn't look completely inadequate standing next to Vincent. After two hours I was down to the ice fairy, Tinker Bell, a sexy vampire, or, of course, the old standby, the black cat.

I was wearing the sexy vampire outfit when I noticed Heather was beginning to lose some of her enthusiasm. She was sitting in a chair that looked like a throne amidst a pile of random clothing. She fiddled absently with the purple feather of a pimp hat. As I scrutinized myself in the mirror, I watched her sigh out of the corner of my eye. She was obviously either bored or upset about something.

"Do you want to leave?" I asked, pulling my hair from the high ponytail I'd made to make myself look more angular and vampire-ish.

Heather started, looking up at me. "No, no . . . that's not it."

I went to sit next to her, tugging the short polyester cloak around my legs. "What's wrong?"

Heather tucked her hair behind her ear and looked away. "Nothing," she said quietly.

"Liar. Come on, you can tell me. Is it something with class?"

She sighed once more and looked at me with those sweet brown eyes. I liked that she didn't wear makeup. She was prettier that way.

"Tell me," I urged.

I saw her debate for a moment and then she said, "Pete . . . did something."

"Okay," I said slowly. "Something bad, I take it."

Heather nodded. Her eyes welled with tears and I shushed her gently.

She swallowed. "It was last night after the club. We were in his dorm room kissing and . . . I could tell he wanted to . . . you know . . . *do* it. But I never have before and I told him I wasn't sure. Then he started giving me this big long speech about how much he loves me and he only wants to be with me." Heather's words were sweet, but the tone of her voice was sour. I could tell this story was going someplace bad. I squeezed Heather's hand.

"Go on," I said. "It's okay."

"Well, I told Pete that I loved him too, but that I just . . . I just wasn't ready, you know?"

"I know. You were right to tell him how you really felt. That was brave."

Her freckled face creaked into a small smile for a brief instant. Then it died and her face grew pale, wrought with dirty shadows. I braced myself for what I already knew was coming. That look on her face . . . I knew that look so well. The same look my mother had for months after what happened.

Hollow.

Broken.

It was a face only a scumball man could put on a woman. I prayed and prayed that I was wrong. That Pete was different.

"He started to get angry," Heather whispered. "Yelling about how I didn't love him at all. That if I really cared for him, I'd just do it."

I winced, shaking my head. If Pete could do this—nice, funny, gangly Pete—then there was really no hope for the male sex.

"I yelled back," Heather said. "He was being so mean . . ."

I drew in a deep breath to steady my voice. "Then what?"

"He said . . . he said he was going to break up with me if I didn't do it. So I . . . I . . ." She choked up and I wrapped my arm around her.

"Heather," I murmured. "I'm so sorry."

She sniffed loudly and said, "So I broke up with him."

I stared. I'd thought she was going to say she did it. I drew back, looking at her miserable tearstained face with a new respect. "Wow," I said. "Well . . . good."

"Good?" she asked. "Good?"

"No," I said quickly. "I didn't mean it like that. I just meant that it was good you didn't let him pressure you into it."

The fire in her eyes died and she nodded.

I released a long breath. "When you first started talking I thought it was going to be something bad. Not that this isn't bad. But it could have been way worse."

She frowned, looking at me like I was crazy. "What else could be worse?"

I said nothing, but there was a lot more Pete could have done.

"What did you think I was going to say?" Heather asked. Her voice was cautious, like she was testing the words as she spoke them.

I scratched my eyebrow, looking around uselessly.

"Faith," Heather said, lowering her voice. "Did you think he *forced* me?"

My eyes hit hers, locking there.

Heather's expression grew shocked as she realized that was exactly what I had been thinking.

"Pete would never do that," she said. "You don't know him."

"I know his kind."

"Kind?"

"Yes. The kind of man that would try to force a woman to have sex with him. The kind of man that says one thing and does another, that lets you down time after time . . . that . . . that does things you can't even imagine. I know that kind of man, and maybe you're too blinded by your feelings for him to see it, but *I* know it's only a matter of time before Pete becomes just as horrible as him!"

Heather's face was stricken.

"What are you talking about?" she asked faintly. "Horrible as who?"

I faltered, glancing around at the sallow cashier, gawking at us. My face flushed.

"No one," I said. "Nothing. Just—forget it."

I got up and flew into the changing room, mortified by my outburst. I hadn't talked about that day in years, but hearing Heather's story had brought it all back and now the memories flooded my vision, just as terrifying and painful as they were when I was thirteen. And now I'd yelled at Heather, too. Antagonized the only friend I had left at CSU. I sat on the filthy carpet, tempted to cry, but I refused. I wouldn't cry over him again.

Heather came in a few minutes later, but I didn't look up.

"Can I sit?" she asked gently.

I just nodded.

We were like that for a moment before Heather broke the silence.

"If there's something you want to tell me, you know you can, right? I'm your friend. You can tell me if there's something Derek did. I know you guys don't speak anymore so . . ."

I whipped around.

"Derek never did anything to me." At least, nothing that involved coercion into sex.

"But someone did," she urged.

I looked away again. I hated to talk about this, but Heather was right. She was a friend. She'd opened up and shared something personal with me. I felt like I should reciprocate. Plus, there was a small part of me that wanted to talk about it—that hoped for some sort of closure.

"It was my mom," I admitted. "She's like, the smartest person in the world, but she's an idiot when it comes to men. The first was my dad. He was a major deadbeat. He left us when she got pregnant. I never knew him. But my stepdad . . .

"Sometimes he was great. The perfect dad—like how my real father should have been. But then sometimes . . . and I never knew what set him off. But I'd hear through the walls. I'd hear him hitting her. He would scream and yell. And then he'd leave for a few hours, come back drunk and when he woke up in the morning it was like it never happened. My mom covered the bruises with makeup and nobody ever spoke about it. It went on like that for years until one day . . ." I blew out a puff of air, releasing the anger with it. "He took it to the next level. He attacked us both. I think that was the final straw for my mom. She could handle him hitting her, but when he hurt me . . . she finally fought back. She's a lawyer and after the whole . . . incident, she got him put in prison.

"But I loved my stepdad, as crazy as that sounds. I was young at the time. I didn't understand what was happening. After everything, I was so confused—still am, I guess. I don't understand how you can trust someone with your entire body and soul, like I did my stepdad, and then they just . . . betray you. Without any warning or purpose. It's why I have a hard time trusting anyone, especially men. Whenever I do, I get hurt." *Just like when Derek cheated on me.* I'd thought he was the only guy on Earth I could trust, but even he'd let me down.

I looked over at Heather then, thinking maybe I'd revealed too much. I tried to cover. "I just . . . when you said Pete did something and I saw that look on your face, I'd seen it before. I'd seen my mom wearing that expression after the incident and . . ." I didn't know what to say. "I'm sorry," I blurted. "I didn't mean to accuse Pete."

Heather nodded slowly. "I understand now. It's okay."

"But what he did was still wrong. It wasn't physical violence, but he tried to manipulate you into having sex. You were completely right to dump him."

Heather turned away with this sad, unsure expression on her face. "I know, but I love him. I kind of want to go see him. Talk to him about what happened."

"Are you serious?"

"I know you won't understand," she said. "And I don't expect you to after what you just told me about your stepdad. But I just feel like if I don't, I'll regret it forever. He was really drunk last night . . . part of me thinks he didn't even know what he was saying."

"He'll lie to you," I said. "He'll lie to get you back."

She didn't say anything.

"And you'll just forgive him?" I questioned, sounding a little harsher than I intended.

"Everybody makes mistakes," she whispered.

I could have argued that, but I didn't. There was no point. She was going to do this no matter what I said. Trying to force her would only drive a wedge through our relationship and I really liked Heather. I just had to be there for her and try to help her as best I could.

But I would never forgive Pete. And I would never forget it, either.

"Let's get out of here," I said finally.

Heather nodded again and got to her feet. I followed suit, and tried to lighten the mood as I surveyed myself in the mirror—still wearing the vampire costume.

"I think I'll just be a sexy vampire tonight," I said pensively. "Vincent might like having someone around who's as pale as he is."

After that ordeal, I was pretty much spent. My brain felt like smoldering ash. I didn't feel like doing anything, let alone going on a date.

But I'd agreed to go and I had no way of canceling, since I didn't have Vincent's phone number. My only other option was to stand him up, which felt too mean. All I could hope was that by the time eight o'clock came, the pain of reliving my life's most traumatic event would have ebbed some.

I still had a few hours to kill before I had to start getting ready and I decided to take care of the laundry that had been accumulating for the past two weeks. If I didn't do it today, I'd be stuck wearing the vampire outfit to class, which was so not happening. I gathered the mountain of clothes spilling over my hamper and plodded off to the laundry room in the common area between the dorm buildings.

I was relieved to find it deserted. The bluish, flickering light of the fluorescents above me made everything look grainy, and I could smell a thousand different kinds of laundry detergent. The floor was sticky beneath my feet as I went to the washing machines.

I set my basket on one of the dented washers, rummaged around in my pocket for some bills and went to the change machine. As I turned around with my coins, I yelped and dropped it all. Quarters rolled across the linoleum.

Lucas Whelan lounged in the corner of the room. He was sitting on a plastic chair, bent and wilting from his weight. His sandaled feet were propped up on a washing machine. He was wearing a thin, white tank top and cargo shorts. All he needed was a Mai Tai and some sunglasses and he'd fit right in on Del Mar beach. Except that his vibe was more befitting of a pro-wrestling champ—enraged and violent.

He stared at me for a moment, eyebrows cocked. Then his deep, grating voice filled the silence.

"Nice to see you alive," he grumbled.

His sarcasm ignited my indignation immediately—I still hadn't forgiven him for last night's rudeness.

"What's that supposed to mean?" I snapped.

"I tell you to stay away from Stone and you get into a car with him?" He eyed me beadily. "Pretty dumb, Faith."

"How do you even know what I did last night? You left Zydeco's."

He just stared at me baldly and I realized I already knew the answer. He'd been watching me. The thought made my knees weak, both because it was scary and tantalizing at the same time. But I couldn't let him see that.

"What I do with my life is none of your business," I said crisply and bent to pick up my fallen quarters. "Besides, I thought you wanted me to leave you alone? Why do you even care?"

"I don't."

"Well, good."

I walked to my washing machine in a huff and focused fully on separating my whites from my colors and not looking at Lucas. Not thinking about his gorgeous dark eyes watching me. Not imagining them changing colors. Not picturing his big tan hands on my . . .

"You got a date tonight?" Lucas asked.

I jumped, my heart racing stupidly. It didn't make sense that I should feel nervous around him—I practically hated him. But his presence made me jittery, almost giddy. I couldn't stop it. I took a deep breath and tossed my clothes into the washer next to me. "Yeah, actually. How'd you know?"

"It's Halloween. Everyone's doing something and I just figured someone like you—you'd have a date."

Someone like me . . . I tried to decide if that was a compliment or an insult. I decided to go with compliment to avoid another fight. But that didn't mean I was about to reveal that I had a date with Vincent in a few hours. I decided to try and divert.

"So are you?" I asked. "Doing anything, I mean?" I looked up with a shy smile on my face to show I was trying to be friendly—

not snarky—but he wasn't looking. He was staring at his clothes in the dryer, spinning around frantically.

"Nah. I don't much like Halloween. Too many freaks wandering around." Lucas paused and I watched from the corner of my eye as his lips pressed together as if trying to stop himself from speaking. "You going with that Derek guy?"

I stared at him, amazed. "How do you know about Derek?"

"I got eyes." He shrugged his monstrous shoulders.

Oh yes . . . he had eyes all right. Deep, brown, beautiful eyes that happened to turn silver whenever he looked at me.

Not that he ever looked at me.

"No," I said. "Not Derek."

"New guy?"

I untwisted the cap of my detergent. "Kind of."

I saw Lucas lift his head and look at the ceiling. "Jeez, how many different ways do I gotta ask you to tell me this guy's name?"

I laughed nervously, getting the feeling that he already *knew* I was going out with Vincent and he was just trying to get me to admit it. I tried to stall.

"I just . . . I don't think you'd like it," I said. "Not that it matters if you do or you don't. I don't know." I concentrated on pouring the Tide into the cap, but I slopped it on my hands anyway. I wiped it off, feeling fidgety and clumsy.

"Faith," Lucas said and I looked up. My heart all but stopped when he said my name. He stood and came closer to me. He was actually looking me in the eyes, but his face was rigid, like he was silently enduring some extreme measure of pain. "Please don't tell me you're going on a date with Vincent tonight."

I could feel my face set into a defiant expression. "It's none of your business," I said stiffly. "Butt out."

Lucas's jaw muscles jumped and I saw his fist clench around the top of one of the washing machines. I could swear his fingers were making impressions in the metal.

"You can't go out with him," he said. His voice was low and threatening and I felt my heart start to pound harder. He was so close to me. He'd never come this close. His muscled form took up all of my vision, like there was nothing in the world except for him. Nothing but Lucas.

"Why not?" I managed to ask, amidst my inner turmoil. "What's your problem with Vincent?"

"You don't know anything about him, but you're willing to be alone with him—"

"He never said we'd be alone," I interrupted. Well, there was the car ride, but I'd been fine with him last night.

Lucas's perfectly shaped lips curled up in a snarl. "Damn it, Faith! Why won't you just listen to me?" His eyes were molten silver, scalding my skin wherever they touched.

I felt my legs back up all by themselves.

Lucas seemed to realize he was scaring me. He closed his eyes and his face smoothed; it was stone again. Hard, emotionless stone. He unclenched his hand from the washing machine and huffed through his nose.

"Never mind," he said. "Go ahead and go out with him if you want to so badly. Lord knows it'll make things a whole hell of a lot easier for me."

He whipped around and returned to his plastic chair, throwing his feet up onto the washer, just as I first found him. I stared, a touch unsettled now.

"What's that supposed to mean?" I asked from across the room.

"Nothin'. It doesn't mean anything." His eyes flew to mine and they were silver again. I gasped as he took a long blink. "You don't mean anything," he said so low, I could barely hear him. He opened his eyes again, but he wasn't looking at me. Then the dryer buzzed loudly, making me jump. Lucas shoved out of his chair, swiped his clothes into a black laundry basket and strode out of the room, leaving me standing alone, clutching my dirty towels as if they were the only things in the world that made sense anymore.

ALL HALLOWS' EVE

en minutes after eight and I was still fussing with my reflection in the mirror, regretting choosing the sexy vampire costume. The skirt was too short, the collar too high, and my hair—this was a disaster. I applied a layer of red lipstick to try and make myself look less peaked since I'd gone overboard with the white powder. But it was no use. I looked more like a rotting corpse than delicately dead, as I'd been aiming for. But I had no more time to fret.

I threw my cell phone into my purse, slid on a pair of spiky heels, and launched myself through the door. As I hit the main floor, I hoped Vincent hadn't already left without me. Or thought I'd stood him up, which I almost did.

My conversation with Lucas that afternoon had unnerved me. Why would Lucas—a near stranger who seemed to hate me—care if I went out with Vincent Stone? Did these two have some kind of bad blood between them?

I didn't know. But I did know that my date with Vincent was the only thing keeping me from crawling under my sheets and wallowing over my conversation with Heather earlier—not to mention discovering that my ex-best friend was dating Courtney. It was a distraction. That's all.

I raced toward the driveway in front of my building, realizing quickly that I'd forgotten my jacket in my room. Cursing myself, and shivering uncontrollably, I turned the corner and saw Vincent standing under a street lamp next to his shiny black car. He was wearing a very peculiar costume. He looked to be some sort of warrior. His chest was bare and draped with argyle cloth that hung over his shoulder. At his side was a rusty scabbard and a fake sword. He wore leather bracers and high leather boots, scuffed with what looked like years and years of use. He looked handsome, to say the least—like a character out of *Braveheart*.

I walked up to him, shaking, and not just from the cold. His odd, callous vibe touched me once I was close enough, but I could also feel that he was in good spirits.

"Hello," he said pleasantly. "Happy Halloween." His dark eyes raked over my body appraisingly, lingering more than was totally necessary on my chest. "What are you?"

"A sexy vampire," I said. I made a little hissing noise, trying to make a joke.

Vincent obviously thought it was hilarious because he burst out with this wild, maniacal laughter. I stared, thinking it wasn't *that* funny. His mirth abated and he stroked my cheek with a gloved hand, still chuckling.

"An ironically . . . appropriate choice," Vincent approved. "But we don't exactly match, do we?"

I shrugged. "What are you?"

"A barbarian."

My eyes found his slim chest, perfectly sculpted and glowing underneath the moonlight. I made myself take a step away from him. I was worried I might do something impulsive. Like touch his abs.

"Yes, we should get going," Vincent said. He bent and swung the door open for me in one fluid movement.

I got in and watched as he walked slowly around the front of the car, as though giving me time to admire the perfect gait of his step. He slipped into the driver's seat, pushed the shifter into first gear, and sped off down the road, heading toward the highway. I wondered where we were going.

"I have to admit," Vincent said after a moment's tense silence, "I did not think you would show."

I immediately thought of Lucas's warning and admitted, "I almost didn't."

"Hmm, yes . . . well"—Vincent said and his lips drew up into a dry smile—"I'm certainly glad you did. It would have been most embarrassing to show up at my own party without a date."

I turned to look at Vincent's profile, surprised. "I didn't know it was your party." I didn't even know we were *going* to a party, but I didn't want to seem dense.

"Indeed. I have always been a fan of Halloween."

Vincent exited onto a long, desolate road suffocated with countless pines on both sides. There were very few other cars.

"Are we . . . going to your house?" I asked.

"No, no, not at all. I wouldn't subject my home to that kind of trauma," he said with a chuckle, giving me a genial smile. "I've discovered the hard way that partygoers tend to leave their host with quite a bit of mess in the morning. No, I've rented a barn in one of the more remote areas outside of Old Town. Don't want to wake the neighbors." He winked at me. I usually didn't like boys that winked—it just seemed forced or lame—but on Vincent it worked. I found myself glad I'd put on so much white powder so he couldn't see me blush.

Twenty minutes later, Vincent turned down an unmarked dirt road. I spotted several other couples and big groups of college kids walking down the lane toward an old barn. In the light of the headlights I watched the various costumes—zombies sporting oozing wounds, petite pixies shimmering with neon glitter, pirates, sexy policewomen, and a guy who looked completely naked except for a pizza box strapped around his waist.

Vincent and I snickered at that last one.

"I always enjoy seeing how creative young minds can be," he commented.

I giggled as Vincent pulled up amongst a gathering of parked cars lining the road. We got out and I heard the deep pounding of music from inside the barn mingled with the occasional girl shrieking with fear. I looked up at Vincent nervously.

"Just a little entertainment for the crowds," he explained. He put his arm around my waist as we began walking toward the barn and his vibe hit me harder than ever—anticipation.

I was starting to grow more and more nervous about what was to come. What kind of entertainment did he mean? I'd had a fear of haunted houses since middle school when one of the guys with knives lurking around grabbed me and pretended to stab me until I cried. I'd gotten him in big trouble, of course, because you're not supposed to grab people, but the event had traumatized me.

As we drew closer, I saw a crowd of people in front of the big double doors angling to get inside. Vincent took my hand and drifted straight to the front of the crowd where a pair of gigantic men dressed as trolls stood, one of whom held a clipboard. Vincent whispered smoothly to the troll and he bent to undo the chains crisscrossing the doorway.

A high-pitched squeal from inside made my knees buckle. Vincent had to tug hard to get me to move through the doorway and away from the annoyed grumbles of the crowd.

At first, I couldn't see much. Smoke machines fogged the place and black lights inverted all of the colors, making everything trippy and distorted. But as we went further in, the smoke dissipated. People were everywhere, sweaty and sticky with glitter glue or fake blood. Rock music blared, glowing drinks drifted around for the taking, and bodies gyrated to the grinding beat of the music. Poofy wigs, protruding costumes, spider webs, someone's amputated arm—it was all a blur.

But I loved it.

My fear of haunted houses was obliterated by the madness. Everything was so completely abnormal that it did exactly what I'd hoped—it took away every bad feeling I'd had up until then. The ordeal with Heather—gone. The squabble with Lucas—nonexistent. Jealousy over Derek—Derek *who*? What did it matter when I could spend one glorious night dancing with Vincent, this indecently perfect barbarian? I could finally crawl out from my tortured thoughts, stop obsessing over what I couldn't change, and have some fun!

Vincent grabbed a Jell-O shot from a blue-skinned fairy wafting by and handed it to me with a wide grin.

"Well, what do you think?" he shouted over the music.

I took the Jell-O shot, but didn't down it. The memories of this morning were still too vivid.

"It's awesome!" I yelled. I was beginning to wonder where Vincent got the money to throw a party of this magnitude. Fancy foreign cars, designer clothes, ridiculously cool parties had to mean he came from money. I was tempted to ask him about it, but my mom always said that asking people about money was rude. So instead I started to ask Vincent if he wanted to dance.

"Hey, do you want to—"

That's when it happened. Something walking by us—something large and furry—suddenly turned and roared in my face, taking my shoulders and shaking me roughly. I screamed and threw my hands across my face, trying to protect myself from the thing's bloody jaws.

But then, as quickly as it had happened, it was over. The thing released me—I thought I heard a hoarse chuckle—and wandered off to frighten some other unsuspecting girl. I held my hands to my throat, heart throbbing wildly.

I heard Vincent laughing and I turned to look up at him, eyes wide, too shocked to work up any anger yet.

"You should have seen your face," he said with a gasp, laughing cruelly. "You almost wet yourself!"

I gulped and tried to slow my breathing.

"What the hell was that?" I breathed. I couldn't hear myself over the music, but Vincent had no problem.

"I believe it was a worgen," Vincent said, as he stopped laughing.

"A what?"

"Some sort of beast-creature—like a werewolf." His eyes glittered mercilessly. "Did it scare you terribly?"

It would have been useless to lie. The whole barn had heard me scream. I just glared at Vincent's shining, pale face and waited for him to take the hint and move on.

He did. He gave me an endearing smile and put his hand on my upper arm, stroking my skin gently with his gloved thumb.

"You were asking me something?"

It took a moment for me to remember. "I wanted to dance," I said dejectedly.

"And so we shall!" Vincent slung me into the throng of wildly flailing bodies and effectively distracted me from my scare. Just like the night before, he was a fabulous dancer.

A ges later, or so it seemed, I was sweating profusely and completely worn out. I brought Vincent's face down to mine, noting enviously that he didn't have a drop of sweat on him, and asked if we could go outside to get some air.

He agreed with a nod and pulled me through the crowd. As we weaved in between a drunken chain-saw murderer and Darth Vader, my eyes found a couple making out in a corner. Strobe lights started up and everything became choppy, like time had suddenly slowed down. The couple's bodies writhed and struggled against each other. I wanted to look away, but as Vincent tugged me across the room, my eyes remained stuck to them as though I was hypnotized.

And then, without warning, the girl's mouth slid to the guy's neck and a spurt of dark liquid erupted from between her lips. Blood—dripping, gushing . . . *oozing* down his chest. My heart sputtered to a stop as I stared, horrified. I wanted to call out, to tell Vincent what was happening, but my mouth didn't seem to work. The strobe lights continued to illuminate the previously enshrouded couple as the guy stiffened and the girl's body wrapped around him like fleshy tentacles. Was she . . . *sucking* on his neck? *Sucking his blood?* The smoke machines went wild again and the room became foggy. I couldn't see them anymore, couldn't see the blood. But I could swear I heard the guy's ragged screams.

Or maybe that was someone else, scared by one of Vincent's entertainers.

Without being able to see them, the whole thing seemed silly— impossible. Vincent pulled me past the bar and the couple vanished completely behind a gust of acid-green smoke. I shook myself. I was being dumb. They'd just been making out. There was no blood, no screaming. And if there had been, it was probably just a prop. Something to encourage the mood.

Still, it was freaky. . . .

Vincent and I went out a back door behind the bar.

The cool air hit me like a bucket of ice to the face, calming my irrational thoughts. The sweat covering my body turned to frost and I was shivering immediately. Vincent placed his bare arm around me, but I jumped back as static electricity shocked me. A wave of excitement flushed through my veins, cold and greedy . . . *exhilarating* . . . but wrong—like it didn't belong there.

My mind went to the last time I'd felt this way—when Lucas's skin had zapped me and the flash of senseless fear had momentarily consumed me.

And then—just as it happened last time—the feeling was gone, leaving only a tiny numb spot on my shoulder where the electricity had stung me. I let out a deep breath, feeling overwhelmed.

"Apologies," Vincent said. "The air is so electric here. I am always getting zapped." He let out a small smile and unwrapped the argyle cloak from around his shoulders, putting it on me instead.

"Thank you," I murmured, still shaken by the incident—both inside the barn and out. I leaned against the moldy wooden wall and stared out at the vast field before me, trying to calm down. I could see the Rocky Mountains studding the horizon, darker than night. Pine trees stood in the distance, their innumerable needles tossed in the icy wind, dancing spookily. And above it all was the moon, close tonight and strangely yellow. Its eerie light touched the slim stalks of overgrown grass, making them look like hair blowing in a sea breeze. It reminded me of home. Of the beach and suntanned bodies glittering with sweat. Crystal sand sticking to bare legs. Derek and I walking in the surf, just after sunset, me dipping down occasionally to grab an interesting shell.

I missed it like crazy . . . missed *him* like crazy.

"You're sad again," Vincent said, watching me intently as he leaned in close, his hand braced against the wall.

I looked away. I didn't feel like talking about it—it was too heavy for a first date anyway. If this even *was* a date. It was more like an excuse to stop being me for a night.

"Won't you please tell me why?" he asked gently.

"It's just been lonely," I said, thinking that that was exactly how I'd felt lately without Derek to keep me company.

Vincent nodded sympathetically. "Missing home?"

"Yes," I said. "And no . . . that's not it, really. I had a fight with my best friend and he hasn't really spoken to me since."

"What did you fight about?"

"He wants to date me," I said dully. "And I just want to stay friends."

"You hold no attraction to this . . . ?"

"Derek," I filled in. "And it's not that. Attraction isn't the problem. He's pretty much perfect for me, to tell the truth."

"Then what is the problem?"

"I can't trust him."

"Why not?" Vincent's voice was smooth, like sand running between my fingers.

"He cheated on me in high school." I looked up into his bittersweet eyes, trying to read what he was thinking.

He just nodded, waiting for me to continue.

Now that I was spilling, it was surprisingly easy to keep talking. Vincent just listened; if he was judging me, he never let it show. Not one flicker of skepticism crossed his eyes.

"He begged me for months to forgive him," I said. "But I'd been let down by someone before . . ." I shuddered. "And I just couldn't bring myself to take the chance. Pain like that . . . you don't forget it overnight." I looked down at the fraying hem of my polyester cloak, tearing at it with shaking fingers. "But I didn't want to be alone, so I said we could be friends. Selfish, I know . . . but I need him."

"And now?" Vincent asked. "What happened to make you fight now?"

"He tried again," I said. "We went camping and he kissed me. I was so dumb, and I let him . . . I kissed him back. I still care about him and a part of me *wants* to be with him. But I can't trust him after what he did."

"So you denied him again," Vincent finished.

I sighed hugely. "Yep. Hence, the not talking."

Vincent blinked and nodded like he understood.

"Believe it or not," he said, leaning in closer. "I know how you are feeling."

I eyed him skeptically. "I don't think so. Most people have no problem falling in love. I don't even know if I *can* love anymore. At least, not the way normal people love. Freely. Openly."

Vincent's voice was low and silky. "But, dear Faith, I also cannot feel love—*true* love, not lust or passion—for any person. Not even myself."

My face fell into a sympathetic grimace. Even though I felt the same way he did—that I was broken when it came to love—it still sucked, and I felt very sorry for him.

Vincent must have seen the pity in my eyes because he backed up, folding his arms across his bare chest. His voice was defiant when he spoke.

"At least you have the *ability* to love," he said. "You do not know what a gift that is, what I would give to feel anything close to that." Vincent's eyes flashed beneath the moonlight, and in that moment, I saw rage . . . or perhaps resentment. I don't know, but for that brief instant when his eyes darted to mine, I was scared of him.

He stepped toward me. "There are things in this world that can take away your ability to feel love and happiness. Things that will destroy everything that had meaning. They will take away your life and all that was in it. Those things . . . those evil beings are real. And once they've touched your life, they never go away. You never feel anything good again."

His vibe had suddenly gone haywire along with his creepy speech. I tried to calm him down. "I sort of know what you mean,"

I said. "Even though that's really dark, I know what it's like to have your life taken away. I'm sorry you had to go through it, too."

Vincent sniffed and looked away.

"You know nothing of life," he said sharply. "And you know nothing of what it feels to have it taken."

I felt anger rush through my veins like acid. He thought I didn't know what it felt like to lose someone I loved? He didn't even know me. Was he really so arrogant?

"Now I can see why Lucas doesn't like you," I said venomously. "You think you're the only one who's ever felt the pain of losing someone? Well, you're wrong." I came away from the wall, closer to the edge of the barn. "There is pain in this world besides yours, Vincent. Pain and loss and grief. What Derek did to me in high school, what my stepfather did to my mom and me—those things *ruined* my heart. I lost who I was. So you might think you're the only one who's dealt with loss, but I'm living proof of the contrary." I glared at him from the corner of the barn, ready to spin around and leave. Sure, it'd been fun to dance with him, to forget myself for a while, but now reality had come crashing down on top of me and I could see that Vincent wasn't at all as nice as I had thought. He was a jerk.

"Take me home," I demanded.

Vincent surveyed me from his spot, ten feet away. "What did you say?" he whispered. I barely heard him over the throbbing music.

"I said, take me home. Now."

I began to walk away, but Vincent was at my side before I could blink. His gloved hand held onto my wrist, preventing me from moving away from him.

"Did you say Lucas?" he asked. "You can't mean Lucas Whelan?"

I tried to snatch my wrist away, but his grip was like an iron shackle.

"Let go," I said, low and firm.

He released me, but his eyes were hard as onyx stones.

"What did he say to you?" he asked harshly. "What did Whelan say about me?"

"He said you were a jerk, which I now believe to be totally true." I spun on my heel and began walking away again. I no longer even wanted a ride from him—all I wanted was to be back in my room. I'd walk there if I had to. But I made it only ten steps before Vincent was in front of me as though he'd materialized out of thin air.

I gasped and jumped back.

"Tell me what that mongrel said about me," Vincent hissed. His face was glowing in the night, his eyes shining with hate.

It was clear that Lucas and Vincent had some sort of feud going on. They despised each other. Vincent had even used the same curious insult Mark had used about Lucas. I wondered for a moment if Mark was somehow involved in all of this as well, but then pressed it aside. If he was, all it meant was that Mark was a jerk, too. They all were. And I wanted nothing more to do with any of them.

I sidestepped Vincent and put my finger in his face. *"Don't* follow me."

Only two steps this time before Vincent was in front of me again. Only now his leather-bound hands were gripping my forearms like pincers.

"Whatever he said is a lie," he snarled. "You cannot trust him. He is a villain."

"A villain? What is this, a Spider-Man comic?" I tried to shake his hands off, but he squeezed tighter and I cried out in pain. "Let go," I said, writhing in his grip. "I'm going to scream."

"Then scream!"

Suddenly, Vincent tugged me against his body. All I could see was the pale, taut skin of his bare chest. I heard a rush of wind and then he threw me into something hard. I looked around. We were in the woods at the edge of the field—about six hundred feet from where we just were. Ancient pines and thick brush enshrouded us in fathomless shadows, blocking out the moonlight. Immediately, I tried to run, but Vincent pushed against my throat to hold me in place.

I started to choke.

"Lucas Whelan is a monster," Vincent said in a low voice. "He is a murderer and a fiend. I am the good guy. He is the villain. Do you understand that, human?"

I nodded, unable to talk with his hand cutting off my air. He released my throat and I dropped to the ground, coughing and taking in ragged breaths.

Vincent stood above me. "How do you know Whelan?" he questioned. "Is he your lover? Is that why your little Derek broke up with you?"

I blanched. "No," I said hoarsely. "Lucas is just my . . . he's not even my friend; I just know him from class."

"Liar!" Vincent yelled and dragged me up by my shoulders. His grip hurt so much it brought tears to my eyes. "You love him, don't you? He's your everything, your world, right?"

I shook my head, crying.

"Say it's true!" Vincent roared.

"It's true, it's true." I'd say anything to get him to leave me alone. *What have I gotten myself involved in?*

Vincent released me and I fell against the harsh bark. To my amazement, and disgust, he began chuckling. "Oh, how lovely," he said to himself. "This is so perfect . . . what an odd coincidence." Then he straightened as if just realizing something. He turned and called out to the woods. "You're here, aren't you? Of course you are. You wouldn't leave her to me." He laughed, bouncing on his heels happily. "Why don't you come out, puppy? Come show your lover what you really are!"

He started clucking and whistling like he was calling an animal. I stared. Confused. Scared. Almost too scared to move.

Almost.

I bolted. I ran toward the edge of the trees so fast I didn't feel my feet didn't touch the ground.

But Vincent was faster. He popped up in front of me and knocked me backward with both hands. I flew through the air and landed in a pile, right back where I started, except now blood trickled down my face.

My vision blurred for a moment and then I saw Vincent's face above me. He was breathing hard, his mouth was open wide. . . . He had *fangs.*

I backed away into a tree behind me. I had to be dreaming. People didn't have fangs. People couldn't move at the speed of light. People didn't have superstrength.

I had to be dreaming.

But I wasn't.

Vincent took off his gloves with one swift movement and put his fingers on my cheek, wiping up the blood. Once more, a sudden wave of emotion hit me, and I realized that it was *Vincent's* emotions I felt inside me. *Greed, excitement, lust,* and above all, *hunger.* The sensation made me gag. When it passed, I noticed groggily that Vincent's hands bore no burn marks, no scars. They were smooth as the skin on his pale face.

He looked at the crimson liquid shining on his fingers and moved it around between them. He smiled and murmured, "So warm . . ." Then he brought his fingers to my lips and smeared the blood over them. I jerked my head away, and he laughed.

"Feisty," he mocked. "I wonder if this will bring your puppy out of hiding."

He grabbed my face and kissed me. His lips were like ice. Like hard, nasty blood-tasting ice. I almost retched. But I didn't have time. I heard a savage growl from off to the side, and Vincent turned his head. He licked my blood from his lips and straightened.

"*There* you are, puppy. I have been searching for you."

From within the shadows of the trees, a colossal black wolf materialized. Its hair was shaggy and matted, and it had teeth the size of my fingers. Silver eyes like cold metal glinted in the scant light. It came toward us, slowly, growling, snarling.

I pressed myself into the tree. I didn't know who to be more frightened of—Vincent or the wolf. For as scared as I was, Vincent was just as calm. Like he skulked in the woods abusing young girls and talking to wolves every day.

"Hello, old friend," he said to the wolf. "It did not take as long to find you as I would have thought. You are getting lazy . . . or stupid."

The wolf gnashed its jaws and started forward.

I jumped and dug my nails into the bark of the tree at my back, concentrating on the solidness of it. The realness.

Vincent was talking to a wolf. *Why doesn't any of this make sense?*

"Come on, puppy," Vincent said, leering at the wolf. "I know you can't hold your form for much longer, so what is it going to be? Will you fight me to save your human or will you wait until the change wears off so that she can see the monster you truly are."

The wolf barked and snapped, its fangs dripping with ropey saliva.

Vincent lowered himself into a crouch. "Bring it, mongrel."

Instantly the wolf tore at Vincent. A scream ripped through my lungs as I watched Vincent dodge with impossible speed and punch the wolf. He grabbed it and sent it flying toward me. I screamed again and launched myself to the side.

I moved just in time. The wolf careened into the tree and let out a yelp as the wood buckled, almost splitting in two.

But the wolf wasn't fazed. It jumped up and barreled toward Vincent. It clamped its jaws around his thigh and yanked.

My stomach churned at the sound—screeching, tearing, muscles separating. Vincent roared and brought both fists down on the wolf's head.

It let go, and Vincent hobbled backward. Strangely enough he wasn't bleeding.

But the wolf was. Blood poured out of his mouth in a stream of gore. Amidst my fear, I felt bad for the wolf, my defender. My savior.

Vincent stepped forward, his face distorted in rage and pain. He lunged, hissing like some sort of evil, giant snake. The wolf dashed away just in time for Vincent to miss his mark. He seemed to be attempting to bite the wolf. Bite him with those inhuman fangs.

The wolf backed away and shivered violently.

Vincent straightened, and a nasty smiled spread across his face.

"I knew you had little time to spare," he said. He strolled toward me, and I shrank away. The wolf growled and trembled again. "So what will it be, old friend? Shall we finally finish this now or will you delay the inevitable once again? We both know you will have lost your leverage in only a few minutes and that is not enough time for you to defeat me." He knelt down next to me, huddled into a heap in the dirt. He faced me and said softly, "What will he do, I wonder. Will he choose to fight these last few seconds to try and save you? Or simply reveal himself and save me the trouble of tearing you apart? For the knowledge of such a thing will surely do just that." He came closer and whispered in my ear. "The knowledge of what your lover really is."

The wolf barked and then whined as a tremor rippled down its spine.

"It would seem that his decision is being made for him," Vincent said pleasantly. "Not that it matters. Either way, Faith is dead." He picked up my arm, which I had clutched to my throat and brought it to his lips. I struggled against him, but his grip was unrelenting. His eyes sparkled at me, darkening until the pupils blacked everything out like an ink spill. Even the whites of his eyes were filled in. I felt the tips of his teeth scratch against my skin, and I screamed.

Suddenly the wolf lunged, catching both Vincent and me by surprise. Its gaping jaws made contact with Vincent's throat, and he let out a choked cry, fighting against the wolf's mighty grip. Finally managing to overcome his shock, Vincent produced a slim silver knife and stabbed it into the wolf's side.

It fell to the dirt and didn't move.

Vincent held his hands over his throat, his eyes wide with alarm. I could hear a gurgling, rattling sound in his chest . . . but there was still no blood.

How can there be no blood?

Vincent limped over to the wolf for a moment, shot one last venomous look at me, and then disappeared in a blur of shadows.

I remained flattened to the ground, staring at the spot where Vincent had just stood. I stayed that way for a long moment before a noise jolted me out of my stupor. I looked over and saw the unconscious wolf tremble and shudder; the air around it seemed to vibrate. I started inching away as the shape of the animal began to morph right in front of my eyes.

The matted black hair disappeared, turning straight and short. The paws became big, tan hands. The tail shrunk away into nothingness, and his massive chest turned into smooth, graceful muscles. Naked muscles.

The wolf had just turned into a man.

It had become Lucas Whelan.

9

REALITY

My mind rejected everything: Lucas, the wolf, Vincent's superspeed and strength. His fangs. None of that had happened. I had to have been imagining things.

But the body lying on the ground told me differently—my scalp burning from where I smacked it on the tree and the coppery scent of blood in the air were unequivocally real. And it was this, the irrefutable evidence lingering in the quiet aftermath that made my head rush. My vision spun, and I felt faint. I managed to stay conscious, but my stomach cramped and I threw up.

As I got to my feet, it dawned on me that Lucas might not just be some sort of supernatural being, but also that he might be dead.

He wasn't moving, and his side was bleeding steadily.

Tentatively I inched toward him, afraid that at any moment he might switch back into a wolf and chomp my head off. He was totally nude, but thankfully his front side was facing the ground— although his backside was spectacular all on its own. But I couldn't dwell on that.

Regardless of the strangeness of what had just happened, there was one thing I knew without a doubt. Lucas—wolf or not—had just saved my life. I knelt down beside his head and put my hand under his nose to see if he was breathing.

He is. That means he isn't dead.

But he was definitely hurt. I pressed my hand over the wound on his side, feeling the gush of warm blood between my fingers. I stifled another wave of nausea.

Only the right side of Lucas's face was visible, but I could see that his mouth was already crusted with dried blood and his cheek was bent inward from one of Vincent's insanely strong punches.

I reached my free hand out and touched the broken skin over his previously perfect cheekbone, gasping when his skin shocked me so violently it left a welt on my finger. But I wasn't concerned about myself. Lucas had just saved my life. I ran my fingers through his thick, black hair, touched that someone would actually risk their life for me.

But it didn't make sense. Lucas didn't even like me. I pushed his hair away from his forehead. It concerned me that I couldn't feel his vibe when I always felt it with him. He was calm, peaceful, so unlike his normal angry self. I prayed that I'd get to see his face crumpled into that familiar scowl again.

I wasn't sure what Lucas was, but I knew he needed a hospital. Fast. The blood flowing from the wound on his side was beginning to ebb so I let it go and cast around for my purse. I found it pasted to the ground a few feet away. Someone had stepped on it, making it impossible to open. I smacked it against the tree, angry that it was defying me in my moment of need.

Realizing that I had no phone and no way of contacting the police, I returned to Lucas and knelt beside him.

"Lucas?" I said softly. "Can you hear me? I'm going to go look for a phone and call 911, okay? I'll be right back, I swear." I waited a beat to see if he'd heard me when I noticed a scab had formed on his stab wound, as though the cut had happened weeks ago rather than minutes. Baffled, I looked up at Lucas's face and found the skin on his cheek wasn't broken anymore—just a bit of dried blood caked over smooth, unharmed skin. I wiped the blood away and ran my fingers over his cheek.

"What the—"

Suddenly a hand snatched my wrist. I jumped back and fell over. Lucas's eyes popped open, and he sprang to his feet. His gaze darted to mine and filled with something close to panic. I stared at him—it was quite a sight—but then I looked away embarrassed. He didn't even make an attempt at modesty. He just stood there above me, whirling around and peering into the forest as though searching for something.

Once more, his eyes fell to me, sprawled on the ground, and he started forward. "You're hurt?" he asked urgently. His tone rang with alarm.

For a second I didn't know what he was talking about. It was rather hard to concentrate with him standing naked in front of me. It *was* the first time I'd ever seen a naked guy before. But I focused on his face and realized he meant the little wound on my head. "No—it's just a cut," I said, reaching up to feel that it had already stopped bleeding. I looked up at him, felt my heart stutter, and averted my eyes.

Then I saw his feet scamper past me, and I whipped around to watch him run into the shadows.

"Wait!" I said, jumping up. "You can't just leave!"

"I'm not!" I heard him call back. "I got clothes back here, you mind?"

I fell silent, blushing all by myself among the trees. A moment later, Lucas returned wearing the same white shirt and khaki cargo shorts he'd been wearing earlier. The wound on his side was completely healed and left no blood stain on the shirt. *How is that possible?* He walked casually toward me as if he hadn't just turned from a big black wolf right in front of me.

I put my hands on my hips.

"You want to tell me what the hell that was?" I asked.

He leaned against a tree and began putting his shoes on.

"What? You can't figure it out?" he said, not looking at me.

"Hey," I said angrily. "I just got mauled and almost killed by your buddy Vincent, I saw you change into a human after being a wolf, and I'm being pretty cool about it all, considering. You'd better come up with a damn good explanation for this in a hurry, and it better be sugarcoated with extra sweetness. No more sarcasm, got it?"

He tugged on the laces of his sneakers and looked up at me. He walked slowly closer, his eyes glinting silver even in the night. They were the exact color of the wolf's—metallic and cold.

"You wanna know what happened?" he said, standing just inches from me.

I was scared of him then. He was so menacing, eyes roiling in fury and his body quivering with energy. But I was also excited. I felt as though I was on the cusp of discovering something unimaginable, something so unreal it just had to exist. I tried not to betray my tumultuous emotions when I said, "Yeah. I want to know everything. Right now."

"What happened was that you ignored what I said about going out with Vincent, which then forced me to change and get my head bashed in. Now I got a screaming headache, Vincent knows where I am, knows about you, knows how to *find* you, and now he's coming after you. That's what the hell happened!"

I backed up, hysteria rising in my chest. "What are you talking about? What do you mean he's coming after me?"

Lucas pursed his lips and cursed savagely. He kicked a pinecone into the darkness.

"Listen," Lucas said, turning on me again. "You weren't supposed to find out about this, and I'm sorry that you did. But now you're kind of stuck knowing about it, so I guess—" He looked to the sky and dragged his hands over his face. "I guess you'd better come with me so I can explain it all."

"I'm not going anywhere with you. You can tell me right here."

Lucas began rooting around in his shorts for something. "It's not safe here," he said. "He heals fast. He'll be back. We've gotta go to my place."

He started walking out of the woods.

I didn't move, nor did I have any intention of doing so. There was no way I was going any place with him. He was just as dangerous as Vincent—perhaps, even more so.

Lucas stopped when he realized I wasn't following him. "You comin'?" he asked, not turning around.

"Nope." I planted my feet. I was surprised to hear that my voice sounded more confident than I felt.

Lucas turned his head and I could see his sharp profile etched out against the yellow moonlight flooding in from the field.

"Look," he said. "You can either come with me nicely or we can do it the unpleasant way. It's your choice, but either way, you're coming with me." He kept his voice low, threatening.

I felt my resolve disintegrate at his words. "Where are we going?"

"My car. We gotta get out of here fast."

"I—I'm not getting into a car with you. Not after what I just saw."

Lucas turned all the way around, and I saw his face soften.

"Faith, this is hard enough for me without adding your stubbornness to the picture. Just trust me. I'm not the one who was trying to hurt you."

I took him in, silently weighing my intense desire to find out what had just happened and my equally strong apprehension of Lucas's abilities—of what he might do to me if he got me alone. Then I looked at his face, his easy, soothing eyes and the tepid energy rolling off of him, and in that moment, I knew I could trust him.

"Okay," I said. "But if you hurt me, Derek's going to kick your ass. He already wants to, so don't give him a reason." I hoped he didn't know Derek and I weren't talking anymore, otherwise my weak threat would be utterly laughable.

Lucas's lips tilted upward in a lopsided smile. "I won't." He turned and began walking, not even bothering to wait for me. I picked up my purse and hurried after him. We crossed the field swiftly and in total silence. Lucas was always several steps ahead of me, never looking back, never slowing down. As we neared the barn, it became clear that the party was becoming crazier instead of tapering off like I would have thought. The music was louder than ever, and the people were drunk. I was secretly glad to be leaving.

We went to the makeshift parking lot, and I saw Lucas's glittery red parked car shining like a bloody gem in the moonlight. He was already inside it by the time I reached the dirt road, and he pulled up in front of me. I heard the door unlock, and I tugged it open, enduring yet another staggering electric shock. I looked down at my hand in wonderment. Another angry welt had appeared beside the one I'd just received when touching Lucas.

First Vincent's vibe had all but consumed me, and now I was being zapped to death. *What the hell is happening to me?*

"C'mon," Lucas said impatiently.

I looked down at him, wringing my numb hand out. "Where'd you say we were going?"

"My place."

"As in . . . your dorm room?" I asked, thinking of Mark's scary description of his community in Gould and hoping it wasn't there we were heading.

"Yeah. Get in. Now."

I obeyed and Lucas took off before I even had a chance to shut the door.

"Jeez," I said. "In a hurry much?"

"Yeah, actually. Vincent might be back anytime now, and the further away from here we are, the better."

"Why would he come back?" I asked, shaking a little because I already thought I knew the answer.

"Because he's got his eye on you now. And I'm pretty sure he had some of your blood, which means he's gonna be able to find you quicker."

I turned to stare at him, aghast.

"Had some of my blood?"

"I'll explain it when we get to my room."

Twenty minutes later, Lucas pulled up in front of the dorms and hopped out. I jumped out too, happy to be back on school campus. It felt safer here somehow.

We got to Lucas's building and went upstairs to the second floor. He slammed his key into the door and held it open for me to pass.

Lucas came in behind me and flicked on a lamp by his bed, which cast the room in deep, orange light. I was surprised to see that Lucas had a single room, complete with a minikitchen and a couch.

I was less surprised to see that Lucas's room was a mess. Mountains of clothes lay in random piles around the floor, and papers hung out of drawers and over books. Old food was piled in the bathroom sink, and I swear I saw socks stuck to the wall.

Lucas cleared a spot on the couch and thumped down, throwing his head into his hands. I stood in the doorway, afraid to move, lest I found something alive in there. He motioned to the chair at his desk and I tiptoed over. I stood by it, tucking my hands into my armpits.

"So," I said. "Tell me everything."

Lucas scratched his eye and kind of laughed. "I've never had to tell anybody like this. Outright, I mean. Usually if somebody sees me change they guess it right away."

"Sees you change," I repeated slowly. "Change into a wolf, you mean."

"Yeah." His eyes searched me, waiting for me to get it. He seemed to realize I wasn't, so he shot me one last pleading look, took in a breath, and held it. "I'm a werewolf," he said in a rush, like saying it faster would make it less incredible. He eyed me anxiously, probably waiting for me to start hyperventilating.

I nodded for a moment, taking it in. Letting the concept of werewolves sink in . . . then remembering that werewolves are *fake* and that Lucas must be crazy.

But then I'd have to be crazy too because I *saw* him change from wolf to human. A naked human. I saw his body shaking, his fur turn to skin, and his fangs shrink into teeth. I saw it.

But I couldn't believe it.

I smiled at him coldly. "This is a joke, right? Some kind of Halloween prank? Did Vincent slip some LSD into my drink to make me hallucinate? Is he going to pop out now and start laughing?"

Lucas shook his head solemnly. "You didn't drink anything tonight," he said.

"How do you know that?"

"Because I was watching you." He said it so simply, so unrepentantly.

The thought of Lucas lurking in the shadows of Vincent's party, his bright, lupine eyes fixed on me and me alone sent a odd mixture of fear and pleasure coursing through my veins. Lucas scared me, yes, but knowing that he cared enough to follow me? I didn't know how to feel about it. But when I thought back on the night, I realized he was right. I hadn't had a sip of anything while I was with Vincent. It hit me then, harder than ever. What I saw was *real*.

"Oh, my God," I murmured. "You're actually serious. You're really a . . . a . . ."

"Werewolf. Yeah, I am." He stood up, and I started backing away involuntarily. He stopped short. His lips thinned. "You should sit. You look pale."

"That's because a crazy person is telling me he's a werewolf and I actually believe him."

Lucas took a bottle of water out of his minifridge. He slid it over to me and returned to his side of the room, crossing his arms over his chest.

"Drink," he said. "I swear there's no LSD in it."

I let out a puff of air. "Jokes . . . right . . . funny." I cracked the seal on the water and took a sip. I inhaled deeply, sitting down. "This is so surreal. So, I guess I have to ask, are you . . . dangerous?"

Lucas's face tightened. "That depends."

"On what?"

"Everything."

"Could you be a little *more* cryptic, please, I think I understand too much."

Lucas's lips twitched. "Sorry. I'm not used to talking about it with people. It's been a long time since anyone has found out. It's kind of freaking me out to talk openly like this."

"Oh, *you're* freaked?"

Lucas just stared at his shoes.

"How many people know?" I asked softly.

"Excluding my family?" His eyes met mine. "You."

My pulse jumped. It was strange and thrilling to know that he trusted me with such a secret. He could have let me die rather than tell me, but he didn't.

"I have to admit," I murmured, "I'm afraid of you. Aren't werewolves supposed to be wild killers? And aren't they only supposed to change at the full moon? And how come your eyes—"

"Whoa, whoa," Lucas stopped me. "One at a time. I still got a headache."

"Sorry. I'm just trying to understand."

"It's okay. You're actually taking it better than I would have thought. I was expecting lots of screaming and fainting. What was the first thing you asked?"

I swallowed. "Are you dangerous?" My voice came out like a whisper, I barely heard myself.

Lucas looked over at me, his eyes flaring silver for an instant. "Around you? Yes."

"All the time . . . or just when you . . . when you change?"

Lucas regarded me for a moment. "The way I think of it," he said, "is that I've got this energy inside me, bouncing off my insides and fighting to get loose. I can keep it locked up, but only for so long. I'm safe while I'm under control, but once something sets me off . . . I'm dangerous, yeah. And it's the worst at the full moon."

I stared. I'd never heard Lucas speak so much. I didn't want him to stop before he told me everything.

"Why is it worse?" I asked.

Lucas's face became shadowy and his voice turned low. "Because the moon triggers its own transformation. When it's full, I'm not quite wolf, not quite man. But I'm strongest at that time. The bad part is that the strength and the power of it pushes your mind past the edges of sanity. At the full moon, I'm not Lucas Whelan anymore. I'm a monster . . . capable of anything." He looked up at me and must have seen the horror on my face because his expression relaxed. "But when it's not the full moon, I'm not all that dangerous when I change. I mean, I wouldn't want you around, because I can't really control my impulses too well. I might hurt you without even knowing it's you. Plus when I change it's . . . violent."

I nodded, imagining Lucas's body exploding in a frenzy of claws and fangs the size of machetes. I shuddered. "Is it voluntary? Changing, I mean?"

Lucas shook his head, almost as if he were sad. "If I were to relax myself, the change would overcome me, but it fades fast. The time I'm allotted in my wolf form depends on how often I've changed recently, what the situation is. If there's someone in danger, I'll keep it a little longer. It's like focus fire. I target the most dangerous enemy in range, and then when the danger's gone, I shift back. Thirty minutes is the longest I've ever held it outside of the full moon."

I took this in, steeling myself all the while to ask what was really scaring me.

"What if you bite me," I asked softly. "Would I change?"

"I would never bite you," he said sharply. A tremor ran down his spine, and I saw him inhale deeply.

"It's okay," I tried to soothe him. "I'm just talking hypothetically. What if you bit someone, not necessarily me?"

Lucas appeared to relax. "I can only infect someone else when I've changed. But you don't have to worry about getting hurt around me, Faith. I've had a lot of time to manage myself. I'll make sure I never lose control around you. And nothing else will hurt you while I'm here either. I'm strong, even without changing. I have keen senses, so I'll know if someone's coming. You're safe with me." He seemed to be convincing himself as well, as though he wasn't really sure if I *was* safe with him.

But I was sure. I looked into his eyes and knew he wouldn't hurt me—not after he'd gone to such lengths to save me tonight.

"So, exactly how strong are you?" I asked, trying to keep my voice light. "Could you like, rip a phone book apart with your bare hands?"

Lucas cocked an eyebrow at me. "I could rip a car apart with my hands." He grinned, white teeth flashing dangerously. I was suddenly aware of how lethal they were.

I felt my mouth slide open slightly, but I tried to disguise my awe by joking, "Am I supposed to be impressed?"

Lucas's smile stayed in place, like he was mocking me. "Hey, you asked." He eyed me for a moment, and then his lips broke into a wide grin. He looked like a little boy on his birthday. "I'm fast, too," he said. "Timed it once with my brother, and I can sprint at close to a hundred miles per hour."

Now I *was* impressed.

"Anything else you wanna know?" he asked, smirking at the dazed look on my face.

I thought for a moment. "Are you really nineteen?"

Lucas's smile faded. "Yes and no."

"Explain," I said wearily.

He took a deep breath. "I was born in Scotland in 1624, the son of a tailor in Kirkcaldy. I was bitten when I was nineteen years old, and I haven't aged since." He paused. "I'm more than three hundred years old, Faith."

"That's impossible." I breathed deeply. Three hundred years old? Born in Scotland? Why did that sound familiar? Then, of all people, Courtney's words came rushing back to me. *He's got a castle off in Scotland or Ireland or something.* So Courtney wasn't lying. Somehow that shocked me more than the fact that Lucas was more than three hundred years old. And not only that, but he would continue to live, long after I was dead. Lucas's life was eternal.

"You can't die?" I asked, hoping desperately that I had heard wrong.

"I didn't say that. I said I don't age."

"Same thing."

"No, I can die. Silver to the heart will do it." He paused, looking pensive. "But even then, there are ways that I could recover. I heal fast, as I guess you noticed tonight." He gave me a heart-stopping grin.

My face got hot as I remembered him lying on the ground naked, and I put my hands up to my cheeks to cool them.

"Are you all right?" he asked. "You handling this?"

"I think so. So I guess, now I have to ask another big question."

"Yeah," he said nodding, like he already knew what it would be.

I took in a shuddered breath and prepared myself for what was about to come—for my world to be rocked, yet again. "If you're a werewolf," I said slowly, "then what does that make Vincent?" I had a terrible feeling I already knew, but that I also had to hear it to believe.

Lucas smiled and his eyes pressed into mine with animalistic intensity. "And now we've come to the bad part."

CONTROL ISSUES

et's see if you can figure it out," he said. "Two plus two?"

I frowned down at my shoes, ruined now from the fight in the woods. "Okay, well, I know he's strong. I know he's fast. . . ." I glanced at Lucas to see that he was nodding slowly. "Is he . . . one of you?" I asked tentatively. "A werewolf?"

The left corner of Lucas's mouth pulled up, crinkling his eye into a smile.

"Nah," he said. "Think about it, Faith. Why have you only seen him at night? Why's he so cold? So fast? So pale?"

"Oh my God," I whispered. Lucas nodded almost sadly. "Vampire?" I breathed, so softly I almost didn't hear myself say it.

"Yup," he said, still nodding.

I tried to breathe normally, but my lungs weren't cooperating. They forced the air up my throat in large heaves. I put my head in my hands and closed my eyes. I felt Lucas stand and move closer to me.

"You okay?" he asked gruffly.

"Yeah," I whispered, "it's just . . . a lot of information for one night. I went from thinking werewolves and vampires were all just imaginary. Now I have to try and wrap my head around the fact that it's all real."

"It's not *all* real," Lucas said comfortingly. He knelt in front of me and peered into my eyes. "Some of it's made up for movies and junk."

"What part of it's made up? Please say that the whole 'I vant to suck your blood' thing has all been a lie?" I gave him a little smile, which he halfway returned.

"No," he said. "That's all true. They drink human blood to

survive. They only come out at night, and a wooden stake to the heart is the only thing that'll kill 'em. Well, that and ripping their heads off."

"Okay." I nodded some more, disgusted at the mental image passing through my head. "What's fake then?"

"Pretty much everything else. Garlic allergies, coffin sleeping, bat-morphing, and pretty much everything you've heard that makes them vulnerable."

"Great," I mumbled.

"Yeah," he said. "It makes it a pain in the ass to kill them sometimes, but we get it done."

"We?"

"My pack. My family. We're the ones who keep the vampires in this area in line. Werewolf packs all have territories. Ours is Fort Collins and most of the Rockies." He smiled, showing his straight white teeth. "We keep you sweet little humans safe from the big bad vampires."

I giggled nervously. "I thought it was supposed to be the big bad *wolf*."

"I can be, if that's what you want," he said. He growled a little, and I smacked his arm without thinking about it.

He stood up quickly, this weirdly strained look on his face. His eyes were so bright I swore they were stars.

"What's wrong?" I asked, slightly scared. Maybe he saw Vincent or something. My eyes flickered to the window.

"Nothing," he grunted, his jaw flexing a bit.

"No, come on," I urged. "You're scaring me."

He stuck his hands in his pockets, looking supremely uncomfortable. "Well, I guess I might as well be honest with you now that you know everything." He looked down and kicked some clothes around. "Don't get mad when I say this. . . . It's just, I don't think you should touch me. I don't know; it might trigger the change."

I stared at him, still looking away, still fidgeting with the clothes on the floor. "Why?" I asked slowly.

His eyes met mine, and they were still bright silver, the pupils narrowed into slits. He took a step closer to me. "Because you've triggered something in me. Something I don't really understand. When I look at you it's like everything I try so hard to repress comes rushing to the surface—I can't stop it."

Suddenly my heart was beating a mile a minute. I remembered the first time our skin had made contact in the Panda Express—the static electricity and the wave of emotions. *His* emotions, I realized now. I'd felt fear. He was scared in that moment, scared that he would change.

"So this is bad," I said. If I was making him want to change, it put me in serious danger. "Really bad."

Lucas nodded morosely. "It's the worst thing that could possibly happen. It's what I've been trying to avoid my whole life. Hurting someone else because of what I am."

I totally got that. I, too, was hurting someone because of my own issues—Derek. Granted, Lucas was talking about literally hurting people, while I was speaking metaphorically. But still, I got what he meant.

"So when you come near me . . . It's setting you off?"

"Exactly," he said, sounding relieved that I understood. "It's called a trigger. I don't know any other werewolves with this problem, and I don't even know if touching you *would* set me off, but I just can't chance it. Not yet. I don't want to hurt you."

"So, what? You're afraid if you touch me you'll turn into a wolf and be too crazed to know it's me anymore? You're afraid you'll attack me?"

"No," Lucas said, looking both disgusted and appalled. Then he sighed heavily. "I don't know. I just don't want to take any chances until I figure this out—until I figure out why being around you triggers the change. Just bear with me for a little bit. I can control myself, given time."

Control himself? He hadn't needed to control himself when he was sucking tongue with Courtney.

"But, why's it so different with me?" I asked, voicing my thoughts. "This doesn't happen with everyone, right?"

Lucas looked directly at me. "No. Never. Humans don't trigger me—or any other werewolf for that matter." He dragged his hands over his face. "And I told you—I have no idea why I'm like this with you, why I'm so on edge. It doesn't make any sense."

"Is that why you're always so short with me?"

"No, that's just me, I guess. I've been told that I'm naturally and incurably grumpy." He shrugged and his mouth curved into a wry smile so cute it stopped my heart. "I'm sorry it's gotta be this way, sorry I'm such a jerk. But it was the only way I could manage—pushing you away, I mean. That's the only way you can be safe when I start to lose it. The problem now is that pushing you away isn't an option anymore."

"Why not?"

"Because now we've got Vincent to deal with."

"Vincent," I said. "Right. Vincent the vampire. God, that's so weird."

"You'll get used to it."

"I doubt it," I grumbled. "What's going on between you two? You really seem to hate each other."

Lucas's jaw tightened. "That's not important right now. What's important is making sure he doesn't get to you. That means you need a werewolf with you from nightfall till dawn until he's caught. You need protection."

I gulped and shot him a look, knowing where he was going with this.

"It doesn't have to be me," Lucas said. "It's probably better if it's not me, actually. I can get one of my brothers to—"

"No," I said. "I want you. I trust you."

Lucas knelt down next to me again. "You do?" he whispered.

I nodded. "Surprisingly . . . I really do."

Lucas's eyes melded into mine, and I stared into their silvery depths for a long time, heart beating wildly.

Finally Lucas looked away. "So," he said softly. "Now that you know what's going on, you gotta know that you can never tell anyone about us. It's the biggest secret you'll ever keep in your life. If you tell anyone, I won't be able to stop the pack from killing you— and whoever you've told." His eyes bored into mine, waiting for me to confirm that I understood.

I nodded jerkily. "It's not like anyone would believe me anyway."

Lucas stood and cocked an eyebrow up. "True." He let his arms fall, and I felt the tension break as they hit his sides. It was as though someone had punctured a gigantic bubble filled with water and I could breathe at long last.

"So," Lucas said. "We can do one of two things. We can either stay in your room or we can stay in mine. I think here would be best since it's a single. We won't have to explain ourselves to anyone."

I nodded as something close to panic fluttered through my chest, or maybe it was excitement. I don't know, but it made my hands tremble.

"I'll sleep on the couch," Lucas said. "You can get some stuff from your room in the morning to keep over here, but for now, I have some spare stuff in the closet. Use what you want." He waved his hand at the door to his right. "I gotta go make some calls, but I'll be right outside the door. I promise you'll be safe."

I nodded again, feeling numb. "I feel like I'm in the witness protection program or something."

Lucas let out a barking laugh. "You sort of are."

Once alone in the bathroom, I peeled off my filthy vampire costume. Looking at my pallid reflection in the mirror and the fake fangs I'd glued to my teeth, I was completely mortified. Lucas must have thought I was the biggest idiot. I showered the grime from my body, taking care to clean the cut on my head so it wouldn't get infected. Afterward, I wrapped myself in a towel and realized I had nothing to wear. I peeked out the bathroom door to ask Lucas if he would lend me a shirt, but found that one had been folded neatly at the foot of the door. It was a black concert tee with LED ZEPPELIN written in bold white letters. It was thin and faded, and I was willing to bet it was an original shirt from an *actual* Led Zeppelin concert. *So cool.*

Thoroughly impressed, I threw it over my head, wishing I had some shorts or something. I thought about wearing some of Lucas's boxers, but that might have been weird. Or stinky. Or both.

I climbed into Lucas's bed and snuggled in his soft sheets. They smelled of him—warm and woodsy. Which made sense, since he probably spent a lot of time in the forest.

God, this is crazy.

Lucas Whelan was a werewolf.

Everything Mark had said about him and his family had been right. Well, except for them being murderers. They were the opposite of murderers. They were protectors. Saviors from the evil in the world.

From Vincent. A vampire who wanted *my* blood more than any other. Maybe it was because he thought Lucas and I were lovers and he wanted to hurt me to get at Lucas. But why would he want to get at Lucas? What was going on between the two of them? What was their history? And how in the world did I manage to get myself in the middle of it?

But I knew how. It was because of Lucas. It was because of my strange fascination with him. Even before I knew what he was, I was drawn to him. Those eyes, his raging vibe, and his incessantly grumpy disposition—all things that should have turned me off but only did the opposite. I wished I knew why, wished he wouldn't be so distant.

He said that he only pushed me away to keep me safe. But safe from what? Why was it that he could hardly bear to look at me or touch me, while I saw him kissing Courtney? What was it about me that got him so charged?

And for that matter, what was it about him that got *me* so charged? Every time he came near me I felt like my face was on fire. I couldn't breathe and my heart felt like it was going to jump out of my chest. It was like what I felt around Derek but stronger.

Suddenly coldness swept through me as I realized that Vincent knew about Derek. He knew what Derek meant to me, about our fight, about everything. What if Vincent hurt Derek to get to me, which would in turn, get to Lucas?

I saw the door handle jiggle and a sliver of yellow light lit up the room. Lucas poked his head in.

"You decent?"

"Yeah."

He came in, and I heard clothes and junk shuffling as he cleared his way into the room. I saw only his silhouette in the faint moonlight, and I looked out the window next to his bed. The great yellow moon looked back at me, more menacing now than mysterious, as it once had been. It was almost as if I, too, could feel its power . . . the danger it caused.

"Lucas?"

"Yeah?" He sounded tired.

"What if Vincent tries to hurt Derek to get to me?"

"I thought of that, too," Lucas said. There was an edge to his deep voice. "I got a pack member on him right now."

"Who is it?"

"Julian. My brother."

"Your brother's a werewolf, too?"

"He's not my real brother . . . not my blood brother, anyway."

"And Derek will be safe with him? He won't change around him?"

"No, Julian's very much in control of himself." There was a note of resentment in his voice that made me want to ask more, to know why Derek would be safe with Julian while I was in danger with Lucas.

But Lucas silenced my thoughts. "We should sleep," he said. "We've got class in the morning."

I watched as he settled himself on the couch. He swiped away a pile of old books and tossed a pillow down. I had to stifle a gasp as he pulled his shirt off and threw himself onto the cushions. I watched his back swell with the intake of a sigh. His bare skin, illuminated by the gentle glow of the moonlight, reminded me of the woods tonight, of how he had saved me. Risked his life—however eternal it might be—to make sure I didn't get hurt.

"Lucas?" I whispered.

"Hmm?"

"Thank you."

He shifted around and looked at me. "Anytime," he said, his voice soft and grating like the low end of a guitar. He looked at me for a long time as some sort of silent understanding flowed between us. The trust of two strangers, bound together by a secret. I watched his eyes slowly melt to deep, dark brown as he said, "Night, Faith." He turned over again.

"Night," I whispered back.

I rolled over and stared at the ceiling, heart thudding sporadically in my chest. I had the strange urge to cuddle up with Lucas on the couch, to hide in his arms, where I knew I'd be safe. But that was a bad idea. Not only did I not want to trigger him, but I didn't want to start anything between us. I felt something for him, something I couldn't deny. But I couldn't act on it. I'd already lost one friend that way, and I wasn't about to make the same mistake twice.

So I continued to stare at the ceiling, imagining little shapes the shadows made in the contours of the plaster. I saw a bunny, the letter C, a tree . . . a girl . . . a wolf. . . .

CONSPIRACY THEORY

I awoke in the morning to a bright light. I blinked and rolled over to find that the sun was reflecting off a dirty glass on the side table and into my eyes. I sat up and stretched, looking over at the couch.

Lucas was still there, sleeping away. I watched him for a while, thinking of last night and all its impossibilities, which were now somehow possible.

I watched his nose twitch and his lips draw up into a snarl. He made a little whimper and I smiled. He was dreaming. I had the desire to go over and run my hands through his hair like I had in the woods after he'd changed. Feel his soft skin . . .

I shook myself and glanced at the alarm clock by his bed. It was only seven. I didn't have class until ten. I debated going back to sleep, but I still had to go to my room and change clothes so I slid down off the bed and landed lightly on my bare feet. I padded over to the bathroom, grabbing my dirty costume from last night. I threw it on with disgust and snagged my shoes. Casting one last look at Lucas's sleeping form, I crept out of his room and into the morning light flooding the hallway.

I raced to my room, praying to all gods in existence that I didn't see anyone I knew. I looked like I'd been through a tornado, and I felt even worse. My pulse accelerated as I went through the courtyard. I knew it was stupid to be scared since Vincent could only come out at night—at least that's what Lucas said—but I couldn't help feeling anxious all the way to the stairs.

I chucked myself into my room and was relieved to see that Ashley wasn't home yet. She'd probably spent the night at Mark's or something. I undressed and threw the costume and the now ruined shoes, phone, and purse in the garbage. I never wanted to see any of it again. I took a short shower and put on my comfy sweats and a tank top. I felt better already. I surveyed myself in the mirror, wondering if this was the same person I knew yesterday. She looked the same, minus the cut at her temple and the lavender circles under her olive green eyes. But something about the girl in the mirror unnerved me. She seemed . . . hardened.

I sighed at myself. Talk about a hangover.

I applied some Neosporin to my cut. Then I grabbed my computer and settled into bed to do some online shopping for a new cell phone. It was as though the dorm phone by my bedside saw me doing this because no sooner had I finished typing "Best Buy" into the address line, than the phone rang.

I jumped about two feet into the air and grabbed it.

"Hello?" I said, straining to keep my voice level.

"Faith, Jesus," Lucas's relieved voice came through the receiver. "Why'd you leave without telling me? I about lost my mind when I woke up and you weren't there."

"Sorry. I didn't want to wake you."

"Don't do that again. At least leave a note or something."

"Sorry," I said again, cursing myself for not thinking of that.

A bloated silence filled the receiver.

"You feeling okay?" Lucas finally asked. He sounded like he didn't know what to say. I didn't either.

"Yeah, you?"

"Tired, but good. Glad you're okay . . ."

"Yep. Well, I gotta go. I'm trying to find a new phone. I think either you or Vincent squashed it last night."

"Aw, I'm sorry." Lucas sounded genuinely upset about this. "I'll get you a new one."

"Oh, no, that's not what I meant," I said hastily. "I can get my own."

There was another long pause.

"Okay, well . . . I'll see you at class," I said finally.

"Okay," Lucas said. I could still hear the guilt in his voice.

"Don't worry about the phone."

"I'm not." His voice was defensive.

"Good."

"Good!" he said, sounding annoyed now. "Bye." He hung up and I stared at the receiver, shaking my head. For being over three hundred years old, Lucas sure didn't have very good people skills.

I put the dorm phone down and turned back to my computer. I pressed enter to bring up Best Buy's home page when the phone rang again. I picked it up, expecting, and maybe even slightly hoping, to hear Lucas on the other end again. But the voice I heard was so far removed from Lucas's deep, scratchy voice that I almost gasped.

"Hi," Derek's mellow voice came through the receiver.

For a moment, I couldn't breathe.

"Hi," I said back. My voice sounded strange, like I was listening to myself on a recording.

"Why aren't you answering your cell phone?" He didn't sound angry. He sounded careful, as though he was trying very hard to keep from fighting with me.

"It broke," I said, deciding not to elaborate lest I spill everything. Derek usually had that effect on me. As soon as I saw him,

I just started spilling my guts. It felt wrong to have this secret lodged between us.

"I broke it off with Courtney," Derek said slowly.

I frowned, choosing my next words carefully. Talking with Derek was now like traversing a minefield, one wrong step and . . . boom.

"Are you okay?" I asked finally.

That was a safe question. It showed I was concerned about him, but that the information didn't necessarily mean anything to me—even though it did.

"I'm just fine," Derek said tartly. "You know I didn't like her, Faith. She was just someone I could . . . distract myself with."

I grimaced at the phone, thinking about what he meant by "distract."

"That's good," I lied. "It's good for you to distract yourself. It makes things . . . easier."

Derek didn't say anything for a moment, and then he said softly, "I miss you, Faith."

I exhaled. "God, I miss you, too," I said in a rush. "Can we just forget about this whole thing and go back to the way we were? Are we done torturing each other?"

"Well, I'm done torturing myself if that's what you mean." There was an edge to his voice that cut me.

I bit my lip. "It's been hard for me, too," I said. "I've been a wreck."

Derek was quiet.

"You there?" I asked tentatively.

"Yeah. I'm here. But I have to go. I'm late for practice. I'll—I'll see you around, Faith."

He hung up the phone, leaving me staring blankly at it again.

What the hell was that about? Does he want to be friends again? Am I allowed to call him, talk to him? I slammed the phone onto the bedside table.

For the next thirty minutes, I threw myself into my search for a new cell phone, but I was unable to find anything I liked. I looked up when the door handle jiggled, and I watched Ashley shuffle in, bleary eyed and frizzy. She wore the remnants of a Halloween costume—a crooked tiara, a rather sad-looking tutu, and a wand tucked into her purse.

"Hey," I said.

She grunted. "You won't *believe* the night I had."

I hid a smile behind my hand and repressed the urge to challenge her. Instead I said, "Oh, yeah? What happened?"

She started pulling her shoes off and said, "Ugh, well, first I went to this party out in the middle of nowhere and got stranded because Mark disappeared."

That was probably the same party I was at, which struck me as strange. Did they even know Vincent? If so, how? And if Mark had mysteriously disappeared, it strengthened my theory that he was somehow involved in this supernatural world.

"So I tried to get a ride with Courtney," Ashley went on, "but she was too busy wallowing over Derek breaking up with her to bother driving me home. Then she got totally wasted and ended up crying on my shoulder for hours. I only now got her sober enough to tell me where her car was."

"Where is she now?" I asked. It didn't distress me much to know she was sad about Derek dumping her. I was sure she'd be over it by the end of the day, as usual.

"I tossed her in her room," Ashley said, waving her hand dismissively. "I don't think she's going to class, so you should just go without her."

I made a face at my computer screen. *Like I'd be waiting for her anyway.*

"Hey," Ashley said, giving me a concerned look. "What happened to your head?"

I reached up to the cut on my head, instinctually trying to cover it, even though I knew she'd already seen it. "I, ah . . . got a little too trashed last night." I shrugged, trying to look innocent.

Ashley seemed to buy it. "Damn," she said. "Take it easy next time. You might hurt something important."

I fought back a retort about how hurting my head was just as important as hurting any other part of my body—if not more so.

Suddenly, Ashley gasped and came skipping toward my bed. She started patting my leg excitedly and said, "Oh, God, did you hear what happened last night?"

My heart all but stopped. Did someone see what had happened in the woods? Did they see Lucas change? Oh, Lord . . . what would they do to him if they found out? The government would surely take him and keep him locked up in some cage made of silver so they could run tests and experiments like he was some kind of lab rat. I felt my hands clamping onto the edges of my computer. I was frightened, but I tried not to let it show in my face.

"What happened?" I managed to croak.

"A girl was found dead this morning, just outside of Fort Collins. They said it was someone from CSU. Someone found her just like all the other ones. You know . . . with the blood drained out of her."

Ashley's final words rang in my ears like a gong going off. *Blood drained from their bodies . . .* why didn't I see it before?

"Oh, Jesus," I whispered.

"I know," Ashley said, nodding solemnly. "Poor girl. They said it happened late last night. It's all over the news, wanna watch?"

"No," I said. "I gotta go."

I launched myself out of bed. I had to talk to Lucas and confirm what I already knew to be true. I got to his building and realized I had no key to get in. I banged on the door, hoping someone would hear.

Nobody came. I cursed and looked around, bouncing on my heels nervously.

A boy with frosted tips sauntered up, looking me up and down.

"Do you live here?" I demanded.

"Sure do," he said, smiling. "Forgot your key?"

"Yes!" I said frantically.

He shot me an uneasy glance, but opened the door for me. I ran through it and took the stairs two at a time to the second floor. I pounded my fist on Lucas's door, and he opened it instantly.

"What's wrong?" he asked, looking around for signs of danger.

"Did you hear what happened last night?" I panted. "It was Vincent. I know it."

Lucas's face relaxed. "You scared me."

I blinked at him. "Didn't you hear what I said? Vincent's the serial killer!"

"Shh!" Lucas hissed, glancing around. He flung me into his room by my sleeve and clapped the door shut.

I looked around and was stunned to see his room was spotlessly clean. It smelled pine fresh and the window was open, letting a crisp, cool wind cleanse the funk. This time, I noticed that the walls of Lucas's room were papered in art. Black-and-white paintings of wolves, of thunderous seascapes, of silent, snow-covered forests and darker things. Things that made me grimace. It was beautiful but overwhelming. I imagined it was something like being inside his mind.

"You cleaned," I said, astonished.

"Yeah," he said, rubbing the back of his neck absently. "I felt bad having you stay here when it looked . . . the way it did."

I smiled at him and put my hand on his arm, but he jerked away with a shiver.

"Oh . . . jeez," I said, flinching. "I didn't think about it. I'm sorry."

"It's fine," Lucas said shortly. "No big deal." He smiled half-heartedly.

I stared at him as he gained control over his instincts.

It was just a brief contact, skin on skin for just an instant, and the change had been triggered. His ongoing need to release what was wild and fierce within him—the thing he struggled so hard to repress—I had ignited it with just a touch. I suddenly felt horrible that I'd made him so uncomfortable, that I'd pushed him past the boundaries of his self-control. I needed to be more careful.

Then I remembered why I came here.

"Lucas," I said urgently. "I'm about ninety-nine percent positive that Vincent is the one that's been killing all those girls in Denver. I mean, think about it—their blood was drained. What else could do that but a vampire? And then a girl was killed last night after what happened in the woods. I'm just guessing here, but Vincent got hurt, so drinking someone's blood probably helps him heal faster, right? That would mean that he killed some girl to help himself heal. He's got to be the killer."

Lucas's brows had knitted together during my little tirade, and he now contemplated me with squinted eyes, as if trying to decide what to say next.

"I'm right, aren't I?" I pressed, unable to stand his silence any longer.

"Kind of," he said delicately. "It's complicated."

"Go on," I said, sitting down on the couch to prepare myself for more information—as if I hadn't already had enough to last a lifetime.

Lucas sat next to me, but stayed pressed against the cushions, as far away as possible.

"We definitely know it's a vampire that's killing girls," Lucas said slowly. "But whether it's Vincent we can't say. He masks his scent, so we can't track him. It *looks* like it's him, but there's been word of other vampires in the area, so it's possible it was one of them."

"It had to have been Vincent," I said, determined to be right. "It's too much of a coincidence."

"You're right, it is a pretty big coincidence, but there are some holes."

"Like what?"

"Well, when vampires feed, they don't just leave their prey out there in the open like that. They hide them so that no one sees these bloodless bodies strewn all over the place. I mean, it'd be kind of obvious to the werewolves in the area what was going on, and the vampires don't like dealing with us."

"Why not?" I asked, slightly overwhelmed by everything.

"Because we usually manage to kill them, once we find their lair," he said, smiling smugly.

"Lair?" I asked incredulously.

"It's their fancy little word for home. They live in broods, usually no more than ten to a group—though I've heard of some growing into the fifties. And they hide out together underground. A vampire's lair is his most guarded secret. I've seen maybe . . . ten of them in my lifetime. But once you get in there, killing vampires is relatively easy in comparison to finding them—at least in most cases. The older they are, the harder they are to kill. So for a vampire as old as Vincent . . . well, let's just say I've been trying to kill him for over three centuries and he's still here."

"Is that just because he's older than you?"

"He's not," Lucas said. "I'm older."

"Then why can't you kill him?"

Lucas ran his hand through his hair. "I told you," he growled. "They're difficult to track down even for the oldest werewolves."

"But you've had three hundred years to kill him and it's obvious you've fought before. If you're older than he is why haven't you—?"

"I just can't, okay?" His face was livid and I pressed my mouth shut, subdued.

"So, what does this all mean?" I asked, referring to the murder last night. "Couldn't Vincent be killing these girls and not bothering to hide the bodies, because he . . . I don't know, *wants* you to find him?"

"Vincent is very old—not nearly the oldest—but he knows better than to leave his prey after he kills it. Werewolves aren't the only reason they make sure to hide the bodies when they're through. The vampires have their own hierarchy, and improper disposal of prey is a punishable offense. If Vincent is the one doing this, which I don't think he would, but *if* he is, then he's got orders to do it from someone higher up than him." He rubbed his fingers into his eyes. "But if I know Vincent, he's not gonna take orders from anyone. Not unless he's got something to gain by doing it."

I watched Lucas glare into the distance, wondering what he was thinking.

"I was so sure it was him," I murmured. "But maybe that's just because Vincent is the only vampire I know. How many are there?"

"It's impossible to know the true number since they're so damn good at concealing themselves. Plus they're constantly creating more and more of their kind. But I'd say over a half a million, conservatively."

I felt my lips part all by themselves. "And are there just as many werewolves?"

"More," he said. "But most of them are wild, living out of society. It's where all those Bigfoot stories and stuff come from."

I nodded, remembering Mark's ghost story and his strange attack afterward. I hadn't told anyone about it yet, but I thought if anyone should know, it was Lucas. He was supposed to be protecting me, after all, and Mark had threatened me.

Plus I was aching to spill.

I eyed Lucas for a moment and then said, "Hey, can I tell you something?"

"Sure thing."

"Two months ago I was camping out on the La Poudre River with some friends, and one of them—his name is Mark—I saw him talking to this guy in the woods in the middle of the night. He was all the way across the river and I didn't see a boat or anything. And then when I walked back to camp, Mark pretty much assaulted me."

Lucas's eyes sharpened.

"He had a gun and he punched me. And then when I confronted him about it later, he acted like the whole thing never happened." I shook my head, trying to sort everything out. "I have a feeling he's involved with Vincent somehow. He was at his Halloween party and then disappeared, probably around the same time Vincent ran off. Maybe he's the one who killed the girl that night. I don't know . . . but he really scares me."

"I'll keep an eye out. You don't have to worry about anyone hurting you, all right? Especially not a human."

I nodded, still unsure.

He caught my gaze in his and held it. "Hey," he said softly. "I may be a werewolf, but that doesn't mean I'm not trustworthy. I'll protect you."

I sucked in a deep breath, letting his words sink in. It was usually so hard for me to trust men, but trusting Lucas was as natural as the beat of my heart. It unnerved me.

Lucas continued to look at me, a strange emotion plaguing his eyes. I noticed they didn't switch to silver as often anymore. Maybe he was getting used to me. Somehow the thought made me sad, but I couldn't begin to think why.

He opened his mouth and looked like he was going to say

something, but then he snapped it shut and turned away, picking at the frayed edge of the couch.

"What?" I said, unable to stand the fact that he was keeping something from me. I wanted to know everything, including the things he didn't want to say.

He turned back toward me and leaned in a little. "I don't like you going out to the La Poudre alone," he said finally.

"I wasn't alone. I had Derek and four other people with me."

"That's like adding filet mignon to the buffet . . . you get me?"

"No," I said, frowning.

"Faith," he said, coming even closer to me. "We've got a mess of vampires in this area. . . . Vampires who drink human blood to live. And one in particular who wants you, more than any other. They can smell blood for miles, and Vincent has had some of yours, making you easier to locate. It would take him next to no time to get to you, even from miles away. Can you see how being out in the woods alone would make me nervous?"

"Yeah," I murmured, shaking slightly and not just from fear. Lucas was very close to me. I could smell the scent of his skin— pine needles and loamy earth—intoxicating me and making my brain fuzzy.

I backed up and Lucas's face tightened. He backed away too, a pained look in his now silver eyes. "Promise me you won't go into the woods alone, all right?" he said gruffly.

"No problem," I said, trying to keep the emotion out of my voice.

"Faith." Lucas eyed me intently. "I mean it. Do not go out there. Ever."

"I won't," I whispered. My heart stuttered unevenly. "I promise." My eyes remained fixed on his. I was unable to rip them away, even as I felt myself being pulled closer. It was like looking at the sun. You wanted to just because it was forbidden. Because you might go blind from its brilliance. Somehow I was closer to him again, but I don't remember either of us moving. I breathed him in.

Then Lucas's phone rang loudly and he jumped up. I stood too, but I had no idea why. I watched Lucas talk on the phone and gradually noticed he wasn't speaking English. I watched his lips move around the strange words, realized what I was doing, and went to the window, skin prickling in the cold air.

Lucas hung up the phone and came to stand behind me—not too close, but just close enough to make my face redden.

"You wanna get something to eat before class?" he asked.

I nodded my head, too breathless to trust myself with speaking. *What is wrong with me?*

After breakfast, Lucas walked me to my first class. We stopped outside of the building and I shivered in the light breeze fluttering through the sunny day.

I looked up at Lucas, kicking my feet a little.

"Thanks for breakfast," I said awkwardly. "I had no idea someone could eat so many waffles."

Lucas shrugged. "I like waffles."

My face broke into a goofy smile, which he returned, looking equally silly. My heart drummed loudly at the sight of one of his rare grins. I needed to stop this. I needed to stop staring at him so much. This was going in a bad direction. I couldn't let myself develop feelings for Lucas—look how it had turned out with Derek. And if Lucas had feelings for me—an unlikely scenario—I didn't want to put myself in a position that might leave me hurting, yet again, no matter how easy it was for me to trust him.

"So I'll see you in a couple hours?" I said. I wasn't able to keep that inexplicable hope out of my voice. No matter how scared I was that Lucas might one day hurt me, I just couldn't quite stop hoping that he wouldn't.

"No," he said.

I felt my face fall, right along with my heart.

"Why not?" I asked.

"I gotta run up to Gould and talk with my dad."

"Your dad?"

"My pack master. We're not related, but we're still family. Rolf isn't *really* my dad just like Julian isn't really my brother, but they're the only family I've got."

"Why do you have to talk to Rolf?" I tried to keep the fear out of my voice, but I think Lucas heard it anyway.

He smiled down at me in this sweet, comforting way that made me feel warm and safe. The vibe rolling off him magnified the feeling. "Don't worry," he said. "I've got everything under control. You'll be safe while it's light out. Besides, Julian's around here somewhere on Derek's tail, so if something happened—which it won't—you'll be taken care of."

"You'll be back by dark, though, right?"

"Yep," he said. He looked around at the almost deserted lawn in front of the building. I looked around too, remembering the first time I'd seen him—those black eyes raging with raw intensity. I realized then that the cause of his hateful stare had been me. If just the sight of me had triggered him, I blanched at the thought of what would happen if we touched.

"You'd better go," Lucas said. "I think you're late for class."

"Shoot!" I said, starting out of my thoughts. "I'm always late for this class!"

"You're always late for everything."

I eyed him, wondering just how much he knew about me.

"Go," he said. "I gotta jet if I'm gonna be back before dusk."

I opened the door of the building and stepped inside, turning to watch Lucas walk away through the door. I pressed my hand against it and let the frigid glass burn my skin. It hurt, but I kept my hand there, feeling the solidity of the glass, the invisible barrier between us—the secrets we kept from each other and held close to our guarded hearts. Those gruesome secrets which made it unlikely that Lucas and I would ever be together.

CAPTIVE

H ours later, I sat in my room, jiggling my leg against the carpeted floor, unable to concentrate on anything. My mind spun in frantic circles, all of which revolved around Vincent's cruel face and his tongue licking my blood from his cold lips. I was tormented by what I couldn't control—the inevitability of nightfall, which would descend upon me in a matter of hours and along with it, danger.

I stood up. I needed a distraction. Since I still had no cell phone after my botched attempt to buy one online, I grabbed the dorm phone on my bedside table, wincing as it shocked me with a loud crack. I stared at the phone, feeling my bones vibrate from the electricity. There was definitely something freaky going on with the zaps, but I had no clue what. It only reinforced my need for distraction. I shook off the feeling of unease and dialed the number I knew by heart. I needed to feel safe and normal for a while, and I knew the exact person who could do that for me.

"Hi," I said into the receiver.

"Hey," said Heather. "How's it going?"

"You hungry?" I asked.

"Oh . . . actually, I'm at lunch with Pete right now."

My heart sank.

"Pete?" I asked. "So you two are . . ."

"Together? Yep, we are. It was like I said. He was just really drunk and he apologized for everything."

I didn't say anything. I could have told her how many times my stepdad tried to apologize for what he did to my mom and me, but it wouldn't have made a difference. They were already back together. Heather had actually forgiven him. But I'd be damned if I was going to do the same.

"Did you want to join us?" Heather offered.

"No," I said, hoping I didn't sound as furious as I was.

Heather began to say something, but I cut her off. "It's no biggie. Talk to you later." I hung up. Seeing Heather and Pete together was not what I needed right now. I'd probably bite his head off if I saw him. What I needed was a friend. And Heather was the only one I had left.

I sat up straight in my chair.

Derek is speaking to me now, right? Sort of? I decided to call him.

"Hey, Faith," said Derek when he picked up. He sounded wary.

"Hi," I said. "Listen, I need to buy a new phone, do you want to come with me?"

Derek hesitated. "I don't know. I've got a ton of homework and a game this weekend so—"

"Please, Derek? I know you're upset, but I wouldn't have called unless I really needed you. I just need to talk to you . . . to feel normal again."

I heard Derek sigh hugely. "Meet me in front of your building in ten minutes. I'll pick you up."

"Thanks, Derek," I said.

Derek hung up without saying anything.

He was still mad at me, or hurt, or both. Maybe going out on a casual trip would smooth over some of our issues. Maybe we just needed to spend some time together, to get back into a routine. And the outing would serve a dual purpose because I needed to hang around someone who wasn't secretly a werewolf or a vampire. I needed normal, if only for a few hours.

After dressing, I raced downstairs to see Derek's silver Mazda parked in front of my building. He leaned over to push the door open for me and I hopped in.

"Hey," I said. I took in the familiar face of my best friend, feeling my heart flip in my chest. "Wow, you got a haircut."

"Yup," Derek said, touching his now much shorter locks. The tips of his hair used to fall into his eyes, but now they stood up straight and away from his face. It was a good look for him. I found myself staring a little.

"I like it," I said. "Very cute."

A muscle in Derek's jaw twitched as he pulled the car out of park and took off toward a strip mall.

"It's great to see you," I said after a way too long silence.

"Mm-hmm," Derek hummed, drumming his fingers over the steering wheel.

"You don't seem happy," I said carefully.

Derek forced his face into this overly happy smile and looked at me for a second.

"Better?" he asked coldly.

I turned away, swallowing hard as a lump grew in my throat. I took a deep breath and decided to face this full on.

"You wanna tell me what the problem is?" I asked. "You're the one who called me and said you broke up with Courtney and that you missed me. I took that as a sign that you wanted to be friends again."

Derek's whole face seemed to ripple with the extreme effort of staying calm.

"Isn't that what you meant?" I asked.

Derek hesitated, glanced at me and then said, "Yeah. That's what I meant. I'm sorry. I'm just having a crappy day."

I searched his face for signs of deceit. If he was lying, he hid it well, but I still got the feeling that I had misinterpreted what he'd meant on the phone and I was now making things worse. And Derek obviously didn't want to discuss it, so I followed his lead.

"What happened?" I asked.

"Nothing. Just junk with football."

"You can tell me about it, if you want."

He looked for a moment as though he was going to tell me off, but he must have decided against it because he started talking instead.

"I haven't been doing so hot in my classes," he said. "And if I don't start doing better I'm going to lose my scholarship. And then my dad called me and chewed me out because he saw the game on TV and saw me miss that pass that lost the game."

"I'm sorry," I said quietly. "I didn't know you were having such a hard time."

"Yeah, well, you wouldn't."

"And that's my fault?" I asked, getting fired up. "*You* stopped talking to *me*, remember?"

"Because you rejected me! I told you I loved you and you completely stomped on my heart like it was nothing."

I stopped short on the comeback I had prepared. I watched his eyes as he focused on the road, the downturn of his lips and the hoarse way his voice had come out. He was right. I'd never paused to think what that night on the La Poudre had been like for him.

He'd put himself out there, kissed me, and then I'd promptly turned him down. In my mind it'd been obvious all along that I would deny him, but Derek had really been holding onto the hope that I wouldn't. And I'd crushed him.

I'd simply expected him to get over it immediately, to act as though it hadn't happened. But now I could see that the reason he'd stopped talking to me wasn't because he didn't want to be friends anymore. It was because he needed time to get over the fact that I would never be his girlfriend. That I would never be able to love him the way he deserved.

In high school, it had taken me months to get over his cheating and he'd waited patiently for me to be ready to forgive him. Now I had to do the same for him.

"You're right," I said.

His frown deepened.

"I was insensitive to what you were going through. I'm sorry."

For a moment, I saw a glimmer of softness pass through Derek's eyes, but then it disappeared and he just nodded silently.

I pressed my fingers into my temples. This was so not going well. "Derek, you just passed the mall. You have to make a U-turn."

Derek cursed and slammed on the brakes. As he did so, the dashboard compartment popped open and I stared at its contents.

There was a gun inside.

"Derek," I whispered. "What the hell is that?"

He glanced sideways at me as he steered us into the strip mall. "What's it look like?"

"Why on earth do you have a gun?"

"I went camping on the La Poudre a few times with Mark—he

left it by accident. It's not a big deal." He reached over and smacked the drawer closed.

"Why haven't you given it back yet?"

"I just haven't, okay?" He thrust himself out of the car.

Weirded out, but unwilling to badger him, I let the subject drop and followed Derek cautiously into the store.

The rest of the trip was spent in pretty much the same manner. Derek remained mute while I made desperate attempts to turn us back into the friends we'd always been. But my attempts were totally wasted. No matter what I did or didn't do, Derek kept his arms crossed over his chest and his responses restricted to non-committal grunts.

We didn't talk on the ride back to my room.

I got out of the car and leaned down to Derek's eye level, clutching the plastic bag containing my new cell phone like it was my lifeline.

"Thanks for taking me," I said in my nicest voice.

"No problem," he said icily.

"Derek, if there's something you want to say to me, you can. I won't get mad or anything. I just want us to be friends again."

Derek squeezed his eyes shut and his knuckles turned white on the steering wheel.

"Faith," he whispered. "Just please go. I'll—I'll call you okay?"

"You promise?" I asked.

"Yeah. I got this thing planned for the first snow in a few weeks, so . . . so maybe you can come. I don't know. I'll call you, okay?"

I felt my face lift. "Okay," I said. "Bye." I shut the door and watched Derek drive away.

I didn't know what to think about him anymore. I stared up at the building above me, dreading going back to my room to be alone or worse, with Ashley. I didn't think I could take her perky smile right now.

My skin felt like it was crawling, itching for something. Then I realized it had been days since I last ran. I wasn't exactly dressed in running clothes—jeans and a thick hoodie—but I was wearing sneakers and that was all I needed.

I tucked the shopping bag into the pocket of my sweater and started jogging down the campus walkway. It was late afternoon, so most people were done with their classes by now. A few couples walked hand in hand, a man in too-tight running shorts jogged by, his earphones dangling. I pushed myself harder, trying to ignore everyone else as I snaked in and out of the elm trees dotting the walkway. I tried very hard not to think about Derek, but the temptation grew, and soon I was close to tears.

I would be more than happy to be friends with Derek again, even after all of this, but he just wasn't going to be happy unless we were together—he'd made that much perfectly clear. And he refused to accept the fact that I didn't want the same thing, that I was scared to trust him again after he'd broken my heart. As much as I might still care about him, might be jealous to see him dating someone else, I refused to let Derek hurt me again.

I ran faster as the tears spilled down my face. My body pulsated with energy, my heart hammering to the beat of my shoes pounding the cement. I could hardly see. Finally, I slowed only because I was concerned that I might hit a tree.

That's when I heard someone calling my name.

"Faith, slow down!"

I stopped and turned to see Mark hustling up to me. He walked like a duck—bowlegged and waddling. It was a wonder that he moved swiftly enough to play lacrosse.

I hastily wiped my face as he approached.

"Fancy meeting you here," he said.

I just grunted and started walking. As he fell in next to me, I gave him a disgusted look. I still wasn't sure if he was working with Vincent or not, but either way, I detested the jerk.

"Still hating me for no reason, I see," he said. "You should get over the dream you had on the La Poudre already. I never did anything to you."

"Yeah, well, you have your version and I have mine. I know I wasn't dreaming."

He chuckled, but I could tell it was forced.

"I saw you out with Derek today," Mark commented.

I made no response. *None of his business.*

"You break it off with Lucas Whelan?"

I swung my head around to look at him. "Who said I was dating Lucas?"

He shrugged. "Word gets around."

"Well I'm not. And how could word possibly get around after one night of sleeping at his place?" I eyed Mark's profile, trying to see what he knew. "Did Ashley tell you I wasn't home last night, or something?"

Mark seemed to relax when I said this. "Oh, yeah, yeah. Ashley told me." But then I knew he was lying. Ashley was out all night with Courtney and she didn't know I'd been at Lucas's.

What was Mark playing at? Why would he lie to me? Before I could respond, Mark elbowed me lightly in the side, winking his beetle-brown eye at me.

"You and Lucas, huh? He any good?"

"Ugh!" I exploded, dodging his elbow. "Can't a girl just be friends with a guy and not be sleeping with him?"

"Not when they spend the night in his room."

"What do you care anyway? Why are you even talking to me?"

Mark picked at a zit on his cheek as he pondered my question. "Just trying to make friends. You *are* my girlfriend's roommate."

"Well, please don't. I think it's obvious that I can't stand you."

Mark just smiled, shrugging his sloping shoulders nonchalantly. I wished he would go away. I was having such a lovely wallowing session until he showed up. I blew out a long breath and turned my face to the sky, trying to calm down, when I noticed it was getting dark fast and I'd run halfway across campus.

Mark and I were standing in a remote area between the tall, brick chemistry labs. I could smell herbs and other foliage growing in the greenhouse at the end of the walkway. I stopped and turned around.

"I have to get back," I said.

"Why? We're having such a fun little chat."

"Oh, right," I grumbled sarcastically. "No, I really have to go." As I started to turn, Mark grabbed my arm. I tried to jerk him away, but his grip was like iron. "Get off," I said, still struggling.

"Just stay," he said. "I'm not done talking."

"Well, I am. So get *off.*" I yanked my arm hard on the last word, but to no avail. Mark was unnaturally strong. I wished I had been watching where I was going. Especially now that the night was coming and my window of sunny safety was waning.

"I just want to hang out," Mark cajoled. "Is that so bad? Am I really such a dick that you won't give me a chance?"

"Well, you're being a dick now. Let go!"

Instead of letting go, Mark grabbed my other arm and steered me toward the greenhouse. I struggled, but there was no way I was getting away from him. I glanced up at the sky as Mark threw open the greenhouse door. I prayed Vincent wouldn't be able to find me here.

Mark slammed the glass door shut behind him and tossed me to the ground. I hit the dirt with my face and promptly sprang back to my feet, ready to fight.

But Mark seemed totally chill. He flipped open a cell phone and was speaking in seconds.

"Got her," he said.

Pause.

"I know, I know . . . sundown. I'll keep her here." He eyed me for a moment and then said, "Hurry."

He slapped the phone shut and put his meaty hands on his hips, regarding me like someone about to scold a dog for peeing on the rug.

"Why do you have to make things difficult?" he asked. "Couldn't we have had a nice walk in the moonlight? Why make me man-handle you?"

"I didn't make you do anything, you psycho."

Mark darted forward and grabbed my chin hard. His face was inches from mine. He stunk like decaying flesh. "Not nice. I'm not crazy, Faith. Just resourceful." He let go of me roughly.

I grabbed my jaw, rubbing it. "What are you talking about?" I asked, trying not to let him see how scared I was.

Mark shrugged his shoulders and strolled the aisles of potted plants. Abruptly, he began knocking them over. The piercing clatter of ceramic shattering made me start every time one hit the ground. "I'm a cunning guy," he said. "I know what I want and I use whatever—or *whomever*—I have to, to get it. In this case, that person is you. My guy says he wants you. So he gets you." He winked at me from across the table, letting another plant topple over.

A chill ran down my spine. Minutes to nightfall—I had to get away. I began edging toward the door, trying to obscure myself behind the lush plant life. "Your guy?" I asked, distracting him.

"I won't tell you his name, if that's what you're thinking. Hell, I don't even know his name. He uses fake ones. Napoleon, Caesar, Barack Obama . . ."

"Well, this is all very fascinating, but what does your *guy* want with me? I haven't done anything."

"You know what you're into," he said. "Same thing I'm into, just different sides of the coin." He sent a table of beautiful crimson flowers crashing to the ground. They looked like droplets of blood scattered in the dirt. I crept closer to the door.

"I don't know what you mean." The air was thick and hot in the greenhouse and I was beginning to sweat.

Then Mark looked up from behind a potted fig tree and I halted. "Why do you fear the night?" he said in a low voice. He stared me down for a long time. "You know what's out there. You know what's coming for you." He looked up through the dewy glass ceiling and into the sky.

I shook my head, and his grin became all the more sinister.

"The vampires," he breathed, eyes glittering. He snickered as my eyes widened. "Don't pretend to be shocked. If my guy wants you bad enough to send me after you, you must at least know about them."

So I was right. Mark was involved with the vampires. As I watched him, I suddenly made a connection I hadn't thought of before. That night on the La Poudre, Mark had been talking to *Vincent*. But Vincent didn't even know me then, or that I knew Lucas, so he couldn't have been trying to get to me. So what had they been discussing?

But now that Vincent thought I was involved with Lucas, he'd gotten Mark to . . . what? Find me? Keep me here? Why? Vincent knew where I lived; he'd picked me up outside my dorm room on Halloween. Why would he need idiot *Mark* to get to me? And what did Mark get out of it all?

I sucked in a steadying breath and made myself focus. None of that mattered right now. All that mattered was getting out of there alive. I had no hope of Lucas coming to rescue me since he didn't know where I was, so I was on my own. I had one chance: if I could keep Mark distracted, I might be able to reach the door in time and make a run for it.

"So I guess now I know who you were talking to out on the La Poudre," I said, trying to sound much braver than I felt. "It was a vampire wasn't it? Your *guy*?"

Mark said nothing, but a smug look crossed his features.

"So why didn't he just kill us all then?" I wondered aloud. "He could have made it look like an animal attack and saved himself all of this trouble."

Mark's smirk widened and he let out a puff of laughter. "He wouldn't do that." The sound of yet another pot cracking in half made me jump.

"Why not?" I warbled.

"Because I told him not to."

Now it was my turn to scoff. "And why the hell would a vampire care what you wanted?"

"Because if he doesn't keep me happy, I won't be willing to do him any more favors, and he'll have to find someone else—he needs me." He lifted his head proudly and glowered at me. "If it weren't for Ashley, I probably *would* have let him kill you all . . . he was hungry."

A shiver rippled down my spine at the thought of what might have happened that night. I knew I needed to play for time so I decided to get a few of my questions answered. "Why would the vampires need you? I mean, they're *vampires*."

"You really don't know anything, do you?" Mark asked, mocking me. "The vampires might be strong and fast and whatever, but for all that, they have some pretty dumb shortcomings."

"Like?" I was actually interested now.

"They can't go into anyone's house without being invited—and that includes dorm rooms."

I blinked. "What?"

"Yeah, I know. Dumb, huh? It usually doesn't matter much, cuz there's plenty of people for them to feed on without having to get into their houses. But for cases like yours"—he said, as he leered at me and began tearing petals off of a tray of flowers—"when a mongrel's stuck his nose into things, it makes things difficult for the vamps. They gotta bide their time and wait for the right moment. And they don't like to wait, see? Rather have a human help 'em out, like I am now."

"So what do you get out of it?" I asked. "I'm sure you're not just helping him for the thrill?"

Mark looked away, still destroying flowers, as I inched toward the door. A few more feet and I was golden.

"You ever get vamped?" he asked.

I stopped for a moment.

"What?"

He shot me a withering look. "I don't know why he wants you so bad. You don't know a damn thing."

"Enlighten me," I challenged.

"Humans can drink vampire blood," Mark said. "It gives them powers, like what the vampires got, but not as strong. And it makes you high if you drink enough."

"You *drink* their blood?" I asked, aghast.

Mark nodded and then looked thoughtful. "Well . . . technically I guess they don't have blood, do they?"

I stared blankly.

"Usually they're empty," Mark explained. "But right after they feed, they're full of it—full of human blood. Once it enters their bodies it gets poisoned, but a human who hasn't been bit can drink it without turning into a vampire."

"And they just *let* you drink from them?"

"Nah, like I said, you gotta help 'em out first. They drain it out for you into a vial or a cup, and then you just take a sip. Just a tiny sip and you're like a superhero. You can run faster, lift more. Hell, I even aced a calculus exam on the stuff."

I sneered at him and he strolled away from me. I didn't give a crap if Mark lived or died right now, but I definitely had to pretend to care if I wanted out of there. Maybe I could make him see that Vincent was using him. Not the other way around. And once Vincent was through with Mark, he was dead meat.

"Listen Mark," I said, scooting toward the door again. "I know it seems like a great deal right now. You help—Vin—your *guy* get his blood and in return he gives you a little, but just think of who you're dealing with. These are *vampires*. Evil, bloodthirsty murderers. You can't trust any of them to keep you alive once you've worn out your usefulness."

"Who said I trusted them?" He held up one of the flowers he had been tearing apart. "This is a saffron crocus flower. See these little antenna-looking things here? It's what people put in their Spanish rice and enchiladas. Saffron. It's fine for us humans to eat, but totally lethal for vamps. They used to burn it in Catholic churches way back when. It's where all those myths about vamps and crucifixes came from. Holy water like acid . . . please . . ." He guffawed to himself, dissecting the flower.

I mustered up some courage, intending to shake Mark a little right before I made a dash for the door. It was full-on dark now. I had to run now or never.

"Saffron?" I said dubiously. "Really? That's it? You're ingesting saffron so that if a vampire sucks your blood, it'll kill him?"

"Yup," he said proudly.

"And who told you about that? A vampire? To give you some insurance, no doubt."

Mark faltered with this dumbfounded look glazing his face.

I smiled coldly. "Yeah. Good luck with that!" I bolted through the door and ran for my dorm room, legs pumping so fast I'd swear they were a blur beneath me. I heard Mark yelling after me. I was a fast runner, but if he had vampire blood in his system he might be faster. He would catch up. I needed Lucas.

The cell phone.

I grabbed it out of my pocket, wrestling with the bag. *Thank God I activated it at the store.*

I pounded the speed dial for Lucas. One ring.

"Where are you?" he snapped. "It's past nightf—"

"Lucas, I need you!"

"Where are you?" he said again.

"Running . . . toward your room . . . Mark . . ."

"Can you make it someplace secluded?"

I heard Mark closing in. Frantic tears bubbled up on me, choking my throat.

"Never mind," Lucas said. "Give me fifteen seconds."

He hung up. I let out a sob and glanced behind me. Mark was less than ten feet away.

"Stop, Faith! He's coming any minute, just give it up!"

I pushed myself harder. *Run. Run. Run. Don't stop.*

I saw the courtyard in front of the dorm rooms in the distance, less than fifty feet away. But I wasn't going to make it. I cast around for some place to hide—there was nothing. *Where is Lucas?*

Then I saw him.

The front end of a massive black wolf crouched in the gap between two buildings on my right.

"God damn it!" Mark roared from behind me. "STOP!"

My legs burned; I couldn't breathe. I wanted to stop. But there was no way I was letting Mark win. I was fast approaching the gap where Lucas hid.

I glanced behind me.

Mark was two feet away, stretching out his hand to grab me. I lunged forward, out of his reach, but tripped. I rolled to the ground, landing face up. My head lolled to the side and found Lucas's hulking body, poised to attack. His eyes were trained on me with an intense hunger engraved in their silvery depths—hunger for the kill.

Then I saw the blur of Mark's body as he leaped over me to avoid tripping. I rolled into a ball, readying myself for his blow, which was sure to come next. But then Lucas pounced. His eyes were still locked on me and for a split second I feared that he wouldn't know me, that he would attack me instead of Mark. I looked into Lucas's fierce metallic eyes as he came at us, and suddenly an electric shock passed through my body, stronger than anything I'd ever felt. Vertigo warped my vision, and my mind felt like it was stuck on repeat. *Attack Mark, not me, not me . . .*

And then the moment was over.

Lucas's body flew over me and collided with Mark. I bolted upright and watched Lucas drag Mark, screaming and struggling, into the darkness. I heard a gurgling, retching noise and then a quick crunch. *Snap, snap . . . drag . . .*

Bile rose in my throat. I swallowed it down and stood, shaking. I slowly approached the shadowy gap. There was no sound coming from within.

"Lucas?" I whispered.

Nothing.

I put my hand on the cold brick wall and leaned in.

"Lucas?" I asked again, louder now.

Two huge hands yanked me by my shirt into the blackness. I shrieked. One of the hands closed over my mouth.

"Shut up. It's fine. Just me."

Lucas let me go with a jerk, but my lips burned from where he had touched them. It was the first time our skin had touched for longer than a second, something I definitely noticed, even if he didn't. Lucas backed against the wall, as far from me as possible, although there was only about a foot of space between us. My body was alive with his nearness.

"What are we doing in here?" I whispered.

"Giving anyone who saw that time to think they imagined it."

"Oh." I could just barely see Lucas's profile in the moonlight streaming in from between the buildings. He was clad in only a pair of shorts. His broad chest took up most of my vision, so I busied myself by looking around for signs of Mark. "What did you do with him?"

Lucas eyed me. "You really wanna know?"

I flinched away. *Definitely not.* I felt fairly certain I wouldn't have to worry about Mark anymore. "What am I going to tell Ashley?" I asked.

"Don't tell anybody anything. You never saw him today, never heard from him, nothing. We'll take care of the police if they get involved."

"How?"

"We have some pack members on the police force." He seemed to sense my uncertainty and gave me a withering look. "We do this a lot, Faith. Cover-ups, I mean. Everyone will just think he went missing . . . a tragedy." He sniffed bitterly.

I nodded and looked up at him. "Did he hurt you?"

"Yeah, right," he grumbled. "Just a human."

"He'd been drinking vampire blood."

Lucas was unconcerned. "They get themselves . . . helpers sometimes. Blood bitches, I call them."

I giggled despite myself.

"But what do they need humans for?" I asked. "I mean, besides what Mark said—getting us out of our houses."

Lucas winced. "I wish he hadn't told you so much."

"Why not?"

His eyes met mine, shining in the scant light. "I hoped that maybe I could spare you knowing the gory details." His voice was gentle for once.

I found myself much too pleased that he'd been thinking of sparing me the horror of his dark world. But that didn't stop me from wanting to know about it.

"I don't mind . . ."

I heard him sigh. "They get humans to do their dirty work, usually people with connections."

"What do they have them do?"

"Just odd jobs, things they don't want to do themselves, or can't. Anything that has to be done during the day, digging graves for their victims or covering up missing people. Taking the fall for their murders."

"*What?*" I couldn't imagine any human being so desperate for vampire blood that they would take the fall for a murder they hadn't committed.

Lucas nodded sadly. "They're like drug addicts, the blood bitches. They'll do anything to get vamped."

"Wow," I whispered. And then I remembered something. "Mark said he was eating saffron to poison Vincent if he ever bit him. Did you bite him? Would that hurt you?"

Lucas chuckled darkly. "They're still using that one, eh?" He smiled down at me. His sharp teeth glinted in the moonlight, making me very aware that he had been a rabid wolf not five minutes ago. "Saffron is just a spice. They invent stories like that to make the humans feel better, feel in control, but there's not much that can hurt a vampire, except us."

We both fell silent for a long moment.

"Faith," Lucas murmured.

I met his eyes, loving the fact that he didn't hide them from me anymore.

"I felt something when I was changed," he said quietly. "Something . . . different."

I furrowed my brow. "What do you mean?"

"It was like . . . for just an instant, I wasn't in control."

"I thought you were never in control when you change?"

"No, that's not what I mean. It was like, someone else was steering me. It was just an instant, but it was unnerving."

My pulse quickened as I remembered the electric shock that

had hit me when my eyes met Lucas's. It was as though our minds had been connected. In that moment, I'd been stalled on those few words, *Attack Mark, not me.* And then Lucas had *obeyed.* He hadn't so much as glanced at me the whole time he was changed. And after Mark had been defeated, he had changed right back into a human. A wild thought occurred to me at Lucas's words. Had I *controlled* him? Or had I just been very, very lucky?

"And you think this has something to do with me?" I asked, unable to keep my voice from warbling.

He surveyed me for a long while, but then he shook his head. "No, I guess not. How could it?"

I just shrugged. I could have told him that I'd felt something too, but admitting it would have made it real. I wasn't sure I was ready to acknowledge that I had an ability. I'd only just entered this underworld of supernatural creatures, but I knew that if what I thought had happened—that I had somehow *stopped* Lucas from attacking me—he definitely shouldn't know about it.

"What's wrong?" Lucas asked when I remained silent.

"I feel like—" I groped for something to tell him that wasn't a lie. "I feel like I can't trust anyone anymore. Anyone could be working for the vampires." And it was true. I felt terribly alone all of a sudden, singled out for no reason that I could see.

Lucas looked down at me. He reached his hand out like he was going to touch my cheek, but lowered it with a sorrowful grimace. "You can trust me," he said firmly.

I met his gaze, wishing with my entire body that he hadn't stopped himself from touching me. "I know," I murmured. And as

I said the words, I knew they were true. If I could trust anyone, it was Lucas.

"Come on," he said. "Let's get inside before Vincent figures out where we are."

Lucas let me go to my place first to gather some things to store in his room. I was wary of being left alone when Vincent could be hiding anywhere, waiting for me to exit my dorm, but Lucas assured me that he had someone watching me. I presumed he meant Julian. Meanwhile, Lucas said he'd be dealing with Mark's body. I didn't even want to think about what he was going to do with it.

I went up to my room. Ashley was sitting at her desk, popping her gum and messing around on her computer, oblivious to what had just happened. I couldn't help but feel sorry for her as I imagined what she'd do when she found out that Mark was missing. She was nice, really—if a little ditzy—and I hated to think that soon she would be in pain.

"Hey," I said as I entered.

She waved, not bothering to turn around. I took a quick shower and felt much better when I got out. I was throwing on some woolen socks when Ashley knocked on the bathroom door.

I came out and she said, "Some guy just came by and left something for you."

"What guy?" I asked, snapping to attention.

"Dunno . . . really tall with brown hair and freckles."

"Freckles?" I said, frowning. I'd thought maybe it was Lucas, but he didn't have freckles.

"Yeah, he was supercute. He left a note. It's on your desk."

I went over to my desk and found that there was a piece of lined notebook paper folded in half lying on my computer. I opened it and something fell out. I bent and picked up a little brass key. Confused, I opened the note.

> This is from Lucas.
> He's going to be held up.
> Go straight to his room when you're
> done packing. Lock the door behind you.
> Don't let anyone in.
> ~ Julian

I stared for a moment. Julian . . . Lucas's pack brother. So he *had* been the one assigned to keep watch on me while Lucas handled Mark.

I tossed the note in the trash and spent the next thirty minutes packing the essentials. I waved good-bye to Ashley, who was complaining that Mark wasn't answering his phone, and ran over to Lucas's room, slamming the door behind me. I locked it firmly and exhaled. I went over to Lucas's desk and flipped on the low light. Not knowing what to do, I drifted to the window and watched the half-moon hanging serenely in the sky with not a care in the world but waxing and waning. I had sick visions of Vincent's face popping up in the window, smiling that pointy smile, licking my blood from his lips.

I had to stop thinking. I needed a task. I set off into the bathroom to put all my girly things in the cabinets. I didn't take up too much room, but I saw that Lucas had cleared out half of everything for me to use. Half the closet, half of the shower, half of the desk drawers.

I shuffled around the pens and papers rattling around in the bottom drawer and my hand found something leather. I pulled it out and found a small notebook. I held it in my hands, rubbing the black leather. I cracked it open and my eyes widened.

It was a sketchbook.

In it were amazing drawings. Pictures of things I could only dream about. There were moons and eyes and wolves and fangs swirling, melding together, angry and tangled up in Lucas's mind. I touched the pages. These drawings were tortured, anguished. I could see a pattern. They started out melancholy, sketches of hands curled against a man's face, tears raking down his cheeks. Then they became more anxious—trees, hunts, and night skies filled the pages. Then I saw drawings of wolves, of moons looming above, taunting him—calling to him. Then the transformation. Angry, raging pictures, some so gruesome I quickly turned the pages. And then the drawings would become mournful again.

I came to the last page, a drawing of a girl—just her face and the spindly branches of an evergreen. Great care was taken in the execution of her eyes, distant and vaguely somber. Her lips pursed into a small frown, her dark hair coiled around her shoulders loose and free. She had a small freckle above her left eyebrow—just like me.

I smiled slightly and felt my heart swell.

Then the door banged open and I yipped, dropping the book on the floor. But it was just Lucas. I exhaled heavily and put my hand to my chest, laughing.

"Lucas! Jeez, you scared me."

Lucas came in and locked the door behind him. "Sorry I'm late. I hit traffic."

"It's okay," I said, still catching my breath. *Where had he gone with Mark's body that involved traffic?*

Lucas walked to the couch and sat heavily, kicking off his shoes. "Sorry I scared you."

"It's fine." I stood by his desk, not really knowing what to do with myself—if I could go sit by him without it bothering him. I saw his eyes fall on the journal on the floor and then streak to mine.

"You looked at it?" he asked gruffly.

"Yeah," I admitted.

"Wish you hadn't done that," he said, standing up. He crossed the little room in two strides and bent to pick up the book. He straightened and flipped through it, looking at me. He was standing very close—closer than he usually did.

"They're amazing," I said. "You're really good."

He nodded like he already knew that. "It's just my way of . . . coping." He closed the book and placed it on the desk. "Some of it's kind of dark, but it helps. Sometimes."

"It's good to have an outlet," I supplied uselessly. "Is that why you're here?"

He stared blankly at me.

"In college, I mean." I imagined that he must have been in college before, seeing as how he was over three centuries old, so I couldn't really understand why he was even at CSU. What was the point?

"Oh," Lucas said, clueing in. "Well, yeah. All my other degrees are in boring stuff—law, medicine, business. When I started drawing, I thought maybe I'd learn more. I got some pieces showing soon."

"Pieces . . . showing?"

"I'm an art major. Some of the students get to show their work at the end of the semester. It's not a big deal." He bit his top lip for a moment. "You can come see them. I mean, if you want." He sounded tentative, almost reluctant.

"I'd love to see them," I said, meaning it completely. "I wish I had talent like you."

Lucas's face was skeptical as he sat at the desk chair.

"No, really," I said. "If I had talent like that, I'd at least know what I want to major in. What I want to do for the rest of my life."

"You don't have a major?" Lucas asked, sounding disbelieving.

I pushed myself up onto his bed, letting my feet dangle off the edge. "Nope. I'm lost. Totally and completely lost."

"I used to feel that way," Lucas said. "Still do, sometimes. But then one day I picked up a pencil and just started going. Stopped caring about being good or bad at it, and just did it for the release."

"Sounds great."

Lucas studied me for a moment. "Try it," he said.

"What? No." I looked away, feeling my face grow hot.

"Naw, come on," he said, standing up. He moved in front of me and leaned in, placing his hands on either side of my thighs. He was so close. Now my face was on fire. I couldn't even breathe. "I promise I won't look," he said, interpreting my expression as embarrassment. "It might be good for you, especially after everything that's happened."

I started to look away, but his eyes caught mine.

"You must be feeling some pretty strong things, Faith. You gotta find some way to get it all out. Maybe this is the way."

"I'm a horrible artist," I said, pleadingly.

"Doesn't matter. Nobody's gonna see it but you." He stepped away from me and grabbed a pencil and some blank paper from his desk drawers. "I'm gonna jump in the shower. Feel free to use these." He pointed at the paper on his desk.

I nodded and watched him shut the bathroom door. I listened as the shower turned on and heard the rustle of the curtain being pulled back. Trying not to let the image of Lucas's naked body invade my thoughts, I reached over and grabbed the pencil and paper from the desk, holding them in my hands.

They were mocking me.

I leaned onto my elbow and put the pencil to the paper. Its blankness was staring at me, waiting for me to make the first move.

I listened again to the water running and stared at the bar of light underneath the bathroom door, thinking of Lucas.

I had to stop . . . I *needed* to stop. I could feel myself falling, and it was a feeling I knew very well. Luckily, it was a feeling I knew how to stop.

At least, I knew how to stop it with Derek.

But everything was different with Lucas. Despite my better judgment, I trusted him almost to the point of stupidity. And everything was more potent with him—every time my heart skipped, every breath that caught in my throat, every tremble of my hands. It was as undeniable and inescapable as nightfall.

Lucas was the night, dark and dangerous, flirting with my senses and making me feel things I shouldn't be feeling but secretly wanted.

And it was that wanting that scared me. Because it didn't matter how much I wanted Lucas, I couldn't have him. In the end, it would be just the same as with Derek. Lucas would eventually break my heart. So I couldn't love him—couldn't love anyone.

The bathroom door creaked open, and Lucas came out wearing only a pair of dark blue jeans hanging unbuttoned on his bare hips. He was clearly not wearing underwear because I could see almost down to his butt. His chest was bare, still moist, and his short hair stood up in little spikes. He ran his hand over it, and I watched the water sparkle through the air and hit the mirror.

"Oops," he said, wiping the mirror off with his hand.

I smiled and blushed. I must have giggled too because Lucas looked over at me, hiking his jeans up and buttoning them. "You care if I don't wear a shirt? I figured you wouldn't since, you know, you kind of saw me naked." His lips spread into a devilish little grin.

I gaped, thinking there was no way he could get any hotter. "No, I don't care."

"Awesome. I hate wearing clothes. I feel like they're smothering me."

I gaped some more, feeling kind of smothered myself.

Lucas came over to the bed and stood near my feet, leaning on the bedpost. "How's it goin'?" he asked, jerking his head toward the pencil I had clutched between my fingers.

I looked down at my paper and was surprised to see the rough sketch of an eye looking back at me. It was big and angular with pupils narrowed into vertical slits.

"Ahh," I mumbled, "It's okay."

"Can I see?"

"I guess . . . but it's just a little doodle. Nothing amazing."

Lucas took the paper and nodded at it. "What was your inspiration?" he asked, looking up at me. His eyes blazed silver and the pupils narrowed. They were two identical replicas of my drawing.

"Oh, shut up," I said, snatching the drawing away. "It just came out. I didn't even know I was drawing it."

"That means you were thinking about me while I was in the shower." He smiled impishly again and moved closer to me. "I was thinking about you, too."

"You're such a jerk," I said, flushing.

Lucas laughed loudly and flopped himself down on the couch. He stared at the ceiling, his hands behind his head. "Julian said you were with Derek today?" His tone was uncaring, overtly so.

"Yeah," I said.

"What'd you guys do?"

"He went with me to get a new phone."

"I told you I'd pay for that," he said sharply.

"And I told you I could handle it."

Lucas fell silent, his face drifting into that familiar scowl. "What's with you two, anyway?" he asked, sounding angry now.

I rolled over to glower at the ceiling. "What do you mean?"

"You say Derek's your best friend, but all you do is fight with the guy. What's the deal?"

I peered at him. "You really want to know? Or are you just trying to be nice?"

"If I didn't wanna know, I wouldn't have asked."

I rolled my eyes. "Fine," I said. "But prepare yourself for some major melodrama." He smiled, and I told him the condensed version of my sad history with Derek and our current status of nonfriends, nonlovers, nonanything.

"That sucks," Lucas said when I was done. "But I don't get it. Why won't you just go out with him? It seems like you really like the guy, so what's the big deal?"

Why didn't anyone understand this, but me? "Because I can't trust him anymore, and pretending to do so would only make things worse. He wants more. I can't give it to him. End of story."

Lucas mulled this over for a bit. "Why can't you give him more?"

"Because I just can't. It's not in me."

"What isn't?"

"Love," I admitted finally.

"Why not?"

"Ugh!" I exploded. "What is this? Make-Faith-uncomfortable night? Can we please talk about something else?"

"Sure," Lucas said. But he didn't say anything.

Silence enveloped us.

"What do you want to talk about?" I said, unable to stand the silence beating against my ears.

"What's your favorite book?" he asked, grinning in my direction.

I laughed as the tension between us broke. "*Cujo* by Stephen King."

"Aw, shut up," he said, throwing a pillow at me and laughing.

13

FIRST SNOW

After that first night, life fell into a comfortable routine. For the next two weeks, I spent all of my time with Lucas. He walked me to my classes, ate lunch and dinner with me, and then I spent every night at his place. He even sat in the bleachers sketching while I was at track practice. He was forbidden from attending any meets—it would have made me too nervous to compete—but I enjoyed having his eyes on me as I ran at practice.

Mark's disappearance had been televised as a kidnapping, and his parents had appeared on the local news station, teary-eyed and begging for his return. The sight had made me sick to my stomach, and I stopped watching the news after that. Mark's roommates—Derek included—and Ashley had been questioned by the police, but since the werewolves on the force kept things relatively quiet, there wasn't much of an uproar from the community. People let it slide as a tragedy—just as Lucas had predicted.

There were no more murders, thank God, and I didn't see Vincent, or hear of him at all. I didn't see Derek either, except once. Lucas took me to a football game, and I saw him play, though I never spoke to him or even let him know I was there. I had been expecting to feel some sort of pain upon seeing Derek, but all I felt was a dull sadness. I missed him, yes. But as time passed, the ache his absence had caused began to fade and I thought of him less and less.

Mostly, I thought of Lucas. Maybe that was because we spent almost every minute together, or because we suddenly got along so well, or possibly because being near him sent shivers down my spine—even after two weeks. But Lucas became my world. We stayed up late, sometimes all night long, just talking. Lucas was a great talker once I got him started. And he knew everything—art, movies, history, books, food—name it and Lucas could tell a wild story about it. He'd traveled to tons of countries and had some crazy adventures in many of them—some involving blood and guts.

But we never talked about his pack or about Vincent. Those were two topics we stayed away from. Nor did I bring up my suspicions about what had happened that night with Mark. If I had made some sort of connection with Lucas while he was changed . . . if I had controlled him, I knew I needed to keep it to myself. Nothing good would come of telling Lucas about it. Besides, I didn't even know if I *had* done anything. Maybe I was just one very lucky human.

Lucas and I never discussed any trouble he was having being around me either, although his eyes flashed silver all the time— while we were laughing, playing cards, or watching TV. Or sometimes during those perfect quiet moments, when we were just content to be near each other. I'd look over and catch him staring at me, his eyes cast in silver. He'd shiver a little and look away quickly, taking deep breaths to control his instincts.

I was careful to stay away from him, never coming too close, never touching him. But sometimes our fingers would accidentally brush against each other or our legs would touch when we sat on the couch together. And each touch was like a fire alarm going off in my brain. I was constantly aware of my body, where it was in relation to his, if I was about to touch him. If I would inadvertently set him off.

I felt myself falling for him, but I couldn't stop myself like I could with Derek. No matter how many times I tried to convince myself of the contrary, I knew deep inside that I trusted Lucas. And knowing that was enough to make me fall harder than I ever had with Derek, or anyone else.

And though it frightened me, that fear was the least of my worries. That was a *good* fear in comparison to what really scared me.

Vincent.

Sometimes I found myself doodling on the margins of my papers, only to see his black eyes staring out at me, a pair of bloody fangs over my neck. I dreamt of Vincent's eyes looking in from the window, the moon melting into his face, so dangerously handsome and terrifying. I heard his silken voice against my ears, saying my name, and that sick laughter. Many times I'd wake up in the middle of the night, crying. Lucas would hear me and come to my side. He never touched me, but he'd just talk to me, distracting me.

He made me laugh when I was down, challenged me into new ways of thinking when I was being stubborn and entertained me when I was bored. Or sometimes he was just there as this constant force in my life, keeping me safe, keeping me company.

That is, until the full moon came.

It was our first full moon together. It was Saturday and I rose late, but right from the moment I woke up I could tell it was going to be a tension-filled day. I found Lucas sitting on the couch, his leg jiggling frantically. His eyes were silver. Bright silver.

"You okay?" I asked, yawning.

"Good. You're up." He stood and grabbed a pack next to his leg. "I gotta get outta here, but I didn't want to leave without saying good-bye." He started toward the door.

"Wait," I said. "You're leaving?"

He didn't look at me. "Yup. I can't be around you today. Not at all. The urge is too much. I'll have Julian on you until nighttime."

"But wait! We didn't talk about this. You can't just leave me alone tonight. What about Vincent?"

"I'm gonna call you as soon as I leave. I gotta go."

With that he thrust himself out of the door.

Two minutes later Lucas called. I snapped the phone to my ear.

"Lucas?" I said, my voice high.

"Yeah." He sounded much calmer. We were both quiet for a moment, each of us absorbing the moment. "I'm sorry," he finally said. His voice sounded pained.

"It's okay," I said instantly. "I didn't realize it was so hard for you . . . you never talk about it."

"It's not so bad. It's been getting better. . . . It's just with the full moon . . ."

"I understand."

I really *didn't* understand, but it was the right thing to say. I jumped out of bed and crossed the room to lie on the couch. I curled up on it, inhaling deeply. I wasn't used to being alone like this—without Lucas.

"All right, so listen," Lucas said, sounding businesslike. "I know we didn't talk about this, but I got a plan for tonight. The thing about vampires is that they can't enter a household without being invited."

"I know," I said. "Mark told me."

"Right," Lucas growled.

"But why can't they come inside someone's house? It seems so silly."

"I don't know why—it's an undead thing. Whatever. The important thing is that you stay inside tonight, just stay in my room, that's the safest—then Vincent can't touch you. Okay?"

"Okay," I said, nodding to myself. "What about Derek?"

Lucas didn't respond.

"Lucas? What about Derek? He doesn't know what's going on. He doesn't know to stay inside."

I could almost *see* Lucas's scowl on the other side of the phone. "You'll have to find a way to keep him inside," he said in a rumble. "You know him better than me, so you figure it out. But keep him outta my room."

"Fine," I snapped at his tone.

There was a loaded silence.

"Are you going to be okay tonight?" I asked. My voice came out as barely a whisper.

"I'll be fine," he said dismissively. "I'm more worried about you—I *hate* not being there. You gotta stay inside, all right? In a household, or someone's room—preferably mine."

"Okay."

"Promise me, Faith."

"I promise," I said, meaning it.

"Okay, I gotta go now. I—" He stopped himself from saying something. "I'll see you tomorrow morning."

"Please don't get hurt."

"Yeah," he grunted. "You either." He hung up.

I kept the phone pressed against my ear, somehow hoping that his voice would come back. After a few minutes, I stood, determined not to waste the day away being lonely. I didn't have any homework, and Lucas and I had already finished the project for humanities, so schoolwork was a no go. I turned and went to the window, wondering if maybe Heather wanted to get breakfast or something.

But the sight greeting me from the window stopped me dead.

It was snowing!

My mouth popped open and I immediately ran downstairs. I launched myself into the frigid air and turned my face to the slate-gray sky. I did the cliché thing and opened my mouth, catching snowflakes on my tongue. I watched some other people throwing snowballs and staring up at the sky, much like myself.

It was the first snow, and an early one at that. After the excitement and shock of watching the world go white wore off, I realized I'd never been colder in my life. I ran to my room to gather up the snow gear I had stowed away somewhere.

I was face first under the bed, reaching for a box in the way back, when my cell phone rang. I banged my head on the bed in my enthusiasm to get to the phone before it stopped ringing, shimmied my way out, and snagged the phone on the very last ring.

"Hello?" I said, panting slightly.

"Hey," said an all too familiar voice.

"Derek! It's snowing, did you see?"

I heard Derek laugh. "Yeah, I saw. I, ah—remember how I said I'd call you at the first snow?"

"Yes," I said, even though I didn't. I'd been trying to block Derek from my mind whenever possible—give him time.

"Well, I'm calling. And I wanted to know if you want to go with me and some people to go skiing."

"Yes!" I said instantly.

This was perfect, now I could spend the day doing something besides making myself crazy, try to reconcile with Derek, *and* figure out a way to keep him inside all night.

I did a little happy dance around the box holding my winter clothes.

"Great," Derek said. "Pete and Heather are going, too."

I curled my lip, ceasing my happy dance immediately. I really didn't want to see that guy. But if it meant making up with Derek, I could deal. I'd just act like he wasn't there.

"That's fine," I said.

"I would invite Ashley, too, but I figured she wouldn't want to go after . . ." He trailed off for a moment and then asked gently, "You heard about Mark?"

I'd only discussed Mark's "disappearance" briefly with Ashley after the police declared him a missing person, courtesy of the werewolves working undercover on the force. I knew it wasn't the truth, but it's not like I could say anything to Ashley about it—not even to ease her pain. Now I still didn't know what to say. I was such a bad liar.

"I heard the police report on TV," I said cautiously.

"Me too," Derek said. "I wanted to call you but . . ."

"It's fine," I cut him off, struggling to sound normal. "It doesn't surprise me, actually. I knew he was into some bad stuff. Drugs, I think."

"Oh, man. I had no idea." Derek exhaled loudly as if purging the negative thoughts. "So, did you, ah . . . want to bring anyone skiing?"

"Nope."

This seemed to make Derek happy because I heard his voice

lift when he said, "Pick you up in fifteen minutes."

"'Kay," I replied and hung up.

I clawed open the box filled with my snow stuff and started layering. Twenty minutes later, I shrugged on my navy blue parka, threw a knit hat over my head, and dashed downstairs. Derek's car was already in the driveway so I got in and smiled at him. He was beaming back at me—a big improvement over the last time I'd seen him. His familiar energy washed over me, warm and wonderful as the sunrise.

"Hey," I breathed.

"Nice hat," he said, holding in some laughter. I gave him a light smack on the arm and he handed me a pair of sunglasses.

"What are these for?" I couldn't imagine needing sunglasses in this weather.

"The sun glints off of the snow and makes it blinding," Derek explained.

"Oh . . . right. Thanks."

Derek took off, and I rolled down the window because it was hot with all the layers.

He got onto the expressway, and I asked, "How long of a drive is it?"

"About an hour."

"Oh . . ." I began to fret over the timing of this little trip.

"That a problem?" Derek asked, sensing that there was something wrong.

"No, it's just that I have to be back before nightfall."

"Nightfall?" he asked, looking slightly incredulous. "Why?"

I searched for an excuse, but came up with nothing. I should have planned this out beforehand. Now I just looked like an idiot.

"Is it because of that guy you've been seeing?" Derek asked, annoyed. "You and him have a date or something?"

"No," I said hastily. "And I'm not seeing him; we're just friends."

"Uh-huh." Derek sounded disbelieving. "Courtney says you never come home anymore."

"How would you know? I thought you weren't dating her anymore."

"I'm not. I just talk to her sometimes. Jeez."

I looked away, silent.

"What do you see in that guy anyway?" Derek asked.

"Lucas?"

"Well, yeah. I'm assuming that's the only guy you're seeing. Maybe I'm wrong."

I shot him a dirty look. "I'm not seeing anyone. And Lucas is different than he looks."

Derek glanced at me. "What's that supposed to mean?"

"It means I like him. And he's a nice guy, so lay off, okay?"

"You *like* him?"

"Yes, Derek. I like him. Wipe that shocked look off your face and get over yourself. Some people aren't what they seem once you get to know them."

"And you know him?" Derek questioned me savagely.

"I do."

Derek squinted at the windshield for a long moment.

"I don't like this, Faith," he said at last. "I don't like you spending so much time around him."

"Look, Derek, you stopped talking to me. You can't expect my life to just freeze because you decided to forget I exist."

I saw Derek's mouth clamp shut. "I didn't mean it like that," he said. "I just don't think he's good for you. There's something about him I don't like."

Hmm, could it possibly be that he's a werewolf who has to constantly suppress the overwhelming instinct to kill me?

I turned away from Derek, angry that he was right and not willing to lie to tell him otherwise.

"Don't worry about it," I said finally. "We're just friends."

We were both silent.

"I didn't invite you out here to fight," Derek said at last. "Let's just forget it, okay? You can date whoever you like."

"I'm not—," I cut myself off. There was no point in denying it. Derek wouldn't believe me anyway—not when he knew I was sleeping at Lucas's place. I had to admit, if it had been the other way around, I wouldn't have believed Derek.

For the rest of the trip, we were content to talk about normal stuff. We fell into that easy, effortless rhythm we had together that always made me wonder whether Derek could read my mind. There was something calming in the way we got along—when we were getting along—that had always drawn me to him. It made my world feel at ease and soothed the worries plaguing my thoughts. We talked about completely normal stuff: football and classes and Halloween—minus the werewolves—and our families.

Derek admitted that computer engineering wasn't what he'd thought, and he'd switched to exercise science—an idea he'd gotten from me months ago on the La Poudre. He said he'd decided on physical therapy and although I teased him about it to no end,

I actually thought it was a perfect fit for him. Derek had always loved sports of every kind, and he was a complete gym rat. But beyond that, I knew his caring nature would be what made this the right track for him. While I'd been scared and intimidated by the thought of rehabilitating war vets or elderly people who'd fallen, I knew Derek would have no trouble. He always knew exactly what to say when I was feeling down or discouraged. Even Derek's parents—who weren't exactly the nicest people in the world—were supportive.

We were both smiling again by the time we reached the ski rental place. Pete and Heather were already there. After throwing Pete my best I-hate-you glare, we all headed into the ski rental store to get fitted with boots and helmets and all the other necessary items to avoid killing ourselves on the slopes. About half an hour into it, Derek and Pete had separated themselves to go stare at the snowboard section and act like they knew what they were doing. Meanwhile, Heather and I sat on a worn wooden bench, trying on boots.

"So . . . " Heather said.

I let out a puff of laughter. "So what?"

She tugged on her boot buckle and looked over at me, trying too hard to smother a smile.

"What?" I asked, grinning too.

"Anything happened lately you want to tell me?"

Oh, nothing much, just evading death at every turn and trying frantically not to fall for a guy who is totally and completely wrong for me. You know, the usual.

If only I could really tell her that. It would have been such a relief to have someone to unload on. But I'd made a promise to Lucas, and I wasn't about to break it.

"Nope," I said, returning my attention to my ill-fitting boots and wrestled them off with a grunt.

"Nothing . . . in the romance department?"

I smiled down at the floor. So that's what this was about. She wanted me to tell her about Lucas. This was the first time I'd seen Heather in over two weeks. She had to know something was up. I just didn't know if I was ready to admit that there was something going on between Lucas and me.

"Derek and I are talking again," I said, stalling.

Heather rolled her eyes. "Obviously," she said. "But I meant with that guy. Ashley says his name is Lucas?"

I wrinkled my nose and faced her. "He's nobody."

"He doesn't seem like nobody. Ashley says you sleep over in his dorm room every night."

"You don't know what you're talking about."

"Exactly," Heather said earnestly. "I *don't* know. You haven't spoken to me in weeks. And now you're sleeping with this random guy."

"I'm not sleeping with him!"

Heather crossed her arms. "I'm not an idiot, Faith. Don't treat me like one."

I looked dead at Heather to show her just how serious I was. "And I'm not lying. I'm really not sleeping with Lucas."

She seemed to believe this, but she still looked upset. "Then what are you doing sleeping over at his place?"

I faltered. I really didn't have an excuse ready for this.

"We're . . . just close," I said lamely.

"So you're dating him?"

"No."

Heather scoffed. "Sleeping at his place, but not dating him."

"It's . . . complicated. Why do you even care? It's really not a big deal."

"I care because I'm your friend. Because I haven't seen you in, like, a month. And because you seem to be pretty serious about a guy you just met. . . . I just don't want you to rush into anything you might regret."

"You mean like with you and Pete?"

Her face fell.

Why am I acting this way—picking fights with all of my friends? Heather is only trying to be nice.

"I'm sorry," I said. "It's just—"

Heather thrust her chin out. "Pete and I are better now," she said. "He apologized a long time ago and I forgave him. You should too." She eyed me pointedly.

I looked away. The way he'd treated Heather was unforgivable in my eyes.

Heather stood up and grabbed my boots from me.

"I just want you to be happy, Faith. And I want to be friends with whomever it is you like so much that you can't spare a moment to talk to me anymore. Maybe that way we could all hang out together."

"You're right," I said. "I'm a lousy friend. Lucas and I . . . We'd love to go out with you." I looked away. "And Pete."

Heather's face brightened considerably.

"But not as a date," I said hurriedly. "We're not dating.

We're just friends."

"If you say so," she said over her shoulder.

As she walked away to get some more boots for us to try on it occurred to me that I'd had to declare Lucas as *just* my friend twice since exiting his room and entering the real world, and it had only been a couple of hours.

Maybe if I kept saying it, eventually it would be true.

Once we were all geared up, we tottered out to the bunny slopes. Heather knew how to ski already so she taught us, which saved us the expenditure of lessons. We spent a few hours not learning to ski so much as falling over. But toward the end, Derek, Pete, and I got the hang of it. So after a late lunch, we hit the real slopes.

There was a lift right next to the rental place and we all got on, me next to Derek. My heart was rattling around in my chest as the lift brought us higher and higher over the woods. It had stopped snowing, but the trees were blanketed in sheets of white powder. It looked like someone had dusted the entire world with sugar.

I glanced at Derek, who was bent halfway over the edge of the carriage, peering down at the wonderland below.

"Derek!" I screeched and pulled him back up. The carriage gave a sickening swing, and I felt my stomach drop. I elbowed him in the side. "Believe it or not, I'd rather you didn't plummet to your death right now."

Derek smiled impishly. "What? Like this?" He tossed his upper body over the railing and I screamed.

"Stop it! Stop it!" I grasped at his parka.

Derek laughed and righted himself on the carriage. "You're such a worry wart."

"And you have zero sense of self-preservation."

Derek snickered under his breath.

We both eyed the upcoming end of the line with unease.

"I'm nervous," I admitted. "I'm going to fall."

"Just keep the skis in line like Heather said."

I gulped and put my skis straight out in front of me as the carriage approached the snow-covered mountaintop where a ski lift worker stood, assisting people off the lift. As he came closer and closer, I sat up straighter, readying myself. Then the carriage sloped downward to the ground, and both Derek and I glided off. The ski lift helper grabbed my arm and steered me out of the way. I glanced over at him to say thank you, and my breath caught in my throat.

This man looked almost identical to Lucas—same straight nose, same square jaw, same slanted eyes, except this man had freckles dusting his olive-toned cheeks and his eyes were bright green. He had a kind vibe about him, easygoing, like water flowing. But an undercurrent of lunacy tainted his energy, and I knew in an instant that he was a werewolf. This had to be Julian, Lucas's pack brother. I stared at him and he winked at me, nodding for me to continue on my way. Suddenly I felt much safer, knowing I had a mythical creature at my back. I should have been terrified by the thought of werewolves hanging around at the full moon, but I knew they would be the least of my worries tonight.

Derek noticed my exchange with Julian and he put his hand on my back possessively.

"Who was that?" he asked in a low voice.

"No idea," I lied. Inside I was screaming, *He's a werewolf!*

Pete and Heather glided up next to us, looking excited. Well, Pete looked slightly ill, but whatever. I felt ill, too. If I made it down this hill alive, it'd be a miracle.

We seemed to be on top of the world. Around us, people on skis and snowboards whizzed by and launched themselves down the steep slope of the mountain. Far below were the ski rental shop and the beginner's slope I wished I was still on. Then I saw a small girl rocket down the slope and I felt like a wimp. If she could do it, so could I.

"Ready?" Heather said, grinning widely. She didn't wait for a response. She popped a kiss on Pete's cheek and sped down the slope. I watched, amazed, as she weaved expertly through the people.

Pete gave us a frightened glance and then shrugged. "You only live once, eh?" And then he pushed himself over the edge, screaming like a little girl.

Derek and I laughed and looked at each other.

"What if I fall?" I asked.

"Then you fall," he said. He leaned down and kissed me on the lips. I jumped back. He beamed at me and tossed himself down the hill.

I glared after him and then mustered up some courage. I followed Derek down the slope. At first I moved slowly, controlled. Then I began to pick up speed as the slope steepened. Trees and people blurred past my vision, and my lungs stung from the glacial air. I concentrated on my skis, keeping them in line, skating around those in my way. I saw Derek up ahead of me, going way too fast.

Then he fell.

My heart dropped and I sped up, pitching myself forward as Derek rolled. He slowed to a stop at the bottom of the hill, and I rushed to his side, half falling myself.

"Derek!" I gasped, unlocking my skis from my boots and kneeling down next to him. "Oh, my God, please don't be hurt."

He pulled his sunglasses off and wiped the snow out of his face. He was laughing.

I started hitting him. "What is wrong with you? You scared me. I thought you cracked your spine!"

Derek laughed harder, fending off my punches. But soon I was laughing, too. I fell on top of him and gave him one last swat. "You suck."

I sat up. Pete and Heather were staring down at us with these annoyingly knowing looks on their faces.

I flushed and let Heather help me up. Derek righted himself and said, "Who's up for another run?"

We went down the mountain what felt like a hundred times. It was late afternoon and Derek and I were on the lift again when I finally said, "Okay. I can't move my legs much longer. This is the last time."

"Yeah," Derek said, rubbing his thighs. "Me either. I'm beat."

"Are we going to make it back before dark?" I hated to bring up the subject again since it had made Derek angry earlier and we were getting along so great, but I had to make sure we'd be back in time. And I still had to figure out a way to keep Derek inside all night. My only thought was either to stay in his room or to have him stay in mine. I didn't care which way it went so long as he was safe.

"Yeah, we should be all right," Derek said. "As long as this is the last run."

"Okay."

"You wanna tell me why you have to be back before dark?"

"Not really."

"I won't get mad," Derek said, fiddling with the zipper on his parka. "I'm just curious."

"I just have a lot of work to do," I tried lamely.

Derek's eyes hit mine, searching them for the lie I'd told. He'd be able to recognize my deception. He always could. I had to distract him.

"Do you want to, I don't know . . . study with me?" I asked. "You know, tonight?"

Derek's eyes brightened. "Yeah," he said, his lips tugging upward at the corners, as if he wanted to smile but wasn't sure he could. "I'd love that."

"Cool." I looked away from his hope-filled eyes and said, "Head's up." We had approached the end of the line and we glided onto the mountain. I caught Julian's eye and nodded discreetly. Hopefully he understood that to mean I was leaving now. He gave an infinitesimal nod back.

Heather and Pete came up next to us again.

"Hey, guys," Derek said. "This is our last run. Me and Faith are beat."

"Us too," Heather said. "Mind if we just take off when we get down? We have a rehearsal at six, and we're already going to be late."

"No problem," Derek said. "See ya."

They both said good-bye and raced down the mountain, leaving Derek and me up at the top again. I stared down at the thick pines below thinking how tranquil it all seemed from so high. It was hard to imagine that the woods were teeming with werewolves, poised to change at the first sign of night. Not to mention the vampires.

"Ready?" Derek asked.

"Okay," I said wearily.

"After you." Derek dipped into a little bow and motioned for me to go. I rolled my eyes from behind my shades and launched myself forward. I slid down and down, enjoying the ride as best I could despite the burning in my thighs.

Then a little boy swerved in front of me. My heart rate exploded as I tried to dodge him, but my skis got all tangled up and I fell, rolling sideways into the trees. Somehow I became righted again and I started careening through the forest, out of control. I screamed, ducking and dodging branches. Then a tree hit me.

Okay, no. I hit the tree. I bashed face-first into the harsh bark of a massive spruce and went sprawling. I must have lost consciousness then, because the next thing I remembered was hearing my name and being shaken roughly awake.

"Faith!" Derek yelled from above me. "Are you okay?"

"I'm okay," I said, gathering my senses. I smiled weakly. "Well, that's one way to stop."

Derek laughed hoarsely and held my face. "You sure you're not hurt? You're bleeding."

I touched my fingers to my nose and brought them down to see a flood of crimson. My cheeks were scraped, stinging. "This is going to look fabulous tomorrow." I pinched the bridge of my nose to try and stop the bleeding. Then the adrenaline wore off and I could feel a shooting pain in my ankle. I winced, trying to unfasten my skis.

"Let me see." He reached down, unbuckled the ski boot and pulled up my puffy pants. He yanked off his glove with his teeth and gently touched my ankle, massaging it and rotating it tenderly. "Any of this hurting you?"

"It's sore, but otherwise no."

"Okay. It's gonna be fine." He smiled at me and put my sock and boot back on. "Guess all my football injuries paid off, huh? I should be a doctor." He stood and helped me up, his hands hovering around my waist.

"I'm fine," I said, though I was woozy. "We should get back." I looked around nervously at the trees expanding in every direction, all frustratingly identical and useless. I looked up and saw the light was fading.

Fast.

My heart began to throb and not in a good way. "Which way do we go?" I asked, looking at Derek for help.

He glanced around and pointed to the right. "That way . . . I think." He grabbed our skis and we started walking, too afraid to ski lest we get out of control again. Plus, my ankle was killing me. After fifteen minutes I had to stop.

"Derek, I don't think this is right. We've been walking too long."

Derek stopped and tossed the skis down. He wiped the sweat from his forehead and turned around in a circle. "I thought this was right. I got turned around when you fell."

"Why didn't we just follow our tracks back out?"

"I dunno. Didn't think about it."

"Well, why not?" I asked, hearing a note of hysteria tainting my voice.

"Why didn't you?" Derek yelled back. "I was flustered!"

"So was I!"

"Stop yelling, just stop." Derek came to me and wrapped me in a hug. "Let's just turn around and go back the way we came, and then we can follow our tracks out, okay? It'll be fine."

"Derek, we have to get out of here before dark. We can't be outside once night falls."

Derek shushed me and kissed my forehead. "I'll get us out of here," he said surely—probably more surely than he felt. "Come on. Let's keep moving. It'll keep us warm."

We walked back the way we came, but within minutes it began to snow—snow hard. It was like a wall of white paint had clouded my eyesight, and it wasn't long before we couldn't see our tracks anymore. Daylight was running low and the night was creeping in on us. I saw it between the trees, peeking around branches, and snickering in the wind. I saw eyes, smiling teeth, heard laughter whispering through my hair. We didn't have much time. Vincent could probably run so fast he'd be here minutes after nightfall, and he knew my blood. He would be able to track me easily. I began to walk faster, not even caring where I was headed, just so long as I was moving.

"Do you think Heather and Pete have noticed we're gone yet?" I asked, breathing heavily.

"They left," Derek said flatly.

"But maybe they waited. Maybe they sent someone to search for us."

"Maybe." He didn't sound like he believed himself. "Do you have your phone?"

"I left it in the car. I was scared it would fall out of my pocket."

"Yeah . . . me too."

I moved faster, keeping my eyes on the snow. "I can't see our tracks." My voice was shaking.

"I know."

"What do we do?" I stopped walking, my entire body shaking now. "Derek we have to get inside. We can't be out here!"

"We'll find a way out soon. Don't worry."

"You don't understand! We can't be caught out here alone!" I began running now. I heard Derek behind me, calling my name, but I couldn't stop. Everything looked the same; everything was so cold. Trees, trees, snow, green, brown, white. So much white everywhere. My lungs screamed. I had to find a place for us to hide. The night was coming!

Then someone grabbed me. I let out a shrill screech and beat against a pair of iron arms.

"Shut up!" said a deep, growly voice. "Faith, stop it!"

I stopped and looked up. How did this person know my name?

Oh, because he wasn't a person.

He was a werewolf.

14

NIGHTFALL

I sagged into Julian, so relieved I didn't even care that he was a stranger, that he was minutes away from changing into a creature that could kill me with a single deadly claw.

"Who the hell is that?" Derek asked from behind me.

"Julian," my savior said. "You guys need to come with me. Now."

"Why?" Derek asked, sounding suspicious. Then realization dawned on him. "Hey, you're the ski lift guy! Oh, man, thank God. We were so—"

"Shut up," Julian said. He pried me from his coat and grabbed hold of my wrist. "We have only minutes, so just follow me and don't ask questions."

I nodded, too scared and relieved to speak. Julian started running, tugging me along with him. Derek ran after us.

"Where are we going?" Derek yelled. "What's the big deal about it getting dark?"

"Shut up and run!"

A minute later we hit a clearing. Inside was a decrepit wood cabin. Julian didn't stop to let me take it in. He dashed to the door and tore it open. He threw me inside, shoving Derek in behind me.

I gave Julian one last desperate look. His big angular eyes were acid green and the pupils were slits of gray. His body was beginning to quake, but he returned my gaze and said intently, "Do not leave. Not for anything."

I nodded jerkily.

He slammed the door shut and I watched him run so fast he was just a blur of tremors. I stared through the dirty glass window, watching the night overcome the woods. I felt Derek come to stand behind me. He put his hand on my shoulder and spun me around.

"What in the hell was that about?" he asked. "Who was that guy? And why are we in this cabin? Why didn't he take us back to the ski rental place?"

I put my hand over his mouth and said, "I can't tell you."

Derek's eyebrows pulled into a frown.

"Shh," I hissed. "Don't. Just believe me when I say you don't want to know about it. You really don't."

Derek peeled my hand from his mouth and said, "No. I definitely do. I want to know."

"If I tell you, it'll put me in danger. Do you want that?"

Derek's eyes became alarmed. "What the hell is this, Faith? Is this about Lucas? Did he get you into this?"

I took Derek's face and forced my eyes into his. "Listen to me, Derek. If you love me, and I know you do, then you'll trust me when I say that you do not want to know about this. Please, just trust me, okay?"

Derek stared me down for a long moment, his eyes like sapphires, hard and unrelenting in his stubbornness. But then they softened and became fluid, possibly recognizing how desperate I was to make him believe me. "Okay," he said finally. "But only because I love you."

I smiled weakly. "Thank you."

I let go of Derek's cheeks and looked around. Dust coated everything in the one-room cabin. A small kitchenette-looking thing stood in the corner, cabinets left open with cobwebs filling the spots where the food should have been. My stomach growled just looking at the toppled-over refrigerator. A torn up couch stood in the center of the room along with a damaged table and a few dead mice. I wrinkled my nose.

There was a fireplace on one side of the room and a pile of logs near it. I pointed to it and Derek began stacking logs in the fireplace. I stood behind him, shivering, when I thought of something that crushed the hope for warmth right out of me.

"No matches," I said.

Derek reached into his pocket and grabbed a cigarette lighter. He grinned at me from over his shoulder.

"Ew," I said. "You're smoking now?"

Derek put the flame to the logs and avoided looking at me. "Only a little with Mark. Not anymore since . . ."

"That's disgusting, Derek."

Derek tucked the lighter away. "Yeah, but I bet you're pretty glad I'm so gross now, huh?"

I rolled my eyes and kicked his thigh lightly.

It took some work, but Derek finally got a decent fire going. When he was done, he tossed another log into the fireplace and sat down in front of it. I crashed next to him, still shaking with cold.

Or possibly fear.

"You know what this place reminds me of?" Derek asked.

"Hmm?"

"That time we drove down to Tijuana for spring break."

A smile broke across my face and I groaned, remembering. "You mean the hacienda we stayed in with Charlie and Gregg?" It hadn't been so much better than this shack we were in now. In fact, it might have been worse.

"Yeah," Derek said, laughing a little. "And Gregg was so drunk he barfed in the oven."

"Ugh!" I groaned again, throwing my hands over my face.

"And we stayed up all night talking because you were scared of the rats."

I laughed, but then we fell silent, remembering the good times we used to have together. The times we had before Derek began wanting things I couldn't give him.

"Can I ask just one thing?" Derek said, looking off into the flames.

"Okay, but I reserve the right to refrain from answering if it'll put me in danger."

Derek looked me up and down incriminatingly. "Why do we have to stay in this hellhole all night long?"

I sucked in a breath and held it, giving him a pleading look.

"Can't tell me?"

I shook my head.

"Well, then I get another question."

I let the breath out and motioned for him to continue.

"How do you know that ski lift guy?"

I scratched the back of my neck, thinking about how best to word my response. "He's Lucas's brother," I said at last. "His name is Julian."

Derek nodded slowly. "You said you didn't know who he was."

"Technically, I don't. That was the first time I'd ever met him."

Derek nodded some more and lay down on his side, facing me. He propped his head on his elbow and looked up. "How did he know where to find us?"

I winced and pressed my lips together.

"Okay, okay," Derek said. "But just so you know, this sucks."

"I know. I'm so cold."

Derek held his arms open. I hesitated, worried that letting him hold me would give him the wrong impression, but I was freezing so I lowered myself down against him, my back to his chest. We stayed that way, listening to the sound of the fire crackling and the wind shearing the snow off of the trees with its raw power. It howled through the branches, sounding like wolves crying, or possibly something much worse. I watched the snow pelt the windowpane, sliding down in clumps of ice.

"I've missed you like crazy," Derek whispered in my ear. I felt his hot breath on my neck, giving me chills. "I hate fighting with you, but it seems like that's all we can do lately."

"I hate it, too. I wish things could be like they used to be before we screwed them up. We used to be good back when we were only friends." I hesitated, wanting to ask something I'd been thinking about for a year. But if ever there was a time to ask, now was it—we seemed to have all night to ourselves. Time to fix the things we'd broken.

"Why did you do it?" I asked quietly. "Why did you cheat on me?"

Derek let out a long breath. "I'll never be able to apologize enough for that, will I?"

"You broke my heart."

"I've told you, it was a stupid mistake. It didn't mean anything." He hesitated and then said cautiously, "Besides, what happened between us . . . It wasn't all me."

"I *never* cheated on you," I said hotly.

"I know, but you . . . you hid yourself from me."

I was silent, trying to understand.

"It was like there was this part of yourself that you wouldn't give me," he went on softly. "And it was so frustrating and *heart-breaking*. Because I loved you so much, and every time you refused to say it back it killed me."

"Derek, you know why I was like that. I thought you understood."

"I do. But I also remember the girl I knew before that. The one who was so filled with joy, who smiled all the time and was never afraid to show me how much she cared. I remember that girl and I miss her. I tried so hard to get you to go back to that. I wanted to be the person to put the light back in your eyes. But I couldn't. And now I see the way you look at that guy. You look at him like . . . well, like the way I wanted you to look at me. Like you loved me. I can't help but feel like maybe you've healed? And now we can be together, be happy like we used to be."

I hated hearing Derek so sad, and I hated that I'd caused him pain, but the fact remained that he'd cheated on me. Not the other way around. And I was still angry about it, even if I'd told him I wasn't. There was no way I could consider being with him again until we straightened that out. Even then, I didn't know if I believed in love anymore. What Derek said about me looking at Lucas had to be wrong. I didn't love Lucas. But I *had* loved Derek, even if I couldn't admit it.

"I know I told you I forgave you for cheating," I said. "But the truth is that I never really got over it. That's why we can't be together, Derek. That's why I said no out on the La Poudre. It's not because I don't love you, or that I don't want you, like you said. It's because I just can't trust you again." I shook my head. "We were perfect for each other and you ruined it." I heard the ugly note of bitterness in my voice, but it felt good telling Derek the truth. I craned my neck around to look at him.

His face was set in a grimace. "I know I did. And I've been trying to fix it ever since, but I can't, can I?"

"I don't think so, Derek. Things between us—they'll never be the same and we just have to accept that."

"What if I don't accept it?" He lifted himself onto his elbow and I looked up into his eyes, desperate and agonized. "What if I never stop trying to fix us? What if I'll always love you, always wait for you? What then?" He reached down and took my hand, squeezing gently. "If I have to spend my whole life making up for hurting you, I'll do it. I love you that much. And this time I'll wait for you to say the words; I'll wait forever. I just want to be with you."

I couldn't speak through the tears that welled in my eyes and spilled over my cheeks.

Derek wiped them away with his thumb, holding my face. "I'm sorry for what I did to you, Faith. It was the biggest mistake of my life. I know I've said all this before, but maybe now you'll believe me. And if you don't, I'll say it again and again, every day for the rest of my life. Please, forgive me."

Derek wrapped his arms around me and I closed my eyes, trying to make myself do it. Trying to force my heart to believe the words I said over and over in my head, *Forgive him, forgive him.*

But I couldn't. Because I could still remember all too clearly the searing pain that tore through my heart when Derek had told me he'd kissed that slutty cheerleader after the football game. I could feel the shattered pieces of trust I'd gathered after my stepdad's betrayal ripping my world apart. I could see myself standing outside the football field with my books in my arms, Derek sweating from practice, his face pale and his eyes filled with tears. I could hear him apologizing over and over, just like he was now.

The words had meant nothing then, and they meant just as much now.

I could never trust Derek with my heart after that.

"I'm sorry," I said softly. "I still can't—"

"Can't you just try?" he whispered. Derek bent his head toward me again, and I felt my spine tingle. He began to whisper in my ear, "Don't you remember that kiss? Just try it. . . . Remember how my lips felt, my hands touching your skin, my body up against yours, just like it is now. I know you liked it. I felt you kissing me back. Don't you want it to be like that, always? Come on, baby, just try."

I felt like I was melting. His words sunk into me and buried themselves in my heart. I wanted them to be right, to feel at home there, but it felt all wrong somehow, as though the words had invaded a place that was already taken.

"I don't want to try," I whispered. "And I don't want to hurt you. I can't—"

"Yes, you can. Trust is a choice, Faith. Just like forgiveness. If you choose to, you can let yourself go, forgive me for that one stupid mistake and trust me again. Just let go, let yourself fall. I promise I'll be there to catch you."

I smiled slightly. My face was so close to his; I saw the little scar on his chin where he'd fallen down the bleachers at practice.

"That's such a cliché," I said, teasing him.

He smiled too, but his eyes were pleading with me. "It's a cliché because it's true. I'm here. I've always been here." He searched my face, waiting for me to say something.

But I didn't know what to say. I pulled back from him and his hands held onto my arms. He didn't want to let go.

He didn't want to let go.

Let go, let go.

The words continued to ring in my ears.

Let go, let go, let go.

But I couldn't. I couldn't let go.

I couldn't. But he could. He had to be the one to do it. If I let Derek go, he'd never accept it. But if he was the one to lose his love for me, then he could finally move on. Then one day, maybe we could be friends again.

"Derek," I said. "You have to let me go."

He started to shake his head to argue with me, but I put my hand over his mouth.

"I'm broken," I said. "I know that. I've known that ever since . . . ever since . . ." I couldn't say the words. I regrouped. "But you can't fix me, Derek. You're not the one who can fix me. I'm sorry you have to let me go."

Derek was silent for a moment. I took my hand away from his mouth and his eyes deepened into a frown.

"Not the one? I'm not the one who can fix you?" He sat up, and his face ripped into fury. "I've always been the one, Faith. I've always been there for you, since the very beginning when I beat up that kid on the playground. I was there for you when you lost everything and I was *still* there after you put yourself together again. Yes, I screwed up once. But that was over two years ago and I've apologized more than enough times. Ever since then, I've been here, standing in front of you. Loving you. Waiting for you. Waiting all these years and racking my brains out trying to figure out how to make you realize that you love me back. And now I find out I'm not the one? I've *never* been the one? Well, who the hell is the one, Faith? Is there ever going to be a man that'll be enough for you? That'll fill this space you've got in your damaged heart? Or are you just determined to be miserable?"

"I'm not miserable," I said in a small voice. "I'm happy when you're not being like this."

"Like what?" he spat. "Telling you the truth? Just because you won't face it doesn't make it any less true!"

I sat up. "No, I'm happy when you're not trying to make me feel something I just don't feel anymore."

Derek let out a noise that sounded like a growl and he stood, heading for the door. His hand touched the doorknob.

I scrambled to my feet.

"No!" I screamed and pummeled him. We both fell to the dusty floor, tangled up together in a mess of coats and scarves and limbs.

"Get off!" Derek yelled, shoving me away. "I'm not sitting in this godforsaken cabin with you any longer." He grabbed the door handle again, and I threw myself around his waist.

"You go out there and you die," I said fiercely.

Derek grabbed my arms and got in my face. "I'd rather freeze to death out there, than spend one more second with a bitch like you."

My body went limp.

For a moment Derek's eyes shone with something close to agony. Then his lips curled into a snarl, and he launched himself into the storm.

I stood in the doorway, frozen both literally and figuratively. The snow bit my face and Derek's words shredded my heart. Then the distant sound of footsteps crunching in the snow met my ears and I yelled into the swirling mess of snowflakes and wind.

"Derek! Come back! I'm sorry, just come back!" I started to cry. I bounced on my feet, clawing at the doorframe, trying to force myself into the night. I had to make Derek come back. Vincent was out there, he had to be by now. He would kill Derek.

I pumped myself up. *Okay. Go. Run out there, Faith. Save your friend. GO!*

I ran headfirst into the night, screaming for Derek. The wind was insane—it snarled hair into my mouth, choking me. It beat against my eardrums and prevented me from hearing anything at all.

Which meant Derek couldn't hear me either.

I ran around in circles, trying to keep an eye on the cabin, all the while searching, praying, begging.

That's when I heard it.

That laughter—that low, hideous laughter. It seemed to come from behind me, so I turned and tried to see through the snow. The shadow of a tall form stood in the light pouring from the cabin. It walked toward me, slowly . . . ever so slowly.

Then I saw a pair of eyes, black and inhuman.

The eyes of a vampire.

15

FANGS

I tried to scream, but I couldn't. I couldn't do anything but stare into the pallid face illuminated before me. Vincent Stone. His lips were spread into a cruel smile and his fangs were barred, dripping with blood.

My hand flew to my mouth. *Derek!*

Vincent was standing over me now, his gloveless hand covering my cheek. It was cold, so much colder than the air. Dead.

"I have been waiting," Vincent said. Somehow I could hear him perfectly over the wind.

"What did you do to Derek?" I yelled, determined not to go down as a wilted flower.

Vincent's smiled deepened. "Oh, your little friend is just fine." He pointed to the cabin behind us, and I saw Derek's limp form draped over the doorstep. His head was bleeding. Badly.

I started toward him, but Vincent cut me off with a movement so quick it was impossible. I glared up at him.

"He had better be alive," I said viciously.

"Oh, he is. He is perfectly fine. Actually, it is lucky for me that you had him with you."

"And why is that?" I asked. I kept my eyes on Derek, hoping to see him move. *Praying* he would move. If I could just get past Vincent and into the cabin, we'd be safe. I had to keep him talking, keep him distracted like I'd done with Mark.

Vincent rubbed his thumb over my cheek. "How else could I lure you outside when you murdered my little aide?"

I jerked my head away. I knew he was talking about Mark, but I feigned innocence. "What's that supposed to mean?"

Please wake up, Derek. Wake up and go inside.

Vincent sighed heavily, ignoring me. "Do you know the cruelest part about losing my emotions to death, dear Faith?"

"No. I don't have that particular problem."

Vincent entangled his fingers in my hair and said, "The cruelest part is that while I cannot feel a thing other than hatred and bloodlust, I am fully and painfully aware of everyone else's emotions. For instance, I can imagine the concern for that boy whimpering in your heart. I can almost *feel* the scalding hatred you hold for me." He tugged on my hair with a swift jerk. "And then, of course, the warm lull of all-consuming love you feel for Whelan is as clear in my memory as if I could feel it myself."

I gulped, trying to be brave. "Oh, yeah? Well, I don't have to imagine emotions. I *can* feel you, and all you have is evil in your heart."

He chuckled. "I do admire your spunk, Faith." He began to pull on my hair, smelling it. I heard him moan. *Oh, crap.* I had to get him talking again.

"And you're wrong about Lucas," I said hastily. "He's just my friend and that's all he'll ever be. You and me, we have one thing in common. I can't feel love, just like you. I told you so on Halloween, remember? You know I don't even believe it exists."

Vincent threw my hair away. He brought his face so close to mine that I could smell his breath, the acrid copper of blood.

"You try and play me for the fool, but I will not be deceived! There is love in this world, I have felt it, known its treacherous depths, and now it has been stolen from me. All because of him! It's his fault that my life has ended, right along with all the things I loved. So why should Whelan have love when I cannot?"

I swallowed and felt tears trickle across my cheeks, blown around in the wind. I looked over at Derek again, still bleeding freely. He was so hurt. I had to save him.

I heard Vincent make some sort of sniffing sound, like snide laughter. I looked around, and his face was placating. "You are not going into that cabin, Faith. Please, stop these sad attempts at stalling. It is pathetic."

"The only thing pathetic around here is you. Don't take your bitterness out on me."

Vincent's eyes sparked with rage. "Are you really so vain as to think this thing is about you?" He laughed softly. "How very wrong you are."

"Well, what the hell's it about then?"

"It is about settling a score! Righting the wrong that has been done to me and making the monster that caused my pain suffer like no being has suffered before!"

"What are you talking about?" I screamed back at him.

"I am talking about Whelan! It is always about him! He has stolen my life and made me this way, made me this hollow shell of a being, too hideous to see the light of day. He walks this earth living, breathing, *feeling*." He grabbed my arms and shook me hard. "He is allowed to love you, while I have been damned for all eternity! How is that fair? How is that just?" He let out a roar, high-pitched and guttural. "I have been waiting over three hundred years for this! To finally cut him the way he has cut me. To settle this once and for all!"

He swiped my hair away from my neck, slashing me with his fingernails. His hand held my head to the side, and I struggled uselessly. I kept my eyes wide open, screaming and clawing, while Vincent slowly lowered his mouth to my neck. I felt his frozen lips close over my skin, even colder than the snow swirling around us. His tongue traveled up and down over the vein pulsating like mad beneath the skin that felt so helplessly thin.

"Please, please no." I strained against him "No!"

Then something hit us both with the force of a train. I fell into the snow, crushed underneath Vincent. His teeth scraped against my skin and then he vaulted away. I sat up, clutching my neck. There was a white wolf standing at the edge of the clearing. But this wasn't a werewolf. It was a *real* wild wolf. As soon as Vincent saw it, he dashed into the trees with a vicious snarl. The wolf followed in a rush, yipping as though it enjoyed the chase.

I didn't hesitate. Not even for a millisecond. I raced toward the cabin and grabbed Derek's feet. I hauled him inside and slammed the door shut. I flew to the window and heard the sounds of savage barking and snarling around the cabin. The werewolves were out there fighting—howling with the wind.

I heard a moan, and I dashed back to Derek. His eyes flickered open and he cringed, rubbing his forehead.

My hands flew to his head and found it uninjured. But how could that be? I'd seen him bleeding. There was blood everywhere, staining the snow and gushing from his skull. I tugged his hair around searching for the wound.

"What are you doing?" Derek asked, grabbing my hands.

"Hurt, you're hurt!" I said, scrambling to get back at his head.

"I'm fine. You're the one acting all nuts. What's your problem?"

I stopped trying to maul him and collapsed into his lap, sobbing.

"I thought . . . I thought . . ."

Derek shushed me. "It's okay, baby. Calm down. Tell me what's wrong. Did you have a dream?"

I stared up at him. He didn't remember any of it. How was that possible? I took in a shuddery breath. "Yeah," I said. "It was just a dream."

Daylight came slowly the next morning, creeping in through the window and sluggishly making its way toward me. I know because I watched it. I'd stayed up all night, listening to the wind die away and turn to smothered silence.

I waited until I was absolutely sure that any and all vampires were safely sleeping the day away, and then I disentangled myself from Derek. I snuck out of the cabin and waited.

I knew someone was coming for us and I prayed it would be Lucas. I prayed that he was safe, that Vincent hadn't found him. Killed him. I waited a long while, trembling in the morning light. The snow lay thick on the ground and heaped over the trees, making them bend under the weight. Branches creaked and crackled as birds landed, twittering to the morning. Snow fell to the ground with random thuds that made my pulse jump, and my breath shuddered in my throat as I struggled to maintain composure. It must have been hours that I stood, waiting for a miracle, but then I heard a voice.

"Hey," it said casually.

I whipped around and saw Lucas leaning against a tree, barechested and grinning slightly. I leaped toward him and flung my arms around him, not even thinking that I shouldn't. All that mattered was that we were alive!

For a moment, I just held him, basking in the warmth of his soft skin and feeling every inch of him against me.

I felt his body stiffen and I drew back, smiling sheepishly.

"I'm sorry," I said. "I wasn't thinking."

His eyes were silver and tired. He looked exhausted, actually. His hair was tangled and his eyes bore purple circles. The side of his face was smudged with old blood.

"It's fine," he said hoarsely. His mouth was set in a stern line. "You wanna tell me what you're doing out here?"

I bit my lip. "I—I got lost."

"Faith, you promised me you wouldn't go into these woods."

"I know, but it wasn't my fault! We were skiing and a little boy darted in front of me and I fell and got lost."

"You fell?" He asked this like it was more important than the fact that I'd almost been bitten by a vampire—like me falling was the end of the world.

I nodded, not looking at him, feeling incredibly stupid.

"Are you hurt?" he asked gently.

"No." I touched my nose gingerly, hoping it wasn't bruised. My entire body felt like it had been through a giant washing machine. Everything was sore.

Lucas's eyes roamed my face, touching the numerous scrapes on my cheeks. They swept downward to my throat. "Did he—?"

"He never bit me," I said quickly, rubbing the spot where Vincent's fangs had scraped my throat. I hesitated, wondering if I should ask. But I had to know. It was killing me. "Is Vincent . . . ?"

My voice was just a whisper.

"We'll talk about it when we get home," he said. "Does Derek know?" His eyes were piercing into me, wondering if I had betrayed his confidence.

"No. I didn't tell him. But last night I saw Derek bleeding, and then Vincent ran off and he was fine. Derek didn't remember fighting with me or leaving or anything. How is that possible?"

"Vampires can screw with your mind," Lucas said. "They hardly ever do it because it makes them weak—almost like a human. He must not have thought we'd come to protect you last night, or he wouldn't have tried it. It explains why he took off running like he did, anyway. He couldn't fight us because he'd used hypnotics to make you guys fight."

"So it was all to get me out of the cabin," I said, mostly to myself. "It was all fake."

"If I had been there I would have told you what he was doing. I'm sorry I wasn't there to protect you."

"But you were, weren't you? The pack came and—"

"After the fact isn't good enough," he said. "You could have died last night!"

I flinched, surprised by his outburst, but also touched that he cared. "Don't be sorry," I muttered. "I'm the one who messed up." I looked down, ashamed that I'd been so naïve. "Did anyone get hurt?" *If someone from his pack had been injured . . .*

"No. Everyone's fine."

"You were bleeding," I said, reaching up to touch his face. Lucas recoiled and I stopped, letting my hand fall to my side.

"It doesn't hurt. I heal fast. You're the one who looks like you got in a fight with a paper shredder." His eyes were warm and caressing despite his joke.

I put my hand to my cheeks. "It was just a tree," I muttered, embarrassed over my fall. "I want to know what happened last night."

But instead of telling me, he just gazed down at me almost sadly.

"Faith," he murmured. I looked up and his eyes touched mine, the only part of our bodies that *could* touch. He seemed to be on the verge of saying something big, something I desperately wanted to hear. His eyes deepened with a longing I could never understand. Then he broke our gaze with a pained expression and said, "Let's go home. Get Derek and meet me out here."

My heart sunk. I'd forgotten all about him telling me what had happened last night. All I cared about now was what he'd been about to say.

Reluctantly, I turned to go and then stopped, facing him again. "You might want to wash your face off and put something on. It's going to be kind of obvious that something's up if you're out here half-naked and covered in dried blood."

The corner of his mouth lifted into a smile. "Get in there and get that boy so we can go."

I turned and went inside to find Derek curled up next to the dusty hearth with his mouth hanging open. I bent and prodded him a little.

"Derek," I said. "Lucas is here to take us home. Get up." I shook him. "Get up!"

Derek snorted and sat up, hitting me in the head in the process. I fell over and clutched my forehead.

"Ow," Derek said, rubbing his head as well. "What's up?"

I stood and threw my hat and gloves on. "Lucas is here. We're leaving."

"Lucas?" Derek asked, his tone incredulous.

I put my hands on my hips, staring at him blankly.

"I knew it! I knew this was about him. Where is that psycho? I'll kill him!" He jumped up and ran outside.

I rolled my eyes and jogged out after him.

Lucas was standing in the middle of the clearing, face clean and clothed in a leather jacket. He wore his customary scowl and lazily looked over as Derek strode over to him. He shot me a look, and I threw my hands up. Derek was going to say what he had to say, and there was nothing I could do to stop him.

Derek marched up to Lucas and shoved him.

Lucas didn't budge.

"What the hell is up with you, man?" Derek shouted. "What did you do to Faith? Why'd you get her mixed up in your crap?"

To my surprise, Lucas actually winced as though he'd been struck. Derek had hit a nerve, and I started forward, angry at Derek for causing it.

"What's going on around here?" Derek continued yelling. "I want some answers now, damn it!" He shoved Lucas again, but only succeeded in unbalancing himself and stumbling backward. "What did you do to Faith?"

I stepped forward and stood next to Lucas. "Stop it, Derek," I said firmly. "Lucas didn't get me mixed up in anything. What happened yesterday had nothing to do with him."

"Then how'd he know where to find us?" Derek snapped.

"Julian told him," I said.

"I still don't get what the heck is going on here!"

Neither Lucas nor I spoke.

"Tell me!" Derek demanded.

"Calm the hell down," Lucas said. "Faith is fine. You're fine. We're all fine. Let's just go home now, all right?"

"Don't you talk to me about Faith," Derek spat. "You don't know anything about Faith or about me, so just butt out and get your own life!"

Lucas's jaw tightened. "Fine," he ground out. "I'm going down to my snowmobile and driving back to campus. Anybody who wants to come along is welcome to." His eyes ripped into Derek. "Anybody who wants to be a dick and stay up here freezing in the snow can go right ahead and do that, too. I don't care either way."

He stalked off into the trees, and I heard the roar of a motor. A second later he pulled up on a giant black snowmobile. I swore I saw a halo over his head in that moment. I jogged over instantly, shoving a helmet onto my head.

Derek stood seething, his body rigid with fury.

"Come on," I called. "Quit being stubborn and let's get out of here!"

Derek seemed to fight off some inner turmoil that probably had a lot to do with testosterone and then stormed over.

"Sit behind Lucas," I said, knowing that I wouldn't be able to hold onto Lucas without making Derek uncomfortable.

Derek looked repulsed. "Why don't you? He's your little boyfriend now, right?"

Lucas turned around and said loudly, "Yeah. I am. You got

a problem?"

Derek and I stared at him for a second, both of us floored. Derek threw a disgusted look at me. He tugged his helmet on and sat down behind Lucas, holding onto the sides of the vehicle. I knew he'd rather fall in the snow and die than touch Lucas.

I got on behind Derek and held onto the sides of the snowmobile as well, too scared to even think about touching Derek.

Well, now there were two people I wasn't allowed to touch.

THE TRIGGER

It was late morning by the time we got back to campus. I had ridden with Lucas since Derek was no longer speaking to me. It was a silent trip, filled with this strange, uneasy sort of comfort. I was so happy Lucas was all right, that I'd managed to keep Derek safe, and that I'd managed to keep *myself* safe amidst my blunders. But now Derek was mad at me again. We had just started to get back to our normal selves, laughing and playing around together. It had only lasted a few hours, but I'd loved every moment of it. I was bummed to think that Derek would probably never speak to me again after what I'd put him through, and I wallowed over it the entire way home.

When we got to Lucas's room, I crammed down a granola bar, washed the blood from my face and crashed. He must have known how exhausted I was because he didn't protest when I hit the sheets. He just gave me this tiny, silvery smile and lay down on the couch, his eyes never leaving me.

It was nightfall when I woke up.

At first, all I could see was this blurry mass of tan next to me. Then I backed up and saw a face—a smooth, tan face with a perfectly straight nose and lips so immaculately shaped it was hard not to think about kissing them. Lucas's black hair was tossed into his eyes, which were closed to the world. His breathing was steady. I looked around, confused.

We were lying on his bed together. I wondered when he'd left the couch. *Had I been crying? Did I have a nightmare?*

I didn't know and I didn't care. I watched him sleep for the longest time, his body so close to mine, yet not touching at all. I'd never been so acutely aware of myself, what my hands were doing, whether or not my legs were too close to his. And now we were so close I could have leaned in and kissed those perfect lips.

Lucas sighed in his sleep, and his eyes blinked open. He didn't move away from me. He just smiled.

"Hey," he said softly. I could feel his breath on my cheek, reminding me of the warm desert breezes I used to feel at home.

"Hi."

"How long you been up?"

"I don't know," I said honestly. I propped myself up and glanced at the alarm clock. "It's midnight."

Lucas nodded.

We were quiet for a moment. I had so many questions, so many things I needed to know about, but foremost in my mind was, "Are you still mad at me?"

"No," Lucas said. "I'm just glad we got there in time."

"So that was one of your pack last night, the white wolf?"

Lucas's lips twitched into a little grin. "No. That was a plain old wolf. When we change we can control the minds of the canines around us. We used the wolf to lure Vincent away from you."

"Why didn't you just come over and get him yourselves?"

Lucas's right eyebrow lifted. "Did you really want a pack of werewolves surrounding you at the full moon?"

I felt my eyes widen. "No."

"Let me see your neck," Lucas said.

I frowned. "Why?"

"I smell venom."

I slapped my hand to the side of my neck and held it there, frozen with terror.

"Calm down," Lucas soothed. "If he'd bitten you, you'd know it by now. I think he might have grazed you though. Just let me see."

I dragged my hand away from my neck and swept my hair back, tilting my head so Lucas could see.

"Yeah," Lucas said. "He got you."

I gasped. "What does that mean? Am I hurt?"

Lucas shushed me. "You have a burn where his teeth scraped you, but he didn't break the skin, so nothing got in. You're fine."

I let out a breath I didn't know I was holding. "I thought I was going to be a vampire."

He chuckled a little. "No, that's werewolves. Vampires have this whole . . . process."

"What do they do?" I asked, equally awed and disgusted.

His expression closed down. "Nothin'," he said, looking away. "I don't wanna talk about that stuff."

"Why? Come on, I think I should know. I'm in this world now, whether or not I like it. I don't want to be ignorant like I was last night."

His eyes creased with distress, and I knew in an instant exactly what he was thinking.

"It's not your fault," I said.

"I should have told you what they were capable of, especially after what happened with Mark. It was *all* my fault. It's a miracle you're not dead."

"Stop it," I said firmly. "I broke my promise. I was supposed to stay in the room. If I'd done that, I never would have needed to know about their . . . mind powers or whatever."

He looked away and I slapped the bed next to his head to get him to look back at me. He did so reluctantly, his eyes betraying the mash of torment he held inside.

"You saved my life," I said. "I don't blame you, I'm *grateful* to you. I just . . . I want to know about this world—even the dark stuff. I think it's important."

He eyed me for a long moment and I could see him deliberating in his head. His eyes deepened to brown and I knew I'd won. "What was the question?" he asked.

"How do vampires make more of themselves?"

"Well, first they bite you and feed you their blood—"

I nodded. "And then?"

"Then they bury you and keep you underground until the next full moon. On that night you'd rise from the earth, a spanking new vampire. But if they bite you and feed you their blood on the full moon, then you turn into a vampire immediately." He smiled slightly at my dumbstruck expression. "It's different for us."

"How?"

"With werewolves, it just takes a bite. One bite and you're just like me." He bared his teeth in a swift grin, displaying his slightly elongated incisors.

I laughed nervously. "What if a vampire bites a werewolf? Does it kill you?"

He shook his head. "It hurts like hell, but it won't change us or anything. And it definitely won't kill us—only silver can seriously injure a werewolf."

"So," I asked. "What happens if Vincent bites me, but doesn't do all that stuff to make me turn? I'll just die?"

"He won't bite you," he said adamantly.

"But . . . what if he does?"

"Then I'll kill him."

I heaved a sigh. "Well, what if he bit some *other* human being?"

Lucas scratched his eyebrow, avoiding my gaze. I stared him down and he rolled his eyes. "You're more stubborn than I am."

I smiled proudly.

"Well," he said wearily, "if they drain you completely then you'd die, obviously. But if the wound's not fatal, it won't kill you."

"Well, that's something," I said, feeling encouraged. At least there was a chance at surviving a vampire bite.

Lucas puffed a laugh. "No. It's not. Vampires have this coating on their teeth like snake venom, but worse."

"So, the bite *would* kill me?"

"No. I said it was worse."

"What do you mean?" I asked irritably.

"Vampire venom doesn't kill you. It spreads a paralyzing agent throughout your entire body. If you're lucky, he'll have bitten your throat or your groin and you'll just bleed out and die that way. If you're not so lucky, you'll survive the bite, but the venom will make you completely immobile. It usually takes about a week for the victim to expire."

"Expire . . . ," I murmured. Such a sterile word. "So the venom *does* kill you, then. Just slowly."

"No. The venom immobilizes you. If you survive the bite, you starve to death. Or sometimes the pain will do it." He shook his head slowly. "I always feel sorry for the ones with their eyes stuck open. They can see everybody staring at them, trying to save them, saying their good-byes."

I shuddered and then thought about what it must feel like to have my mom standing over my paralyzed body, crying, begging someone to do something. She wouldn't understand why I couldn't move, why I was dying. Derek wouldn't understand either. He'd get angry, start raving. And I would be laying there watching it all. But would I feel better if I couldn't see them? Stuck laying there, hearing their voices, and longing to see their faces?

"No," I said. "I'd want to have my eyes open. . . . I'd want to see my friends, my family." I stole a glance at his stony face. "See you." His eyes flickered to mine and then turned silver. "Sorry," I said quickly. "I didn't mean to . . ."

"Don't," he said. He put a finger to my lips, and my heart flipped over. He was touching me, actually touching my skin, my lips. But he quickly removed his finger and whispered, "Don't be sorry." His eyes deepened, the metallic color of them broken by the black of his hair. I reached to sweep it out of his eyes. His face tightened, and I paused. I didn't want to overwhelm him. Make him change. But he reached up and put my palm to his skin. It was like rubbing my fingers against a sea stone—as though his skin had been polished by the relentless waves of the ocean. But in Lucas's case, his body was worn away by time. By his immortality. Human imperfections faded year by year until his skin was flawless. It grew warm beneath my touch—hot, even. I pushed the hair away from his face, and I heard his breath shudder in his throat. I withdrew my hand, but he grabbed it.

"It's okay," he said. "You can touch me. . . . I can handle it." His eyes dissolved into that human brown color as though offering proof to his words.

Carefully I returned my hand to his face and swept it slowly down his neck, his chest. His eyes shifted to silver and stayed that way as he gazed at me. His body grew hotter, almost burning me.

"You're hot," I said.

He smiled. "Why, thank you."

I laughed nervously and said, "I meant your skin. It's crazy hot."

"My temperature rises when I change."

I froze, my heart beating harder. He must have seen the fear in my eyes.

"It's okay," he said softly. "I'm under control. It's easier after the full moon."

I nodded and ran my fingers through his thick, black hair. I looked into his eyes, silver and strange. Like an animal's eyes. It was so rare to have him look at me like this. I felt as though he was swallowing me up in his gaze.

"Your eyes are—"

"Silver? Yeah, I know. It's why I can't look at you around people. The eyes are the first to go."

I swallowed. Somehow I was closer to him. "And—and the shivering? I've seen you shiver before . . . like a tremor."

"That comes next. I can usually repress it from there, but if you see my fangs drop—"

"Fangs?"

"Yeah," he said, smiling. "You see them drop, start running and don't stop for anything."

I smoothed my fingers over his eyes. He closed them and sighed, almost like a dog settling in for a long nap.

"Have you ever killed anyone?" I asked tentatively. "Besides Mark, I mean."

He didn't hesitate. But his eyes opened, slightly pained. "Yeah," he said.

"How many?"

He shook his head, and I knew the number was too great to count.

"Do you regret it?" I whispered.

"Not the ones like Mark—the ones who would have hurt others if I hadn't stopped them." He lowered his eyes. "But I do regret the accidents. The innocent ones who got too close, got me too angry, and I couldn't . . . I couldn't stop it."

I tried to imagine what it must be like to worry about not killing people every time you were with them. Every time you felt instinct start to take over, having to press it back, so that you don't feel it at all. So that you don't kill those around you, the ones you love.

I put both my hands on his face and inched closer.

"It's not your fault," I said. "You didn't ask for this. You can't help what you are."

His voice was hard when he spoke next. "What I am is a murderer. A monster."

"No," I said earnestly. "That's your curse. But you? You are a person. And people screw up sometimes. The fact that you feel guilty about it just proves how *good* of a person you are."

He turned away, but I held his face harder, making him look at me.

"How many people have you saved?" I asked. "You told me that your pack dedicates itself to helping and saving us humans. How many people have you helped? Saved the lives of?"

He shook his head a little. "That doesn't take away the people that are dead because of me. Saving others won't give them their lives back."

"No," I agreed. "It won't. But it proves that you're not a monster or a murderer. Those deaths were accidents."

"You don't get it. Those times when I can't control myself, waiting for something to tip me over the edge—it's maddening. I spend my life in repression—constantly fighting off the change, until the full moon when I can't control myself anymore. When the monster takes over."

"It must be terrible," I murmured. My mind flashed to his journal and the gruesome drawings in it. "It's . . . manageable," he grumbled.

I tilted my head. "What do you mean?"

"I'm older, so it's easier for me. I've had more time to gain control, to find ways of coping. It's why I can live this . . . *semi*normal life. Most werewolves can't do that. A lot of them take to the wild. I guess they think it's better that way." His eyes grew distant and blank as though seeing something far away.

"Are you very old, compared to the others?" I asked.

"I'm up there. Rolf's the oldest I know. He's going on half a millennium." Lucas smiled at the shock on my face. "He has a measure of control I don't think I'll ever have. He's all but human except for once a month."

We fell silent for a moment.

"When you repress it," I said, "does it hurt?"

He shook his head, eyes delving into mine with intensity. "The only thing that hurts is the thought of what I might do to you . . . if I lose control."

He was so afraid of hurting me, but I knew Lucas could never do that. He was a protector. A savior. Underneath the layers of anger he put up to keep me back, I knew he was good. I'd seen the vulnerable side he kept hidden, and it had revealed the softness of his heart. This fear of hurting me was so unnecessary, and suddenly I wanted to prove it to him.

I smoothed my hand across his stubbly cheek and over his lips. He shivered violently and his eyes hit mine. He snatched my hand away.

"Don't do that," he said.

"It's okay. I know you won't hurt me."

"Faith . . ." His eyes were frightened, pleading.

I went closer to him and put my hands over his chest, around his neck. Slowly . . . so very slowly I pressed my body against his.

"Stop," he said. His voice was hoarse. He said the word, but I knew he didn't want me to stop. I knew he was just scared.

I put my forehead against his, bringing my lips closer. "You won't hurt me," I said again. "I trust you."

I brought my lips to his throat and touched them to his skin. It was so hot, but he shivered as though he was freezing. I moved my lips closer toward his and kissed him again along his jaw. I felt a surge of heat under my lips, his temperature rising.

Suddenly he grabbed me by the waist and pushed me back. He shoved his hands into the sides of his face, digging his fingers into his skull. I heard him take in several deep breaths.

"Hold on," he muttered. His eyes were squished shut. He was like that for a long time, and I sat up against the wall. I kept my back to it, staring as Lucas overcame his instinct—his will to change. It was an amazing sight, like watching something wild become tame. But I didn't understand. Why couldn't he kiss me when I saw him kissing Courtney with no problem? He seemed to be triggered by some kind of emotional response, but if I'd set him off from the moment he saw me then it didn't make sense. What emotions could he have had upon merely looking at me? Attraction, perhaps? Could that have triggered him? But if so, then why didn't he want to change every time he saw a pretty girl? There had to be something else—something he wasn't saying. What was so different about me? Lucas looked up at me, and his eyes were dark, dark brown. He didn't come toward me.

"I'm sorry," he said. "We can't do that, Faith."

I peeled myself from the wall and leaned in closer. He held his hand out in front of him. I stopped.

"I know you won't hurt me, Lucas."

"I won't *mean* to hurt you, but I might anyway."

I laid down again, sidling closer to him. "No. You won't. I know you. I know your heart. You can withstand this."

"You don't know how close to death you were just seconds ago. It took every piece of self-restraint I have to tell you no."

"Then don't tell me no," I said. He looked away, scoffing. I brought my hand to his face, and he didn't shake me off. "This is new for me, too," I murmured. "I've never felt this way before, either. I've never wanted anyone so much. I didn't even think it was possible. I've never believed in . . . in something like this. But I feel safe with you. And I know you can control yourself. I know you won't hurt me."

I moved even closer to him before he could push me back. I

wrapped myself around him again, and I felt his back stiffen.

"Are you determined to kill yourself?" he asked in my ear.

"No. I'm determined to make you see that you're stronger than you think you are."

"Faith . . ." His voice was agonized. "If anything happens. If I lose control—"

"You won't. I trust you."

He put his hand over my back, clutching me close. I felt the heat of his skin through my clothes and my heart did a flip. His other hand took my cheek, burning me.

"What if I don't trust myself?" he whispered.

I pulled his head toward me and kissed his cheek, my lips just barely touching the corner of his. I kept my lips on his skin, letting him adjust, letting him gain control. Then I kissed the other side of his mouth, lingering . . . waiting. I could feel the heat of his skin. I knew I was triggering the change.

But he didn't make me stop.

Instead he took my face in both of his hands and pressed his lips against mine. They were so soft, so warm and perfect. My breath caught in my throat. Then as fast as it had happened it was over.

He drew back, his face clenched in concentration.

"Just a sec," he said. He took in two breaths, keeping his eyes closed. "That was . . . amazing."

"Yeah," I said, panting a little. "Can we do it again?"

His eyes opened and they blazed with silver fire. He brought my face closer and tilted it to the side, kissing along my jaw to my ear. His mouth pulled on my earlobe, and I felt my body go wild with anticipation. I held to his arms and let out a little sound. Lucas shivered, and I felt his lips break into a smile over my cheek.

"You're testing me," he said.

"Wouldn't dream of it." I closed the distance between our lips and kissed him, longer this time. It was perfection—the best kiss of my life. And all I wanted was more. I knitted my fingers through his hair, pressing my body to his and rolling on top of him.

Then Lucas pushed me away again. His body convulsed and I held his face, looking straight into his eyes.

"It's okay," I said urgently. "Focus. You don't have to do this. You can overcome it."

Lucas swatted my hands from his face, and he was on the other side of the room in an instant.

"Go," he said, still shaking. "Go, Faith. Run."

"No, I'm not scared."

I watched him shake, and shake, trying desperately to stop the change. His face distorted into a snarl, and I heard a low, guttural sound escape his lips.

"GO!" he yelled, slamming his fist against the wall.

I started to back up, realizing that he wasn't going to be able to stop himself. I'd pushed him too far. He looked up at me, his eyes tangled in fear and something else . . . something *wild*.

Then his fangs dropped.

SUMMONED

L ucas let out a roar so loud my teeth chattered. His body became deformed, arms curling into themselves and fingers cracking into paws. He fell onto all fours. A gigantic shiver rippled down his spine, tearing his clothes and sprouting black hair down to his feet. His face was gone, eyes wide and glowing metallic. And teeth, gnashing at me, dripping with saliva. A low, bubbling growl sounded in his throat; his hot breath filled my nostrils. I pressed myself against the wall, half amazed, half terrified.

Then the door was pounding. I heard yelling on the other side. It was a man. I prayed it wasn't Lucas's next door neighbor coming to complain about the racket we were making.

"Lucas! Let me in!"

The wolf barked loudly, and my eyes flickered to the door. The voice out there sounded familiar.

"Don't make me break the door, Lucas. Faith, if you're in there, open the door! NOW!"

Lucas advanced slowly. In his eyes, there was nothing but savage intent—the instincts of a killer. This was no longer the Lucas I had come to know. This was an animal. And I definitely needed to get away.

I had only one chance—get to the door. But every time I moved even an inch, he was watching, poised to attack.

Then I thought of something so crazy it just might work.

"Lucas?" I said gently. "It's me. It's Faith. . . . I'm getting the door because I think it's someone who's going to stop you from eating me." I started inching off of the bed, coming disconcertingly close to Lucas's jaws. "Don't worry," I said slowly. "I'm just getting the door."

"LUCAS! OPEN THE DOOR, DAMN IT!"

My eyes connected with Lucas's just before he pounced. Just as I'd hoped, electricity pulsated through my body, shocking me and sending my mind into a haze. In the milliseconds I had while Lucas came at me, I focused on one word, *NO!*

I lunged for the door, and Lucas roared after me.

It hadn't worked. I could feel Lucas's hot breath on the back of my neck as I stretched for the door handle. *No, no, no!* I tried to do what I'd done once before—to create the connection between us, but it wasn't working.

Miraculously, I managed to fling the door open, and Julian jumped over me, charging Lucas. They hit each other full on with bone-crunching force. Lucas snapped his jaws at Julian's neck, but he twisted away at the last moment. I slammed the door shut, hoping to God that nobody was hearing this. They scuffled; Lucas trying desperately to get at me and Julian holding him off with his powerful arms. Finally, Julian held Lucas around his thick, furry throat. Lucas made coughing, hacking sounds as his airway constricted.

"Stop it!" I yelled. "You're hurting him."

Julian ignored me. "Change!" he commanded, squeezing harder. "Change, Lucas. Now!"

Lucas wriggled stubbornly one last time and then slumped in defeat. His body jerked with the change, and he morphed back into a buck naked human. I sagged against the door, still holding the handle in a death grip.

Julian let go of Lucas and stood up. He tossed a bed sheet over to him, and Lucas wrapped it around his waist, coughing loudly.

He put a hand on Julian's shoulder. "Thanks," he puffed.

Julian's jaw clenched as he regarded his brother. His kind green eyes were a mess of anger, magnified by his vibe. "That was close, Lucas. You're pushing your luck around this one." He jerked his head in my direction.

"I've got a handle on it."

"Doesn't seem like you do. You would have killed her if I hadn't been here. It was sheer luck I was coming to see you."

Lucas winced, his eyes troubled. "I know. Thank you." He turned to me. I was still pressed against the door, clutching the handle so tightly it made my hand cramp. He took a step toward me, and I put my hand to my throat, gasping. Lucas stopped, his face fluctuating from pained to hard and emotionless. "I'm sorry," he said, voice breaking. "I thought I was under control. . . . I'm so sorry, Faith."

My heart broke at the sound of his voice. I'd confirmed to him the thing he feared the most, and I couldn't stand being the one to have caused him this torment. I ran to him, wrapping my arms around him, stubbornly refusing to be afraid of him. He hugged me back tightly. "Some first kiss, huh?" he said, a hint of laughter in his voice.

I laughed too, realizing I was crying at the same time.

Julian cleared his throat, and we both looked over, not releasing each other.

"I got bad news for you," Julian said to Lucas. "Dad's calling you."

Lucas's arms stiffened around me.

"What? Why?" he asked, his voice tense.

"I think you know why," Julian said, as his eyes flickered to me. "And he wants you to bring Faith."

Lucas cursed and crossed the room, rubbing his hands over his eyes. He spun and rounded on Julian. "If he thinks I'm bringing her into this he's crazy! I'm not doing it. I won't."

Julian looked unconcerned. "You don't have a choice, Lucas. He's summoning you."

Lucas swore again and punched the bedside table. I heard the wood splinter and I jumped. Lucas's back quaked.

"Calm down," Julian said. "Maintain control or I'm going to have to kick your ass again."

Lucas let out a puff of strained laughter. He turned around, shaking his head defiantly. "I'm not bringing her."

"You have to. I don't want to get people hurt any more than you do. But Dad's being . . . Dad. You have to bring her."

Lucas ground his teeth, glaring at his brother.

"Lucas, you have to—"

"Fine!"

Julian seemed to deflate, and his eyes grew gentle. "Good. I'm on your side, Lucas. We won't let them do anything that'll hurt her, all right?"

Lucas sneered at him and said, "Just get out."

The two werewolves stared at each other for a long moment, and then Julian said, "I'm on your side, brother." And he left, brushing past me in a blast of wind that blew my hair back.

Lucas glared at the door for a long time and then looked over at me. His gaze was contemplative, and I wondered if he'd felt me try and control him again. If he did, he didn't mention it. After a moment of silence, Lucas sighed.

"So," he said with a half-smile. "You wanna meet my parents?"

L ucas woke me at eight the next morning with a kiss on the cheek that felt like a fire poker. I jolted awake and saw him smiling down at me.

"It's so great to know I can touch you," he said, putting his hand against my face as if to prove his point.

I smiled back at him. "I like it, too," I said. "Now, why are you waking me up so early? Class isn't till ten."

"Got a long trip ahead of us. We're going up into the Rockies." His face turned stiff. "Gotta meet my parents, remember?"

Oh, do I ever. "How long of a trip is it?"

"Couple hours. But we gotta get going. I don't wanna spend the night up there. Some of the newbies get a little . . . frisky."

I laughed and sat up. "That's a nice way of putting it."

Lucas grinned at me, wiggling his eyebrows.

"Aren't you worried one of them is going to lose control?" I asked, pretty worried about it myself.

"Nah, I'm with you."

"Oh, well, that's comforting, considering last night."

He gave me a withering look. "It won't be like how we've been for the past few months. This intense urge to change—I only feel it with you. Around any other human, I'm in control. The other werewolves will be in control, too—the older ones at least. And if any runts come around, I'll be there to protect you, all right? You're safe."

Satisfied, I got ready to leave. Lucas and I ate a hurried breakfast and then piled into his tiny car. We headed north onto the expressway toward Gould. As we drove, I looked over at Lucas's perfect profile and said, "Don't think you're getting out of telling me what happened in the woods just because you changed last night. I have no mercy for you today."

Lucas frowned dubiously.

"I have a million questions I still want to ask you," I said, pressing forward.

"And I have a million answers I won't give you."

I rolled my eyes. "What's going on between you and Vincent? I know there's something bigger than just werewolf-vampire drama." I glanced at him, but his face showed no reaction. I pressed on, trying to strike the nerve that would get him talking. "Vincent said the other night that it was your fault he was dead."

"He did that to himself!" Lucas shouted.

I smiled. *I'd struck a nerve.*

"Vincent is demented," Lucas said. There was distinct note of disgust in his voice.

"I know *that* much. What I don't know is the details. If he became a vampire out of choice, like you say, then why does he hate you so much? Why is he trying so hard to kill me? Is it just to hurt you?"

Lucas's scowl deepened.

"Come on," I urged. "I tell you secrets all the time. I'd never told anyone about the time I stole my mom's slutty lingerie and danced around singing 'Like a Virgin,' but I told you. It's your turn to spill."

Lucas laughed despite his discomfort. "All right," he said. "I guess you gotta know anyway since you're involved. Plus you're so damn stubborn. I'll never hear the end of this until I tell you."

He gave me a pointed look, which I returned with a triumphant smile. "So I told you I was born in Scotland in 1624, right?"

"Yeah."

"Well, Vincent was my best friend when he was alive. We both worked in my dad's shop and our families were close. When my dad died, Vincent was there to help me through it. We were like brothers. But one day everything changed. When we were nineteen, we went hunting with some friends. We got separated from the group and got lost. Night fell and we heard wolves. We ran, but that was useless. One bit me. Vincent escaped, thinking I was dead.

"But I wasn't dead. I'd been infected. Eventually, I found my way back to my village and told Vincent the whole thing. He didn't believe me at first, but soon my instincts overcame my small measure of control and I was able to show him exactly what I was.

"Those first years were nightmarish. . . . I was tortured by the beast inside me. The moon was my catalyst, forcing me past the edges of my restraint and turning me into what I feared the most. Turning me into the monster I am." His voice was strained with emotion, and I put my hand on his knee, trying to comfort him.

"Vincent was there with me," Lucas went on, "helping me through the pain, helping me gain control. He had to leave me when I changed, of course. And there were some very close calls. . . . I almost killed him many times. We were lucky. But Vincent saw how this new life tortured me, and he wanted desperately to help me. So without telling me what he had planned, he went back to the woods and searched for the werewolves. But it wasn't a werewolf that found him. It was something darker, something much more dangerous.

"Vincent was made vampire that night. He was missing for months before he found me again, and I knew exactly what he was. I could smell the dead flesh on him, the blood. His eyes were wild with bloodlust. His need overcame his every thought. I had to fight him off and protect my village from his hunting. He would come every night, sneaking through the alleys, preying on hapless humans." Lucas paused and his knuckles turned white on the steering wheel.

He drew in a breath and said, "And then one night he found my baby sister, my Reece. He told me that I was to blame for his transformation, that I was the cause of his death, his trip into madness. We fought, but I was wounded and unable to stop him from killing her. He killed my sister and drained her in front of my eyes." His voice broke, and he cleared his throat.

I stared at his shadowed, tortured face, thinking I could never understand the pain he felt, when I suddenly realized that I did— at least a little. Lucas's best friend, someone who had been like a brother to him, had betrayed him, just as my stepdad had betrayed me. It wasn't exactly the same, I knew. Seeing your sister drained of her blood was a whole different level of horror than what I'd gone through, but still. It was pain. And I understood now where his hatred for Vincent came from.

I closed my hand around his, clenching it tightly.

"After that," Lucas went on, "any love, any feelings of pity or friendship I had for him were gone. We've spent the last three centuries locked in an eternal war, neither one of us able to kill the other. The things we've done to each other . . . the people that have been hurt and killed because of us . . ." He looked away, his eyes hooded. "I just want it to be over now. I tried to run from him, to start a new life here with my pack. But his thirst for revenge has possessed him. He won't stop now . . . can't stop anymore. This war will last until one of us kills the other—for good."

I didn't know what to say, or even how to react. Lucas glanced at me. "So now you know the truth," he said. "You know why he wants to kill you. Why he hates me so much. Why he'll never give up, no matter how long it takes. Why I have to find a way to get you out of this mess alive . . . hopefully this meeting with my pack will help with that last part."

"Hopefully," I whispered.

"Are you freaked out?" Lucas asked, casting another glance at me.

"I'm just . . . absorbing."

"What are you thinking?"

"I'm thinking how alike we all are."

"Alike?" he asked, a little dubious.

"Yeah," I said, still working it out in my head. "You, me, even Vincent, we all have this same hang-up. . . . We can't feel what's supposed to be the most natural thing in the world and it eats at us, making it impossible to live like normal people."

Lucas glanced at me, eyes fierce. "You're wrong. I can feel everything just like a normal human. Vincent? I don't think there's much more human left in him. It's just bloodlust . . . and vengeance." He turned his eyes to me. "But you," he said more gently. "You have what both Vincent and I have longed for since we were changed. You have life . . . mortality. And everything that goes with it. The ability to love, to feel freely without having to worry about killing anyone. You don't know what a gift that is."

"Yeah," I grumbled. "Vincent said the same thing. But what neither of you get is that I'm as screwed up as you two. I don't have some freaky supernatural thing going, but I have my own issues."

"You don't *want* to feel love—or won't let yourself, I don't know."

"That's not it."

"Then what?"

"It's that I don't believe there's any love in this world at all."

Lucas shook his head at the windshield. "Jeez, what the hell happened to you that made you so cynical?"

"Nothing."

"You're a terrible liar," Lucas said. "Why don't you try the truth?"

"I just—I had something happen to me when I was younger. And it made me see the world for how it really is—a horrible, evil, loveless place."

"You wanna tell me what happened or am I gonna have to guess?"

"I don't want to talk about it."

"Yes, you do," he said softly. "You need to."

I stared out the window, watching the trees streak by, blurring into a mass of evergreen. My eyes clouded with tears. I heard the words in my head, begging me to say them out loud. Begging to be felt. To be accepted—something I was never able to do no matter how hard I tried because the more I thought about it, the harder it was to deal with. Talking about it with Heather had been more than enough, and I hadn't even told her the whole thing.

"What happened, Faith?"

I didn't want to talk about it, but I knew deep down that I would never recover if I didn't. And I wanted to be better. I wanted to trust Lucas, not just with my life, but with my heart. I wanted to love him like he deserved. It was now or never, and if anyone could understand, it was Lucas. He always did. It was as though there was a part of our souls that simply *got* each other.

I took a deep breath. "My stepfather . . . he went to prison. When I was thirteen."

"Why?" Lucas asked.

"Because he . . . did something to me and my mom."

"What did he do?"

I swallowed hard, trying to stave off the tears I knew would come. "He was a drunk. And he—he beat my mom. Terribly." The tears strangled me, and I took a second to steady myself. Lucas waited patiently. Not touching me. Not saying anything. The wind rushing by the car was all I could hear, deafening wind. "I loved him so much," I said, choking. "He was my dad. We used to bake pancakes every Sunday; we used to go to the beach together; he used to sing to me when I was scared at night. He was my dad and then he—and then he"—sobs racked my body— "and then he wasn't him anymore. He got drunk and went crazy . . . stopped being my dad and became this . . . evil person." I took in a breath to steady my voice. "And then one day I came home from school, and he had a gun in his hand. He was raving around, and he . . . he beat my mom and then he shot me when I screamed for help."

For a moment there was utter silence.

"He shot you?" Lucas's voice was uncharacteristically calm. I nodded and rubbed my upper thigh where the scar still shone bright pink against my skin.

"And they put him in prison?" Lucas asked. I could hear a hint of bite in his voice now.

"Yeah," I whispered. "I've never told anyone about this before . . . not the whole thing, how it really was. Derek is the only one who knows."

Lucas pulled the car onto the shoulder of the highway. He turned toward me and put his hands over my cheeks. He bent and kissed them, mopping up the tears with his lips. I turned toward him, and his lips brushed against mine, so feather light I might have imagined it.

"I'm sorry," he said. "I'm so sorry that happened to you. There's so much evil and wrong in this world. But it's what makes the good things so precious. Things like love."

"There is no love," I said dully.

"There is. I know it because I feel it. I used to think like you. I used to believe that love was this made-up thing for books and movies. But if you open your heart—if you ignore that voice scream-ing at you to keep it closed—then you'll see that there is love, and kindness and goodness in this world. You'll see it, just like I have." He laughed a little. "It's kind of ironic when you think about it."

I sniffled. "What is?"

"That you—the nonbeliever—would be the one to make me believe. To have faith."

I smiled and a few tears leaked out of my eyes. "I don't know if I can believe it. I want to trust you. But I'm scared of what will happen."

"Faith, look at me." Lucas's voice was like steel, hard and unbend-ing. "Look at me and hear this. If you hear nothing else I'm telling you, hear this. I will *never* hurt you. You have my word on that, okay? Hurting you is the last thing I'd ever want to do. It goes against my very nature. I'm meant to protect you from harm—not cause it."

I wrapped my arms around his neck and pressed my face against his cheek. I felt his words deep inside my heart—sinking in and soaking up my fear and hurt with the absolute certainty that Lucas would never hurt me.

"I believe you," I murmured into his shirt. "Even though I know I shouldn't, even though that voice is screaming at me. I know you'll never hurt me."

He turned my face toward his and did something we both knew we shouldn't do, something that would likely kill me. He kissed me.

And he didn't stop.

18

GOULD

The rest of the trip's conversation was considerably lighter. It felt amazing to get that thing out of me—to voice it and face it head on with Lucas at my side.

We stopped for lunch at a Wendy's and then got back on the road, both of us silent for a while. I listened as Lucas hummed to the radio and watched the sun climb higher in the wintry white sky.

"There's something I don't understand, though," Lucas said.

"Hmm?"

"You said that the incident with your stepdad is the reason you can't trust men, but you trusted Derek enough to go out with him?"

"Yeah. I mean, he was with me throughout the whole thing. He stayed with me in the hospital, talked with me during the . . . bad times. He was my best friend. And when he wanted more, I felt like if there was anyone in the world I could trust with my heart it was him, right? He helped me hold onto it in the first place."

"So what happened?"

"He cheated." My voice was clipped. I didn't want to go over this again. But Lucas still had more to say.

"So that ruined any trust you might have salvaged." It wasn't a question and I didn't say anything.

"But now . . ." Lucas said. "What about now?"

"What do you mean?"

"I mean, why are you with me?"

The words struck me, and I turned to look at him. "I mean," he said gently, "How can you trust me when you don't trust anyone else?"

I turned away again, pondering his words. Why *could* I trust him? When I thought about it, it didn't really make sense. He was a dangerous mythical creature, after all. He was completely unpredictable in every sense of the word, and it was more of a possibility with him than with anyone that he might hurt me.

But there was something steady about him as well. Maybe it was carried over from his human self, but when I looked into his eyes I saw peace. I saw compassion and warmth. I saw love. All along it had been disconcertingly easy to trust him with my life because . . .

"It's because you saved it," I murmured.

"Huh?"

I looked over at his profile etched sharply against the forest-green blurring outside the window. "You saved my life on Halloween and again, the other night. You can't go through something like that with someone and not trust them. Every time I've ever had to put my life in your hands I've done it. No questions asked. It's like I know in my *soul* that you'd never hurt me."

"I wouldn't," Lucas confirmed.

"It's something I've never felt with anyone else—even Derek. When he promises me he won't hurt me, I'm skeptical because he told me that before and he broke his promise. Even before he'd cheated, though, there was always a little part of me that didn't believe him. It's like you silence that part of me, the part that disbelieves."

He smiled and took up my hand. "I'm glad," he murmured and kissed my skin.

I looked down at our clasped hands, molded effortlessly together. A closeness I longed to feel in my heart. It was so difficult for me to let go—to give Lucas everything I'd been keeping prisoner inside my heart. But I was trying, ignoring the voice of doubt, and that was the first step.

I t was late afternoon when we pulled off of the main road and onto a dirt track, shaded by ancient evergreens and pines the size of skyscrapers. I took in a nervous breath. *We must be getting close.*

"You look scared," Lucas said as we bumped along.

"That's because I'm about to meet a pack of potentially dangerous werewolves. Not to mention your parents."

"If if makes you feel any better, they're not technically my parents. That's just how pack members refer to them. And anyway, nobody's gonna hurt you." He looked over and must have seen how pale my face was because he grabbed my knee. "You wanna know a secret?"

I laughed, but quickly stopped because it sounded psychotic. He was trying to distract me. How sweet. How useless. But I'd play along. "Sure," I said. My voice cracked.

Lucas glanced at me again and said, "My name's not Lucas."

I whipped around. "It's not?"

"Nope. It's Whelan. Whelan O'Connell."

For a moment I was speechless. "Why'd you change it?" I asked at last.

"Well, Whelan started getting me strange looks, so sometime around the turn of the century, I changed it."

My head spun at his casual use of "turn of the century." "Why'd you pick Lucas?"

"It was my dad's name."

"But isn't your whole pack named Whelan?"

"No, they all have their own surnames," he said. "When I came to Fort Collins, I wanted to try to live normally so Rolf told everyone in town that he and his wife were my parents—the Whelans. The pack lived a pretty quiet life until I showed up. Nobody in town really knew they were there so everybody pretty much accepted them as the Whelans."

"Why did you even want to live normally?" I asked. "I mean, you said you wanted to go to CSU to learn more about art, but why would you even bother? Why not live in the woods? Wouldn't that be easier for you?"

"Easier, sure. But lonely. The other werewolves—the ones who live like you're talking about—they're not much in the way of company. Most of them are nuts, to tell you the truth." He shrugged. "And plus, living incognito as a human made it harder for Vincent to find me."

"But he *did* find you."

"Yeah," Lucas grunted. There was a bleak glint in his eyes now. "Don't I know it."

I mentally kicked myself for bringing Vincent up—it always put him in a bad mood and I was eager to ask him more about his life. But Lucas's glowering came to an abrupt halt as he glanced at me.

"Wanna know another secret?" Lucas asked, his voice light now.

"I don't know," I said, teasing. "I'm kind of scared now."

"That wasn't such a bad secret. It's just a name."

"Would you be so calm if I suddenly told you my name was Judy?"

He snickered.

"So what's the secret?" I asked, bracing myself.

We pulled into the driveway of a massive log cabin that looked more like a cabin/mansion/five-star hotel, and Lucas put the car in park. He turned to me and brought my hand to his lips. He kissed it and pulled me close. "You sure you wanna know?" he whispered in my ear. My heart vibrated in my chest.

"Yes," I said softly.

Lucas brought his lips over mine and brushed them against me. "My secret is that I love you."

I smiled against his lips. "I hate to tell you this, but that wasn't a secret."

I felt his lips break into a grin, and he kissed me. I slid my hands around his neck and tangled my fingers up in his hair. His hand held the small of my back, and I could feel the heat surging in his lips, in his mouth. I wondered briefly if I should pull back, but I couldn't sustain the thought for more than a second before I was swept away.

Eventually Lucas withdrew, panting against my lips. "We'd better go in there," he said hoarsely.

I nodded, breathing heavily. Lucas gave me one last devastating peck and then turned the car off. I flipped the sun visor down to check myself out and winced. My face was flushed and my lips were bright red. I groaned. *Nice first impression, Faith.*

Lucas flicked the visor up. "You look beautiful. And besides, they're all hiding behind the curtains watching us. We won't be fooling any of them."

I felt my mouth drop. Lucas pushed my chin up and smiled

devilishly. He got out and strutted around the front of the car. I got out as well and started scanning the countless windows of the house for peepers. I noticed twelve or so fancy foreign cars parked in the giant U-shaped driveway, and the lawn, though dead from the winter, was immaculately kept. Even from the outside, I knew the Whelans were wealthy.

I felt inferior before I'd even crossed the threshold.

Lucas seemed to sense my unease because he took my cold hand in his warm one. I smiled up at him, and his skin flared with heat. I wondered at the reaction since I knew the heat meant he felt the change, but after the kiss-fest in the car it seemed out of place.

"Lucas?" I asked as we crossed the snowy yard.

"Hmm?"

"Is it easier now?"

"Is what easier?"

"This," I said, indicating our hands intertwined. "Touching me. Kissing me. Is it easier?"

A small smile tugged at the corners of his mouth. "You know, it's odd, but in a way, yes. The more we touch, the easier it is to halt the change. Maybe it's just because I expect it now. Before, most of the caution was because I didn't know what would happen. I didn't want to chance it, you know?"

"And now that you know you won't kill me—"

"Don't say that." His eyes cut into mine, fierce and feral.

"Sorry," I whispered.

We walked silently up the icy slate steps to the front door, which was twice as tall as me and made of finely polished oak that blinded me in the setting sun.

Lucas turned and faced me before entering. "Look," he said gruffly. "I can't even think about it—hurting you, I mean. Thinking about it makes it a possibility and then I can't . . . I can't justify kissing you or even being with you. And that's not something I'm willing to give up." He smiled sadly, taking my cheek in his warm hand. "It's selfishness, really," he murmured deeply.

"No," I said, stepping close to him. "I want this just as badly as you do. I don't care if you could hurt me because I know you won't."

A dubious light played in the depths of his gaze, but he bent and kissed me lightly. His eyes were silver when he pulled back, and a stabbing pang sliced my heart. I wished my touch didn't affect him that way. I didn't want to cause him any more pain than he was already dealing with. But whether it was selfishness, as Lucas claimed, or something else, I knew I wasn't willing to sacrifice our relationship either. I needed him and I suspected that he needed me now, too. I was just happy it was getting easier for him, whatever the reason.

"Let's get this over with," Lucas grumbled and turned to the door. He didn't even bother to knock. He pulled the wrought iron handle and ushered me inside.

Immediately I was wrapped in the warmth of the house, and not just because of the temperature. The main room was a huge recessed living area, filled to the breaking point with couches, cushy armchairs, and big pillows strewn about. Art cluttered the wooden walls and punctuated the room in the form of sculptures and woven tapestries from all over the world. The lifestyle was obviously opulent, but it still felt homey and rustic.

Lucas put his hand on my back and led me past a gigantic stone fireplace that crackled gently with fire. The mantelpiece was topped with a painting of water lilies. I stared at it and stopped; I'd seen it before somewhere.

Then my eyebrows hit the ceiling.

"Is that—is that—," I said and then turned to Lucas. "Is that a *real* Monet?"

Lucas glanced up at the painting. "Yep. Met him once. He was a pretty cool guy. A little nuts, but all artists are, huh?" He flashed a grin and tugged me through the kitchen to the backyard. My mouth was still parted when we came to the French doors that opened up to the patio.

I looked around and was surprised to see that in addition to the big house, there were several smaller houses arranged in a circle, their back porches all facing inward. Now I knew what Mark had meant by *community*—there must have been more than one werewolf family living here.

Lucas hung his arm around my shoulders as we reached a large group of people sitting in lounge chairs surrounding a big fire pit. The faces were all different, but somehow they bore a resemblance to Lucas. All had big eyes of varying colors and thick unmanageable hair that looked more like fur than anything else. Kids swarmed the place, running and screaming around the adults who sipped glasses of red wine and talked loudly.

I felt my heart thumping as we got closer. I wondered if they were all werewolves. I fretted over the state of my hair, of my lips. Were they still red?

A woman with auburn hair who looked to be in her late twenties waved when she saw Lucas. The group turned toward us with big smiles, and I felt a collective wave of anticipation hit me from the group, a vibe of carefully concealed raging energy, much like the one Lucas had.

"Hey," Lucas said coolly. "Everybody, this is Faith. Faith, this is my pack. Well, some of them, anyway."

They all smiled even more brightly with glittering, sharp teeth and some waved.

"Lovely to meet you," the auburn-haired woman said. She seemed to be in charge here because everybody kept looking at her as if gauging how to react to me. "I'm Nora Nocturn." She had a stern, yet gracious energy, reinforcing my impression that she was in some way a leader.

I returned her smile timidly.

Lucas turned to Nora. "Where's Dad?"

"He's not here," Nora said, taking a sip of her drink.

"What? Where is he?"

"He felt the call."

"He's *hunting*?" Lucas asked incredulously. "We come all the way up here and he doesn't even have the decency to be here. That is so *Rolf*."

"Oh, honey, bitter doesn't suit you," Nora said. "He'll be back in the morning. You and Faith will just have to spend the night. We have plenty of room. Go in and get yourselves settled, and then come back out and join us."

"No, thank you," Lucas spat.

Nora's face fell, and I was immediately frightened of her. As Lucas's hand clenched around my waist, I could feel her vibe turn powerful and threatening. The energy began to overwhelm me, consuming me much like the times when Lucas's and Vincent's feelings had overwhelmed me. But those times, I'd been touching them, and the feeling had lasted only seconds. Now it was as if I was being slowly drawn in, feeling her emotions crush me.

Lucas glared at her for a long moment, grinding his teeth. Then he spun around, breaking the growing connection I'd felt to Nora's anger, and tugged me along behind him. As soon as we entered the house, Lucas took a right, pulled me up a flight of stairs, and down a long hallway. We stopped at the last room on the left, and Lucas pushed the door in. He stalked through and shut the door behind us.

He flicked the lights on, and I took the room in while he fumed. It was huge and papered in art. Not famous art—Lucas's art. And everything seemed to glow in red hues for some reason. I walked to the big king-sized bed and sat on the scarlet comforter, letting my legs dangle over the edge. I folded my hands in my lap and waited for Lucas to get over himself.

I, too, needed to calm down. Sensing other people's vibes was becoming more intense, and it was really starting to unnerve me. First I had only felt them when I met someone. I'd get a brief feel for their emotions and then it would go away. But then, with Lucas, I'd constantly been aware of his energy, like a hum in the back of my mind. I'd just attributed that to the fact that he was a werewolf and that his vibes were stronger than a normal human's. But now I was feeling these intense waves of emotion as well. What was happening to me? It was like this vibe thing was evolving, changing as I delved deeper into Lucas's world.

And if that were true, then maybe I could learn to control it, to feel others' emotions at will. . . .

A sound made me lose my train of thought. Lucas had kicked a chair over. I watched him pace around the room grumbling unintelligibly and then finally turn to face me, hands on his hips. I held my arms open for him. He let out a big breath and crossed the room to hug me. His cheek brushed my neck as he settled in and the contact zapped me. I winced. The static electricity was getting worse, too. Maybe, the zaps had something to do with what was happening to me.

"I'm sorry," Lucas rumbled in my ear.

I sighed, coming back to the situation at hand. "It's no big deal. I don't mind sleeping here. I already missed one day's worth of class, two is no big deal. I can catch up easily."

"That's not what I'm worried about," Lucas said.

"We'll just stay in here. It seems comfy enough." I smiled suggestively at him.

Lucas rolled his eyes. "I'm not sleeping in this bed with you."

"Why not? You've done it before."

"Yeah, and look how great that turned out. If Julian hadn't been there—"

"Stop," I said, not willing to consider the fact that he would have hurt me.

He bent and caught my gaze. "I'm sorry, but lying in bed with you blows past my control levels—not that they're so great to begin with."

"I think they are. You couldn't even look at me without changing and now you're kissing me. I think you're stronger than you think you are."

"And I think you have a death wish. Just because I'm able to do this much, doesn't mean I can do any more than that."

"You mean . . . ?"

"Yes, I mean that," Lucas said curtly.

I watched him sadly, pitying him almost.

He shifted his weight, seeming to fluff himself up a little bit. "It's not like I've *never* done it," he said. "When I was human, I was with a lot of women. I was what you might have called a rogue. Or I guess the term now is man whore." He grinned crookedly.

I smiled at his joke even though I felt my heart sinking for some reason. Probably because I was now the only virgin in the room. I knew it was dumb for me to have thought Lucas was a virgin. The guy was over three hundred years old. That's a hell of a long time to wait. But still, it would have been nice.

"Is it the same for all werewolves?" I asked, trying to mask my dejection by interrogating him.

"Mostly," Lucas said. "We usually only date within our race, that way if we lose it and change too close to each other, nobody gets hurt. It's safe." He regarded me with somber eyes. "Relationships with humans usually end badly."

I looked away. I didn't want to think about the end. Not when it had just begun.

I steered the subject around and said, "So have you ever . . . with another werewolf?"

His eyes met mine, giving me the answer. "It's been a long time." His voice was soft. "I don't date werewolves anymore."

"Why not?"

"Because it always ends. There's no relationship strong enough to last an eternity. And eternity is a long time to deal with an ex-girlfriend."

My heart sunk even lower, almost paining me with the ache of it. I shouldn't have felt that way. I wasn't immortal. We didn't have to worry about an eternity of awkwardness. If we ever broke up, he'd only have to deal with me until I died. But knowing Lucas didn't want to spend eternity with me was a sting. An irrational and totally premature sting, but a sting nonetheless.

Lucas seemed to sense my distress because he went on, trying to bolster his argument. "Werewolf relationships are usually just one big mess, Faith. Especially in packs. We all run together during the full moon and if anyone's fighting, they usually get into it pretty good. Sometimes there are deaths. I don't want any of that."

I nodded slowly. It made sense when he put it like that. If I had some crazy ex-boyfriend trying to kill me every full moon, I might not be too keen on dating either. "So you only date humans," I said, letting it marinate. "But you can't go any further than kissing."

"Well, I guess I *could*, but I don't. Risking lives for the sake of my libido doesn't really sit well." He gave me an anxious, lopsided grin, as though worried about how I was taking this.

"How do werewolves even have sex?" I asked. "I mean, you don't . . . change do you?"

To my surprise, Lucas laughed—a rarity that I usually enjoyed but which only made me feel idiotic now.

"No," he said between chuckles. "It doesn't work like that. We stay human."

"But you said that you might change too close and hurt the other person. What if you changed in the middle of it?" My face felt like it was on fire as I asked the question, but I was too curious to let it drop. I wanted to know exactly what type of danger I was dealing with. Then I could decide whether or not I wanted to brave it.

Lucas pulled his hand over his face, seeming to agonize over how he would answer. "We can feel the change before it overtakes us," he said. "So it's just a matter of getting away quickly to keep from hurting the person we're with. If someone's too close, the violence of the change would tear them to shreds."

Yikes. Not a good idea.

Lucas saw my reaction. "It's very rare," he soothed. "And it only happens with younger werewolves, ones out of control. But like I said, most werewolves don't like to chance it. They don't even consider dating humans as an option, that way there's no temptation. We're supposed to protect humans, not endanger them."

"But you're old, right?" I asked, trying to find a chink in his armor. "Can't you control yourself?"

"I'm old enough that changing wouldn't be a problem, and if it were anybody but you, we could try it. But sometimes just looking at you triggers me." He rubbed his thumb over my hand, eyes dark and sorrowful. "I'm sorry, but I can't justify chancing it."

I nodded, crestfallen and frustrated. But then I realized that Lucas had never said he couldn't have sex with a human—just that he didn't want to. A ray of hope I had to explore. If it was getting easier for him, then maybe one day . . .

"Have you ever tried it with a human?" I asked.

Lucas's face collapsed into a mingling of hurt and anger, but at what I couldn't know. He didn't answer for a long time. I felt the silence stretching out into infinity.

"Once," he admitted finally.

"What happened?" Something in his voice made me fearful of what he would say next.

"The experience was . . . unpleasant," he said, maneuvering around my question.

"Lucas," I said warily.

"Fine," he growled. "It was when I was still a runt. I was lonely and out of control . . . stupid. I got with this girl; we started kissing and I changed. She was too close and she got hurt. She spent the rest of her life in a wheelchair because of me, so I don't think we'll be doing that anytime soon."

"Well, I didn't say I wanted to anyway," I shot back.

He clamped his jaw, and I saw his eyes shift silver.

I frowned. I was going to ask it, just come right out and go there. I knew it was stupid to ask about ex-girlfriends, but whatever. I had to know this or it was going to eat at me forever.

"Lucas," I said slowly. "I want to know something."

He sighed heavily and his voice was calmer. "Sure, why not? I've already told you everything I've been trying to hide, so go for it." He pulled away and lay down on the bed, his hands behind his head.

"I want to know why I'm the only one that sets you off. Why you have trouble even touching me when I saw you kissing Courtney with no problem? And . . . and I know you did more than that with her, so . . . so I know you can do it." I'd never heard them through my wall—thank God—but it seemed out of place to think that Lucas wouldn't have had sex with Courtney. She was hot, or so everyone seemed to think, and Lucas was a guy. It wasn't rocket science.

I turned and looked down at Lucas to see his troubled eyes

fixed on the ceiling. "Why do you think I did more with her?"

"Because Courtney does it with everyone, and she was going on and on about your abs, so I put two and two together."

Lucas's lips twitched into a stiff smile. "I can kiss or touch any girl I want, so long as I don't have any real feelings for her. I never had sex with her. It's why she dumped me. I think she thought I was gay."

I giggled, feeling my spirits lift. My mind flashed to that first conversation I had with Lucas, the one where dating had come up. His words floated through my head and suddenly made sense: *I date a lot of girls I don't like.* He dated the ones he didn't like because it prevented him from feeling anything for them.

"So it's emotions," I said, confirming my theory. "Your feelings trigger the change." I wanted to say feelings for me, but that felt like hoping for too much. He openly admitted that he dated girls he didn't like. Was I just another one of those girls?

"Yeah," Lucas said. "Intense emotion triggers the change. Anger mostly. But fear will do it, too. And even happiness if it's strong enough." He sat up and looked at me full on. I saw his eyes turn bright, ice cold like metal. "Arousal . . . and love, as I'm finding out now, will set me off, too."

"Love," I said, feeling my pulse speed up.

His eyes remained on mine. "I never thought I'd experience anything close to it. I've trained myself not to feel anything. Anything at all. And then I met you . . . and I've never felt such intense, sudden, emotion. Such inexplicable attraction. To a complete stranger, no less. At first I couldn't figure it out. I didn't know why I felt the change coming every time I even looked at you. But then I saw you with Vincent and I felt jealous. Crazy jealous. I've never been jealous of anyone before. Not like that. I thought of everything he'd do to you if he got the chance. How he'd torture you, kill you.

"That's when I felt the rage. It's why I missed so much class that first month. I kept changing . . . thinking about you. But then that rage turned soft . . . turned to something I couldn't pin. I thought it was just protectiveness. Or maybe fear for your safety, my werewolf instincts kicking in, you know? Protect the weak." He smiled, almost resentfully.

"But then I got to know you and saw how alike we are." He put his hand over my cheek, warming it with his palm. "And I realized that the reason I felt such a strong urge to change when I was with you, was because I'm in love with you. I've loved you since the moment I saw you."

I felt tears drag down my face. I looked into his silvery eyes, so bright with happiness.

"It's amazing," he said. "I never thought I could have this. Have love, I mean. I've spent so much of my life trying to feel nothing, and now I feel everything all at once. And it's all because of you, because of what you've triggered in me. It's something so strong, something so intense . . . something I know I can't live without anymore." He pulled me close. "I'm gonna make sure you're safe, Faith. I'm gonna make sure Vincent never touches you. I'll die if that's what it takes."

I grimaced, not willing to even consider the possibility that I'd lose Lucas. I nuzzled my face into his neck, inhaling his musky, sweet scent. The comfort of having him hold me, of knowing that he'd always be with me, filled my every thought and I knew without a doubt that I was in love with him, too. It was a terrifying realization and it took every ounce of determination I possessed to keep from squashing it back. Instead, I decided to do the impossible.

"Do you want to know a secret?" I whispered.

He pulled back and looked into my eyes, nodding.

I felt my entire body shaking and my mind was centered on the three words waiting to be released. "I didn't say it back before," I murmured. "Because I was scared. I'd convinced myself that loving someone was impossible after everything that happened to me. But I was wrong." I closed my eyes and pressed my forehead to his, feeling the heat sink into my skin, strengthening me. It came out in a rush of relief that warmed my soul. "I love you."

T he morning came much too soon. Lucas and I spent the night in his room in the same way we spent all nights together. The only difference was that we were constantly entwined with each other and broke up the talking with random kissing sessions, which always ended in Lucas fending me off with jokes and death threats. We were so wrapped up in each other that we didn't even pause to eat dinner.

It was close to nine when I opened my eyes to the red light streaming in from the window and finally figured out the cause of the redness in Lucas's room. The sun filtered through his crimson curtains, bathing the room in bloody light. I rolled over to see Lucas sleeping upside down on the bed, his way of remaining celibate throughout the night. I don't know why being upside down prevented him from kissing me, but it seemed to have worked just fine. He hadn't touched me at all while I slept.

At least, I thought he didn't.

I flipped over and rested my head on his chest, breathing in the scent of his thin white tee shirt. I was glad he didn't smell like a dog. It was more like pine needles mingled with the earthy scent of his tan skin.

"Morning," Lucas rumbled, snuggling his face in my hair. "You been up long?"

"No," I yawned. "I'm dreading going downstairs."

"You and me both."

"What's going to happen?" I felt the familiar tingling of fear prickle at the back of my neck.

Lucas ran his fingers over my arm, causing tingles of a different sort. "Wish I knew," he said. "I can only guess that Rolf knows something about the murders and he wants me to help."

"So why'd you have to bring me then?"

"That's what's worrying me," he said grimly. "I have no idea."

I gulped. What use could a house full of vicious werewolves have for a weak human like me? I couldn't help them catch the vampire that was killing people in Denver. I couldn't even figure out what I wanted to major in! I turned toward Lucas, ready to unload all of this on him, when the door banged open. We both turned our heads upside down to see who had come in.

It was a pretty girl who looked to be a few years younger than me. She was tall with short black hair. She stood straight as a rail and wore a bright green tank top and a toothy grin. I knew in an instant that she was a werewolf—the crazy energy sparkling around her indicated as much.

"You know you guys are upside down, right?" she asked, her yellow eyes twinkling.

"What do you want?" Lucas asked.

"Dad's home. He wants to see you. Right now." Lucas and I started to get up, but the girl said, "Just Lucas."

I looked at Lucas, trying to gauge what this meant from his expression. His jaw was hard as he turned to me. I saw him swallow. "Go with Katie and get some breakfast. I'll meet with Rolf and then we'll leave. It's gonna be fine."

I nodded jerkily. He planted a kiss on my forehead and smiled down at me.

"Bring me some waffles," he said.

I tried to smile back, but it might have looked more like a grimace. Lucas threw on his leather jacket and brushed past Katie on the way out of his room. I listened to his heavy footsteps thud down the hardwood floor in the hallway. My eyes shifted to Katie, standing with her arms crossed and an impish smile on her petite face. Her cheeks were rosy with excitement. I wondered why Lucas had left me with her. She didn't seem all that safe.

"Don't worry," Katie said. "I promised Mom I'd be good."

I laughed nervously. "Who's your Mom?"

"Nora." She waved me over. "You hungry?"

I nodded. I was starved.

"Come on then," she said. "Julian and Melanie made steak and eggs."

"'Kay," I said, jumping from the bed and sliding on my flats. I followed Katie down the hallway.

"So," I said, eager to fill the silence. "Is Lucas your big brother?" I was curious about whether Nora was his mother since Lucas hadn't said anything about it. She seemed to have some sort of authority over him, but he'd completely disregarded her invitation to hang out with the pack last night without much thought, so she couldn't have been *that* important to him. But then I didn't really understand the pack politics since Lucas and I hardly ever discussed them.

"He's my pack brother, not my bio brother," Katie said. So Nora wasn't his mother, just someone influential in the pack. "Julian is my real brother."

"Really?" I asked, intrigued. "You both got bitten?"

"Yup."

I hesitated before asking my next question, wondering if it was a sensitive topic. "Do you mind if I ask how it happened?"

"My dad bit us."

"Your *dad*?"

"Uh-huh," Katie said happily as we trotted down the stairs. "He let us decide if we wanted to join the pack and we both said yes."

"So . . ." I struggled to understand. "Werewolves' kids aren't born werewolves?"

"Nope. It's not genetic, more like an infection in the blood. But most kids join the pack when they get old enough."

"How old are you?"

"Sixteen. Dad wanted to wait until I was older, but I caught him at a weak moment and convinced him otherwise." She grinned slyly.

"So how long have you been a werewolf?"

"Only a few years. But I'm almost all the way under control. Hardly anything triggers me anymore . . . besides cute boys anyway! The Council is really impressed with me. It usually takes a lot longer for werewolves to get themselves under control. But I'm a prodigy!" Katie smiled toothily.

We rounded the corner of the living room and entered the dining room, which was flooded with early morning light from a large bay window. A table as long as a school bus stood in the center, and it was packed full of people. The savory aroma of steak and eggs, buttery grits, and flaky pastries wafted over me. My stomach growled even though I wasn't much of a breakfast person. After skipping dinner last night, I felt like I could have eaten the table and been sated.

"Sit by me," Katie said. She plopped down into a chair at the end of the table and I lowered myself into the one next to her, glancing around nervously as though something might jump out and bite me. Then again . . . something might.

Everyone at the table had hungry eyes. I didn't feel any kind of antagonistic vibe from anybody, so I tried to be calm. I smiled to myself. I sounded just like Lucas. *Be calm!*

I noticed that none of the older people from last night were here. It was all adolescents and kids. I was willing to bet that the adults had convened in that pack meeting Lucas went to.

"Why aren't you at the meeting?" I asked Katie.

She moved a bowl of grits toward me and said, "Because I haven't been initiated into the pack yet. I have to prove myself before I can be a full member." She made a face and tore into one of the three steaks piled onto her plate.

"Oh," I said and scooped some grits onto my plate, smearing butter into them. "What do you have to do?"

"I don't know exactly. They like to keep everything a secret so we can't prepare. But from what I've dragged out of Julian, a lot of it has to do with self-control and fighting abilities. And vampire tracking, of course."

"Of course," I agreed. I wondered whether Lucas had to pass this test to get into the pack. The thought of him running around at night chasing vampires made me cringe.

"Is it dangerous?" I asked. "The test, I mean?"

"Oh, sure," Katie said. "Everything is dangerous when you deal with werewolves." She chuckled as she poured ketchup over her monstrous plate. She eyed me for a moment and then said, "You like Lucas a lot, huh? I can tell he likes you a lot, too. He's never brought anyone back here before."

"Well, he didn't exactly have a choice."

"Still." She smiled knowingly. "I can tell he likes you. And don't worry about what Rolf says. Lucas is pretty high up on the food chain around here. He can do almost anything he wants, short of directly disobeying Dad. He'll make sure nobody eats you."

I choked on a bite of grits and Katie beat me over the back with the force of a jackhammer. "Joking!"

"Katherine, stop hurting the human," said a voice from the doorway. I looked up, still coughing and saw Nora standing there. Her hair fell in one perfect sheet down to her waist, and her hazel eyes were piercing.

"I'm not, Mom!" Katie said, looking abashed. "She was choking on her food."

I felt my face flush. *Nice.*

Nora turned her gorgeous face to me. "Rolf would like to see you now, Faith."

My stomach gave a nasty twist. I nodded and stood up.

"Bye," Katie piped. "It was nice knowing you!" I felt the color drain out of my face. Katie noticed and then said, "Kidding, kidding!" She laughed and stuffed steak into her mouth.

Nora placed her hand on my shoulder and steered me through the living room.

"Ignore my daughter," Nora said with a note of exasperation in her lilting voice. "She likes to cause trouble. You are in no danger here. We protect the humans, remember?"

I couldn't even begin to respond. I felt my entire body aching to be near Lucas, aching to feel him beside me, keeping me safe.

We stopped at the fireplace and Nora pushed against a place on the wall where there was a nifty hidden door. We walked down a short flight of stairs and then came to a big room with lots of couches and chairs scattered in random disarray, although the basic shape was a circle. The lighting was low and orange, coming from a fire crackling on the back wall. All eyes turned toward us when we entered. I searched them for a pair I recognized, but they all looked the same—all large and slanted, not quite human.

Then someone stood and it was Lucas, his familiar face popping out of the crowd. He held his hand out for me. I willed my feet to move toward him and then somehow I was holding his hand. He lowered me into a chair and sat down next to me, dragging my chair closer to him. He put his arm over my shoulder in a comforting and somewhat possessive gesture.

I didn't mind.

He leaned in. "You forget the waffles?" I could hear the humor in his voice.

I choked a laugh out, watching as Nora sat down next to a man with a long braid and freckles just like Julian's.

"Hello, Faith," said a voice to my right. I looked over, and a man sitting in front of the fire was smiling at me. Really, he looked more like a bear. He was hulking and hairy and I swear I saw claws where his hands should've been. He couldn't have been more than a few years older than Lucas when he'd been infected, but there was something about him that alluded to his ancient age. The eyes, intense and focused. His vibe, too, was raging with power and I knew in an instant who this massive beast was. He was the pack master.

I swallowed and said, "Hi." My voice sounded strangled and small. Lucas's arm tightened around me.

"I am Rolf," he said pleasantly. "And I have a great favor to ask of you."

19

STRATEGY

I felt my stomach drop. I glanced at Lucas and saw a muscle in his jaw vibrating. I took a deep breath.

"I'll help if I can," I said, trying to sound brave.

This seemed to please Rolf. He leaned back in his armchair and smiled. His eyes flicked to Lucas and then back to me.

"I'm sure you have heard of the murders in Denver, and now in Fort Collins as well," Rolf said. He had a bombastic voice and perfect enunciation. It made me feel slightly inadequate.

I nodded in answer to his question. So this was about the murders, after all. I wished knowing that made me feel better, but it had the opposite effect. What did these people think I could do to help them? Wasn't staving off vampires their deal?

Rolf gazed at me intently with eyes like hot coals. "Then I am sure that you have realized that they are vampire killings."

More nodding on my part.

"The killings are out of character for a vampire of Vincent Stone's age and experience. However, we had a stroke of luck at the full moon. We were able to catch his scent and match it to the one at the crime scene of the last murder." He dipped his head in a little bow. "We have you to thank for that, Faith."

I frowned. "Why are you thanking me? I did everything wrong. I fell for his trick."

"Yes, you did. But if you had not lured Vincent into the open, we would not have been able to match his scent to the one at the crime scene. Now we can be sure that he has killed at least one girl, and I believe it is a safe assumption to say that he is responsible for the ones in Denver as well."

I heard mumbles of agreement from around the room.

"But why he is doing this, is beyond us," Rolf continued.

"Doesn't matter why!" shouted a voice from the back.

"Yeah," said another, a girl this time. "Any dead vamp is one less to worry about!"

"Let's bring him down!" a man roared. Shouts and whoops erupted around the room, but Lucas didn't make a move. His eyes remained fixed on the far wall.

"Enough," Rolf said, and the shouting died down. "We are all anxious to have this matter settled. Since the killings are out of character for someone Vincent's age, I would venture to think that he has orders from a higher up." He sighed a little, as if exasperated. "However, Lucas thinks that is unlikely."

"Why?" I asked, turning to Lucas.

"Vincent doesn't take orders," Lucas grunted. "Not the Vincent I knew, anyway."

"Well, you said that the Vincent you knew was lost," I said. "Maybe the newer, more evil Vincent found a way to get to you by murdering these girls, so he did it because it'd hurt you."

"How would that hurt me?" Lucas asked arrogantly.

"Well . . . I mean, this is your territory right? It's your responsibility to keep the vampires from killing humans, so if you guys fail to do that, wouldn't that piss you off? Make you angry?"

Lucas just clenched his jaw.

"And then if you're angrier," I said eagerly, "it'd make you change more . . . make you more impulsive and more likely to make a mistake. It'd make it easier for him to kill you."

Lucas made no reaction, so I looked around to Rolf, who was nodding.

"Very good," he said to me. "But regardless of Vincent's motives, he cannot be allowed to continue his killing spree." His voice became hard. "We cannot have a vampire on our territory, killing on a whim with no consequences, especially when he does it with no concern for subterfuge. His boldness has drawn the attention of the human authorities. He is putting all of us in danger now."

He looked to Lucas. "I am sorry, son, but this feud has gone on long enough. It is time we stepped in."

Lucas's eyes glared with silver fury. "This is *my* fight," he said loudly.

Rolf's eyes burned red instead of silver. "Not any longer. He has involved all of us now—our land, our reputations, our families are in jeopardy! We've stood by and watched the two of you torture each other for years. You cannot defeat him alone."

Lucas leaped out of his seat. "Don't tell me what I can and can't do. I'm strong enough to kill that leech without any of you!"

Rolf's tone was gentler, but still firm. "Lucas, there is no shame in accepting help. We are your family, your pack. Let us help you end the suffering."

Lucas's body heaved with deep breaths.

"I have a plan," Rolf said firmly. "Sit down and be calm."

Lucas obeyed begrudgingly. "I don't know what you think is so different about this time. I don't care how many of us are out there—you're not gonna catch him if he runs. And he *will* run."

Rolf nodded slowly. "It is different now because we know what he wants." His eyes flickered to me.

Lucas vaulted out of his seat again.

"She's not bait!" he roared, his body trembling. Several people around us rose out of their seats, looking anxiously from Rolf to Lucas. I saw a few of the bodies in the back shiver.

My heart pounded. I prayed the room wouldn't erupt into a mess of angry werewolves. I definitely wouldn't fare well in that scenario. I gripped the edges of my seat, staring up at Lucas's shaking form.

But Rolf stayed calm. "Everybody sit." His voice took on this sonorous yet somehow hollow nature, and everybody sat immediately—even Lucas, though he didn't look happy about it.

"Lucas," Rolf said calmly. "Think about it, son. We wait until the full moon, when we are at our strongest, and then we place Faith in a given position."

I heard Lucas let out a low, guttural noise.

"Stop that," Rolf said, his voice creepy and hollow again. Lucas stopped, looking slightly choked. "We place her in a spot where she will be safe and then we wait for him. We can ambush the vampire and find out if he serves a master, as I suspect. Once we find out what we need, we will dispose of him."

"You've lost your mind if you think I'm letting you do this," Lucas said in a low voice. "There's no way."

Rolf looked unconcerned. "You know I do not have to ask your permission, Lucas." His tone was pointed.

Lucas's eyes flashed. "You do that and I leave the pack!"

Several people winced and gasped.

Rolf narrowed his eyes at Lucas. "How else do you expect to finish this? How long can you keep her safe from him? You already put her in danger once."

Lucas cringed, his face breaking with torment. I put my hand over his, glaring at Rolf.

"That wasn't his fault," I said. "He told me what to do, and I ignored him. Don't blame Lucas for something I did to myself."

"Regardless!" Rolf barked. "How many more innocent lives must be taken because of your stubbornness, Lucas? We cannot sit idly by and watch him disgrace our territory!"

"I don't care about the stupid territory!" Lucas yelled. "I care about Faith. I'm not letting you put her in danger."

"Lucas," Rolf warned. "Do not make me do this. Do not make me force you."

"Go ahead and force me," Lucas said between his teeth.

They glared at each other for a long moment, eyes burning. I felt their furious energy rebounding against each other, commanding and unrelenting. I watched Lucas's livid profile in slight amazement; he would give up his pack just to keep me safe. As touched as I was, I couldn't let him sacrifice that for me. His pack was the only family he had, and I of all people knew what it meant to have a family that wasn't a wreck. I had the power to help Lucas end this war that tortured him so.

"I'll do it," I said. I stood and turned to Rolf. "You don't have to force Lucas to do anything. I'll help you kill Vincent."

Lucas rounded on me. "Like hell you will! I don't need your help!"

"Yes, you do. It's okay to need people." I put my hand on his cheek. "You taught me that. I want to do this, Lucas. I want to help you get rid of your demons, just like you're helping me get rid of mine."

Lucas shook his head, his jaw set with stubbornness and his

metallic eyes desperate, yet fierce.

"You don't understand," he growled. "I'll die before I let this happen."

I could see that he meant it and no amount of convincing on my part was going to sway him. I turned to Rolf for help, but he, too, seemed to realize this wasn't going to work. If Lucas wouldn't cooperate, it threw too many obstacles into an already problematic plan.

"Fine," Rolf rumbled. "But we must act. This cannot continue."

Lucas leaned back in his seat with his arms crossed over his chest, expression closed. I sat too, watching him. I'd never seen him so angry. Well, except maybe on Halloween, when Vincent had shown his true colors and attacked me in the woods outside the barn. The tumultuous energy he was emitting now was very similar to then.

Oblivious, or perhaps merely unaffected by Lucas's fury, Rolf scratched his bearded chin. "What we need is an advantage. If we could only locate his lair . . ."

"Can't you?" I asked. "You said you caught his scent, so can't you just follow it to his . . . ah . . . lair?"

Rolf's bushy eyebrows drew together. "Under normal circumstances we could, however it has proved difficult with all the snowfall. We lose the scent somewhere on the outskirts of Fort Collins."

"Is there anything around there?" I was grasping at straws, trying to make something click in my head.

"Only some residential buildings, a few warehouses, an abandoned barn. Nothing likely to attract a vampire. They prefer to live underground."

But then, something *did* click.

The barn.

"Lucas," I said suddenly. "Vincent threw his Halloween party at a barn. Maybe it's the same one."

Lucas gave me a patronizing look. "It is the same one, but we've checked it, Faith. All of the buildings have been checked."

"Maybe you missed something," I said stubbornly. "I mean, you said the snow covered the scent."

"It's highly unlikely that we would have missed him," Rolf said. "He is hiding someplace else. Perhaps in Denver. I know there is a brood there, and quite a large one at that."

I fell silent. I was so sure that was where Vincent would be. It seemed like the perfect vampire hideout. . . . But then, maybe that was just because it had been decked out to look like a haunted house at the time. There had been creepy beasts "attacking" guests, detached limbs on the floor, and blood and—

"I saw someone drinking blood that night," I said at once.

Everyone stared at me.

"What?" Lucas asked cautiously, as though he thought I'd lost it.

"I saw a woman bite this guy. They were hiding in a corner of the party, but the strobe lights came on and I could see them. She bit him. There was blood everywhere. I thought it was a prop for the party, but now . . ." I looked hopefully up at Lucas.

He was staring at me like he couldn't quite believe what he was hearing. Turning to Rolf, he said, "We need to check again. If there was more than one vampire there, it might be a lair."

"You would have smelled them," Rolf argued.

But Lucas shook his head. "There were too many humans that

night. They obscured everything." Rolf still looked skeptical, so Lucas cut his hand through the air and said, "Look, it might not be Vincent's lair specifically, but he still might stay there sometimes and we just missed him with all the snow. C'mon, Dad, it's all we've got. It's worth a try."

At last, Rolf seemed to agree. He pointed at two werewolves to his right and motioned for them to leave. In a blink they were gone. "They will look again. You are released for now."

The pack members began to stand and murmur to each other, but the energy I felt emanating from Lucas was so tumultuous, I felt it was best to be silent. Then Lucas stood in a motion so quick it startled me.

"Come with me," he growled and strode out of the door. I followed in his wake. He stopped in the hall leading to the kitchen and rounded on me. "What in the hell is wrong with you?"

I blinked. "What do you mean?"

"How could you volunteer to do something like that? Be bait for a vampire? Do you have any idea how dangerous that is? How many humans get killed doing exactly that?"

"I was just trying to help. You don't have to get so mad at me."

For a moment, Lucas seemed to struggle with himself and then he yelled, "I'm mad at myself! I'm mad that I dragged you into my screwed-up life. I'm mad that I finally found someone I love more than I love anything and now I have to put her life in jeopardy because of what I am. I'm mad that it's just the same thing, over and over, no matter how hard I try to stop it. I'm always hurting you. Always putting you in danger. And I'm mad that I can't keep you safe. That I have this vulnerable time when

I can't be with you. And yes, I'm mad at you, too!"

"How is any of that my fault?"

I saw his eye twitch. "It's not. I'm mad that I had to pick the most stubborn and willful person in the world to love. I need someone who'll be this damsel in distress, someone I can lock up somewhere and guard the door. I can't keep you safe because I never know what you're gonna do! Any normal person would have told Rolf to stick it. But no. I pick the girl who charges in headfirst with no concern for herself!"

"Well, sorry I care about you!" I yelled back.

"Don't be sorry, just—just, damn it!" He turned away and slammed his fist against the wall—not hard enough to break it but enough to make me flinch. He inhaled deeply, shaking. "I can't handle you getting hurt because of me, all right?" He looked sideways at me. "That's the truth. So no matter what happens when we go back in there, I don't want you putting yourself at risk for me. Is that clear?"

I bristled at his tone, but I was touched by his words. So I nodded. He seemed to calm down after that, and he leaned against the wall, glowering toward the basement we'd soon be returning to. I leaned against the opposite wall and folded my arms over my chest.

"Do you think they'll find anything at the barn?" I asked.

"It's possible. It wouldn't be the first time we've missed a vampire's scent—they're very elusive. It makes a difference when you find their individual fragrance, but they alter it every so often so that we have a harder time tracking them. But we might get lucky. Vincent might not have altered his yet. And we never rechecked the barn once we found it because Rolf thought it was an unlikely place for a lair. They might find something now."

I could only hope.

An hour later the door down the hall popped open and Nora called us back into the basement.

"Already?" I asked Lucas.

"They're our fastest runners," he grumbled.

Once inside the basement, we resumed our seats along with the rest of the pack, and I watched Rolf hang up a cell phone. Silence fell as Rolf contemplated whatever he just heard.

"They were able to detect traces of Vincent's scent at the barn," he said at last.

My heart leaped. Excited murmurs fluttered around the room.

"It may have been remnants from the party Faith spoke of," Rolf went on, "but it's the most promising lead we have."

"So what's the plan?" asked the man with the braid sitting next to Nora. He looked important, and I was willing to bet he was on the Council Katie had mentioned earlier.

"We will take some pack members and raid his lair on the next full moon."

Malicious smiles appeared among many of the werewolves around me, but not Lucas. His face was somber.

"Who will volunteer?" Rolf questioned.

Immediately several people stood. Nora and the man sitting next to her rose together. Julian stood as well, as did ten or so others I didn't know.

And, of course, Lucas stood.

"Excellent," Rolf said, looking around from under his eyelids.

"We reconvene here on the next full moon." Rolf started to leave, but Lucas wasn't satisfied.

"We do this on one condition," he said darkly. "You can all come and help me get the jump on Vincent, but I'm going to be the one to finish it. Nobody else." He glared around the room, his energy imposing and his eyes narrowed in intensity. "I'm the one who kills Vincent Stone."

AMBUSHED

The details were hashed out afterward. I wasn't allowed in the room, but Lucas filled me in on the way back to CSU.

"Basically we're raiding the place," he said matter-of-factly. "We gather at the mansion, Rolf will corral us—that might take a little time, given the excitement. We haven't raided in a while." He grinned at me. "Anyway, then we'll run to the barn together. At that point, it gets tricky, because if Vincent hears us, he'll run and then it's over."

"So how do you keep him from hearing you?"

"We'll send in our best trackers first to see if he's there."

"Who are the best trackers?"

He smiled again and I admired the flash of his white teeth. "Me," he said. "And Julian. I taught him everything I know. So he's good. Real good." His smile widened and I could see the pride he had in his pack brother.

"So once team badass goes in, what then?"

He chuckled. "If he's there, we corner him and call the rest of the pack in. Get the exits sealed and I'll attack."

My face dropped as fear overtook me. "Does it have to be you?" I whispered.

He glanced in my direction. "It's been over three hundred years, Faith. He killed my sister, killed countless others—some I cared about and some who were just in his way. And he tried to kill you. Nobody else has as much riding on this kill. I have to be the one to finish this. Only then can I rid myself of him forever. Only then can I be at peace—or as close to peace as I can get."

"Do you think you can beat him?"

I expected a cocky retort, something along the lines of "I can beat anyone" so I was surprised when he turned thoughtful. "I've fought him hundreds of times. Sometimes he'd come real close to killing me—luckily I was able to fend him off and run. But those times when I was the one about to do the killing . . ." He curled his lip as if disgusted. "Something always stopped me. I have no doubt in my mind that I have the ability to kill him. It's just—"

"What?" I couldn't understand why he hadn't done it before now. He'd killed countless vampires without remorse and Vincent was so obviously evil. After everything he'd done—draining Lucas's sister, murdering people, and trying to kill me and Lucas—how could Lucas have let him live? Vincent deserved death.

"He wasn't always a vampire," Lucas said softly. "I guess some part of me keeps hoping that he'll, I don't know . . . change. Go back to being my best friend." He laughed coldly. "But I know it won't happen. He'll just continue to become more and more evil. I have to kill him." His eyes met mine, level and deadly. "I *will* kill him."

But as sure as Lucas was about his fighting abilities, I knew there was still the chance that Vincent would get the upper hand. That Lucas might be the one to die that night and I would lose the only man I'd ever loved. That I would be alone. Again.

The full moon wasn't due for close to three weeks, which, at first seemed like an eternity to wait. But time seemed to slip away from me like water falling through cupped hands. I probably should have been worrying more about the coming raid, but strange as it sounds, I didn't. The first two weeks were the happiest of my life.

We spent them much as we'd always spent time together, talking, laughing, teasing . . . only now there was the added bonus of kissing. We went to football games together, mostly so I could catch a glimpse of Derek, and—to keep my promise to Heather—we went to the movies with her and Pete, both of whom were annoyingly happy that I was dating someone. I even went to Lucas's art show, which got me thinking about art as a major. Lucas and I would sometimes sit outside and sketch silly pictures of each other, mine always had big pouty lips and crazy hair, while I usually drew him with some sort of wolf part. I wasn't the most amazing artist in the world, but when Lucas got me a new camera for my birthday, which happened to fall on the half-moon, I soon found that I made an excellent photographer.

I started snapping pictures of Lucas at random moments—mostly just to bug him. But then I started clicking all the time, loving the way the light hit his face in the morning, or the shadows his hand made over mine.

I'd taken a photography class in high school and always liked it, but never seriously considered it as an option. After going to Lucas's art show and seeing his, and the other art majors' work, I realized that he'd been right. Art was a good way to let out some tension. I still wasn't sure if photography was for me, but I was having fun with it nonetheless.

Thanksgiving found Lucas and me sitting in Panda Express, sharing a cup of noodles and talking about my dorky high school days. I had been planning on going home to see my mom during Thanksgiving break, but as luck would have it, she had to go on a last-minute business trip for her firm. As much as I was dying to see her, she was on the verge of making partner and I knew missing this trip would cost her. So I didn't make a big deal. It turned out to be fun, if a little unorthodox. Chinese food and a werewolf. Perfection.

Cross-country track tapered to an end during the same weeks as my final exams—all of which I passed, thankfully. Not having track to run off my steam left me with a lot of pent-up energy. Lucas had only come to a few of my practices, but when I confessed to him how much I missed it, he confessed a little truth of his own: he was a runner, too. Apparently, it was a werewolf thing. After much cajoling, I allowed Lucas to run with me in the afternoons, racing him on the abandoned track circling the soccer field. At first I'd rejected the idea since Lucas was so obviously faster than me, but it turned out to be great. It was another way we could connect and I loved it . . . loved him.

But the happiness I'd experienced with Lucas during those first two weeks soon turned sour. As the moon waxed, so did my anxiety. The night began to frighten me again. Lucas and I began to snap at each other more often as the tension grew. We both knew that these last few days before the full moon might very well be the last we'd ever have together. Sometimes it made me so sad, I felt like my world was crumbling to ruins, and other times I just felt angry and cheated. I would lash out at my friends or at Lucas, and then my heart would break all over again, thinking of never seeing him again and having our final days destroyed by senseless fighting.

It was an odd, tumultuous time, and the night before the full moon was the worst. Our last night together. The weight on my chest was so heavy it felt as though it would cave in. We lay together on the couch in the darkness of Lucas's room. We were both quiet. It wasn't an uncomfortable silence, so much as uneasy. I think we could both sense how nervous the other was. Lucas's eyes had been silver all night.

"Do you think he'll be there?" I asked after a while.

My head was lying on Lucas's bare chest, and I heard his sigh through his tan skin. "Hope so."

"What happens if he's not?"

"The pack will probably disperse. Without a set goal or a vampire in the vicinity to focus our aggression on, everyone will just go their own way. But Rolf will probably leave a couple scouts there just in case Vincent comes back."

"And if he does?"

"Rolf will herd us all together again and we'll go back."

"He can do that?" I asked. "Make you listen, even when you're all crazy?"

"He's the pack master," Lucas said simply. "Rolf can make us do pretty much whatever he wants."

I was silent, trying to imagine what it was like for Lucas when he changed. Did he have any comprehension left? Any rational thinking? Or was it all madness and bloodlust? He must have had some kind of control if Rolf was able to order him around.

"How does he do it?" I asked. "Make you listen, I mean."

Lucas stroked my hair as he pondered my question. The sensation of his fingers brushing my neck made my heart flutter. "Well, when I change it's like the world turns red, in a way. I have very little control over my actions, no self-restraint. If something triggers me, I don't have any chance to press it back. The beast just takes over and that's it. Whatever I've targeted is dead. Usually."

"But Rolf can make you listen."

He nodded. "It's like a voice in my head that overrides everything else. He can only give us simple instructions, mind you. Run. Attack. Come. But that's all he needs. When we hear his voice, we obey."

"But doesn't that feel, I don't know . . . intrusive? That he's in your head?"

"Well, it's not ideal," Lucas said. "But it's the only way the pack can have some semblance of organization on the full moon. It's how we get things done, like the raid tomorrow night. If we didn't have Rolf to corral us, we'd all scatter."

"And if *I* were to talk to you when you were transformed?" I heard the hesitancy in my voice. I knew he didn't like to think about me being anywhere near him on the full moon. He usually never even entertained the thought. But I was curious. "Would you understand me?"

"Yes," he said. His tone was curt, but he went on anyway, maybe because he now thought it *might* be possible that I'd meet him on the full moon—if things went badly tomorrow night. "I understand what humans say, I can hear them begging me to stop . . . trying to make me recognize them. Sometimes it gets through, sometimes it doesn't. Vampires always seem to get through to me, probably because they're supernatural, too. Like we run on the same wavelength. But most of the time I'm too crazy to know what I'm doing."

I flinched, thinking how frustrating it must be to lose your mind, and how terrifying. If it were me, I would worry constantly about killing innocent people or doing something else truly horrible and being unable to stop myself.

"Do you remember anything afterward?"

Lucas passed his hand over his face, groaning. "You have a lot of questions tonight," he grumbled.

"I'm curious. You never let us talk about this stuff. I'm taking advantage, while I have you at a weak moment."

"I'm never weak," Lucas said stonily.

I decided not to dignify that with a response. Instead, I cuddled into his burning skin, hoping his warmth would stay with me when he left tomorrow.

"So do you remember?" I asked.

His voice was very different when he spoke next. Somber. Haunted. "Yes. I remember everything."

I was silent, then, rolling everything over in my thoughts. Absently, I watched Lucas's chest rise and fall in the white light streaming in from the window. I ran my hand down his arm, marveling at how smooth his skin was, when I felt a rough spot—the small scar on his forearm I'd noticed when we'd eaten lunch together all those months ago. I smiled to myself, remembering how I'd thought the scar was from his accident at the high school. I'd known then that Lucas hadn't been entirely truthful about what had happened when he fell off the roof of the gym, but I'd been too nervous to press him about it.

"Lucas, what really happened on the roof last year? When you fell?"

"Do you have to know *everything*?" he asked wearily.

"Yes." What a stupid question.

"What happened up there doesn't matter."

"It does to me," I said. "I don't like that you lied to me."

"Technically, I didn't lie . . . sort of."

I sat up and folded my arms across my chest, looking down at him. "I find it hard to believe that you tripped. You, the agile werewolf."

He grinned at that and ran a hand through his hair. He seemed to know my stubborn streak was kicking in and I wasn't about to drop this. "You're not gonna like it," he warned.

I shrugged. I didn't like a lot of what he told me, but that never stopped me from wanting to know more.

"Remember how I told you I don't date werewolves?"

I nodded and resumed my place, nestled into his side. I put my hand on Lucas's flat stomach, feeling its swells and dips as I listened to him.

"Well, that wasn't always the case," he said. "When I was younger I used to date. Most of the girls died out over the years, but there's still one alive that I know of. My most recent girlfriend."

My heart was growing colder and colder with each moment. Part of me—the jealous part—hated hearing this and wanted to tell him to forget it, but another more self-destructive part wanted to know everything. I swallowed, hoping to keep my voice even when I spoke. "What does that have to do with why you fell off a roof last year?" I tried to make it sound like hearing about his ex-girlfriend was no big deal.

"We used to live together," he said. "At the mansion in Gould."

"Wait—so you've lived in Fort Collins before?"

"Yeah. I needed a large pack, and Rolf's is one of the biggest in the U.S."

"Why would you need a big pack?" I asked.

"I needed to escape Vincent. We'd just had one of our rows up in Ontario, and I was on the losing end. I needed time to rethink my strategy. A bigger pack meant more protection, so I came here."

"I see. So you came to Fort Collins and met . . . what was her name?"

I looked up and saw Lucas's brown eyes grow distant for a moment and then he said softly, "Danielle."

Somehow just hearing her name pass through his lips sent a slither of jealousy through my heart. I didn't even want to think about all the hot werewolf sex they'd had—the sex Lucas and I would never get to have. "So what happened?"

"It was a while back," he said. "Her dad was the old pack master and had just died. Rolf took over as the new leader, and everything was kind of a mess. Since she was the ex-pack master's daughter, she had to deal with the politics of changing pack masters. There was a lot of fighting. A lot of bloodshed."

"Why?"

"When one pack master takes over another, he replaces the Council as well—the people he relies on to make decisions. When those people don't want to give up their power, it gets ugly."

I grimaced, imagining, but tried to appear composed. "Go on."

"Well, being her boyfriend, I had to defend her. I got into a lot of fights. It went on for years and I was tired of it. I was trying to lay low. Vincent was in the area." He puffed out an unemotional laugh. "It was a lot like it is now, actually. Only, back then I didn't mind dumping her to be free of everything."

I frowned up at him.

"Don't look at me that way. I almost got my head chewed off once a month for over two years. Literally. It was exhausting and back then I thought no woman in the world was worth dying for." His eyes grew soft at that last statement and a small smile tugged at his lips.

"So you broke up with her," I said.

He nodded. "And left Colorado for Russia. Vincent was close by, so I needed to ditch soon anyhow. Danielle was really pissed when I left, but she never came after me. Had too much to deal with here. The next time I came to Fort Collins was a few years back, like I told you. I was friendly with Rolf and convinced him to 'adopt' me. I tried living normally as a human, and for a while it worked. The only problem was that Danielle was still here. She'd fallen out of grace with Rolf and the Council and was living in a hovel of disgraced pack members out in the woods. She found me about a year after I came here and started stalking me."

My face betrayed my shock. "That's so creepy."

"Tell me about it. I managed to keep going like I didn't notice, but eventually she got so obvious that I felt I had to say something. I told her off, tried to get her to leave me alone. But she'd gone crazy living in the wild. We fought every full moon for months, but once she realized she couldn't beat me, she took on a different tactic. She found me at the high school. On the roof where I *was* drawing." He fixed me with a meaningful stare, one that said *I wasn't lying completely.* "Danielle attacked. I fought back. I got the advantage and went in for the kill. Except I couldn't. I had loved her once. And beyond that, she was a werewolf, and killing my own kind. . . . Well, that's not cool in my book. So I hurt her bad enough to prove my point—that I didn't love her anymore and I wanted her out of my life—and told her to go someplace else." He passed his hand over the back of his neck. "And for all I know, she did it. I haven't seen her since."

I stared, overwhelmed with the story. "But that still doesn't explain how you fell."

He cracked a wry smile. "Oh, yeah. Well, she wasn't too happy about what I said and I guess her pride was wounded at being beaten by me. Again. So she caught me while I wasn't ready and pushed me off the roof. I think she wanted to hurt me because of how we'd left things. It *did* hurt like hell." He rubbed his back as if remembering the pain and then shrugged. "Or maybe she just wanted to cause me trouble. I don't know. Like I said, she was crazy." He looked at me with a cautious glint in his deep brown eyes. "You pissed?"

"No, just surprised I guess. I never knew you had so many vendettas hanging around from your past."

"Yeah, well that's why I don't date werewolves anymore. Too much drama."

"Oh, right," I said. "So what we're going through isn't drama?"

Lucas wrapped his arms around me. "This is different."

I snuggled closer, inhaling the stubbly skin at his throat. "How? You dumped the last girl who got too troublesome. What makes this any different?"

"The difference is that if you died, it would be the end of me."

My heart swelled, but I teased him anyway. "So really, saving me from Vincent is for *your* benefit."

He kissed the top of my head. His voice was soft in my ear, his warm breath tickling my skin. "Everything I do is for you, Faith. You're my world."

I turned my face to his and kissed him, feeling the warmth surge in his perfect lips. But the kiss wasn't as sweet as I expected. A bitter, frightened feeling bloomed in my heart as I contemplated that this might be our last kiss, our last night together. Lucas could die tomorrow night, and the cruel reality of it hit me hard. I kissed him eagerly, arching my body closer to his, wishing I could melt right into him.

He kissed me back more fiercely, urgently, as though he too thought this might be our last one. His hands touched me every-where—the hollow above my collarbone, across my stomach, down over my hips, my thigh, pulling my leg around his waist. I knew we both wanted the same thing, but that it would never hap-pen. In a few moments he would pull back, tell me he loved me, and kiss my forehead.

But he didn't.

We went on like that for what seemed like forever, until the heat of his body became almost too much and I was the one who pulled away.

"Lucas, I don't think this is safe anymore."

He was shaking beneath me. "I know," he whispered. I could hear the resentment in his voice. "I'm sorry."

"Don't." I kissed him gently and pressed my forehead to his. We breathed heavily, our hearts slowing together as if they were one. I reveled in how lucky I was to have found my Lucas, some-one I could connect to on more than just a physical level, someone who understood me. He was a part of me now and I didn't know how I would recover if I lost him.

I wanted to tell him all of this, but as I opened my mouth to say the words, I looked into his eyes and realized he already knew.

I had to tell him good-bye the next morning.

I watched from the bed as Lucas rustled around the room, gathering what he'd need for the trip to Gould. My heart was in shambles, but I'd already sworn to myself that I wouldn't cry. If I started, I wouldn't be able to stop.

Finally, Lucas was finished packing and he turned to me, duffel bag slung over his shoulder.

"Well, I guess this is it," he said. His eyes were rimmed in silver, just as they always were when the full moon was close. I wished I could see them deep brown one last time. . . .

No. I can't think that way. Lucas is going to be fine tonight. He has to be.

"I have something for you," he said. He took a step forward—not coming too close because the likelihood of him changing was increased today—and held out what looked like a foot-long pointed stick about as thick as my wrist.

I took it and frowned up at him.

"It's a stake," he said. "If something goes wrong tonight or if he's sent someone else to get you . . . Well, I don't know how much use it'll be, but I'll feel better knowing you have a chance."

I couldn't manage a smile, but I nodded and tucked the stake into the pocket of my hoodie.

Lucas adjusted the duffel bag and stepped back again. "I'll

see you tomorrow, Faith." His tone was more convincing than reassuring.

I managed another jerky nod.

I wanted to tell him I loved him, to say good-bye, but I was terrified that if I said the words, if I let good-bye become a possibility, then I would never see Lucas again. And that was a reality I wasn't prepared to handle.

So I remained quiet, restraining the tears until they became too much. I looked up, desperate for something to comfort me.

Lucas's metallic eyes met mine, frustrated and yearning. I could tell he wanted to close the distance between us and hold me—and God, did I want him to—but the danger was just too great. Instead he gave me a small, heartbreakingly sad smile and left.

After two hours of crying, I spent the rest of the day and part of the night asleep. Lucas and I had stayed up the entire night before, so I was pretty exhausted. It was my cell phone that woke me at one thirty in the morning. With a jolt, I realized that Lucas would have changed by now and that he and the pack were already on their way to Vincent's lair.

Groggily, I reached for my phone and had to do a double take when I saw the caller ID.

It was Derek.

Derek and I hadn't spoken at all during the past few weeks, except once, right after we'd returned from skiing. I had gone to his room to get my phone, which I had left in his car. I wanted to smooth things over with him too, but when he gave me the evil eye and chucked my phone at me from across the room, I'd decided it was time to leave.

"Hello?" I answered.

"Hey, Faith," he said. His soft, deep voice was like a warm blanket surrounding me, comforting my fear for Lucas. I'd missed Derek's voice. "Listen, I want to talk to you. Can you come down?"

As much as I missed him, I wasn't in the mood to deal with any Derek drama right now. My nerves were already too frayed. "Why can't you just tell me whatever it is over the phone?"

Derek hesitated. "I need to see you. It's about what's happened between us. I wanted to say—" He cut himself off and made a funny strangled noise. "Look, can't you just come down?" His voice was hard now, almost reluctant.

I rubbed my eyes. "That's not possible, Derek. I'm in the middle of something right now."

"I'm outside in the courtyard. Just meet me down here." I heard a sharp intake of breath and then, "Please." But the word sounded harsh, ugly.

"*Wait*—you're outside? In the dark?"

Derek was silent, probably trying to figure out why it mattered that he was in the dark. But I knew why it mattered. He couldn't be outside during the night because if something went wrong during the raid and Vincent decided to come for me, he'd find Derek—the perfect bait to get me to leave Lucas's room.

Or there might even be a werewolf out there—it *was* a full moon.

No, Derek definitely needed to come inside.

"Fine, I'll be right down to let you in. I'm in Lucas's building, so go there."

I hung up and threw my shoes on. Flying down the stairs, I realized just how much danger I was putting myself in. If Vincent or some other creature was out there to get me, I was doing them a huge favor by coming out to meet them. But I didn't have a choice. I couldn't leave Derek. But I'd just go to the door and crack it open for him. I didn't even have to cross the threshold.

But when I got to the front door, I peered through the glass pane and saw that Derek wasn't there. Cursing, I opened the door and peeked around the corner of the building, still keeping my hand on the door.

"Derek?" I called quietly.

Nothing. The courtyard was illuminated in a stale yellow light that cast black shadows in every crevice. Thick foliage heaped in snow surrounded the buildings, providing the perfect hiding place for anything that might have been lying in wait.

Then there was a blast of wind in the center of the courtyard and two people materialized as if from nowhere. My heart caught in my throat and I closed the door immediately, staring through the glass pane in horror.

It was Vincent.

He stood covered in blood with a body pressed close to his chest. His sardonic gaze was locked on me, and his pointed teeth were bared in a bloody grin.

But I wasn't looking at him. All I could see was the human caught in his grasp, the crystal blue eyes pleading with me and the rigid jaw, grimacing in pain.

I pressed my hand to the door.

Derek.

21

ESCAPE

omething had definitely gone wrong during the raid, that much was clear. If Vincent had smelled the werewolves before Lucas had a chance to call in the rest of the pack . . . I stared in horror at the blood ringed around his mouth. *Lucas . . .*

Vincent moved slightly and a glint of silver flashed at me. A knife. Held at Derek's side and pressing into his skin.

My immediate reaction was to go out there. I grabbed the door handle, but stopped short. Going out there was exactly what he wanted. And he would probably kill Derek either way. . . . At least inside, I had some leverage. I removed my hand and propped it firmly on my hip. I caught Vincent's eye and shook my head meaningfully. I wasn't going out there.

His smile widened. Derek suddenly gasped and arched his back. My hands flew to the door handle again.

Vincent crooked a finger at me, still smiling as if he knew some deadly secret I had no knowledge of.

I cracked the door, still keeping my feet planted on the inside of the threshold.

"Let him go," I said. "I'm not coming out."

Vincent's voice was nothing more than a murmur, but I heard him clearly. "Then he dies."

"Faith, *don't* come out." Derek's voice, hoarse and pained, but still adamant. "I'm sorry. . . . I really did want to see you. I was in my car about to call you and then he . . . whoever this is, saw me. He made me call you and tell you to come down. I'm sorry. . . ."

"It's not your fault," I said numbly. "You didn't know."

"Just stay inside."

But I couldn't stand here and watch Vincent stab Derek to

death. I had to do something. I started to protest, but Derek cut me off, his voice firm. "Look, I didn't go all this time without you—realize that I can't live without you in my life—just to let you be murdered by some random psycho. Go inside and call—" Then he grunted loudly, holding in his pain.

"Enough," Vincent said. "Your adolescent sentiments bore me. Come outside now."

I didn't move.

"This knife can go deeper," Vincent said calmly. "I have no interest in killing him. As you can see"—he said and then licked his scarlet lips—"I already ate dinner. But I'll gladly stand here all night, pressing this knife deeper and deeper. Over. And. Over."

Derek gasped again and cursed. Blood was beginning to accumulate at his feet.

I closed the door again, keeping my eyes on Derek. His eyes were clearly telling me to go inside. To call . . . what? Call the police? Poor Derek had no idea what we were dealing with. Vincent would be gone long before the police got here and he'd take Derek who-knew-where to kill him. There wasn't a doubt in my mind that Derek was going to die if I didn't go out there.

So it was him or me.

I wanted to cry, but refused to let Vincent see me lose it. So I made my hand take the door handle. Made my arms pull the door open.

"Faith, go back inside!"

I shook my head. "I'm not going to watch you die." I turned my eyes to Vincent. "Let him go and I'll step outside."

Vincent's smile had finally gone and his eyes narrowed into slits.

He regarded me carefully for a moment.

"No. Come outside and he will be unharmed."

Slowly, I put one foot over the threshold, feeling a swell of frigid air. "Now let him go."

"Faith—"

"Shut up," Vincent spat and dug the knife into his side. "Enough from you. All the way out or your friend is going to be in an unbearable amount of pain. You have two seconds."

I stepped out of the building, keeping my hand clenched on the door.

Vincent's smile reappeared, twisting his face in the sallow, yellow light. "Excellent." He shoved Derek to the ground and slipped his knife into his coat. He stepped over Derek and strode up to me, extending his hand.

I tried to scramble back inside, but I knew before I even started that it was silly. He was so much faster. His hand clamped onto my upper arm and it was over. I looked up at him, hating him so much I thought it would come pouring out of me and melt his disgusting, handsome face.

Then Derek was standing again, breathing hard.

"I'll kill you," he grunted.

Vincent didn't even bother to turn around. He just smiled down at me. "Ready, darling?"

"Go to hell," I breathed, barely able to make my voice work.

He crooked a rueful grin. "Already there." He pulled me close and yanked me hard.

I heard Derek yelling for me as I was whisked away to Vincent's car, parked next to my building. He threw me into the passenger's seat and rocketed around to the driver's side. I had just enough time before Vincent sped away to see Derek running after us. He leaped into his car, parked beside Vincent's, as I reached for the door handle, hands shaking.

Then there was a sharp pain in the back of my head, stars bloomed behind my eyelids, and then . . . darkness.

I awoke to a cold, clammy feeling on my forehead. Vincent leaned over me with that sick gleam in his eyes. His hand was on my head, and he removed it when I looked at him.

"Apologies," he said. "Most of you women take to screaming when placed in stressful situations. I find it's less taxing on my delicate hearing if I render you unconscious." He straightened and offered his hand to help me up out of the car.

Blinking away the pain in the back of my head, I ignored his hand and got out by myself, staggering as I stood up. I looked around blearily. "Where are we?"

But then, I already knew where we were. I'd been here before. On Halloween. We stood outside of the barn where Vincent had held his party. The shadowed structure loomed over us—its large windows pits of ebony and the moon above like a pearl. I glanced around at the desolate snowy field surrounding us in all directions, halfway hoping to see the pack barreling out of the woods in the distance. But they were nowhere to be seen.

Something had definitely gone wrong.

"Why did you bring me here?" I asked quietly.

"To wait for him."

Ice cold relief ran through me. *Lucas is alive.*

Vincent seemed to sense what I was thinking. "Yes, he came here tonight. Unfortunately for him, I was elsewhere. I smelled the disgusting mongrels as soon as I returned, however, and I thought this was my best chance to get to you." He leered at me. "It would seem that I was correct."

"So why haven't you killed me yet?" I hated to ask the question, but I also hated not knowing. I decided being upfront was easier than admitting to myself just how frightened I really was.

Vincent sighed melodramatically. "Questions, questions . . ." He put his hand on my back and pushed me toward the barn, which was now infinitely more terrifying than it had been when it was a haunted house. "Let's talk inside, shall we?"

As we walked silently toward the barn, I looked up at the moon, the perfectly round orb taunting me up there in that black sky. I narrowed my eyes at it and then turned my attention to the inside of the barn.

It was then that I saw them: four pinpricks of gleaming light from within the inky darkness of the barn door. Eyes. I could feel a deranged energy coming from within, sparkling like fireworks, and I knew in an instant that there were werewolves hiding in there, left behind to await Vincent's return.

Vincent realized it at the same moment I did and threw me to the side with a shriek.

I hit the snow and looked up in time to see two werewolves thrust themselves out of the barn. Vincent met them halfway, leaping nimbly over their heads and landing in a pounce. He hissed viciously as one of them spun around and attacked.

The other, much smaller and russet colored ran through the field, toward the woods, letting out a shrill howl that echoed through the night.

He was going for help.

A sound like a blast of thunder made me turn. Vincent and the werewolf were fighting, their bodies clashing together, biting and scratching. Vincent was whippet quick, his reflexes bordering on precognition. In his hand was a blade, silver and already coated in blood. Each time it bit into the werewolf's flesh, a yowl sounded, twisting the ache of nerves in my gut. Vincent was magnificent, a blur of precision fighting.

But I marveled at the werewolf. His body wasn't shaped like a wolf at all—more like a gigantic man than anything. His back was hunched and layered with ropey gray hair; his arms were thick, bulging with muscle, and ending in gnarled claws. His face was the most wolfish, a snout and two glowing eyes, jagged teeth like steak knives.

His strength was like nothing I'd ever seen. Once he managed to land a blow, it sent Vincent flying, skidding through the snow. But somehow Vincent always got up, always charged again, his face a crazed mask of fury.

I didn't know what to do—some part of me was yelling, *Run!* But my eyes were glued to the fight. My heart pounded, adrenaline flowing as I watched. The terrible beauty of it stunned me. I wanted the werewolf to win, wanted it like nothing else, because I knew that if Vincent lived, I would be the next to die.

They were a mess of limbs. I couldn't see what was happening until—*crack!*

The werewolf went limp and Vincent sprang away, his eyes alight with victory. For a moment, there was no sound, just the rushing of my blood through my veins and the stopping of my heart.

He'd lost.

My one hope . . . gone.

The werewolf's body jerked and shivered. For one golden moment, I thought he was still alive. But the werewolf's body morphed back into a human—a man with light brown hair and staring blue eyes. Eyes that would never see again. Vincent bent and took the man's head between his hands. He twisted it and, with a sound like feet squelching in the mud, tore it off.

I gagged, looking away.

A thunk—the head hitting the ground.

Tears raked across my cheeks, nausea swimming in my stomach. I risked a look and watched Vincent take the knife and plunge it into the man's chest. A flash of silver and it returned to his coat.

The werewolf was dead, his blood pooled in the snow spreading against the white like an oil spill. I stared, entranced by the gore.

Vincent's swift footfalls reached my ears as he came to me. He tugged me to my feet and I sagged, unable to support myself.

His chuckles in my ear were like the rustling of forest leaves. I looked up at him, hate in my eyes.

"Disappointed?" he asked with a mocking grin.

I lifted my chin defiantly, pushing away from him. "The other one got away."

"I *let* him leave, darling. How else will your boyfriend know where to find us?"

I swallowed hard, angry that the one small victory I'd been

clinging to had all been part of Vincent's plan.

"Lucas will kill you," I said, mostly to comfort myself.

Vincent cocked a slim eyebrow and ushered me forward. We crossed the threshold of the barn, Vincent's lair. It was starkly empty when compared to how I'd last seen it. Blue light filtered in through the hayloft above us, giving Vincent's chalky pallor a spectral glow. He'd never looked less human to me. I jerked away from his hand on my back.

"Why does Lucas have to be here for you to kill me?" I asked, although I thought I knew the reason.

He came closer to me, his mouth by my ear, smooth voice just a whisper. "I want him to watch as I drink the life from your veins, as your warm blood flows into my mouth and through my body. I want to *see* him suffer. And then I am going to kill him." I smelled his breath, ripe with the rot of decay, and had to suppress a gag. "His little lookout will tell him I've returned and then we shall have some fun." He smiled at me.

As horrifying as that speech was, something about it stood out. It didn't seem as though Vincent knew the entire pack was coming. Otherwise, why wouldn't he kill me now and leave before they got here? He must have thought Lucas only elicited the help of a few. He had no idea what was coming.

But I knew better. I knew it was only a matter of time before the fury of the pack descended on Vincent—and me.

A tremor of alarm rippled down my spine as I realized I'd still be here when the werewolves arrived—if I lived that long. Would they know not to attack me?

Somehow I didn't think so. I knew without a doubt that I had to get out of there, and fast. There wasn't a chance I could fight Vincent so that meant talking my way out of this. Vincent seemed fairly confident in his ability to kill Lucas. Maybe I could weaken it.

"How do you know Lucas won't kill you?" I asked, surprised at how normal my voice sounded. "It's the full moon."

Vincent's black gaze sharpened on me. "Lucas and I have fought when he is at his strongest more times than I can count. He has all but killed me time after time, but never once has he delivered the death blow."

"Why not?"

"Because no matter how much he hates me, a part of him remembers what we were. Brothers." Vincent's voice was cold and uncaring. "Lucas will not kill me tonight," he went on with supreme confidence. "I have no fear of that."

"And you don't think your feelings for him will get in the way?"

Vincent sneered at me. "I have no feelings left for that dog. I will destroy him tonight."

Dread consumed my thoughts as the force of his words hit me, and I was unable to speak anymore. *How in God's name am I going to get out of this alive?*

"All this concern for your mongrel," Vincent said speculatively. "But none for yourself. Does it not concern you that I'll be biting you in a matter of minutes? That you will die tonight?"

Oh, it concerned me all right. But I wasn't about to let him see it. If I was going to go down, I might as well do it my way.

"So go ahead and do it," I challenged. "Bite me."

Vincent's left eyebrow twitched up and he chuckled deeply. I looked away. "I will miss your spunk, Faith. It makes you such a joy to be around. Almost as though I, too, am alive." I felt his eyes on me, but I didn't look up. "I do not have to kill you, you know. . . . There is another way."

I frowned, confused.

Vincent leaned into me, brushing the hair away from my throat. "The one I serve has burdened me with the task of creating new vampires to join our army of undead . . . *many* more vampires." He regarded me thoughtfully, his face much too close to mine. "It is quite difficult to turn a woman, especially a young woman. . . . Their souls are so rooted to their bodies that it is hard to separate them." He smiled evilly. "And they taste so sweet it is hard to stop before you kill them. Hence, the abundance of bodies you humans have been whining about." He stroked my throat with a wintry-cold finger. "Apologies, but I did do my best by them. Is it my fault they're so delicious?"

I kept my face blank, but inside my mind was racing. Was he actually doing this? Telling me outright that he was the serial killer as I had suspected all along? It even made sense now that the only victims found were young women because Vincent said they were harder to turn. And if that was the case, there might have been tons of others he had successfully turned that the human world had written off as runaways or missing people.

And it was just as Rolf had said. He wasn't doing this on a whim; his superior was making him do it. But why? Why would the vampires let Vincent risk their most guarded secret—their existence— just to create more vampires? Couldn't they do it and still remain inconspicuous? After all, that's what they'd been doing for centuries.

I had to try to find out more. But I couldn't be too obvious or else I risked Vincent growing suspicious and killing me before I could manage an escape. I tried for nonchalance, putting my hands into my hoodie pocket and shifting my weight.

That's when my pulse skyrocketed and hope shone in my chest like the rising sun.

The stake.

It was still in my pocket from when Lucas had given it to me this morning. He'd said it probably wouldn't do me any good, but now I could have kissed him. If I could somehow manage to distract Vincent enough I might be able to stake him and get the hell out of there before the werewolves showed up.

But I had to stay calm. I couldn't let him suspect anything.

"*You* serve someone?" I asked, trying to seem only vaguely interested. "What, like you're a slave?"

His vibe prickled with annoyance. "I serve only the one who created me and no other being—living or dead."

"Is that because you have to or because you choose to?"

"I do it because it is vampire law," Vincent said. "To refuse the word of my sire would put me at the mercy of the strongest vampires on this earth. No vampire crosses them without good reason."

"So do *they* know your sire is letting you leave exanguinated girls strewn all over Colorado?"

His eyes glittered malevolently in the moonlight, seemingly pleased that I'd figured out he was the killer. "Of course. They ordered it."

"And why would they do that—let you leave your corpses lying around in the open? Doesn't that risk your entire existence? What if the humans find out about you?"

His perfect lips twisted into a smile. "Soon it will not matter if the *fearsome* humans discover us," he mocked.

I faltered. "But why not?"

"That is not for your human ears to hear, sweet Faith." He reached out and touched his clammy fingers to my earlobe, tugging on it gently.

I flinched with disgust. "You're forgetting about the werewolves," I said, trying to keep him distracted from me. "They'll never let you continue doing this."

"*Let* us?" He released a barking laugh. "As if those canines *let* us do anything. We are vampires, little human. We do whatever we like. We need no permission from a pack of mangy mutts whose existence on this earth is soon to be at its end."

My body went numb. "What are you talking about?"

Vincent's eyes became manic. "We will destroy them!" he exclaimed. "All of them, every puppy, bitch, and brute out there! They will all rot under our feet where they belong!"

I was silent, awed by his outburst. Somewhere in the night a wolf howled. It had a grating, violent undertone, and I knew it was a werewolf.

Vincent heard it too. "He is coming," he whispered in my ear. "Are you ready to die, Faith?"

I lifted my chin, but I felt my bravado shrivel. Tears began to sting behind my eyes, but I pushed them away. Crying wasn't going to help. I needed to act. Fast.

I took a breath to calm my nerves. I needed to think of something to distract him—throw him off for just an instant. That would be all I'd need.

Another shrill howl sliced through me and I cringed.

"Are you frightened?" Vincent asked in a low voice.

I made my voice strong. "To die? No. Death is easy compared to living without him." I gripped the wooden rod with sweaty hands, readying myself. "That's why I—I want you to turn me."

That was it. The second I needed. Vincent's eyes widened with shock, and I whipped my hand out of my hoodie. I plunged my hand toward his heart.

But that second of shock wasn't long enough. Vincent swatted my hand away and the stake rolled off into the shadows. He gripped my wrist in a vice and snarled in my face.

"That was very stupid," he said.

My wrist felt like it was on fire despite his frigid skin, but I remained strong. "Can you blame me?" I grunted. "Wouldn't you do the same in my position?"

"Challenge a three-hundred-year-old vampire? No. I would not be so foolish." He pulled me closer to him, keeping me imprisoned in his iron arms. "But what a tantalizing suggestion you've made. Turning you, the love of my dearest enemy." An evil hunger shone in his black eyes. "I must admit, I quite like the idea."

I struggled against him, refusing to let my fear show through my eyes. "Lucas is going to kill you," I said through my teeth. "If you hurt me, you only ensure your own death."

Vincent's eyes erupted with malice. "But what's taking your precious Whelan so long to rescue you? Perhaps he has decided that you are not worth saving after all—that you are better off dead rather than alive." His deathly white fingers traced swiftly over my throat, his nails ripping into my skin. "But don't fret,

Faith. I will still want you when you become like me, when your skin goes cold and the light fades from those delicious green eyes. We shall be together forever. An eternal torture for your beloved Whelan."

The thought was so repulsive I almost gagged as I tried to get away from him. I glared up at Vincent. I was no longer afraid that Lucas would come, I was praying for it. Whatever chance there was that Lucas would kill me was a hell of a lot smaller than my chances with Vincent. "Lucas is going to be here any second," I yelled. "He's gonna kick your skinny ass!"

Vincent grabbed my face and squeezed so hard I heard my bones creak. I let out a cry of pain.

"*No*," he said viciously. "No one is going to save you. I am finally going to have my revenge on Whelan." I felt my feet lift off of the floor, and I struggled for breath, kicking my legs wildly. Vincent seemed unconcerned. His voice was as cool as his breath. "I thought at first that I would simply kill you, but then that would leave you dead. And I have to say, Faith, that is such a shame. You are *so* lovely." I saw his pupils dilate as the moonlight streaming through the window hit his eyes.

Vincent continued, "Since I am under instructions to create new vampires, I might as well do two things at once." He ripped my hoodie down over my shoulder, and I gasped from the cold. "And to make things even better, now I will have the added bonus of torturing you along with your mongrel lover. And this torture will last an eternity, sweet Faith. It never stops." His hand stroked my cheek and his face glazed over with the ecstasy of feeling my skin. He placed me on my feet.

I set my jaw, stubborn to the last millisecond of my life. "Lucas is coming," I said.

Vincent shoved my head to the side and ran his fingers over my throat. I felt my blood rush faster, betraying me. Then I felt Vincent's lips just above my collarbone, and a scream tore through my chest. I pushed against him. Lucas wasn't going to get here in time. Vincent's lips broke into a smile over my skin, his mouth was like ice. I fought against him, but his arms were unmovable. Panic consumed me—this couldn't be happening to me.

"See you on the other side," Vincent said over my skin. The tips of his teeth pressed against the hollow over my collarbone and terror took over. I screamed again, the sound ripping through the night.

"Faith!" A voice sounded from behind us.

Vincent froze and I heard a deep growling sound in his throat. I wriggled around enough to see who had called my name.

It was Derek.

He ran at us, his hand in the pocket of his coat.

I screamed his name. Vincent let out a guttural snarl and launched himself toward Derek, but Vincent only made it a few steps. Then the sound of a gun going off rang through the night and Vincent's body jerked. I gasped, watching him crumple to the ground.

Stunned, I looked up at Derek standing in the doorway with Mark's gun in his hand.

22

SACRIFICE

E ven from a distance I could tell Derek's hands were shaking. I glanced from Vincent gasping on the floor to Derek, standing still as a statue. Vincent moaned, grabbing his stomach, but unless those were wooden bullets Derek had in that gun, Vincent was going to heal. Fast.

"Derek!" I yelled. "What are you *doing* here?"

"I came to . . . to make sure . . ." He was still staring vacantly at Vincent writhing on the ground.

I threw my hands over my face. He'd come to make sure I was all right.

"How did you even find me?" I gasped.

"Followed the car," he said blankly. "I got lost . . . took forever to find you . . . Jesus, I just shot someone."

I couldn't be happier that Derek had shot Vincent, but now he was in serious danger. I had to get him out of here before Vincent healed.

"Derek, we have to go."

Derek seemed to snap out of it, his arms dropped and he started forward. He ignored me and asked, "Are you okay? Did he hurt you?"

"No, but we have to leave. Now."

"Wait—shouldn't we, I don't know, call someone?"

Vincent began to groan and grab at his chest.

"Holy hell, is he still alive?" Derek said, gawking at Vincent.

"Derek, let's go!" I yelled.

He didn't need to be told again. Without a word, he took my hand and together we raced out of the barn. I threw a look at Vincent before smashing the door closed. He was on all fours now.

He was healing. My heart stuttered.

"Hurry!" I shouted as we ran for Derek's car, parked out front near Vincent's.

We reached it, but Derek was having a hard time with the key. His hands were shaking badly.

"Derek," I pleaded. "Hurry."

The car doors clicked open and I began to get in.

That's when the barn door flew off its hinges, and Vincent stood silhouetted in the doorway. I screamed again.

"Get in the car!" Derek yelled.

I vaulted into it and slammed the door shut. Derek started the engine. And just when I thought we'd get away, Vincent appeared at the hood of the car smiling his evil smile.

He cocked an eyebrow at me and then disappeared underneath the car. I heard Derek floor the gas, but we didn't move.

"What the—?"

Derek's question was cut off by my shriek. The car lurched forward and then back. I held to the dashboard, bracing myself as the car was lifted into the air. Derek and I were both screaming now.

"Hold on!" Derek shouted.

Then Vincent threw the car into the snowy field. We hit the ground hard and skidded several feet before coming to a halt. The airbags exploded, burning my arms and face. Before I had time to react, Vincent was before us again. He picked up the car and tossed it onto its side. I heard Derek cry out, cursing as he fell onto me. His window blew out on impact and glass rained down on us. I closed my eyes, trying to keep myself upright as I felt the car lift into the air again. This time Vincent threw it further.

He obviously wasn't trying to kill us or we'd already be dead. It was a scare tactic—and it was working.

As we hit the ground again, I felt my head crack against the window. My vision swam, but I managed to stay conscious. Derek too, although he looked like he was in major pain. He lifted himself off me, gasping.

I looked out of the window and saw that we were close to the woods surrounding the vast field—the very woods where I had first discovered this world. I found it morbidly ironic that I would die in the same place.

Derek groaned and grabbed his sides. "I think my ribs are broken," he rasped. "Are you okay?"

"I think so, but—"

Vincent tore my door off and yanked me out, dragging me away by my feet. He threw me to the side and I landed in a heap, covered in freezing snow and blood. I knew this was it. I knew my life was coming to a close, but Derek could still get out of here alive.

"Derek, run!" I yelled hoarsely.

But Derek had other plans. He pulled the gun out of his pocket and began shooting. The sound was deafening. One, two, three shots—he clipped Vincent in the arm. His pale face glowed with wrath. He made a hissing sound, clasping his injured arm.

Then he turned his attention to Derek. He ran in a blur and jumped over the car, landing nimbly next to the driver's side.

Derek pointed the gun at him. But Vincent beat it away with a flick of his wrist and it went flying. Derek scrambled backward through the car, his eyes as big as dinner plates.

"Run!" I clambered to my feet and raced toward them. "Derek, run!"

But it was too late. Vincent seized Derek from the car and took hold of his face, shooting an ugly, triumphant look at me.

"Say good-bye to your friend," Vincent said, his fangs glistening with moisture.

I started screaming, running and screaming. I couldn't let this happen, not my Derek. I reached the car just in time to see Vincent lower his mouth to Derek's throat.

"No!" I cried.

But Vincent's fangs sunk deep into Derek's skin.

I dove forward and collided with Vincent. It was like hitting cement. My bones crunched, but Vincent didn't even falter. I began beating his back, yelling. He shoved me aside as though I was nothing more than an irritating bug and continued drinking. I rammed backward into the car, hitting my head. I lost vision for a second and then saw Derek's blood leaking into the snow, staining it deep scarlet.

With what looked like a great deal of effort, Vincent pried his mouth from Derek's throat and licked his lips. Derek was screaming, the sound delayed in reaching my ears, and it made my head swim with rage.

Vincent shoved his sleeve up and bit his own wrist, not even wincing.

"No!" I yelled.

I ran at him again, not even caring that nothing I did would help. I wrapped my arms around Derek and pulled at him, trying in vain to steal him from Vincent. Derek's body was like a limp noodle. He was paralyzed now. . . . The venom had already taken him. He was so pale. He was dying.

But I wouldn't let him become a vampire. I pulled at him, crying, but Vincent pushed me away again, harder this time. I went flying and rolled to a halt some ten feet away. My body was weak with exhaustion; it took every ounce of my energy to lift up to my hands and knees. I heard that shrill howling again somewhere in the distance—my werewolves, coming to save me . . . or kill me. Either way, it was too late for Derek.

I saw Vincent lay him down in the snow. He opened his mouth and tilted his wrist over it, letting the blood flow into Derek's body. I struggled forward, unable to stand and Vincent looked up at me. He was smiling.

Hatred coursed through my veins, revitalizing me.

I hated Vincent more than anything I'd ever hated in the world. I wanted to kill him. My whole purpose for being suddenly became centered on the fact that I needed to kill this vampire bastard. And I was going to do it with or without the pack.

A glint of silver reached my eyes. The gun, laying not two feet away from me. I crawled to it and took it in my numb fingers. I pulled the cylinder open and saw that I had two more bullets. Two chances to shoot Vincent. I'd stun him long enough to retrieve the stake—and then I'd kill him.

I rose to my feet, stumbling. The adrenaline made me quake violently, but I pushed forward, forcing my feet to move. My body was alive with heat, though my clothes were soaked with freezing snow. I could hardly breathe as I flew at Vincent. I was so close. I aimed the gun—

But Vincent grabbed me before I could shoot. He beat the gun out of my hand and held me to him. "A valiant effort." He laughed. "But ultimately so futile. Do not fret, young Faith. This will not hurt." His eyes were filled with blackness, even the part where the white should have been. He was consumed with bloodlust. And I was next.

But then there was a vicious growl from right behind us and Vincent spun around, still holding me tightly.

A creature stood before us. It looked like a wolf, but elongated. It stood on two feet, and it had a chest like a man. Its body was covered in thick, jet black hair, and its hackles were raised along his hunched back. Its face was that of a wolf, bright white fangs dripping with saliva and shining silver eyes glinting dangerously beneath the full moon.

I knew in an instant that it was Lucas. His vibe, though mangled with insanity, had the essence of the man I loved. But this wasn't my Lucas anymore. The moon had transformed him into a mutated creature, neither totally man nor wolf. He was truly a monster.

I looked into the distance and saw the trees banking the field start to shake. Then ten or so creatures of varying shapes and colors ran from the woods to stand behind their brother.

I'd never been so relieved and so frightened at the same time. The energy bubbling from the werewolves was manic. The same unpredictable, erratic energy my stepdad had when he hurt my mom and shot me. I tried to tell myself that this wild animal heaving in front of me was my Lucas, but I knew better. I knew what it would do to me if it got the chance—if I messed up again.

Vincent backed up and sidestepped my dying friend on the floor. He snatched my wrist, holding it to his mouth, much like a criminal would hold a gun to his victim's head when the cops showed up.

"I'll bite her," Vincent said. There was an unveiled note of panic in his voice. "One bite and it's over."

Lucas roared and bent over, scratching at the ground as if itching to charge Vincent. He had claws—like bear claws but longer. I couldn't believe this was Lucas.

The werewolves began to encircle us. Vincent glanced around, and I was glad to see the fear in his eyes. I was right—he hadn't been expecting the entire pack to show up just for him.

"Stop!" Vincent commanded, yanking on my wrist. "Get back or I'll bite her, I swear I will!" His voice was harried. He knew he was cornered. He turned on Lucas, his eyes shining with hate. "Am I really so strong that you had to cry to your pack to come and help you? Can you not defeat me on your own?"

Lucas jerked forward, gnashing his massive jaws together.

Vincent backed away. "One more step and she's dead," he whispered. "Do not test me, old friend. You know I will do it. I have waited much too long to be thwarted now. Even if I have to die to make you scorch with pain for the rest of your days, I'll do it." He brought my wrist closer to his mouth, and I strained against his grip, feeling tears drag down my cheeks.

"Lucas," I said, breathing desperately.

My voice seemed to trigger something in Lucas. His big silver eyes blazed and without any kind of warning, he lunged. He was fast, so fast I didn't see his paw shove me away as his body collided with

Vincent's. I hit the snow and scrambled away, bumping into Derek.

Lucas and Vincent were a ball of limbs, screeching and yowling. The pack watched, barking in encouragement and excitement. I saw Vincent's fangs dig into Lucas's shoulder, and he roared, sending my body into chills. The silver knife raked over his back, blood spurting everywhere. I couldn't watch. I heard Derek groan and I dragged myself to him, bringing my ear by his bloodstained mouth. He was barely breathing. Sobbing, I put his head in my lap.

I shushed him as he began to moan and writhe. I guessed the venom wore off once you were fed vampire blood? I didn't know. All I knew was that the sounds he was making churned my stomach. I combed my fingers through his hair and cried, knowing that he was turning before my eyes into something not quite dead, not quite alive. My sweet, baby-faced Derek was becoming a vampire.

A loud scream made me look up. Lucas had Vincent pinned to the snow, his claws were forcing themselves into his pale skin.

"You . . . don't have . . . the guts," Vincent spat. I could feel the hatred, the fury in his voice. "You have had over three centuries to do this and you have yet to follow through. Now is no different. You are weak, Whelan. . . . And your weakness will be what kills her."

Then I could swear I saw that familiar smirk flit across Lucas's wolf face. He threw his head back and let out a deafening howl that jarred my bones. It seemed to go on forever, Lucas's body, shining underneath the moon, his coat stained with blood, his teeth, white and deadly. Then Lucas raised a massive claw and ripped Vincent's head right off, sending it flying into the snow where it landed with a sickening thunk.

The rest of the pack began yipping and howling. Some of them darted forward and shredded into Vincent's dead body. I felt bile rising in my throat and I looked away.

I knew I should leave. I knew that I was in the middle of a werewolf feeding frenzy and that any second one was going to turn on me. I knew that my best friend was turning vampire in my arms and that he was no longer the Derek I once loved.

I knew all of these things . . . but I couldn't accept them.

I couldn't accept that Derek would be a vampire. *Not my Derek. Not my best friend.* There was only one thing I could think to do, one small hope. I wasn't sure it would even work, but it was all I had. Lucas had to bite Derek. The werewolf infection might cancel out the vampire magic or else save him from becoming undead. It was a long shot, but I had to try.

Adrenaline began to surge through me again, but this time it was more potent. My body vibrated as though bolts of electricity were shocking me. I recognized this feeling, only now it was magnified ten times stronger than it ever was before. I embraced it, letting it spread and flood through my veins from my heart to my fingertips.

"STOP!" I shouted, standing up by Derek's writhing body. Every one of the celebrating werewolves froze. "Lucas!" I yelled. I stepped forward into the mass of colossal werewolves. Some of them snapped at me, but I ignored them, sure now that they wouldn't hurt me with my connection secure. I went to the one I knew to be Lucas. I looked straight into his eyes, feeling the connection strengthen. I focused my mind on only two words and I spoke them aloud to make sure he heard them this time. *"Bite him!"*

My boyfriend just stared at me, but I knew he understood.

"Lucas, bite Derek! Turn him into a werewolf. I can handle a werewolf. I can't handle a vampire." Again, I focused on Lucas's eyes, willing him to obey me. *Bite him!*

Lucas's silver eyes shifted to Derek. I could somehow *feel* him hesitate, but I urged him with my mind. *Do it!*

Lucas started toward Derek.

Then the biggest werewolf, who had to have been Rolf, came between them, growling furiously. I tried to make him move, but Rolf paid no attention. He was old enough and strong enough to resist me. As he stood between Lucas and Derek, his knifelike teeth barred, I could understand all too clearly what he was saying, though he couldn't voice it. He was forbidding Lucas from biting Derek.

"No," I said, turning to Lucas. "Go bite him. Go save him!"

Lucas just stared down at me, his eyes vacant and glittering with madness.

"Save him!" I yelled with both my mind and my mouth. And again, as if I were steering him, Lucas took a step toward Derek.

But Rolf was having none of it. He let out an endless roar that weakened the connection I had with the pack, and Lucas stopped. The toll the connection took on my mind was exhausting and every second I held on, the task grew more strenuous until I could barely feel the energy anymore. Rolf's hold over Lucas was more powerful than mine, and I was weakening by the second. It was then that I realized I wasn't going to be able to do it. I couldn't make Lucas save Derek. . . . He was going to die. And so was I. The connection was the only thing saving me now, and once I let it go, they would descend on me.

I fell to my knees at Lucas's feet, my face in my hands and Derek's blood pooling beneath me. I looked up into Lucas's silver eyes. "Please," I begged with my voice breaking. "Please, Lucas. Save him."

But his eyes were indifferent to my sorrow. They were empty and cold, reflecting the opalescent moon above us that controlled his world. I looked down at my hands, smeared with Derek's poisoned blood. I knew that it would only be a few more moments before Lucas's instincts took over. He would smell the vampire blood, and it would drive him to attack. He and the pack would kill us both.

For a long moment, the only sounds were Derek's ragged breaths and my desperate sobs. I could feel what was left of the connection waning, the electricity ebbing until there was only a tiny spark left. I felt Lucas and the pack's erratic energy, their crazed bloodlust. I knew death was coming, and I thought one last time, with every inch of my heart, *Please . . . bite him. Please . . .*

Then I heard the crunching of snow as something rushed by me. I looked up, hardly daring to believe.

Rolf roared again, but Lucas picked Derek up in his gigantic arms. He gave one harried look at Rolf and then his teeth tore into Derek's arm.

23

AFTERMATH

erek began screaming and making these awful guttural sounds. Lucas dropped him, his teeth shining and his eyes bright with the taste of fresh meat. He turned toward me, and I felt fear smother my senses. His eyes no longer bore any resemblance to my boyfriend's eyes. They were completely and totally feral.

I had no time to try and stop him. Lucas lunged for me.

Then Rolf attacked Lucas.

The rest of the werewolves clashed in an explosion of fangs and chomping jaws. Bodies crushed together, barking, snarling. I didn't know what was happening, but I did know that I had to get the hell out of there. Now. I weaved through the hairy bodies, tripping and falling several times and narrowly missing the bloody jaws of a spotted werewolf whom I guessed was Julian.

I dove for Derek. "Get up!" I screamed. I grabbed underneath his arms, hefting him as hard as I could. He barely stood as I draped his arm over my shoulder and began stumbling out of the fray. I was able to steer him away, fueled by the adrenaline pumping in my veins.

Werewolves tussled and rolled by us. I smelled blood in the air, and it was only a matter of time before they noticed us. I tried to ignite the connection, to make my body electric again, but I was too distracted. I pulled Derek along as he moaned and staggered. My feet slipped in the snow and my muscles protested, but I continued until I reached Vincent's car.

It was then that I realized I didn't have the keys to this car. Derek began to claw at me, gasping. He was fading. Panicking, I pulled at the car door, hoping for a miracle.

It opened.

Vincent had left his keys in the ignition—probably having no fear that anyone would steal his car way out in the middle of nowhere.

Crying out with relief, I managed to stuff Derek into the backseat and slammed the door shut. I heard feet pounding the earth and I whirled around. A black mass of bodies was hurtling through the field straight at me. The werewolves had finally gotten organized again. And they smelled fresh meat smothered in vampire blood.

I flew to the front seat and turned the key. Derek's voice rose into a high-pitched scream and I spun around. He was limp.

"Derek!" I shouted and jostled him. "Derek!"

Then I heard barking, and the first werewolf skidded to a halt in front of the car, illuminated in the headlights.

I threw it into reverse and screeched down the dirt road and onto the long, desolate highway behind me. I shoved the car into drive and slammed my foot down on the accelerator. I heard howling behind me and glanced in the rearview. They were chasing me!

I pushed harder on the gas as the car climbed to eighty, ninety. They could still go this fast. Lucas had said that he could run a hundred miles per hour. I felt something hit the back of the car, and I swerved, almost losing control. I pressed harder on the gas . . . a hundred . . . a hundred fifteen. It couldn't go faster. This was it.

I glanced in the rearview again and saw the werewolves falling back. A big black one stood at the front and let out a shrieking howl. I saw its eyes glint silver in the moonlight. Then I rounded a bend in the road and lost sight of my boyfriend and his family, baying to the full moon.

I drove all night and didn't stop, even when I got to civilization. At first I didn't know where I was going, I just knew I couldn't stop until daybreak. I pulled over on the side of the road somewhere around four a.m. to check on Derek. He was unconscious, but he was alive. I prayed to everything I knew that he would make it through this. *If Derek dies because of me . . .*

Then I began heading in the direction of Gould. It was the only place I could think to go. I couldn't take Derek to the hospital—a vampire and a werewolf bite would be hard to explain—and I knew that the pack would be normal again by morning. They were the only ones who could help now.

About an hour after the sun had risen, I reached the werewolf mansion. There was no one around—no sounds, just me. I couldn't carry Derek, so I left the keys in the ignition and went to the front door. I knocked using the big wrought iron door-knocker and waited.

A woman answered the door. She was easily the oldest person I'd seen around there, but she could only be forty or so. She had a warm smile, but it was tainted with concern and maybe even suspicion.

"Yes?" she asked. She had a deep voice like an owl's cry. Somewhere in the back of my mind I was surprised to find that I couldn't feel her vibe . . . but maybe I was too tired to feel anything anymore.

"Is Lucas back yet?" I asked.

"Who are you?"

"I'm Faith. His girlfriend." The woman made a face like my name meant something to her. I wondered what they'd been saying about me. But I didn't care anymore. I cast a look back at the car and said, "My friend got hurt last night. I need to bring him inside and see if there's anything . . . anything they can do."

"The pack should return shortly," the woman said. "Come in and I'll get the boys to carry him."

"No, I'll wait here."

The woman looked me up and down for a moment and then said, "As you wish." She closed the door, and I walked back to the car. There was no way I was leaving Derek alone here. Part of him was possibly a vampire, and I didn't want the werewolves getting any ideas. I opened the backseat up and put my hand on Derek's skin. It was like ice, cold and clammy.

Like dead skin.

I felt tears springing up into my eyes and I grimaced, looking around into the early morning light. The sun's gentle rays warmed my skin, melting the ice in my heart. I worried briefly about whether the sunlight would hurt Derek's skin, but I pressed the thought away, refusing to accept that as a possibility. He couldn't be a vampire. He just couldn't.

I heard the door open and looked around. Three boys a little younger than me strutted forward. They all looked close to identical—tall, black hair, kind of gangly, but muscled.

I stood back and watched two of them lug Derek out of the car. I followed close behind them up the front steps, into the living room, and up the stairs to a bedroom. Inside were the older woman and two other younger girls bearing washcloths and first-aid equipment.

The boys lowered Derek onto the bed and stood at the back of the room, eyes wide. The older woman waved her hand at the girls, and they started unclothing Derek.

I looked away and then felt someone stand in front of me.

"What happened?" the older woman asked.

"He was bitten by a vampire and fed his blood. . . . Then he was bitten by a werewolf." I didn't want to tell her which werewolf had done the biting.

The woman's gray eyes crinkled into little slits. "No werewolf would have done that. Vampire victims hold no interest for werewolves."

"Yeah, well . . . one bit him."

The woman scrutinized me for a long while and then turned to the boys. "Out!" she barked, and they scurried away. She turned around on her heel and went to Derek. I let out a long breath and leaned against the wall, exhausted. I watched the woman inspect the wound on Derek's throat and the one in his forearm, the latter of which looked much worse because of the size of Lucas's teeth.

She began shaking her head and clucking her teeth. "Stupid . . . stupid, stupid . . . ," she muttered to herself. "A few broken ribs, but that will heal itself." She continued her examination and then looked around at me. "There is nothing to do but wait."

I took a step forward. "What do you mean?"

"I have never seen two bites from both races on one being. There is no telling what the result will be. He might die from the mixed magic. One magic might overpower the other, or they will blend and he will be the start of a hybrid race. God only knows what that means." She shook her head almost sadly.

"But can't you help him? Can't you . . . I don't know . . . *do* anything?"

"There is no helping this one now," she said brusquely. "We will know what he is by the next full moon. If he lives that long." She turned to the girls, who were swabbing Derek's body with warm cloths. "Clean the wounds well," she said. "Come and find me if he wakes." She started to turn around and then stopped, looking around the room as if just realizing something. "Close the curtains. No light." She strode out of the room.

I sank to the floor, my back pressed up against the wall. My body shook with sobs, but there weren't any tears left. *My Derek . . . my sweet Derek.* My best friend, the one who stood by me through everything and anything, was going to become some sort of undead hybrid vampire-beast because of me. I couldn't stand it. Derek had come out there to help me, and I had gotten him hurt.

Maybe I should have let him stay vampire. Would that have been better? My mind rejected the thought, but he might be something so much worse now. Had my attempt to save Derek from a life of walking the earth as an undead corpse doomed him instead? Instead of a half-life, now he might not even have that much. He might die.

I heard a door slam downstairs and then cursing and yelling. Two men and a woman. The girls cleaning Derek exchanged furtive glances. Then feet pounded up the stairs and down the hall. I stood up.

Lucas bashed through the door, and we all jumped. His eyes found mine, and he darted to me, wrapping me up in his arms.

"God, I'm so sorry," he said in my ear. "I'm sorry, Faith. You're alive . . . I was so scared . . ."

"It's okay," I said. "I was scared, too." I started crying, thoroughly relieved that he was okay. I held his face and smiled into his deep brown eyes. "You saved me," I said, still in wonder over it. "You saved my life . . . and maybe Derek's, too. I—I don't know what to say."

Lucas smoothed his thumbs over my cheeks. "You don't have to say a word. Just come here." He pulled me to him again and enveloped me in his arms. He was shirtless, and I felt the warmth of his skin sink into my body. For a moment, I closed my eyes, loving it . . . loving him, relieved beyond words that we had both made it through the night with our lives. Happy that Lucas was in my life, loving me enough to risk death for me.

I was so warm and so filled with love. But suddenly I couldn't stand it. I couldn't stand feeling this small measure of comfort while Derek lay dying on the bed beside me.

I pulled away.

Two more people entered the room: the older woman and Rolf, both of whom looked furious. I guess the lady had figured out who'd bitten Derek. I wondered how much trouble Lucas was in for disobeying his pack master. Julian, Nora, and a girl with chestnut-colored hair stood in the doorway, their faces grave.

I turned my eyes to Rolf. He moved toward Derek, and Lucas started forward as though protecting Derek.

"He will not be allowed to live," Rolf said. "This creature could be a monstrosity—a mutant. You do not know what danger you have brought unto this household. I will not put our pack at risk."

"He's not a mutant!" I yelled. "He's a person!"

"Shut up," both Lucas and Rolf snapped. I stared up at Lucas. He gave me an apologetic glance and then rounded on Rolf. "We don't know what he is yet. We can't kill him. Maybe the magic cancelled itself out, and he'll be normal. We don't know."

Rolf rolled his eyes dramatically and turned to the older woman. "Is that true, Yvette?"

"It is more likely that he will die," the woman said. "The blood of the two races is not meant to mix."

"But *if* he survives?" Rolf thundered.

The woman made a pained face and said, "There is no way to know. There are legends of beasts like this one, but I have never seen anything like it before. We must wait until the full moon. That is when his true form will manifest."

Rolf rounded on Lucas. "You have disobeyed me," he said. "And you will be punished for it. But your true punishment will be the knowledge of what you have done to this boy, if he survives the change." He stabbed a finger at Derek. "Every time you look at his mutated form, you will know that it was your doing. That is your true torment."

Lucas looked away, his face crumpled in defeat. I knew the anguish this would cause him if Derek died or if he became something horrible.

"It's not his fault," I said, stepping closer to Rolf. "I made Lucas bite Derek, so if you want to punish someone, you punish me."

"*Shut up*," Lucas snarled in a whisper.

"You know not what you have done," Rolf said. "But soon you will see that this . . . *thing* you have created must be destroyed. You have only succeeded in elongating the pain for your human friend.

I hope you are happy." With that he stormed out, blowing past Julian and the others huddled in the doorway.

The older woman, Yvette, followed after him with a tight-mouthed nod to both of us. I watched Julian grab the hand of the chestnut-haired girl and go along with Nora, leaving Lucas and I alone with the girls and Derek.

"Are you hurt?" Lucas asked as soon as the door shut.

I shook my head.

"Let me see your wrist," he commanded.

I held out my hand and let Lucas inspect it. He pulled back my hair and ran his fingers over my throat, checking to make sure I was unharmed. "You sure you're okay?"

"Derek's the one I'm worried about." I hesitated for a second, watching the agony wreak havoc in Lucas's eyes. "Are you in big trouble?"

I saw the girls sneak looks at us. Lucas glared at them, and they left the room, gently closing the door behind them. "Yeah," he said. "Big trouble."

I cringed, leaning my head against his chest. "I'm so sorry. . . . I never should have asked you to do this. I was just so desperate." I felt a sob sneaking up on me, but I pushed it back, taking in a big breath. "That's no excuse," I said firmly. "I shouldn't have asked you to disobey your pack master. I'm sorry."

Then Lucas lifted my face, his expression knowing. "It felt more like you made me do it, rather than asked me." He didn't sound angry, more like he was just waiting for the truth.

I knew it would be useless to deny what I'd done if Lucas had felt it. "Do you think the others know?" I whispered.

"If they felt anything different, they haven't said. And besides, if Rolf even suspected anything like what you did, you'd already be dead."

I swallowed.

"What *did* you do anyway?" he asked.

"I wish I knew," I said morosely.

"But it's happened before," Lucas said. "That time with Mark, I told you I felt something different—like someone else was controlling me. That was you, wasn't it?"

I met his eyes, scared he was angry with me, but he only looked curious. "Yes," I admitted. "But I didn't know what was happening. I didn't know what I was doing."

"Had it ever happened before?"

"No—well, kind of. Once with you, your skin zapped me, and I kind of got a rush of emotions that didn't feel like mine. I think they were your emotions. And it happened again with Vincent. Maybe it has something to do with you guys being supernatural creatures."

"Maybe . . ." Lucas said thoughtfully. "And last night was the first time you did it voluntarily? The first time you controlled it?"

I nodded. "But I wasn't very good at it. . . . Rolf almost usurped me."

"Well, he *is* pack master. He has a pretty strong influence over us."

"Are you mad at me?" I whispered. "I know I should have told you about this earlier, but I didn't really understand it or even accept it until last night."

He considered me for a long while. "No, I'm not mad," he said at last. "Hurt, maybe, that you didn't trust me, but I guess I understand why. It's a very dangerous gift." He held my face in his hands, his eyes trained on mine. "Nobody can ever find out about this. If anyone even guesses, it means you're dead. No questions."

I nodded shakily. "Why do you think you can feel it when I control you and nobody else can?"

He sighed, contemplating. "Maybe it's because I'm so close to you, like I'm attuned to you." Lucas squeezed the back of his neck. "I don't know, but let's just be glad they can't. There's no way Rolf will let someone with that kind of power live. He can't have someone around challenging his authority over us."

I let him tug me into his arms and hold me, but my eyes wandered to Derek, sleeping away, peaceful now.

"What if Derek dies?" I whispered. "Because of what I did?"

"He would have died anyway."

"Maybe that would have been better." I shook my head. "Maybe Rolf is right."

"Rolf doesn't know what he's talking about. He's old and he's powerful and he's pack master, but he doesn't know everything. Derek could be . . . all right."

I flinched, hearing the falseness in his voice. "What if Rolf tries to kill him?"

Lucas's face hardened. "Then I'll protect him."

I'd never loved anyone more than I loved Lucas in that moment. I hugged him fiercely, fighting off the surge of tears that threatened to overcome me.

"What are they going to do to you?" I asked, unable to keep the fear out of my voice.

"Nothing good."

I watched his perfect face, gauging his response. "Will they hurt you?"

"No," he said, but I could tell he didn't believe it. "I'll probably just have to do dishes for a month or something." He forced out a laugh.

I grabbed his face and made him look at me. "Are they going to kill you?"

Lucas rubbed the back of his neck, sighing. "The punishment for disobeying the pack master's orders is the silver room on the night of the full moon." His voice was hollow, unfeeling. I knew it was masking the terror he must have felt.

"Silver will kill you," I said.

"No. It makes us weak. If it hits out hearts, it'll kill us. Being in the silver room prevents us from changing, and on the full moon . . . it's enough to make a person lose their mind."

"And you're going to let them do that to you?" I asked angrily.

"Hopefully it won't happen. I get a trial." He hesitated. "And I can always leave the pack. Start my own, someplace new."

I nodded, letting everything sink in and struggling to make sense of it all.

"Lucas?" I asked. "Is Vincent really dead . . . for good?"

A strange look flowed across Lucas's face. Sadness, remorse, maybe even regret? But he nodded. "He's really dead. You don't have to worry about him anymore." He brushed his knuckles over my jaw, sending thrills through my heart.

"I'm sorry," I said. "I know he was evil in the end, but I know he was your friend, too."

Lucas looked away, his jaw muscles hard as granite. "I just wish we could have found out what we needed from him. . . . The whole thing went so wrong."

"He told me," I said.

"What? What are you talking about?"

"Vincent told me what you guys wanted to know. He said he was under orders to create new vampires."

"Whose orders?"

"His sire."

"Did he say a name?"

"No."

"Did he say why he was doing this? Or if he was acting alone?"

I thought for a second. "No. . . . He mentioned an army of undead."

Lucas furrowed his slanted brows, deep in thought. "And he never said why he'd just left his victims out in the open?"

"He said it was because soon it wouldn't matter if the humans knew about the vampires." I watched him mull this over. "What do you think it all means?"

He just shook his head again, thinking. He didn't say anything for a long time.

"They want to eliminate the werewolves," I said softly as I remembered Vincent's wild tirade. "Lucas, I think they want a war."

His eyes met mine, narrowed and contemplative.

"Don't tell anyone about this," he said at last. "It might help for me to be able to offer the pack information. . . . For my trial, I mean."

I nodded and felt my body sway. Lucas put his hand on my back. "You should get some sleep. You look beat."

"I *am* beat," I said. "But I want to stay here in case Derek wakes up."

Lucas's eyes grew pointed. "You wanna sleep in here? I don't think that's safe."

"I won't sleep then."

"That's not what I meant," Lucas said. "I'll send someone to stay with you in case he wakes up."

"I don't need—"

The look on Lucas's face shut me up. Defeated, I tugged an armchair closer to the bed and collapsed into it. I bent and put my hand over Derek's. It was still. No tremble of life, no pulse thudding beneath his skin, no warmth.

Lucas stood next to me, and I saw his fists balled up at his sides. Was it because I held Derek's hand? He couldn't possibly be jealous. He knew how much I loved him.

"I gotta go talk to Julian," Lucas said.

"Why?" I asked, stroking Derek's mangled arm.

"I gotta get as many people on my side as I can."

"Can I help at all?" I looked up at him.

"No, but I wish you'd go to sleep."

"I can't." I returned my eyes to Derek. "Not while he's like this . . ."

"Right." Lucas's voice was stiff. "I'll be back." He started to move away and an unthinkable feeling washed over me—the feeling that he *wouldn't* be back.

I grabbed his arm, vaulting out of my seat. I felt desperation welling in my eyes.

"Promise?" I asked. "Promise you'll come back?"

Lucas put his hands over my cheeks and pressed his lips

against mine, lingering until my heart felt so full I thought it would explode.

"I'll always come back to you," he said against my lips.

He kissed me again for a long time. I pressed back the gates that had started to guard my heart again and let myself feel. I let myself fall into Lucas for that brief moment.

And then I was alone.

Alone again. But now I had a terrible burden on my shoulders. I had Derek's life clutched between my fingers. I held his hand up to my lips and kissed it. I felt the calluses on his palms from playing football, the game he loved, the game he might never be able to play again. I went around to the other side of the bed and scooted up next to him, stroking his short blond locks. I wound some around my finger, crying silently. Even his hair was cold.

I wondered what he would be when he woke up—if he woke up. Would he still be my Derek? Or would he be like Vincent, crazed and evil, thirsting for my blood? Or he could be like Lucas, a vicious beast concealed inside a human shell. Or worse still, a miserable, tortured mixture of both races. A grotesque monster. Would he try to kill me? Would we have to kill him first to stop him?

Were the horrible events I'd just escaped repeating themselves?

There was no way to know—only the full moon would tell me. Only the night, creeping slowly, coming ever closer, would reveal the secrets locked tight behind Derek's sleeping eyelids. I knew now that the danger would never end. And not even Lucas could keep me safe forever.

I closed my eyes, rubbing my nose against Derek's cheek. I

kissed his skin, hoping that somehow the warmth of my touch would flow into his body and heal him.

It didn't.

Derek slept, his body growing ever colder, his wounds healing much too quickly, and his face becoming ever more lifeless.

And then, four days later, his eyes fluttered open.

ACKNOWLEDGMENTS

Wow, I never thought I'd be writing this. That my dream of publishing a novel came true is still unbelievable to me. And I know that it most certainly never would have happened without the awesome people around me who offered their unfailing support. Thanks to all of you are definitely in order.

First, to my mom and dad. You are the best parents in the world. And I know everyone always says that, but with you two, it's true. You always have my back, even when I screw up. And I have. A lot. So thanks for loving me through it all and for giving me the opportunity to follow my dreams. Without you, I would never be here. And that's not just because, you know . . . you created me.

Second, I have to thank my husband, Mat. You have always been behind me, even when everyone else doubted my ability to do this ridiculously difficult thing. Not that I blame them. The chances were small. But you never let that stop you from encouraging me to forge ahead through the bad times. Because of you, I've made it here. (Just to be clear, these are the good times.)

My kids. You're too little to read this right now, but I have to thank you, too. For your patience, and your smiles, and for putting up with me. I love you both more than words can say. And that's significant coming from a writer.

My sister, Britt, deserves a huge thank you as well for being my first unofficial editor, and for dealing with my late-night freak-outs. It was your encouraging words that kept me going when all I wanted to do was quit. Best sister ever.

And, because I am a fanatic music lover, I must say a thank you to the artists on my "writing playlist." Anberlin, Florence + The Machine, Mumford & Sons, Paramore, Death Cab for Cutie, and The Republic of Wolves. Did I mention Anberlin? ANBERLIN!

Also, I must thank my cousins Pedro Sostre and Chris Rivera at Weblift for creating my author website. I never thought I'd see the day I'd call myself an author, and having my own site made it seem all the more real. Plus, it's just really pretty. Thank you!

Next comes my biggest thank you yet, to my rock star agent, Tamar Rydzinski. You took a chance on me when nobody else would. For that, you have my deepest thanks and my eternal respect. Seriously, I could gush for about an hour. Thank you, thank you, thank you!

To Kelli Chipponeri, my first editor. You deserve a gigantic thank you for taking on the daunting task of rescuing my book and turning it into a story worth reading. To Lisa Cheng, my second editor, thank you, too, for picking up where Kelli left off and taking the story to a whole new level of awesome. And for all the smiles along the way.

To everyone at Running Press, Ryan Hayes in particular, who designed the cover, I cannot thank you enough for all the hard work you did. You took *Blood on the Moon* from a mess of words on a screen to an amazingly beautiful book.

And to you, reader! The biggest thank you of all goes to you, because you picked this up and read it. And hopefully, loved it as much as I do.